Sede, Seed of Eden

volume 1

Kathleen Nennemann

Sede, Seed of Eden

ISBN: 978-0-692-23303-0

Library of Congress Control Number: 2014910685

Copyright © 2014

Published by Kathleen Nennemann

Prepared for publishing by: Orion Productions, LLC.

PO Box 51194
Colorado Springs, CO 80949
www.orion316.tv

Editor: Daphne Parsekian

Disclaimer:

I the author wish to assure you the reader that any of the opinions expressed in this book are my
own and are the result of a fruitful imagination. This is a book of fiction and not intended to be
guidance in theology. Although Noah and his family existed, little is known of their daily lives. My
attempt is to stir within you the reader a curiosity in ancient biblical history through the media of
entertaining reading.

Contents

I dedicate this book to Jesus, the "Promised One" who fulfilled prophecy.

Preface

With the turning of the first page of *Sede, Seed of Eden*, you can almost sense Sede beckoning you: *'Come... follow me on a journey into a faraway land and time'!* As you follow her footsteps, you'll discover the quiet and predictable life she loves. But danger is looming on the horizon, like a threatening storm, blowing its way into her life. What will become of her innocent, yet brave heart; the people she loves; and her village that has remained secluded and safe for centuries? How will this change her? She must choose, and with the choosing; bend like a reed in the wind while the storm rages around her. The momentum builds as you turn each page and discover where she leads you.

Sede's story began its conception during my first year in Bible College. The class of 'Old Testament Studies' sparked a fascinating interest in ancient Biblical history. It seemed the people who lived then - lived by amazing faith. They overcame in the most perilous of times. History has declared them to be our forefathers; and examples of those who live by faith.

In my search of resource material I discovered: The Book of Enoch, Book of Jubilee, Book of Jasher, Book of Bees, Book of the Cave of Treasures, and most importantly - the Holy Bible. With the reading of these ancient manuscripts and books, I found inspiration, which ignited by imagination of a world that existed before the flood. I began to ask myself questions about what life would have been like for them. What was the culture of the time? What spiritual understanding did they have? How did God interact with them? What were the women like, who looked to Yahweh (God), for help in time of need? From these questions came the idea of a young woman named "Sede", who would be of the family of Noah.

Writing on the book continued for the next two years until I graduated. At that time I set it aside for a year. Looking back I realize what I had written so far needed time to lay dormant. My book had become as its theme… a seed. It needed time to germinate until new inspiration came. And it came through my sister and friends. It was my sister Renee, and my friends: Connie, Cynthia, and Tom; who watered the seed with their encouragement to finish the book. And then sunshine came from my publisher, Jenna, and editor, Daphne, with their rays of professional support that encouraged the seed to take root. Without the love and support of these people, the seed of this book would have never bloomed.

There are several themes I developed within the story. The main theme is the seed. As you read you will discover it has several meanings. A seed goes through many stages before it becomes what it is intended to be. Another theme is the parallel worlds of 'innocence' and 'corruption'. I attempted to describe both the subtle and overt evil in which mankind had fallen, as well as the dark powers that directly influenced them. *For the more sensitive reader,* I encourage you to keep in mind that the description of the corrupt world and the behavior of fallen mankind, were written to bring you to the conclusion: that the days in which Noah lived were so wicked and corrupt, that God had to judge the world in order to save mankind. And last of all, is the underlying theme of endearing love. All love is tested, and in the testing, love has a choice. As you read Sede, Seed of Eden, you will see love's choice unfold. It is my hope you enjoy Volume I of the two-volume story. I was both inspired and blessed to write it; and it is my hope you will be inspired and blessed as you read it.

Chapter 1

The Festival

A soft breeze blew the embers, sending flickering sparks into the night sky. Sede folded her hands behind her head and nestled back against the soft furs. As she watched the tiny bursts of light rise toward heaven, each spark seemed to add to the multitude of stars. Ah…the night sky, the smell of the fire, the sounds of her people…a deep satisfaction settled within her. Inhaling deeply, she closed her eyes to take it in: the music drifting from distant drums and flutes, the women's laughter while they served food, children squealing with joyful play in the firelight shadows, and the rise and fall of the elders' bellowing discussions. She loved it all. This was the annual feast of the Sethites, her kin. Pleased by her senses, she pondered how the day began.

She woke at dawn by the blowing of the tower horn announcing the first arrivals. Throughout the morning a steady flow of worshipers streamed through the great archway at the village gate. Families shouted from their doors, waving to their relatives to come and join them. Others set up tents on the village outskirts. Soon a multitude of tents surrounded trees and lined the village walls. The streets buzzed with excitement as musicians played from street corners while children ran here and there, excited to be free from the caravan and their parents' watchful eyes. More and more came throughout the day. They streamed through the great gate, flowing through the city like tributaries of water and creating a moving river of people. This annual feast brought them to worship at the "Village of Leaders": Taasa-toka. It was here that Noah lived, the 10th from Adam, serving the people of God and offering the sacrifice. She had stood at the door of their hut waiting with her father and Dosta. When they spotted her aunt and uncle, they joyfully waved them to come inside. They had journeyed, as they did every year, from the Agkib region and would stay in the spare room reserved just for them. By the time Adah and Hattil had settled themselves, the village had calmed from the excitement of the day.

As the sun began to set over the western hills, the tower horn blew once more, sending the call to worship. Drums beat in slow, methodic rhythm as the villagers reverently left their huts and tents and walked the earthen streets to the altar. Sede walked in silence, feeling the unspoken anticipation of those around her, which only added to her own. As they drew closer, she saw the great altar. It stood tall and magnificent, its white stones glowing in the setting sun. Being the tallest structure in the village, it towered solitary and unmistakable on the open grassy knoll. Built long ago by Seth, it was as old as the village. Seth, Adam's son, had been the first to offer the spotless white lamb as the yearly sacrifice. And for over a thousand years the sacrifices had been made. Throughout the generations that followed father Seth, each leader had been faithful to continue this one tribal ritual that united their people in faith. All had come tonight: old, young, and infant. It never ceased to fill her with wonder as she looked out over the sea of people rising like a tide around the glowing altar, all there for the same reason: to worship Yahweh.

As long as she could remember, she had stood by her father and his friends: Noah, Gruetat, and Erud. They were his dearest friends and their children hers. Noah held a soft place in her heart. Not only was he her uncle, the brother of her mother, but he was the chief of elders and leader of the Sethites. (For among all Sethites, there was no greater respect or honor given but to the elders and leader of their people.) The tower horn blew once more, and a hush fell on the great multitude. Noah climbed the worn steps that spiraled upward, worn by a thousand years of footsteps from leaders of long ago. A great platform extended near the top, and it was there that he looked down upon the people of God. He stood tall, strong, and confident. The glow of love and compassion radiated from his face. He was a man of great stature and strength and looked most dignified with his white hair and well-groomed beard. For a man of 500 years, he showed no frailty or weakness but was vibrant and full of life. In the lifespan of Sethite humans, he was but middle aged and in the prime of his life. His forefather Seth had lived to be 912. It was her uncle's strength and confidence that she admired as well as his quiet, strong love for Yahweh and his people.

Raising his voice, he began: "Beloved Sethite people, today we offer the sacrifice that our ancestor Seth established for all generations. This lamb represents a pure sinless man—the second Adam—the one Yahweh promised to Adam and Eve. This perfect man will restore what Adam and Eve lost for themselves and all mankind. He will be, for us, the ultimate sacrifice! We look to Yahweh to fulfill his promise! People of God, raise your hands and prayers to heaven!" She could feel the mounting excitement in the air. This would be the moment heaven and earth would meet! Everyone began to raise their hands, speaking their own prayers to Yahweh.

She heard little Adat at her side. Looking down on tiny hands lifted up and a face aglow with pure innocence, she heard her childlike prayer, "Thank you for making this world. I love the birds, and flowers, and trees. I love my mebba and abba and my sisters too, and…I love you, Yahweh." Sede thought that perhaps she had never seen such radiant beauty. Little Adat was only four, yet the beauty of holiness was upon her. Closing her own eyes, she lifted hands and face. As she listened to the rumbling prayers around her, the air seemed electrified with an atmosphere of love. Standing next to her, the deep voice of her father rumbled, "Yahweh, great and powerful God, thank you for the 'Promised One' to come. I trust you to fulfill your promise. I give you my praise!" Sede joined in, echoing his prayer, "Yes, Yahweh, send the 'Promised One.' May we live to see him in our generation!"

At that moment all the people were of one heart, mind, and soul. A crackling bolt of lightning flashed from heaven, and its power shook the very ground beneath them! As the smoke cleared, she looked to see. The lamb… it was gone! Only ash remained. Roaring shouts exploded from old and young alike. The Sethite sacrifice had been accepted! Although she'd seen the supernatural power of Yahweh every year, it still thrilled her. The same God who made heaven and earth had touched them this night! From where she stood, she could see the gathered multitude below. A sense of wonder filled her as she considered such a people as these; a people who had joined their love to worship the one True God.

As the last shout faded, a song rose from the people, a song all Sethites knew. It was the song of the "Chosen and the Blessed." The beautiful power of the men's voices resounded strong and mighty; the women's, ethereal and pure. Their harmony blended, creating a song of beauty.

From the altar of <u>our</u> hearts, the fire of love <u>ascends</u>   the women sang the heart of the people
Flames of the called, the chosen, the welcomed, the friend.

From the altar of <u>My</u> heart, the fire of love <u>descends</u>   the men sang the heart of God
Flames consuming Eve's 'Promised One,' for sins choice amends.

The burning altar now is <u>one</u>, the fires of love <u>unite</u>;   the women and men sang in unity
Flames of yours, mine, and ours, restoring Eden's life!

As they sang the melody over and over again, she took Adat's small hand and smiled. Both their voices lifted and blended with the others, rising to heaven like a prayer. These were the people of God—the Sethites, her kin.

As they continued to sing, Noah gathered the altar's ash in a carved wooden bowl. Engraved on its side were the names of the Sethite regions: Estoloph, Agkib, and Makkedaz. As he descended the winding stairs, Sede held her breath. She knew what was coming. There, there is was! Yahweh's glory descending from heaven! Everyone lifted their faces and hands to see and feel the sparkling cloud as it gently descended. Its light filled the darkened sky. Ah, the hush of peace… heaven had touched earth. As they all closed their eyes and absorbed the glory, it was a moment like no other. Hearts were gladly receiving Yahweh's love and the sweet breath of His presence. The moment of love lingered, settling and refreshing the innocent of heart. (For this was the one quality that characterized the Sethites; their innocence of heart.)

As Noah stepped forward, the people instinctively began to form a line before him. Using his thumbprint, he marked ash on the forehead and heart. This was their reminder: Yahweh would be forever in their thoughts and in their hearts. Without a word spoken, they silently paused before him as he marked them and then moved on. One after another they came. When Sede stood before him, he marked her forehead and then her heart. Leaning forward, he softly whispered, "You, Sede, are the blessed seed of the Lord!" Surprise filled her. Even though the words came from Noah's mouth, it seemed as if Yahweh had spoken them. Oh! The words! They felt like warm oil gently flowing through her. Stunned by what had just happened, she stepped aside to listen if he spoke to the next person. He didn't. She knew then that this was a word from the Lord just for her. 'I have been given a gift,' she thought. A peaceful calm filled her as she followed the steady flow of worshipers to the council fire.

And now, the ending of the day and the gathering around the council fire. The day had brought her to this moment. As she continued to watch the fire send sparks into the starry sky, she softly sighed from the pleasure of the moment. The visiting chatter slowly began to still, and the music faded to a stop. Noah stepped to the platform to read from Enoch's parchments. These writings were the Sethite's treasure. Written within them was the foundation of what they knew and believed. Every time they were read, she saw something new and wonderful about the great God they served, her people, and herself. Tonight was no different. This night's reading was about mighty angels sent to help mankind: messengers called "Watchers." Enoch, their forefather, was well familiar with these angels, having walked and talked with them. His parchments recorded his many adventures for future generations to read. These angels taught him how to write and develop the Sethite language and gave him insight into the creation of the world as well as the final judgment against the unholy and disobedient.

As Noah read, he explained that these angels, called Watchers, were created with the ability to choose just as humans had been. The Watchers Enoch had known chose to obey their Creator, but others had chosen to disobey. From these disobedient ones, mankind had been directly affected. Eve had been deceived by their leader, and the rest of his disobedient followers vowed to unite, rebelling against Yahweh, the Most High God. He would judge these fallen angels along with those who followed their evil ways. As she listened, she wondered how these fallen angels could know the perfection of heaven and yet want something else; to be perfect and complete but yet dissatisfied. What could possibly motivate them to resist the love of God? As she listened, leaning against the soft furs, she wondered what it would be like to meet a Watcher. She had never seen one, but some of their elders had. Would it be heaven and earth touching, like Yahweh's presence after the sacrifice? These Watchers seemed shrouded in mystery.

After Noah had finished, she smiled to see her father stand. Tolmaka would be the elder telling tonight's story. She knew his humor. He would have fun with his attentive audience. She loved these familiar stories: Adam and Eve; the two brothers, Cain and Abel; their forefather, Seth; and Enoch's amazing adventures in heaven. Slowly, he paced before the council fire and began the story of the first home of mankind, the Garden of Eden. He described the lush green grass, the beautiful misty waterfalls, the great whispering trees, and the animals with their gentle ways. Like a gentle breeze, the faint songs of angels filled the air, praising the Creator for making such beauty and crowning Adam as its king. This Adam had given the animals their names, and they expressed with their own voices their joy in being part of his world. Adam and Eve especially enjoyed the delectable fruit that fell from the rare and fragrant trees. With a sly smile, Tolmaka reached into his robe and suddenly withdrew apples, throwing them into the air. "Run, run, children! Catch the falling apples from Eden's tree!" Parents broke out in roaring laughter as their little ones scurried to catch the apples before they fell to the ground. Everyone enjoyed this special time that bonded them to each other and their history.

As the children settled once more in their parents' laps, he described the "cool of the evening," when Adam and Eve walked with Yahweh, enjoying his presence. Sede let her imagination wander…She could imagine that distant time and Eden place and could see herself there in the beautiful Garden. As she walked in the "cool of the evening," she could feel the soft green grass beneath her bare feet. Shafts of light fell on her face through the draping willow trees. Straining her ears, she heard the faint song of a bird. He was singing his sweet melody just for her! A warm, soft breeze brushed her cheek. 'A kiss from God,' she thought.

The Festival

The air was filled with a fragrance like no other. It smelled of flowers and spices all blended together. A stirring and fluttering gently moved within her, like the moving of butterfly wings. She was feeling the presence of the Lord, for He was walking beside her. Even in her imagination, this place felt like home. A spark landed on her hand and brought her back to her father's story.

"Why were they driven from this beautiful place?" he asked his listeners. The young children excitedly raised their hands, waving them to be chosen, even though they had heard the story many times before. As the story came to a conclusion, he recited the promise Yahweh had given Eve. From her "seed," the "Promised One" would come and crush the serpent's head—the serpent that had tempted and beguiled her in the Garden. Noah had just read how the leader of the fallen angels had disguised himself as this serpent.

Tolmaka paused and stood still, every eye fastened on him. Pointing his finger, he slowly approached a young maiden and asked, "Could you be the one to bear the 'seed'? Or could you be the one?" he asked the next. "Or is it you?" as he pointed to Sede. With a whirl, he turned, lifted his hands, and clapped twice. "Come, young maidens! Come dance the dance of celebration!" The drums began their rhythm, and the people gave a shout. All began clapping to the beat while Sede and the young maidens rose to dance. She grabbed a ceremonial robe and excitedly tied the sash. Playfully pulling their hands, she drew her friends Shoda and Ne-el into the circle of maidens. Laughing joyfully, they swayed and turned in unison as they danced the dance of the maidens. The sound of celebration rose in the night sky as heaven looked down on the joyful people of God. It was a great way to end a great day!

After goodnights were given to her family, she drew the curtain to her room. In the quiet, she settled in the nest of furs piled high on her cot. She would sleep well tonight. As she relaxed, she was drawn to the night sky through her window. The stars seemed even more beautiful than when she lay by the council fire. In a whisper, she prayed, "Yahweh, I sense your awesome wonder. Tonight you told me, through Noah, that I am your blessed seed. Your words felt like a gift given to me. I desire to give you a gift in return. The only thing I really own is my heart. So Yahweh…I give you…my heart." As the glow of love continued to warm her, she closed her eyes and drifted into peaceful sleep. The sleep of the innocent and the blessed.

Chapter 2

The Hunt

The wonderful smell of Dosta's pottage greeted Sede as she woke. Her aunt was a wonderful cook and enjoyed making things comfortable for her and her father. Dosta came to live with them when Sede was born. Lettah, her mother, had died in childbirth, and it seemed the right thing for both Tolmaka and Dosta since she had neither husband nor children of her own. Sede loved her aunt's kindness and happy spirit. She had one of those laughs that came from the belly. When she hugged her, she felt like a soft pillow for Dosta was as round as she was tall. In her heart, she was relieved that Dosta was good at domestic work and that she loved it. Relieved, so she could be free to hunt with her father.

In those days, the elders recognized the talents and potential in both the young sons of Adam and the daughters of Eve. Young women were not abandoned to domestic duties, and there was no expectation for all young men to hunt. Young men could learn weaving, tanning of leather, music, and the art of writing as well as the study of Enoch's parchments. Young women, if they had skill and courage, could be trained as hunter/warrior. Sede showed both skill with the bow and a strong spirit. The elders gave her permission to hunt when she was only twelve. That was five years ago. It saddened her at times when she thought about her hunting days coming to an end. When the young female hunters became betrothed, they could no longer "go out and come in" with the hunt but entered a "time of preparation." From then on, they exchanged their hunting skins for robes befitting the married. When she thought about her future, she would dismiss it and tell herself, "That time is far away; I have today with my father and the thrill of the hunt!" She hunted with her friends, Shoda and Zara, and the sons of Noah: Shem, Ham, and Japheth. Like all hunters from her tribe, they hunted in packs. This was her pack, and their pack leader was her father, Tolmaka.

The village was quiet and still asleep when she and her father prepared to leave. Although it was the time of festival, the people still had to eat. All the hunting packs would hunt to feed the visitors for it was considered a great honor to feed your guest. Taasa-toka was a large village compared to other Sethite villages, boasting ten hunting packs. Their pack was waiting when they arrived at the village gate and gave each other the customary greeting: hands to forearms, touching foreheads, and a whispered, "Ha-la-lah." With a rush of excitement and eagerness in her voice, she asked, "Where will we hunt today?" "Today we hunt east," Tolmaka answered, pointing his spear to the rising sun.

It was dawn when they left the village; the other packs had separated in different directions. The mist that rose each night to water the earth was still hovering over the ground, and shafts of light were rising from the horizon. As they kept an even running pace, the thumping of their sandals on the soft earth set a rhythm, like the beating of a heart. As she listened to the steady thumping, it matched her own heart's rhythm. Her father's long braided hair swayed as he ran before her, and his breath puffed as he exhaled in the cool morning air. A wonderful sense of oneness with her pack filled her. She was a hunter among her kin!

As the sun rose higher in the sky, they continued until the rolling hills led to an escarpment. Scaling the rocks, they crested the ridge. The wind whirled, blowing up the rock walls that lined the valley below. At the far end, an opening in the wall led to the prairie beyond. Splitting up, they searched for shade to establish camp. Shoda called out, "I found water!" Following her voice, they descended to a small clearing between two rock ledges. Several trees shaded a pool of water, and mist filled the air from the cascading waterfall overhead. It would make a good camp for their return.

The men fell prostrate at the water's edge. The cool water was refreshing from their long run. "We'll scout the area," offered Shem.

"Wait," cautioned Tolmaka, and he untied his leather strap. Handing Shem the horn, he continued, "I saw strange tracks. They look to be the tracks of a

Nephilim. Sound the alarm if you need us." The three brothers scaled the rock wall and disappeared over the ridge.

Shoda knelt by the water's edge. Drawing the water to her mouth by cupped hands, she lost most of it through her fingers. Sede laughed and shook her head. "Better to lay on your stomach and drink." She dropped to her stomach and drew in deeply. Tolmaka chuckled while he and Zara knelt nearby and filled their water skins.

Sede stretched out in the soft grass, resting from the long run. It was nice to take a break. As she watched Zara wade in the water, trying her luck at spearing fish, Shoda knelt beside her. "It's a great day, isn't it?" Shoda said as she sighed and leaned back. "The morning is so clear, and I sense such a peace."

Sede smiled, for she, too, had felt the same things. "Shoda, I'm so glad we not only share friendship but also the hunt. This morning I'm realizing how wonderful it is being a part of what we do together."

Smiling, Shoda softly chuckled. "We've both come a long way from the inexperienced hunters we were five years ago. Now that we're really good at what we do, we'll soon be learning new skills at something completely different."

Sede pondered her words. "Yes, I wonder what our lives will be like when we can no longer 'go out and come in' with the hunt; when we begin our own families. I fear I'll miss it terribly."

"I've thought of that too. I've tried to comfort and tell myself that I will be ready to make that change when I have to. I'm beginning to see Yahweh prepares us to accept change when our hearts are open and willing for something new." She softly laughed and then continued with a twinkle in her eye, "I'm hoping that's the way it turns out." Their quiet moment was suddenly interrupted by the sound of the horn.

Sede looked at her father. He nodded to Shoda and Zara. In confident control, he spoke, "Time to go!" Sede grabbed her bow and quiver, Tolmaka his spear, Shoda her sling, and Zara her boomerang. Following each other's footsteps, they climbed from rock to rock until they reached the top of the ridge. From there they could see below. Suddenly they dropped to the ground. Straight down the rock wall was a 12-foot Nephilim! He hadn't seen them, but she felt the grip of fear. Adrenaline surged through her arms and legs, and she could feel her heart pounding in her chest. She knew what was about to happen would result in either victory or death. "Steady," whispered Tolmaka, "Steady." Sede nodded, feeling herself respond to his words.

"Shoda, you circle right, and Sede, you left. Zara, you stay with me. Keep low and wait for my signal." As the Nephilim faced the rock wall, he roared and feverishly clawed at the cave in front of him. The breeze blew his foul scent up the valley wall, making them nearly gag. He smelled of rotten meat and horrible body odor. Dried blood and pieces of meat matted his thick hair. A leather tunic hung loosely across his chest and about his loins, and old scars marred his body. He roared once more, and the fierceness of rage flamed wild in his eyes. His fingers were now bleeding from feverously clawing the rocks. Shem's horn blew again, the sound coming from below. The Nephilim let out another deafening roar as he clawed at the rocks with increased zeal. He pulled the dagger from its scabbard and jabbed at the cave.

"Shem and his brothers must be trapped in the cave," Tolmaka whispered. Still crouching, Sede drew her bow back, and Shoda loaded her sling. Zara gripped her boomerang, waiting for Tolmaka's word. "Ha-la-lah!" he shouted and stood, hurling his spear. The women rose in unison and released their weapons. It was amazing! The whistling sound of projectiles could be heard as they flew through the air. Tolmaka's spear lodged below the Nephilim's rib cage, and Sede's arrow pierced his left eye. A cratered hole was bleeding where Shoda's stone was lodged between his eyes. The razor-sharp edge of Zara's boomerang stuck in the side of his neck.

It all happened so fast that the Nephilim didn't know what hit him. He staggered on his feet, pawing at his eye, while blood flowed down his forehead and neck. Screams came from his throat, sending chills through them; the hair on their necks raised in fear. At that very moment, Shem leapt from the cave with his dagger drawn. Landing on the Nephilim's chest, he clung to the giant's leather skins. With one deep slash, he slit his throat. The giant staggered while weaving back and forth. Finally, like a falling tree, he fell straight back. The weight of his great body caused the earth to rumble and shook the very rocks beneath them.

Leaping from his chest just as he hit the ground, Shem rolled and stood to his feet. Lifting his dagger in victory, he shouted "Ha-la-lah!" His chest rose and fell with the adrenalin of battle pumping through him. And just as the Nephilim's roar had echoed off the rock walls, now Shem's shout filled the valley with the sound of victory. It sent a new surge of adrenaline rushing through them all.

Tolmaka looked below to see Japheth helping Ham out of the cave and limping on one leg. Spontaneously, Zara and Shoda climbed down to join them. The Nephilim had jabbed his dagger into the cave, slashing Ham's knee. His discomfort was obvious for his face writhed with pain. Shoda helped Japheth shoulder his weight while Zara grabbed their weapons. Slowly, they began their descent while Tolmaka followed close behind. Sede climbed down to meet Shem, who was retrieving their weapons from the dead giant. "That was amazing how you jumped on him and slit his throat! It happened so fast!" Excitement was evident in her voice as she marveled at what had just happened.

"Yes, it did! I didn't even think about. I just did it!" He took the dagger that was still clutched in the giant's fist and untied a pouch that hung at his waist. With excitement still pumping through them, they climbed over the ridge and down the other side to join the others.

When Shem reached the grass near the water's edge, he dropped to his knees and rolled on his back, resting his knife on his chest. He felt his breathing calm as he slowly exhaled the tension that felt like a knot in his chest. 'That Nephilim was fierce in his desire to kill us,' he thought. 'Good that we found the cave in time; good that we had Tolmaka and the women; and good we had Yahweh's favor.' He exhaled once more, rolled back to his knees, and washed the blood from his blade. This was his first Nephilim kill, and he had lived to tell of it!

Shoda busied herself rinsing the blood from Ham's knee. Pressing her hand against the cut, she waited. She knew the bleeding would soon stop. Sede marveled as she watched her friend. Shoda was every bit the strong hunter/warrior, but she had this softer side too. She watched as Shoda slowly and gently smoothed mud over his wound and then reassured him with her soft words. It was though she was watching a secret between them and felt their bond. In her innocence, she blushed and looked away. Not only were Shoda and Ham hunters of the same pack, but someday they would marry. Their parents had made the arrangements long ago. She was happy for her friend. Ham was an honorable man, brave, and the son of her uncle, Noah. Shoda would become her relative through marriage. Since childhood, she had been her dearest friend and often called her sister.

Her attention shifted to young Zara. She stood near the water's edge, sharpening her boomerang edge with a whetting stone from her waist pouch. Zara was but thirteen and the newest addition to their pack. Tolmaka had been wise to keep her close to his side during the battle with the Nephilim, for though she was brave and fearless, she had a lot to learn about hunting and warfare. Sede watched as she gave her boomerang a light toss and caught it in its return. The smile on her young face reflected the great satisfaction she felt. She had helped bring down the giant!

As the sun began to set, the small valley darkened quickly. Tolmaka started a fire, and they gathered around. Opening the wrapped skins, he pulled off a piece of dried meat Dosta had prepared for them and passed it to the others. With legs crossed, he pondered the battle and the dead Nephilim over the ridge. Grabbing a stick, he poked at the fire and mumbled to himself, "Nephilim."

Sede heard him say something. "What did you say, Father?"

"Oh, I was thinking about the Nephilim we brought down."

"Tell us of the Nephilim," she asked. "We've heard the stories of Enoch, but the parchments tell us little about them, only that they exist."

"Yes," chimed in Japheth. "Where did they come from? If Yahweh made all things good, why are they evil and different from humans?" The others nodded, wondering the same thing.

He was silent for a while and then mumbled, "Yahweh did not create them. They were made by others." With puzzled expressions, they drew in closer, tightening their circle. He looked at Noah's sons. "Your father does not read all that is written about the Nephilim. In his wisdom, he knows our people would live in fear if they knew how fierce and threatening they were." He paused as if collecting his thoughts and then continued, "When Adam and Eve began to have children and their children had children, mankind multiplied on the earth. Yahweh sent mighty holy angels called 'Watchers' to teach them the knowledge of the Lord and watch over them. Two hundred of these Watchers rebelled against their assignment to serve mankind. They saw that the daughters of man were beautiful and to be desired! These Watchers devised an evil plan to create families for themselves and boast themselves to be like the 'Most High.' Yahweh had created a family for himself, and in their arrogance, they wanted a family too. Rebellion consumed them, and they chose themselves wives. They prey upon both Sethites and Cainites but favor Sethite maidens. They desire the most virtuous women. Our maidens are innocent not only in body but in soul. My own wife's sister was stolen. It grieved her sorely. Even with her last breath, her thoughts were for her lost sister." Sede's eyes widened, for rarely did he speak of her mother. She sensed his grief was still near even though many years had passed.

He continued, "Yahweh created angels with a different glory than man's glory. There is a unique glory for angels and a unique glory for mankind. Yahweh never intended for these two glories to mix and unite. Every seed was to produce after its own kind. Man was to create after mankind and not mix his seed with angels, animals, fish, or birds. Yahweh had given man and animals the command-ment to be fruitful and fill the earth. He had not given that commandment to angels, although they possessed the seed of life within them. In comparison, it is just as the tree of 'Knowledge of Good and Evil.' It was put in the Garden, but Adam and Eve were told not to eat from it. So in like manner, angels have the seed of life within themselves but were not to share it with mankind or among themselves. Angels were not intended to produce after their own kind. They were created for a different purpose. Perhaps this was a temptation for them, as the tree of 'Knowledge of Good and Evil' was for Adam and Eve. Anyway, it was not in Yahweh's design for angels to reproduce. Only mankind and animals were to reproduce after their own kind. Yahweh has set boundaries within his creation, and this command for each seed to produce after its own kind was one of those boundaries. It is also an interesting thought that angels were created with Yahweh's spoken word, but mankind was fashioned by his own hands and given his living breath—the 'roo-akh' of God. Both man and angel each have their own created purpose. Mankind are Yahweh's children; angels are his servants. Because Yahweh wants his creation to worship him freely, he gave both man and angels a free will. They both have the ability to choose 'good' and abide within his commandments or disobey and turn from serving and worshiping him. These fallen Watchers chose to lust for women and blend their seed with the seed of mankind. Nephilim are the offspring of fallen angels and the daughters of men."

Sede's mouth dropped open. Never would she have imagined such a thing possible! The thought of it made her sick to her stomach. Something rose up within her and made her speak, "This is a defilement and contrary to the ways of the Lord!"

"Yes, daughter, it is! These Watchers rebelled against the boundaries of creation, exercising their own willful plan and ignoring Yahweh's will and plan. The perfect angelic seed within them that was never to be given to any they chose to mix with mankind. Enoch wrote that they defiled themselves with mankind. It was considered a defilement to blend the seeds of creation. Even Nephilim bodies are an abomination and a perversion. Giant in size, some rip open the womb of their human mothers at birth! They have two rows of teeth, with six digits on both hand and foot. Their skulls are elongated, unlike humans, and they vary in height. Some are a foot or two taller than man, and others are as tall as cedar trees. They breed with humans, thus polluting the seed of man. Some Nephilim are grotesque like the one we destroyed today, but some are regal and known as 'Mighty Men of Renown.' These other Nephilim show great intelligence and build mighty fortresses and wonders. These angels gave their sons the knowledge they possessed from heaven. They taught them to understand science, mathematics, the path of the stars, and seasons. Some even have the knowledge to manipulate the soul, stealing the innocence from within them! With this angelic knowledge, they seduce and deceive the Cainites to worship them as gods. They plunder the Sethites and corrupt them to do their bidding. These fallen angels also teach their wives the secrets of root cutting, spells, potions, and tattooing. They perverted the music of heaven, transforming it into sounds that summon demons, whom they eagerly embrace. All the knowledge that the Watchers knew from heaven has been twisted and perverted into evil. It became known as 'dark knowledge.' Yahweh will judge these fallen angels with an everlasting judgment. Enoch was shown this and recorded it so we, the Sethites, would know Yahweh's righteous judgments. Noah read about these Watchers just last night. It's interesting that we would encounter one of their offspring today and speak of this tonight. I'm surprised that we would see one so far into the wilderness. I haven't encountered a Nephilim since they raided our village centuries ago."

His hunters perked up when they heard about this raid. They knew the tales of the great 'Battle of Taasa-toka' but knew little of the details. Shem spoke up, "I've heard stories about the Nephilim raid on our village. Tell us of this great battle." The others eagerly looked at him, wanting to hear more.

"Well...I was a young hunter in those days," he began. "That was nearly 400 years ago." Tolmaka was middle aged, as was Noah. "It was a time before our village had walls and towers, but Taasa-toka was a large village even then. My hunting pack included Noah, Gruetat, Erud, and three female hunters: Lettah, Karan, and Tein. All packs hunted together; not as we hunt today. We had individual packs but hunted our game from one herd and returned to the village at the same time. On this particular day, as the sun was setting, we drew near the village. When we crested the eastern hills, we saw it! It was a raid, and the village was on fire! When we drew near, what we saw was not raiding Cainites but Nephilim. Jair, our leader, was the one who organized us that night. We surrounded Taasa-toka as though we were approaching a hunt. With stealth, we found our position and waited for the sound of his horn. When it came...we struck! A spirit of power and might came upon us, the like I've never felt since! I believe to this day it was the power of Yahweh helping us in battle. We fought throughout the night, and at dawn, the last of the giants were dead. There were none left alive to return and tell of our wilderness village. The giants were fierce in battle and hard to bring down, just as we saw today. The battle for Taasa-toka was a day of wonder, glory, and might! After that battle, we rebuilt our village, building the walls and towers we see today. For 400 years we have had peace." They sat in silence, pondering his words.

Tolmaka poked the fire again, making the embers come alive. Shem grabbed the pouch he and Sede had found on the dead Nephilim. Opening it, he saw strange objects. "What are these?" he asked.

Tolmaka looked with knowing eyes. "The strange stones are objects used for sorcery, and the carved figures are images of the angels they worship." Shem looked at them in disgust. "Yes," said Tolmaka. "Foul indeed! Cast them into the fire!" When Shem threw them in the flames, the sound of screams rose and disappeared into the night. Startled, the young hunters fell back. Only Tolmaka sat still and silent. "I have seen this before, long ago, when I was a young hunter. I was lost from my pack and found a great city near the sea. It was the city of the Cainites. I saw their sorcery and evil culture. They sacrificed their newborns to the fallen angels and summoned demons with their drums and incantations. These demons did foul things to their maidens while their elders laughed and lustfully watched. It was a place of great spiritual darkness and evil that could be felt. It was only by Yahweh's mercy I escaped with my life."

Ham seemed especially curious and asked, "Being from the seed of righteous Adam, why do Cainites welcome evil into their lives?"

Tolmaka settled back on his furs, giving thought to his question. "The Cainites have forsaken the ways of their father Adam. Cainites, like Sethites, have a choice to serve and obey Yahweh or disobey and yield to evil. The Cainites choose to lust after every evil imagination of their hearts. You remember the story of Cain and Abel's sacrifices they offered to Yahweh. Abel's was accepted, but Cain's was not. When Cain became angry, Yahweh told him that sin was crouching at the door of his heart. He was to have mastery over his own heart. But instead, Cain opened the door of his heart to sin and yielded. He murdered his brother Abel, and sin became his desire. All Cainites do the same. They hold no restrictions upon their desires. Evil consumes them continually. They prey upon the innocent and pervert their young. No innocence remains in them. They have no spiritual foundation for their people as we do. This is why Enoch's teachings are so valuable to us. They show us the way of the Lord. Only by teaching and caring for each new generation will our people maintain lives that honor Yahweh. This is why the Sethites earnestly train the next generation. Above all—and I say this to you, my sons—you must protect the innocence of your children. It was innocence that was lost in the Garden when Adam and Eve sinned. This is why Sethites value innocence so highly. It will be your responsibility to guard and mentor your children's innocence, as I do my daughter's. Innocence has its own time to grow full bloom. At some point in a life, wisdom embraces innocence.

Innocence is not lost but becomes a thing of beauty—full and mature!" He looked at Sede with loving tenderness. "It's not only for the daughters of Eve that innocence is to be protected but for the sons of Adam as well. I see that your father has done well in you, my sons, and yours as well, Shoda and Zara." The young hunters felt the power of his words, and comfort rested upon them. Their fathers *had* watched over and protected their innocence.

Tolmaka poked the fire once more as his thoughts shifted. "There is a great gulf between the two earth families. The Sethites have kept themselves pure and innocent but, I say, only with Yahweh's help. The Cainites are so corrupt that if the Sethites and Cainites blended their seed…there would be no righteous seed upon the earth. No righteous seed could be born to crush the serpent's head and fulfill the promise given to Eve. May we live to see this 'seed' in our generation!" As his words settled within them, they drew close to the fire. Sleep would welcome them, and morning would come soon enough. Yawning, Tolmaka said, "When the sun rises, I will send Ham on his way with Japheth, Shoda, and Zara. Sede and Shem will stay behind and hunt with me. Take your rest, my children. Tomorrow will dawn a new day."

Ham left early as Japheth and Shoda shouldered his weight and Zara carried their weapons. Slowly they began their way back to the village. "Come, let us continue our hunt and find food for our village." Tolmaka waved them forward and took the lead. They slowed their pace when they came to a grove of trees. "Stop," he said in a hush. "Shem, see these tracks?"

"Yes, the tracks of the olumba."

Tolmaka smiled. "If we be blessed today, we'll feast tonight!" The three crawled, inching their way forward. When they reached the edge of the underbrush, they caught the scent of the olumba. A large herd grazed in the clearing beyond. "Shem, you circle left and wait until they move forward. We'll come up behind them and make easy prey of the stragglers. Sede and I will wait here." Shem moved out of sight while Sede and her father settled in the tall grass.

Lying on her back, she felt the warmth of the sun on her face and inhaled the sweet scent of grass. She could hear the low of the olumba as they grazed. She loved these quiet times on the hunt. It put her heart at ease. As she relaxed, her mind wandered while she gazed through the top of the trees to the blue sky beyond. She began to think of her future with Shem. "Father, when Shem and I marry, how can I give my heart to him and still love you? Won't my heart be divided?"

Tolmaka smiled at her innocence. "Oh my daughter, your heart has the ability of greater love than you know! You have known the love for friends, kinsmen, and me, but when you give your heart to your husband, you will begin to understand the love you were created for. Yahweh has put this love in every woman's heart. It was put there when Eve, mother of all women, was created. This love made Adam complete. Your husband's deepest needs will be met by that love. It will create a 'oneness' that will fill you both with wonder! Your mother gave that kind of love to me. I came to understand that I would have never been complete without it. The best thing of all is that our united love created you, Sede. I see the oneness of our love in you—part of her, part of me. Our love created a life."

As Sede pondered his words, her thoughts turned to Adam and Eve's promised 'seed.' "Father, I wonder who will be the woman to bear the 'seed,' the 'Promised One' who will crush the serpent's head. Her love and his love would really be something to create a man that could do that!"

"Yes, my daughter. He really will be something! The great love of the universe will create him. This 'seed' that becomes a life will be to us…everything! All Sethites live with that hope. All that our father Adam lost in the Garden will be restored to us. Enoch wrote about this. It blesses me that you ponder such things. I know Yahweh is with you." Tolmaka had done well to protect her innocence and wait until she was ready to learn more about life. He knew that she had centuries, giving her "time" to learn. He was beginning to see the glory of wisdom embracing her innocence and was pleased with her progress. As he smiled at her, she saw the pride of a father for one who is cherished. His wisdom and counsel always brought her comfort.

She recalled the day he told her of the Sethite tradition of choosing a mate for their child. This was considered a great honor for the father. It was determined before they even had children that Tolmaka and Noah would join their children in marriage. They were more than kin; they were bonded friends.

The Hunt

They had shared many adventures hunting, uniting their hearts in both friendship and trust. It was only after Noah became the Sethite leader that their paths took different directions. Instead of hunting, Noah turned his heart to seek Yahweh. He needed His guidance to lead the people in righteousness and the ways of Seth. They determined that their firstborns, Sede and Shem, would be united. Since Tolmaka had but one child, Noah chose the children of Gruetat to unite with his other sons: Ham and Japheth. Gruetat had three daughters: Shoda, Ne-el, and Adat. Shoda had been pledged to Ham and Ne-el to Japheth. This pleased Sede. She knew that her beloved friend would become her sister through marriage. Their lives would always be a part of one another's.

Her thoughts continued to drift as she considered Shem. 'He is now my friend, but someday I shall know love for him.' She remembered the first time she felt something special between them. They had taken three young hunters on a training hunt. It was customary for more experienced hunters to help train the younger hunters—those who were not yet assigned to a pack. This gave the young hunters experience in tracking and use of weapons and the older hunters experience in leadership. On this hunt, Shem and Sede were mentoring Ma-la, Te-mar, and Ro-nad. They had found a small herd of calandra and positioned their young hunters strategically. Calandra is a small game, similar in size to a small wild boar.

They were ready to rush the herd when a pack of wolves charged. The frightened herd began to stampede, making Ma-la's position vulnerable. Shem saw the threat and bolted forward, running with the thundering herd. Through the cloud of dust and roaring hooves, it was an amazing sight to see. He ran alongside her, not slowing his pace. With one great swoop, he lifted her up and under his arm. The cloud of dust was so thick he couldn't see what lie ahead. While the herd ran over the steep face of a canyon, Shem, too, started to fall. In the split second of decision, he threw Ma-la from his cradled side into the air to catch a tree branch hanging over the canyon edge. Grabbing the limb, she hung in midair as Shem plunged forward into the rising dust. Unable to see, Sede and the children thought he had perished far below. Ma-la climbed from the tree while the others peered over the edge. Through the rising dust, they saw his hands climbing the rock wall. When he stood to his feet, Sede eagerly hugged his neck in relief. To her surprise, she felt him respond to her hug. His arms surrounded her not as a hug but as an embrace. He communicated his affection, which gave her a start. Never had they hugged but in friendship. She felt something different this time.

At that moment, something was awakened in her; something she didn't know was there. It was confusing yet exciting all at the same time. As this strange and new feeling subsided, a strong admiration rose in its place. He had risked his life for another. He had thought nothing of his own safety but only his responsibility to protect his young charge. Later that night, young Ma-la told her story to the elders around the council fire. Sede remembered how she felt when Shem stepped forward and the elders honored him, giving him praise for his bravery and trusted position as 'teacher of the young.' As she watched, it began to dawn on her—this man would someday be her husband! That was the first day she began to feel a connection with him.

The olumba began to move, and Tolmaka and Sede prepared themselves for the chase. They faintly heard Shem's signal. It was the signal their pack used to alert each other: the call of the conoka bird. They rose at the same time and rushed the herd. Stampeding hooves lifted the dust as they closed in. Tolmaka's spear flew through the air, lodging below the shoulder of his target, and the beast fell on the spot. Sede spotted her olumba. She released her arrow, hitting its neck with a thud. The olumba stumbled but regained his footing and continued to run. Shem threw his spear and dropped her hit. They had gotten their prey! As the herd ran into the distance, Tolmaka joined them, smiling at their success. "Well done, hunters. You worked as a pack! Your spear felled him, Shem, right through the heart. You'll be honored tonight."

"You as well, Tolmaka."

Sede crouched to tie the olumba's limp legs while Shem pulled the spear and arrow from it side. Lifting the olumba, Shem shouldered its weight. Tolmaka lifted his too, balancing it across his shoulders. Sede followed from behind while darting several fowl that she hung from her belt. They had gotten their prey, and there would be songs sung tonight.

The sun was setting as they followed their own tracks west, and vultures circled overhead when they passed the rock escarpment. It was the feast of the

Nephilim. "A fitting judgment for the 'accursed'!" Tolmaka spouted.

"Aye," answered Shem.

"Aye," echoed Sede.

When they stood atop the hill, she saw their village in the distance. A great crowd had gathered at the gate, welcoming several packs returning with their game. As they drew near, she spotted wild flowers along the beaten trail. "Oh! Folendia, my favorite!" Without stopping, she withdrew her knife and cut a handful as she passed. "I'll hang these in my room." The thought pleased her as she continued walking, smelling their sweet fragrance. Shem gave Tolmaka a little wink, and they both smiled. She, too, had a softer side, and both men had seen it. As they approached the greeters at the gate, a deep pleasure welled up within her. Her pack had brought food for their guests. When they entered the gate, their kinsmen began clapping and singing in delight. They sang the "Hunters Song."

Open fields sing their song
To the mighty, brave, and strong
Come to me and search my lands
And prove your skill of hand

My game is great, my herds abound
With thundering hooves upon the ground
They roam, they graze, they wait
For the trap, the plan, the bait

As spear and arrow bow the sky
Your prize upon the ground will lie
Skill was proven true through you
Your value, worth, and praise are due

Home to happy, cheerful hearts
For you have done your part
Your song and praise are due
You worthy, brave, and true!

Over and over they sang while the three hunters made their way to the council fire. Other hunters had brought numerous olumba, shosposcus, dworta, deer, wild boar, calandra, and baroths along with countless wild fowl. This *was* a reason to celebrate! At the council fire, the hunting packs presented the hunters that had felled their prey. Shem and Tolmaka sat in the long row of hunters. She was happy for them, for she, too, had sat in the seat of honor from other hunts. Fellow hunters passed by the seated, bowing at the waist, and giving the customary praise: "Thank you my brother/sister, my kinsmen, for your courage and skill. You have fed our people this day." As she paused before Shem and bowed, she was suddenly struck by how confident he seemed. She felt admiration for him but then suddenly blushed. Shocked, but then instantly curious, she wondered why she had blushed. 'This is the same feeling I had when he embraced me after saving Ma-la,' she thought. Shem smiled at her. "You helped make this honor possible, Sede. It was your arrow that slowed my prey, making him an easy mark."

She smiled and bowed once more, crossing her bow over her chest. "You are worthy to receive praise, Shem. It is my honor to give it." Graciously, she smiled and dismissed her pondering questions. Joining her father and Dosta and her aunt and uncle, she began to feast.

As the night came to a close, she felt the weight of the day. It had been a long two days of hunting. She and her father slowly made their way home while the rest of their family lingered. Lamps flickered in hut windows along the way, and the glow of the moon softly lit the path before them. As she listened to the festive, distant music, she suddenly realized how wonderful her life was. She slid her arm around her father's waist and gave him a loving hug, resting her head on his shoulder as they walked. "I love our people and our ways," she softly said. "This has been a wonderful night. In this moment, Father, it feels as though there's an invisible bow string threaded from our people to my heart. This night has been the arrow sent from that bow. I feel the bond I have with this world of the Sethite, my kin." He looked down into her sweet face, and his eyes glistened with tears. She was his daughter, a true Sethite indeed. He saw the promise of the woman she would become—the mother of their people—when Shem would take

Noah's place. His heart warmed as he thought, 'How wonderful for the future generation to have a woman like Sede to love and cherish them.'

Chapter 3

Sethite Games

The rising sun greeted her, streaming warmth and light through the bedroom window. Squinting, she slowly yawned and stretched but then sat up with a start! There would be no hunting today. This was the day for Sethite games! She quickly dressed and braided her hair, breaking a blossom from the Folendia she'd hung on the wall and slipped it into her hair. Muffled voices could be heard. Breakfast was waiting.

After each year's sacrifice, the villages competed with each other in Sethite games. Any hunter could compete, but of course, it was the more seasoned hunters who excelled. They competed with great delight, for it was not so much a matter of competing with each other as demonstrating skill and mastery of the weapons used in hunting. They were, more or less, testing their own precision with their weapon of choice. She began competing at twelve, and won once, when she was fourteen. She looked forward to challenging her skills today.

After grabbing a quick bite from the hearth and giving hugs all around for her family, she went in search of her pack. It was from the council platform that the games were announced. There, different hunting skills were demonstrated through competition: the spear, slingshot, bow and arrow, boomerang, and knife. But there were also two other challenges. These were held just for the fun of it and included rope climbing and foot racing. The foot race was everyone's favorite because from anywhere in the village, the hunters could be seen racing above them on the village wall. The wall's width was roomy enough to pass those ahead, and the circumference afforded a very long track—an amazing 320 rods!

Sede, Seed of Eden

Excitement could be felt as the noisy crowd gathered and waited for the games to begin. Sede found her pack visiting with Lebna, the elder who announced the games. In hurried excitement, he was making last minute preparations with his son Tolin, who had made the wreaths that would crown the winners. Stepping to the platform, he lifted his horn. With a long blast, the crowd stilled. "We will begin with spears!" The spear would be thrown at a painted bull's eye on a round cut of wood. Eager hunters lined up with spears of different lengths. Shem left the pack and stood last in line. With a little chuckle, Shoda whispered to Sede, "The best waits till last!" She knew his skill and that his mark was always in the heart of his kill.

A tall, strong female was first to hit the center. Five more struck the bull's eye. After the long line had thrown, it was now Shem's turn. Stepping to the mark, he prepared to throw. Drawing back, he caught Sede's eye and winked. She shook her head, for she knew—as he did—that his skill far surpassed those he was competing with. He threw and hit dead center. She and Shoda squealed in delight, shouting, "Ha-la-lah!" The seven formed a line as the target was moved forward. After each had thrown, two remained: the tall female and Shem. With growing anticipation, the target was moved again. The female drew back and threw, releasing the spear to arch high in the air. It fell short and lodged in the ground but a hand's span from the bull's eye. An "ooh" of disappointment echoed through the crowd. Shem stepped forward, and the crowd stilled. Drawing back, his large arm muscles flexed to the force of his anticipated throw. Catching Sede's eye once more, he smiled in confidence. Releasing the spear, it spiraled through the air. It seemed the whole crowd inhaled as he threw and then suddenly exhaled in praise as it hit the center with a thud. Cheering and shouting erupted as Lebna beckoned him to the platform. As he passed, the female hunter slapped him soundly on the back and spouted, "Well done, hunter, well done!"

Stepping forward, Lebna placed the winner's wreath on his head. The crowd continued to cheer as Sede and Shoda gathered around and echoed each other's praise. "Well done, Shem, well done!" Noah and Ezmere were delighted too. Noah gripped his shoulder with pride. "Your skill was proven today, son! That was a joy to watch!" Throwing her arms around his neck, Ezmere gave him a loving hug. Whispering in his ear, she shared her affection. "That was amazing, son. I'm so proud of you." He was then pulled away in conversation with Tolmaka.

Taking Noah's arm, she reminisced, "I see you in him; that same confidence and control. I remember a time when I thrilled to see *you* compete."

He smiled, remembering too. He had loved being a hunter. Looking into her eyes, he smiled once more. "And I remember your arms around my neck when I was honored. You are still most fair, my wife." Laying her head on his shoulder, she watched Shem as his pack gathered around him, enjoying his moment with them.

"He will make a fine leader, will he not?"

"He will, my wife. I see Yahweh preparing him even now. Wisdom has begun to embrace his innocence." He grasped her hand and tenderly kissed it, touching his forehead to hers. She smiled and sighed, enjoying their moment of endearment....

As Lebna announced the slingshot throw, Shoda stepped forward to form the line. The target was a small gourd stuck on a pole twenty cubits away. Nodding his head, Lebna signaled Shoda to begin. She chose a stone and whirled her sling, building momentum. Faster than the eye could follow, her stone shot through the air, exploding the gourd. Both Shem and Sede yelled above the cheering crowd, "You did it, Shoda! You did it!" The cheering continued as each hunter took their turn. After all had thrown, only Shoda and another female hunter remained. The target was moved ahead. But to increase difficulty and prove true skill, three gourds were lined up spaced five cubits apart. The stone had to hit the first gourd and continue in line to hit the second and third. With hushed silence, the other hunter began. She whirled her sling, winding it faster and faster. Releasing the stone, the first gourd exploded but ricocheted off the second pole. The crowd responded with disappointment. Tension mounted as Shoda stepped to the mark on the ground. Catching the eye of her father, he nodded. It was his nod that triggered her confidence. Smiling, she slowly exhaled. Confidently, she whirled her sling. Faster and faster it whirled and began to hum with speed. The stone shot from her sling, and instead of exploding the targets, it cut a perfect hole through each gourd. Her mouth dropped open, hardly believing what she saw. The cheering went on and on as Lebna rested the wreath on her head.

Sede came alongside, amazed beyond words. "How did you do that, Shoda? That was unbelievable!"

The wonder in her voice brought a blush to Shoda's cheeks. "I'm just as surprised as you are, Sede! I have no idea how I did that!" They laughed and hugged, for it was the same wonder they experienced on the hunt when their weapons struck their racing game at just the right time and in just the right spot. Gruetat and Mersta, along with her sisters, huddled around, laughing and hugging her in excitement.

Adat slipped her small hand into Sede's. "You'll win too, Sede. I know you will! I'm going to use a bow when I grow up and be a mighty hunter just like you!" Laughing for the sweetness she saw in her, she picked her up and swung her around in a circle. She knew Adat admired her and didn't mind that she followed her around. In fact, she called her "my little shadow."

Zara's competition was next. For only thirteen, she was an amazing hunter; skilled with the boomerang and fierce in spirit. That fierceness made her very valuable to the pack. She was not afraid to take risks, although she needed discipline in the risks she chose to take. Tolmaka was careful to guide her and bring her skill under his watchful eye. Foolish risks could put all their lives in jeopardy. Zara's weapon of choice was the boomerang. She had been mentored by an elder from another village when he had seen her interest in this unusual weapon as well as her lack of fear in handling it. It was his joy to teach someone who was hungry to learn.

Their target was the same as the slingshots. One after another, the hunters took their turn, propelling their boomerang through the air and severing the gourds. The poles were moved forward, narrowing down the competitors to two: Zara and an older hunter. But in the end, he was declared the winner. Zara so admired his skill that she followed him around the rest of the day, desiring to learn his secrets, which he was happy to teach her. Erud and Tallma beamed with pride to see their daughter compete. They loved her zeal for life and supported her decision when she desired to train as hunter. The elders, too, supported the decision and put their upmost trust in Tolmaka to mentor and protect her.

It was now Ham's turn to compete. This game showed skill with the knife and required amazing hand–eye coordination. There were three different targets.

The first was a bull's eye; the second, a small stuffed bag attached to a rotating wheel; and the third, a gourd thrown in the air. Many were eliminated by the bull's eye alone, and only Ham and two others remained for the last two challenges. The two were eliminated by the rotating wheel, and Ham was declared the winner when his knife was pulled from the rotating bag. But he wanted to test his skill and continue with the gourd toss. So Lebna calmed the cheering crowd, and Tolin handed him a small gourd. Drawing it below his knees, he thrust it up, tossing it high in the air. As it reached its highest point, Ham threw his knife. When the gourd hit the ground, it rolled to a stop. Imbedded in its side was Ham's knife. His pack joined arms to shoulders and circled around him. As they cross-stepped in dance, they chanted, "Hu-rah, Hu-rah, Ha-la-lah! Hu-rah, Hu-rah, Ha-la-lah!" all the while smiling and laughing in celebration for one of their own. But it was Shoda who truly praised him. Her affection was evident when she stepped from the circle and gave him a loving hug!

The pack then split up as the call for the foot race was announced. Sede had no particular interest to race but knew Japheth and Ham planned to; they both ran like deer. Finding her aunts, she visited with them for a while. The sisters, Dosta and Adah, had a great time together giggling and talking about the old days. Although they hadn't been hunters when they were young, they had known the thrill of adventure. They had been captured once by Cainites and barely escaped. Another time they were lost in the forest and rescued when Tolmaka tracked them. Once they tried to cross a river and nearly drowned, but a Watcher suddenly appeared and saved them. When she told Sede their stories, she humorously pointed out that hunters weren't the only ones to have adventures.

After she spotted Shem, she excused herself, and they began walking through the bustling crowd. Elders from visiting villages gathered around them to honor and encourage him. They knew he would someday lead their people. He in turn showed them great respect, folding his arm across his chest and graciously bowing when they greeted him. He had learned from his father that only through uniting the Sethites in a bond of mutual love and respect could they maintain their culture and way of life. As Sede listened and observed, she welcomed the opportunity to meet these elders. They acknowledged her too, knowing she would be his wife and someday the mother of their people.

As she looked past an elder, she caught sight of Ham, watching from a distance. She smiled and nodded in recognition. He had noticed the elders crowding around his brother, and as he watched, he sensed the honor they were giving him. He often thought of the mystery of how birth order dictates the destiny of a life. Had he been the firstborn, he would be standing in their midst. Dismissing his thoughts, he smiled and happily waved at Sede. Japheth came alongside him, and they were soon lost in the crowd, talking and walking arm to shoulder.

Shem's conversation ended with the elders, and they continued walking through the crowd. Ever so lightly, she felt him slip his hand into hers. He turned to meet her eyes and gave her a warm smile. She felt a sudden flutter and was unsure of what the feeling meant. She knew this was more than a gesture of friendship. She remembered the embrace he had given her when he saved Ma-la, and now he was holding her hand! She sensed something was changing between them but wasn't sure what it was. Even though she felt the uncertainty of what was happening, she liked it all the same. It was then she realized…she, too, was going through a change of her own. Certain feelings were starting to come alive that she had never felt before.

The horn sounded, interrupting her thoughts. The foot race had begun. It was amazing to see the flash of hunters pass by as they ran on the high wall. They lost sight of them as they turned in the distance, but then they reappeared in their approach. Only a few sped past the finish line, the rest lagging behind. When the race ended, Japheth and Ham had tied for third place. Twin female hunters had won first and second. Their parents were overjoyed for them and beamed with pride in their abilities. They, too, had run like deer!

It was after the noon feasting that Sede returned to the hut for her bow and quiver. It was time for the archers to begin their competition. A thrilling rush went through her as she joined the line of hopefuls. Giving her a hardy slap on the back, Shem spouted, "Show us what you're made of, Sede!" She gave him an exasperated look and shook her head. There were many archers ranging from the very young to the old. Through the next half hour the competition dwindled to four, Sede being one of them. As she scanned the crowd, she saw her pack. Her father's confident smile brought her courage. To spear her on, Japheth raised his fisted hand in his usual playful manner. "You can do it, Sede; right through the heart!" Shoda gave him a nudge with her elbow. "Quiet. You'll make her nervous!" Laughing, he elbowed her back.

As they continued to compete, two remained from the four: Sede and another young female hunter. The target had been moved forward several times and was now fifty cubits away. Tolmaka whispered to Shem, "Let's see what my little girl can do." Shem felt his heart warm, sensing the pride of a father for his daughter. He admired Tolmaka's strength as a man but also his ability to express his heart.

Smiling, Shem responded, "I think we're in for a surprise!"

The female archer stepped to the mark on the ground. Pulling back on the bowstring, she released her arrow. As it sailed high through the air and whistled over the target, a unanimous "ooh" was exhaled by the onlookers. Nodding to Sede, she stepped aside. This was it! The moment that would prove her skill! Adrenaline surged through her as she stepped to the mark. The crowd stilled, and she took a deep breath. With her arrow in place, she pulled back on the taut bowstring. Looking one last time toward her pack, she saw Shem. He had such a look of admiration on his face. It warmed her heart to know he felt this way about her. Spotting her target once more, her muscles flexed with the tension of her draw on the bow. Exhaling, she released the arrow. With a loud thud, it landed in the very center of the bull's eye. The crowd exploded with cheering and shouting. She'd done it! "Ha-la-lah!" rose from her pack as they jumped up and down in excitement and hugged each other. One of their own had proved her excellence! Lebna beckoned her forward and marveled; her skill *was* impressive! She smiled in excitement as he placed the wreath on her head.

With a chuckle and a twinkle in his eye, Tolmaka gave her a shoulder hug. Seeing her questioning look, he whispered in her ear, "You both look like you've been crowned king and queen, standing there next to each other."

She hadn't noticed, but Shem was at her side, beaming with pride; and they were wearing crowns—wreath crowns! She blushed, which made him chuckle all the more. It was then her little shadow, Adat, appeared at her side. Beaming, she clasped Sede's hand and said, "I knew you'd win, just like I said. Someday I'll be standing beside you, and we'll compete together." Sede laughed and knelt on one knee to hug her. In that moment she felt such happiness knowing the love of so many.

Rope climbing was next, and Japheth took his place by one of the many dangling ropes that hung from the tree above. From top to bottom, it was an amazing fifty cubits! Lebna gave the signal, and the hunters began to climb. Some fell after climbing only halfway to the top. Others slowed the higher they climbed. Zara shouted above the cheering, "Climb, Japheth, climb; higher, higher!" As the few approached the limb, it was Japheth who gave the shout, "Ha-la-lah!" Cheers ascended from far below. Pulling a piece of leather from his belt, he wrapped it around the rope and slid down. Leather zinged as the rope smoldered from the friction. The crowd went wild, thrilled with the flash of his descent! Tolmaka was truly impressed and slapped him soundly on the back.

Ezmere jokingly said, "I still see the boy in you, son, and I like it!"

Noah beamed and affectionately grabbed his shoulder. "Well done, son! That was amazing!"

As Tolin set the wreath on his head, he, too, commended Japheth's display of strength and speed. In his joking way, Japheth cocked his wreath to one side of his head and smiled. He loved to find the humor in this sudden show of attention. Shoda joined in the praise, clasping his forearms and saluting him with a "Ha-la-lah, brother. Ha-la-lah!"

As the sun was setting, the council fire was lit. Those who wished gathered around. Music played in the background while content Sethites settled into warm conversation with each other. Sede's family lingered at the council fire, but she felt the fullness of the day. It was the calm of her room that she desired. She walked back to the hut, passing the quiet tents and huts along the way. In the stillness of her room, she smiled and hung her wreath on the wall. It had been a great day! Settling on the velvety furs, she felt her body relax. She thought about walking hand in hand with Shem and recalled the unexpected flutter she had felt. A warm blush rose up again. They had met the elders and had been honored by them, recognizing that they would marry one day. She smiled, thinking about her father's comment of them looking like a king and queen. This was all pointing to the life she and Shem would someday share together. She remembered what her father had said when they rested beneath the grove of trees. "Your heart is capable of more love than you know. This love will rise in your heart for your husband and be a wondrous thing!" And what was this love of the universe he spoke of—the love that would create the "Promised One" to come? It sounded like a wonderful mystery. 'Father has helped me see new things,' she thought. 'Things I have never considered before. What will this love for Shem be like—this wondrous thing he spoke of?'

Her thoughts turned to what she saw outside her window: the vastness of the night sky, the stars…and Yahweh had made them all. "Yahweh, God of Adam, I whisper by prayer to you. May the love I give to Shem someday be pleasing in your sight. The life our love creates…may that life be blessed." As she lie silent for a while, she pondered the mysterious promise Yahweh had given Eve. She felt her heart stir, and a yearning rose up within her. She heard her mouth speak the words of her heart, "Yahweh, if any maiden could offer themselves to bear your 'Promised One,' may it be me. I offer myself to be the one to bear the 'seed'—the 'Promised One.'" A warm, soft breeze brought a hush over her, and the fur next to her face slightly moved from the gentle movement. It was though Yahweh was on the breeze…She heard his still and gentle voice. "I love you, Sede, daughter of Eve, and hear your prayer. It pleases me that you have offered yourself to fulfill my promise. My 'Promised One' will not be born for many generations. But he will come. And your father is right. The love that will give him life will be a special love. It will be the love of the universe…my love! You will be part of the generations that will bring forth this 'seed.' You and Shem will live to see a new world, and your descendants will cover the earth. From you and your husband's lineage will come the body I will use to bring this 'seed' into the world. My hand is upon you, my child…I love you." As His words lingered in her heart, a calm silence filled her room. With awe, she whispered, "Thank you, Yahweh…Who am I that you would speak to me and choose me? This is so precious and dear, beyond any words." Peace descended on her like a warm, comforting fur, and her thoughts settled into restful sleep.

When she woke in the morning, her heart leapt! The words she had heard from Yahweh were still fresh within her. She could hardly wait to tell her father. Joining him as he ate in front of the hearth, she burst with excitement. "Father, I must tell you what happened last night as I lay upon my bed!"

"Say on, my daughter," as he continued to eat.

"Last night I prayed to Yahweh about my husband. I offered to be the woman that would bear the 'Promised One' and fulfill the prophecy."

"Yes, a worthy prayer all Sethite maidens should pray," he thoughtfully responded.

"Yahweh spoke to me on the breeze that blew from my window."

Tolmaka's eyes widened, and he set his bowl down. "What words did you hear, my child?"

"He told me that I wouldn't be the one to bear the 'seed' of promise but one of Shem and my descendants would! He would come from our lineage. The love of the universe *would* create this 'seed' within the woman. Shem and I would live to see a new world, and our descendants would cover the earth."

Tolmaka was silent and trembled, hardly believing what she had said. "Oh daughter, this is a wonder! Not since Lamech have our kinsmen heard such a word about the 'Promised One'! I must speak to Noah of this. He must know!"

As they stood, he softly touched her shoulder and said, "Yahweh has blessed you, my daughter, and I am pleased." She stood at the door as he left the hut, watching him hurry down the street with his robe flopping behind him as he took long strides. 'I have two fathers,' she thought. 'The hunter father and this village elder father.' It amazed her how easily he could change from alert hunter to composed elder. 'My words have brought him great excitement. I wonder what he and Noah will discuss.'

Tolmaka hurried up the path to Noah's hut. Built on the highest hill, it was like a beacon overlooking the whole village. Knocking on the door with his staff, he waited for Ezmere's welcome. When she opened, he excitedly blurted, "I must speak to Noah. Please call him." Sensing his urgency, she bid him to sit and disappeared to find her husband. Settling on the floor mat, Tolmaka tapped his staff against his sandals. 'What should I make of these things?' he pondered. 'My daughter has been given a prophecy! She has been told her future and the future Sethite promise of the 'seed.' And what of this new world to come?'

While he was pondering these things, he heard Noah's footsteps. Tolmaka stood, and they greeted each other with the customary greeting: hands to forearms, foreheads touching, and, in unison, a whispered, "Ha-la-lah."

"What brings you here on this busy day, my friend?"

"My daughter has heard the word of the Lord, and you must know of this!"

Noah gestured to the mat, and they both sat. "Say on, my friend."

"Last night my daughter prayed that she would be the daughter of Eve to bear the 'seed' of promise. Yahweh came to her on the breeze and told her that she would not be the one. The 'seed' would not be born for many generations, but He would surely come! The 'seed' would come from her and Shem's lineage, and He would be born from the love of the universe…*His* love! She and Shem would live to see a new world, and their generations would fill the earth."

Noah was silent as he considered his words. With trembling hands, he grasped Tolmaka's arm. "This is the word of the Lord! This confirms the words I, too, have heard from Yahweh. Tolmaka, I will tell you what is to come…It is just as our father Enoch has written. Yahweh is sending his judgment upon the wicked. It has grieved Him that He has made man. All the Cainites have gone the way of wickedness: polluting themselves with fallen angels, perverting their innocent ones, and corrupting the knowledge of the Watchers. Yahweh plans to destroy the world with a flood. He will totally cleanse the world from this corruption. He plans to make a new world, as Sede was told. We both need to seek Yahweh in these matters. Our children will need to be considered, for they are part of Yahweh's plan."

Tolmaka weighed his thoughts and then spoke. "I will leave for the wilderness tomorrow morning. There, I will seek our God."

"Brother and friend, I, too, will seek the Lord from here, in the village. I have yet to send our kinsmen back to their homes. When you return from the wilderness, we will discuss what we both have received from Yahweh." Tolmaka stood to bid his friend farewell. With hands to forearms, they touched foreheads and whispered, "Took-la-say, a-lay-nay." (These were the blessed words of the Sethite farewell.)

When Tolmaka returned to his hut, he bid Adah and Hattil farewell. He would leave early in the morning.

Chapter 4

Tolmaka's Journey

He left early, bidding Sede and Dosta farewell. When he returned, he would have the counsel of the Lord and be able to guide Sede in the prophecy she had been given. He journeyed west, passing the familiar grazing grounds his hunters used to find their prey. After two days he arrived at the foothills of the mountains. He remembered this forest from his youth. His father had brought him here once to pray in a special place. He knew if he walked a half day's journey through the foothills, he would begin the ascent. Halfway up the mountain, he would find a cave. In this special place, he would pray for his daughter. Every night he made camp he felt as though someone was near. His hunting instincts kept him alert. He had seen many different tracks of creatures that had been there before him. That night as he kindled his fire, he again felt someone was near. A Watcher suddenly appeared before him, and he fell back with fright! There before him stood a radiant angel; power and light streamed from his body. The light was so brilliant that it lit the dark forest around them.

"Fear not, Tolmaka. I have been sent to help you on your journey and bring you to the cave."

Tolmaka trembled as he spoke. "Are...are you the one I have sensed with me these two days?"

"Yes," the Watcher answered. He was magnificent in appearance: muscular, tall, and fair. His presence commanded a sense of awe. "Your conversation with Noah has troubled your heart, and Yahweh knows the hearts of men. **He is omniscient!**" The forest reverberated with waves of power as he spoke these words. Even the ground rumbled. When all became quiet once more, the Watcher continued, "Come, sit near the fire and we will talk."

Tolmaka felt peace enter him as fear evaporated. He took a seat by the Watcher, who glowed with a light that seemed to come from within. "You know of Watchers through your sister's testimony and your ancestor Enoch's writings."

"Yes, I know of your kind." He marveled that their conversation flowed so effortlessly.

"Yahweh has sent me to help you see what you must do. You will find the answers to your questions in the cave. Come and rest for the day has known its end." Tolmaka settled next to the fire. Slowly, a strange sleep swept over him. Meanwhile, the Watcher stood nearby with his arms folded across his chest and his legs planted apart. Determination was set on his face as he watched over his charge.

When he woke in the morning, Tolmaka thought he had dreamed a strange dream until he looked up and saw the Watcher. Startled, but then remembering, he exhaled. He was standing where he had last seen him—tall and erect like a statue. No, it wasn't a dream. 'What wonders will this day bring?' he thought. He gathered the few things he had, and they continued their upward trek through the forest.

When they arrived at the mouth of the cave, Tolmaka stepped forward to enter. The Watcher caught him by the arm and said, "Wait, I must clear the way." He raised his hand toward the dark cave and closed his eyes. He spoke, as but a whisper, the language of heaven. Tolmaka wondered at the sound of the words. They seemed so beautiful. "Now we may enter," the angel said. The moment he took his first step, the cave ignited with light. The walls, ceiling, and floor lit with light coming from underneath the stone's surface. This was not what he and his father had seen.

The Watcher looked at him intently. "I have removed the veil from the eyes of your flesh. You now see with the eyes of the spirit. You see the cave as it truly is. You and your father saw this cave, those many years ago, with the eyes of the flesh." He paused, letting Tolmaka absorb what he had said. He then continued, "There is a veil that covers the eyes of man. This veil first covered Adam's eyes when he ate from the forbidden tree." The angel's knowledge and understanding amazed him. How different things looked seeing in the spirit. The walls were not black as he remembered but shimmered like the Keytosa stone, sparkling and glistening as though they were alive!

"Come, Tolmaka, we must go farther." As they entered a small chamber at the back of the cave, he saw before him a table of pure gold. On the table lay a body wrapped in white linen. He looked at the Watcher and knew…"This is Adam!" he whispered in wonder. How amazing it was that he knew without being told.

"Yahweh has shown you, Tolmaka. This is the Cave of Treasures your ancestor Enoch saw and wrote about." To the right of the body was a bench where the Watcher motioned for him to sit. "Come, I will tell you the things you must know." Tolmaka trembled in awe as he sat next to him. The "power of life" was radiating from the angel. It was though he were a sponge, drawing this life into his parched soul. He absorbed more and more of this life, feeling it fill and satisfy him. 'Oh the glory. Oh the wonder!'

After a brief silence, the angel continued, "Noah told you that Yahweh is going to destroy the earth because of the wickedness and violence that has filled the earth. This has troubled you because of the great love you have for your daughter. You fear for her safety and future." Tolmaka nodded, unable to speak. Grief and sorrow held his throat like tight hands. His daughter, his precious one, how would this affect her? "Your daughter has found favor with Yahweh, Tolmaka, and will be saved from this judgment. She will be one of eight who will survive. Your eyes will be spared from seeing the wrath of the Lord on the wicked."

Tolmaka was overwhelmed. The presence of Yahweh began to envelop him, embracing him with peace. The warmth of liquid love flowed though him, filling him with a divine wholeness he had never known before. The Watcher gently gripped his shoulder. "This great peace and love you feel will be yours when Yahweh receives you in death. 'Precious in the sight of the Lord is the death of his favored ones'." Tolmaka bowed his head and worshipped. Words were not spoken, for what words could describe what he felt and knew at that moment? Only his heart could say what his mouth could not. (And so it is…from the heart, man worships his God.)

When the moment was right, the Watcher spoke again. "I am here to tell you what you must do to help your daughter prepare for the future. You must see that she marries Shem. Perilous times lie ahead, and they will need each other. Together they will have the strength to do Yahweh's will. They will both live to see the dawning of a new world—a world that has been cleansed by the flood of judgment. After they become settled in their lives, Yahweh will receive your spirit. You will rejoice greatly as you are ushered into His presence. But there is a warning you must give Noah. A great evil is coming to your villages. This will happen before the great judgment. All of your lives will change because of this evil. Tell him what you have seen and heard here in the Cave of Treasures. Your words will bring comfort to his soul and give him strength. Yahweh will speak to you on the breeze as He did your daughter. Listen, and you will hear what you are to do. Now, Tolmaka, remain here in the presence of the Lord and be refreshed. Tomorrow will greet us at sunrise. It will be then we leave for your village."

Tolmaka lost track of time. When the Watcher appeared, he could hardly believe it was already morning. He had been up all night basking in the glory of Yahweh. When they turned to leave, he asked, "May I touch my father, Adam?"

"Yes, Tolmaka, you may touch him."

The moment his finger touched the linen cloth, frankincense burst forth and filled the chamber. Every cell in his body was ignited as he inhaled the holy fragrance. Something deep within him had been instantly made alive, and he staggered in sheer ecstasy. The Watcher caught him by his arm to keep him from falling. "This is the life that awaits you in heaven, Tolmaka. All this glory awaits the righteous. This awaits your daughter, her husband, and all their descendants. For your Father in Heaven, the Great Yahweh, loves His own and desires them to be with Him always. He has great wonders for them to possess and behold. 'For the eyes of man have not seen or their ears heard, neither has it entered into their hearts, the things that Yahweh has prepared for those who love him.' You, Tolmaka, have experienced but a glimpse."

As they made their way down the mountain, Tolmaka was quiet. All that he had seen; all that he had heard; the fragrance; the presence; the glory; he felt warmed and calmed in a way he had never known. His thoughts echoed his heart…'I have learned from the ancients about Yahweh, but now I know His glory. I have been changed in His presence.'

After two days, he arrived at Taasa-toka. The village was now quiet from the annual festival, and daily life had returned. There in the hut was Dosta and his beloved Sede. Squeals of joy erupted when she saw her father; his face shown with a light she had never seen before. Touching his cheeks, she looked into his eyes. "Your face shines, Abba. Like the face of an angel!" Tears came to his eyes. Not since she was a little girl had he heard her call him Abba. She threw her arms around his neck and lovingly hugged him. "I've missed you."

"I have missed you too, my daughter. After our evening meal, we'll talk, and I'll tell you what Yahweh has shown me."

"Good father, I want to hear everything!" In joyful excitement, she danced and playfully whirled toward the door, almost singing her words. "I'm meeting with Shem. He's going to help me re-feather my arrows. My mark has been short, and I know it's the balance of my arrow. Farewell, Father. I'm so happy you're home!" Tolmaka watched as she left, dancing on her way. Little did she know what lie ahead of her. Her whole world was about to change, and he had been given the warning. Under his breath, he prayed, "Thank you, Yahweh, for what you're about to do for my daughter. I give you glory."

That evening after their meal, as they reclined in front of the hearth, Tolmaka beckoned her close. "Come, Daughter, and we will talk." She slid under his arm and nestled next to his heart. She felt as though she was under the soft, warm wings of love. She could hear the beating of his heart, and each beat resounded in her soul. She thought for a quick moment, 'I was born from this heart of love.' "Yahweh has told me many wonders," he began. "I will start with you, my child. Remember how we spoke of the love between a husband and wife?"

"Yes, Father, I remember."

"Well, the time for you to marry has come. Yahweh wishes it."

In a flash, she thought, 'This will mean I can no longer 'go out and come in' with the hunt.' She felt a pang of sadness. She knew this day would come, and now it was suddenly here. 'I will know the mystery of love,' she told herself. 'I must think on that. That is my future.' In her own innocence, she was trying to comfort herself. But still she wrestled with the sudden news. Under her breath, she whispered softly, "Yahweh, help me accept my future and embrace this mystery of love for a husband."

As he continued to sooth her with his words, she was silent. "You have time to think on these things, my child. I have yet to speak to Noah. He will have to give his consent, but I know he will. Yahweh wishes it. The other wonders I experienced will wait for another time. For now, this is much for you to consider. So come; let us welcome sleep and find a place for all these things in our dreams." He knew his daughter's heart; that hunting was her whole world and that she loved it dearly, and this sudden news had been a shock to hear.

Tolmaka arrived at Noah's early in the morning. After greetings, they settled to talk. "I have returned from the Cave of Treasures and have words to share with you from a Watcher sent by Yahweh. He instructed me to tell you all things."

"Say on, my brother." Noah said in eager anticipation.

"Yahweh knew my heart was troubled by your words of a flood and my concerns for my daughter. He confirmed that a flood would take place to judge the wicked. But the righteous will be saved. My Sede will be one of them. She and Shem will live to see the dawning of a new world. He told me to make preparations for Sede and Shem to marry and see them established in their lives. He also allowed me to experience His presence, giving me a foretaste of heaven itself. It was glorious, and my heart longs to be with Him. I am thankful that He has warned me so I am able to make things right for my daughter. The Watcher also gave me a warning to pass on to you. There is a great evil coming to the villages of our people. It will change all our lives. He did not explain what this evil was, but I am here for you my brother, my friend. I will support your decisions and help you in any way."

Noah was silent as Tolmaka's words settled in his heart. Then, with full assurance, he answered, "Yes, I will consent to our children uniting and will make every effort to see them established in their lives. Thank you for sharing the words of the Watcher. I feel strengthened in some strange but powerful way. I, too, have heard the word of the Lord as I sought Him here in Taasa-toka. I discerned that our simple way of life will soon come to an end and fear that this has been the last festival you and I will see. I will tell you what Yahweh has shown me. Yahweh has told me to tell no one but you. He revealed to me that your eyes will not behold the destruction that is coming. Yahweh will spare you this great sorrow." Tolmaka struggled to hold back his emotions for he saw the great working of Yahweh weaving all things together and showing His secrets to whom He pleases. Noah was to also know he would not see the new world. Noah continued, "Yahweh will open the windows of heaven and the fountains of the deep. The earth will be covered with water, and none shall survive but those who will hear the message He has given me and believe it. If they believe Yahweh's message of turning from evil and returning to the ways of the Lord, they will be saved. But if they do not, they will perish. He has instructed me to build a great ark. This ark will save us so that we will live to see a new world; a world where all evil has been washed away. He has supernaturally given me the knowledge of how and where to build this ark. He also said that I would know when to start its construction. Brother Tolmaka, we are about to see the end of one age and the beginning of another. It is all in the plans of Yahweh to make it so." They continued to talk and fellowship into the late hours of the night.

Chapter 5

Stampede

Tolmaka woke early the next morning and met with Noah once more. They would begin preparations for their children's marriage. Sede knew when she returned from today's hunt that she would begin her "time of preparation." The elder women would instruct her, preparing her for her new life as Shem's wife. This hunt would be her last. She had mixed emotions. Her heart desired to greet her future, but her past held her close. She loved the life of the hunt. She grabbed her bow and gave Dosta a quick hug. "Where will your last hunt take you, Sede?" Dosta asked tenderly, discerning her sad heart.

"I don't know, but it will be one to remember." They hugged, and she walked the long street to meet the others at the village gate. Her cheeks flushed when she saw Shem. She knew their lives were about to change. He would no longer be her friend but her husband.

As she thought of her pack, she searched each face: Shoda's adventurous spirit, Zara's risk taking, Japheth's humor, and Ham's seriousness. And then there was Shem, with his quiet strength. They had been her life. No longer would they spend their days together. No longer would they hunt as a pack. This would be their last hunt together. Everything was changing....

As the others visited, Shem drew close to her side. "Father spoke to me last night. He told me that he and Tolmaka would counsil today concerning our union." He slipped his hand into hers and looked intently into her eyes. "Today is a turning point in both our lives. This will be your last hunt and your last day with the pack." Tears came to her eyes, and he squeezed her hand gently. "I know how hard this must be for you, Sede. I know your love for the hunt." It felt so good to hear his words. She needed to hear them and was glad they came from him.

Japheth interrupted their conversation, not realizing they had been talking. "Today the hunt falls to me. We'll hunt the eastern fields!" Japheth lifted his spear to the sky and shouted, "Ha-la-lah. Let's go!"

As they ran, Sede tried to clear her head from her troubled thoughts. She wanted to enjoy this one last hunt. She set her mind to concentrate on what lie ahead. For nearly an hour, they ran until they spotted a large herd of shosposcus. They were peacefully grazing in the distance. "Let's split up and circle the herd. I'll signal when it's time," Japheth said as he secured Tolmaka's horn to his belt.

"Aye," they answered as they broke up, moving in different directions. They circled the herd and took their positions.

It was then that the lead bull flared his nostrils. Sede wondered if he'd caught their scent. She froze and dropped to the ground. It wasn't their scent the bull had caught but a wind and a cloud of dust that followed it. She waited, knowing of these winds. They would pass, and a calm would follow. All they had to do was wait.

Shem circled her left to remain downwind of the herd. The wind did not settle but rather increased with strength, blowing harder and lifting more dust into the air. The herd sensed the change and began to panic. Soon their panic turned into a stampede. Their backs rose and fell as they thundered in a massive rush forward. The noise was deafening. Sede couldn't see her pack. Where were they? Shem stood and motioned for her to come his way. But while he was standing, a gust of wind caught him and blew him to the ground. The air was now filled with so much dust Sede could hardly see. In the panic of the moment, she knew she had to make a decision. Should she stay where she was and wait for the wind to pass or run with the herd? The dust stung her eyes, swirling and pulling at her skins. Fear gripped her. At the top of her voice, she shouted into the wind, "Yahweh, what should I do?" She heard His voice speaking to her heart, "Run with the herd, child." She frantically ran with the noise of the herd, faintly catching sight of shadowy tails through the blowing dust. As the swirling wind blasted against her body, she pulled her cape over her nose and mouth. 'How can a wind last so long?' she thought. 'When will it calm?'

The cloud of dust had confused Shoda's ability to see landmarks that would give their position, and she had lost her sense of direction. Shoda, like Sede, tried to get her bearings but couldn't tell which direction she should run. Panic gripped her heart. She could hear the pounding hooves coming closer and closer. Several shosposcus ran past her, brushing her shoulder. Instinctively, she began to run in the same direction. All of a sudden she felt something hit her back, sending her flying forward to the ground. She felt a sharp pain to her head and lost consciousness.

Ham strained to see through the cloud of dust. Ghostly figures ran past him, and he instinctively followed them, running full speed to keep from being trampled. Suddenly his head butted a tree that was shrouded in the thick dust. He flew backward from the powerful force of the collision. All around him swirled thundering hooves, parting at the tree. He scrambled up the trunk. His head pounded as he hung over the limb.

Zara saw the herd as it raced by her. 'I know what I'll do!' she thought. She began running with the herd and mounted the back of the shosposcus nearest her. She raised both hands in the air as she sat astride the beast, the full thrill of adventure coursing through her veins. She stayed on for several minutes until the shosposcus realized she was on his back and bucked her off. Landing near a fallen tree, she scrambled beneath. One after another, shosposcus leapt over the top of the trunk while she crouched safely beneath. She laughed as she saw their underbellies flying over the top of her. Here she would wait out the stampede and be none the worse.

From Japheth's position, he saw the herd turning and scurried up a boulder. The only hunter he saw briefly was Zara riding atop the back of a shosposcus. 'Fool of a girl,' he thought and then couldn't help but laugh. He knew her too well. "Wish I'd thought of it!" he mumbled to himself. He lost sight of her when she was bucked off but knew she was quick on her feet. From his position, he could see the great herd below and the cloud of dust rising above them. He was struck by the awesome power of a stampede. No one could have stopped them or had the power to calm them. Even the lead bull no longer led them. The momentum of a thousand hooves now rushed behind him, forcing him forward.

Shem felt fear. Not for himself but for the others. He had only seen Sede, and that was just briefly. Where were the others? Even though Japheth was lead for today, Shem was the oldest, and he felt responsible for all of them. He strained to see them, but it was impossible to see anything. He felt a sudden blow to his back. Butted from behind, he was sent flying to the ground, rolling and sliding. As he continued to slide, he tumbled into a hole and landed on his head. He lay at the bottom, unconscious, while one after another, shosposcus leapt over the gaping hole. Several stumbled as they anticipated the hole, falling headlong to their death and landing next to Shem's body. By some miracle none had fallen on him.

Sede continued racing full speed. Surely the wind would calm and she would be able to see in front of her. Hearing the faint sound of squealing, she slowed her pace and stopped just in time, teetering her feet over the edge. One more step and she would have had the same fate as the shosposcus. Below the cliff, there was no cloud to obstruct her vision. The whole herd lay dead in heaps. She dropped to her knees, adrenaline pumping through her and making her weak in the legs. Her arms went limp. "Oh Yahweh!" she uttered. She crouched, pulling the cape around herself, while the wind blew against her back.

Suddenly she jerked. When her thoughts cleared, she realized she had passed out from exhaustion. She threw her cape back to see a clear sky. Coughing, she cleared her throat from the dust on her cape. All was silent except for the call of a hawk overhead. She waited a few minutes, trying to clear her head. Still weak from running, she struggled to stand. Below, in the canyon, was a sea of dead shosposcus. Beyond them was open prairie to the horizon. She turned in a circle to get her bearings. Reasoning, she knew the herd ran east when the wind began to blow, but because of the dust, there was no way of knowing if they changed direction during the stampede. The sun was directly overhead so she couldn't determine east from west. To her right were mountains and to her left the forest. A multitude of hoof prints and dead shosposcus stretched as far as the eye could see behind her. She knew if she followed the tracks, the search for her pack could take the rest of the day. But if she had a higher vantage point, she could spot them. 'I have no high place to see this flat plain,' she thought. 'From the higher hills, I would be able to spot them or catch sight of the river and meet them there.' She clutched her water skin bag. 'Good, I still have water.' The pouch of food Dosta had prepared for her was gone, lost while running in the stampede.

She headed toward the hills of the mountains. As she ran, her thoughts were filled with questions. Where was her pack? Were they safe? How would they find each other? As hunters, they were sometimes gone for a week. Her father wouldn't know she was missing. No one would know where to look for her. She didn't even know where she was. She ran at a steady pace toward the hills until the sun began to set. From the top of the hills, she scanned for signs of her pack. Still the hills were not high enough. 'I must climb higher, but the sun is setting. In the morning I'll continue my climb, but for now I must make camp.' The open hunting lands were barren of trees and provided little shelter. After cresting a small hill she saw, to her surprise, a grove of trees. 'Yes, that will do. Surely where there are trees, there is water.' Her search proved futile; there was no water.

She gathered small branches and twigs from beneath the trees and started her fire. The sparks from her flints ignited the dry, matted grass she had stuffed beneath. She gingery coaxed the smoldering mesh, blowing softly. She remembered the first time she learned to make fire. Smiling, she recalled the morning the young hunters gathered early for training. Gruetat, Shoda's father, was to teach them the way of fire. It was a mystery to her, how fire could come from striking two stones together. The young hunters took turns building the kindling, striking the stones, and coaxing the flame. Some struggled, while others brought the flame easily. She softly laughed, remembering her youth and the lack of experience she had then. Now her training would serve her well if she were to see her father and her pack again.

She darted a small rabbit and roasted it on her makeshift spit. The food satisfied her hunger, and she felt strengthened from the exhaustion she experienced from the wind storm and stampede. Building a nest of dried leaves, she settled down and covered herself with her cape. The fire would keep the animals at a distance, and the leaves would keep her warm. She was alone and lost, yet she felt no fear. She had been lost before and found her way home. A peace calmed her, and she knew she would be all right.

As she lay beneath the stars, her thoughts wandered. With the great vastness above her and the open hunting lands around her, she thought of Yahweh, who had made them all. This *was* an amazing place. How she marveled at His greatness… She knew the world of the hunt but not the world of marriage. Would she find this same wonder she saw in the hunt as Shem's wife? Marriage, too, was a creation of Yahweh. To share a lifetime with another would be an amazing thing. To see love grow and become a thing of beauty would be an adventure. Her father knew this mystery and said it made the heart complete. Shem's heart was not complete. Her heart was not yet complete. When they became one, this would change. He had said they would know a wholeness and completeness that they were created for. She felt her heart yearn to know these things. She knew she was innocent, but with her people, that was a precious thing. 'For everything, there is a time and a season, and a purpose under heaven. Yahweh makes everything beautiful in its time.' This is what she had been taught. This was now her time to know the love of a man and to learn to love him in return. Her innocence would mature and become as Yahweh intended: beautiful, pure, and strong.

She slept soundly, which surprised her when she woke. The fire had gone out, and the sun was one hand high on the eastern horizon. She opened her water skin and took a long, deep drink. 'Time to go,' she thought. The hills didn't afford the vantage point she had desired, so she decided to climb the mountain before her. The face of the mountain was easy to climb, not jagged like the rocks where they had killed the Nephilim. This seemed a peaceful place. The rocks were exposed, and small sprigs of tender grass and wild flowers grew between them. It was a wonder to her how such delicate beauty and life could struggle to live in rock. She sensed there was a spiritual lesson in what she was discerning. (Beauty can grow in the most unlikely places.) Stepping from rock to rock, she pulled herself higher and higher. When she reached the top, it seemed she could see the whole world. It took her breath away. Turning in a circle, she took in the panoramic view. Wow! From this vantage point, she could see the cliff and the dead herd of shosposcus with the forest beyond. She looked for the river that ran past their village. She knew it would lead her home. Where was the river? It should be there. On the other side of this mountain, a great desert stretched as far as she could see. But she saw something. What was that?

Chapter 6

The Wall

With both hands, Sede shaded her forehead. There, in the distance, she saw an amazing green land surrounded by a brilliant wall. Within its boundary were trees, rolling hills, meadows, mountains, waterfalls, lakes, and streams. The wall had an arched gate. Something sparkled at its entrance, but she couldn't make out what it was. The walls reflected the noon sun, and she wondered if it was made of gold. The stones seemed to absorb the sunlight and burn like fire. 'How could sunlight turn stones to fire?' Over the enclosed land was a sparkling, transparent, celestial dome. Arrows of light pierced the covering and shot upward in all directions. She heard herself gasp in wonder of what her eyes beheld. Never had she seen anything so beautiful. It was like a precious stone shining in the sunlight. 'What is this place?' Something within her heart stirred. This place felt strangely familiar. It seemed as though it was drawing her, calling her.

She closed her eyes, letting the beauty of what she was feeling overtake her. "Yahweh," she whispered, "What is this strange place that it would speak to my heart in such a way?" A wind suddenly whirled around her, fanning her hair and rustling her skins. She steadied her stance, planting her feet against the rock beneath her. "Yes, Yahweh. I will hear you…" The wind passed as quickly as it had come. Now a soft breeze blew upon her. "Go to the wall, my child. You will find your answers there." She felt the warmth of love gently flowing within her heart. It was that same warmth she had felt the night Noah spoke to her at the altar and when she had heard Yahweh's words for the first time. From where she stood, the land was barren from the foot of the mountain to the wall. It was amazing that a beautiful green emerald, circled in flame, could be in such an arid place.

The climb down the mountain proved slower than the ascent on the other side. By the time she reached the base of the mountain, the sun was setting. She would have to wait until dawn to cross the desert. After scouting the area, she found a good place for camp. Cut into a large boulder was a small cave. This would be the shelter she needed. She gathered dried grass from between the rocks and looked for wood to build a fire. This side of the mountain was barren compared to the lush green on the other side. As she continued to search, she noticed a tree limb hanging over one of the surrounding boulders. Scaling the great rock, she climbed halfway down the tree when she spied a bird's nest. 'Could it be?' she thought. Inching closer, she saw two large eggs. "Ha-la-lah!" Happy with her find, she continued down. At the bottom, she found enough wood for a fire and circled the boulder. It was then she realized that had she gone around the boulder, she would have found the wood and spared herself climbing down the tree. Laughing at herself, she thought, 'Oh well, I would have never found the eggs if I hadn't been in the tree.'

After she settled in her bed of dry grass, she rolled her eggs near the fire. She would let them slowly cook in the hot sand and then peel the shells. Reaching for her water skin, she drank sparingly. 'I must save enough water to cross the desert.' Her thoughts turned toward her father, and she yearned to hear his voice. She wondered of Shem. Was he safe from the stampede? The last time she'd seen him was when he stood and motioned to her. What of Shoda, Ham and Japheth, and Zara too. Had they found their way home? Were they searching for her? And what of the walled land in the desert? What did Yahweh mean when He said she would find her answers there?

When she opened her eyes, she was surprised it was so late in the morning. Gathering her water skin and bow, she looked to the sky. The sun was already two hands high. 'I must pace myself. The desert will try to steal my strength.' She slipped her cape over her head and set off for the wall. From the mountain lookout, the wall could be easily seen, but from the desert floor, it was only sand to the horizon. She kept a steady walking pace until the sun rose to the center of the sky. Sitting to rest, she tipped the water skin to her lips. The water was hot, and she felt pain from her cracked lips. 'Where will I find water? I'll need water for the journey home.' The water skin lay limp in her hands as she felt the bottom. 'Two more swallows,' she thought, 'and still I don't see the wall.'

She stood to her feet and stepped forward, the sand grinding in her sandals. With each step, the sand seemed to swallow her feet. 'One step in front of the other,' she thought, 'one step in front of the other.' As her legs began to tire, her thoughts drew her back to a memory. She was very young and walking with her father and his friends. While he was talking, he didn't realize she was no longer at his side. She was struggling to keep up with his stride. Her little legs moved swiftly, putting one foot in front of the other. She felt so tired. As he looked over his shoulder, he realized she was struggling to keep up. Walking back, he scooped her up, laughing. "Here, ride on my shoulders, little one!" He lifted and whirled her in the air. She felt such a thrill, like a bird flying. The world looked different from his shoulders. She could see farther than she'd ever seen before. What a sense of safety and rest she felt being carried. 'One step in front of the other,' she thought, 'one step in front of the other,' as she plod through the sand.

The wind began to blow. It started slowly at first and then mounted, lifting and rising from the desert floor. Swirling and whirling, it sent large clouds of sand in the air, blowing stronger and stronger. It was though the sand had become a partner with the wind; pushing against her, whirling around her. She wrapped her face with her cape and leaned forward, bracing her body against the force of the blasting sand. The wind was merciless. Like daggers, sand pierced her skin and stabbed her arms and legs. A gust of wind pushed her, and she lost her balance, falling to one knee. She held her knee and felt blood. Straining to stand, she shaded her eyes and looked for the sun. She knew the sun would orientate her to the direction of the wall, but all she saw overhead was grey, swirling sand. 'I must press forward!' she told herself.

She pushed against the wind and struggled with each step she took. Sand collapsed around her ankles as she raised her foot to take the next step, feeling as though weights were tied to them. She knew she was weakening, and her body began to tremble from the fatigue in her legs. She staggered, stumbling to her knee once more, and then, all went black. When she woke, she felt dazed. She shook her head and coughed sand from her mouth. What was that weight on her back? Instant panic gripped her as she began to push and struggle. She was buried to her neck. When she had collapsed, she had fallen face down. The blowing sand had covered her. Pushing with all her might, she rolled out of the sandy grave and faced the sun. Heat waves penetrated her body. Her head pounded, and everything around her seemed to spin. She lost consciousness once more.

When she opened her eyes, she squinted. The sunlight was blinding. She didn't know if she had slept through the night or if it was the same day she had started across the desert. She rolled over on her stomach and drew herself to her knees. With weakened, wobbly arms, she managed to push herself up. She tried to focus on what was before her. There, not three feet away, was a wall. She stumbled forward and felt her cheek hit the smooth surface. As her eyes followed the wall up, she gasped! It went straight up as far as the eye could see. "I did make it," she mumbled. Her knees buckled as she turned and slid down, sitting with her back against the wall. With trembling arms, she raised the water skin to her mouth. The hot water burned as she swallowed, making her cough and hold her throat. "Oh Yahweh…help me!" Fatigued and exhausted, she drew her knees up, resting her forehead on folded arms. All was silent. No wind. No song of bird. Nothing. Her ears strained to hear a sound. Instead of a sound, she felt a presence.

She raised her head and blinked. What? She looked again. Standing before her was a beautiful angelic being. His face shone with a light that seemed to come from within. He stood silent, tall, and strong and was dressed in white. The belt around his waist glistened with golden light. A staff was at his side, and the end stuck in the sand next to his sandaled feet. "Sede, I have come to help you, and Yahweh has something to give you." His words were wrapped in compassion and love, with a tone that calmed her to the core of her being. Peace swept over her like a cool breeze, and she exhaled with an "ah." She wondered if she could speak. "Who…who are you?"

"I am a Watcher sent to help you. Yahweh heard you on the mountain and has led you to this place. Come, drink, for your body is weak from the heat."

The Wall

With his staff, he struck the base of the wall and water bubbled from beneath its stones. Soon a pool formed and she, without even thinking, fell face forward in the water. Her sunburned skin screamed. The water was cold. She drank deeply as she pushed her head beneath the surface. "Ah!" Water flew from her hair as she threw her head back. Feeling strengthened by the water, she splashed her face and then each arm. Surprisingly, the water began to sooth her screaming skin. Leaning forward once more, she took another deep, long drink. Now refreshed, she rested her back against the wall, realizing it was made of gold, or something like gold—a transparent gold. Now composed, she spoke. "From the mountain across the desert, I could see the enclosed land. At that distance, I didn't realize the wall was so high. It seems to reach the heavens. What is this place?"

The Watcher bowed his head in reverence and said, "This is…the Garden of Eden." She looked at him and blinked. Did he say what she thought he said? How could this be? *The* Garden of Eden? He continued, "This golden wall surrounds the Garden, and the sparkling light you saw at the arched gate is the flaming sword of the Cherubim that forever guard it. Do you remember how you felt when you saw this place from the mountain?"

She nodded, remembering the awe she felt. "I felt that there was something familiar about it, and it seemed to call to me."

"Yes, you should feel those things; for this was the paradise Yahweh intended for all mankind. This Garden is planted in the heart of mankind, and the heart knows its true home. This is where Yahweh led Adam to live; to keep it; to dress it. Here Adam named the animals. They came and bowed before him and communed with him, sharing this paradise with him. Here Adam slept while Yahweh formed Eve from his side and then took her by the hand. She walked with Him, and they fellowshipped while Adam slept. He gave her the eternal secrets that only the heart of a woman would possess. It pleased Him to see such glory. When He woke Adam, He placed her hand in his. With His hand over theirs, He blessed them and saw that what He had made was very good. His creation was complete. They were His crowning glory, and He set His love upon them. It was then the morning stars sang together, and all the sons of God shouted for joy in what Yahweh had created. I was one of them who sang!" What Sede felt was indescribable! She was being told what only those in heaven knew about this moment in creation. Who was she to have such knowledge? A trembling humbleness settled within her, and she bowed her head in reverence.

She then remembered the words he had spoken to her. "Tell me. What did you mean when you said Yahweh had something to give me?" She waited for his response.

"Yahweh has a gift from Eden for you, Sede. Take your hand and reach deep in the pool." Leaning forward, she reached into the water up to her shoulder. "Now feel with your hand, and you will find your gift."

She grabbed handfuls of watery sand and swished her hand back and forth. "There, there it was!" Something hard and round. She pulled her body back, water dripping from her arm. It felt light in her hand. Opening her hand, she saw a seed. It was smooth, round, and green. "This is my gift?" She wrinkled her eyebrows together.

The Watcher smiled as though he read her thoughts. "A treasure is not determined by its covering but by what lies within. Eden's gift will be a treasure to you, Sede. This gift is seeds within a seed." Sede had another puzzled look on her face. "You will come to understand these words when Yahweh reveals them to you," he said with confidence. The seed moved slightly in her hand. Frightened, she pulled her hand back, dropping it on the sand in front of her. "Yes, the seed is alive. This seed is from the Garden of Eden just like this pool of water. Both are full of life. To you, Sede, has this gift been given. Yahweh has wished it so. This is why He told you to come to the wall when you were on the mountain. It is a rare privilege to see the Garden of Eden for only with the eyes of the spirit can it be seen. It is hidden from the eyes of the flesh. Don't be afraid. Pick it up, and hold it to your ear."

Intrigued, she cupped the seed to her ear. She smiled, closed her eyes, and exhaled softly. "What is this beautiful music I hear? I've never heard such a wonderful melody!"

"Yes," smiled the Watcher. "What you are hearing is the music of heaven. Come now, Sede, you must eat. Throw your cape on the sand before you." The Watcher touched her cape with his rod, and a small cake of bread appeared. He touched it once more, and a cluster of dates appeared. Kneeling, he sat across from her. "Eat, for you have a long journey ahead of you. Shem has come searching for you, and I will bring you to his camp." She ate as the Watcher patiently waited. There was great comfort in his presence. With each bite, she felt renewed strength, and the weakness she had felt seemed to evaporate. When she finished, she submerged her water skin, filling it with the water of Eden. After she put her seed in her belt pouch, the Watcher spoke again. "Let us be on our way."

When she had taken but a few steps, she turned to look one last time at the pool of water that had saved her life. It was nowhere in sight. The wall was gone too. Shocked, she looked at the Watcher. He smiled and said, "The wall and the water of life are now veiled." She pondered these things as the hours passed while she followed the Watcher out of the desert.

The sun had set when the Watcher announced, "Up ahead, at the river's edge, is the camp of Shem." As they drew near the river, they saw the light of Shem's campfire through the trees. Shem heard the sound of rustling grass and cautiously rose to his feet, taking the stance of combat. Pulling the dagger from his belt, he gripped it tightly and waited. "Hail, Shem, son of Noah!" the Watcher proclaimed as he stepped from behind a tree. His glory was brilliant and cast light on the surrounding trees. Just then, Sede stepped out from behind him. Shem was in utter shock and slowly lowered his dagger. He felt the angel's heavenly presence, and a flood of peace swept through his soul. "Who are you?" he asked in wonder.

"I am a Watcher sent by Yahweh to return Sede." Turning to her, he glowed in brilliance. "I must leave you now, Sede. Shem will guide you to the village." Sparkling into a mist of light, he disappeared. They both looked in amazement at the place where he had stood. One moment he was there, and the next he was gone. Then realizing they were together again, they said at the same time, "You're alive!" and grabbed each other in joy.

When they settled next to the fire, Shem asked her, "Tell me, what became of you after the stampede and meeting this magnificent angel?" She replayed her three days of wandering: the first night under the grove of trees, the climb to the mountain lookout, seeing the walled land, and making second camp in the cave.

She told him of her struggle in the sand storm and how Yahweh sent the Watcher to give her water and food. Pleasure filled her as she shared the wonder of being at the wall of Eden. She hesitated. 'Should I tell him about my gift; the seed?" She was quiet and, clasping her belt pouch, she felt the seed within. 'I will tell him one day,' she thought.

As they continued to talk around the fire, she asked of the stampede and the welfare of the others. When he had regained consciousness after falling in the hole, he found Japheth and Zara. Then together they searched for Ham and Shoda late into the day. He took her hand and, with sadness in his voice, said, "I have ill news for you, Sede. Shoda and Ham are dead. The herd trampled them, leaving nothing for us to recognize of their bodies."

Sede couldn't believe what he was saying. "No!" she said, hardly able to breathe. "No, I don't believe this!" She searched his face, for surely he was wrong. Tears filled his eyes as he saw how hard she struggled with the news. Bowing her head, the tears flowed down her face, leaving wet tracks in the dust on her cheeks. Sede's mind was awhirl. Shoda dead? Ham dead? She felt stunned and frozen. The feelings of loss swept over her. All the memories: the days of hunting together, saving each another's lives, dancing at festivals, and happy times in each other's homes. They had been friends since childhood and trained together as hunter/warrior. What of Gruetat? What would he do without his beloved daughter? And Ham; Ham, too, was gone. Her head pounded from the tension of grief, and she felt great tightness in her chest. Shem put his arms around her and pulled her to himself, and she sobbed as she buried her head in his chest. She cried and cried until she had no more tears.

Slowly her body began to relax as she felt his arms around her. He pressed his cheek against her head and whispered, "Shoda and my brother were loved. May they shoot like an arrow, straight to the heart of Yahweh, and there find a place of rest in His embrace." She felt hot tears on the top of her head and heard him cry softly. She began to feel comfort from his words. They were like soothing water releasing the tension she felt from the grief that had gripped her heart. How wonderful to be in his arms, hearing his words. In that moment, she felt so comforted and so loved. She tightened her hug around his chest and gave him a loving embrace.

After a long silence, he asked, "Would you feel better if you refreshed yourself in the river?"

'Yes, water to wash the dust, the sand, and my tears away,' she thought. As she lowered herself beneath the cool water, she felt her body relax. She floated on her back and looked at the night sky. It was a full moon. Their village would be celebrating the new moon with feasting and laughter. But what could she rejoice in? Her friends were dead, their bodies mangled by brutal hooves. It was good that she hadn't found Shoda. She couldn't bear the thought of her being any way but strong, beautiful, and full of life. Tears welled up in her eyes again and stung with pain from her heart. She heard Shem call her from the camp. "Is all well, Sede?" Through a tightened throat, she replied, "All is well." As she floated, the water soothed her, and she began to feel better.

Her thoughts turned toward Shem. He had tried to comfort her, and she had felt it. He had shared his tears with her. 'I have known him as hunting companion, friend, and kinsman.' Still looking at the moon, she thought, 'How can my heart change from friendship and know love for a husband?' While she floated on her back, she whispered into the night, "Yahweh, help me as I learn about this love." She was surprised how much better she felt after she got out of the river. From her skins, she cut a leather strip and fashioned a necklace to carry the pouch that held her seed. It felt good hidden beneath her skins next to her heart. She braided her wet hair as she walked toward the fire and sat next to Shem.

Staring at the fire, she softly spoke. "We are to marry soon."

"Yes," he answered.

Looking tenderly at him, she asked, "How do you change a heart of friendship to love, Shem?" He searched her face and saw the beauty of her innocence. Oh, how lovely she was.

"I have wondered this also." Almost like a whisper he said, "Father told me that love is like a seed that grows. It begins small but gradually grows into a magnificent tree, strong and alive, bearing much fruit." She was surprised by his words. He spoke of a seed. She pressed her hand against her hidden necklace. 'Seeds within a seed,' she thought.

"What are you thinking, Sede? You seem deep in thought."

"I'm trying to find a place in my heart for all the things that have happened. Thank you for your words of comfort, Shem, and sharing in my grief." She leaned back into his arms, and they fell asleep next to the fire.

They journeyed all the next day and arrived at the village as the sun was setting. Gruetat sat waiting at the gate. He had been watching for their return. Japheth and Zara had brought news of Shoda and Ham's death, and he had sat at the gate each day waiting for a sign of Shem and Sede's return. Sede was dear to his family, and they often called her daughter. He knew the bond she had with Shoda. When he recognized them, he stood to his feet. She ran into his arms, weeping in his fatherly embrace. "You have come home to us, my daughter. I will not have to mourn for you as I have for my Shoda."

Shem placed his hand on Gruetat's shoulder and said, "I am sorry for your loss. My heart is with you, Gruetat." His words were warm and caring.

Tears welled in Gruetat's eyes as they turned to enter the gate. "Sede, we will stop at your hut and tell Dosta of your return, and then you will come to my home. Your father has left for the wilderness to pray for you. We will send word to him that you have returned." Tenderly, Shem touched Sede's forehead with his, bidding her goodnight.

As they walked the quiet street to Sede's hut, she took Gruetat's hand and held it to her heart. Her heart was breaking, and she knew his was too. After she embraced Dosta and she had calmed from her tears of joy, Sede left her bow and quiver in her room and walked with Gruetat to his hut. When they entered, Ne-el and Adat ran to her, crying as they held her. "Oh Sede, we're so glad that you have come back to us. We thought we lost you too when you never returned."

Mersta came softly behind, wrapping her arms around her. She gave her a loving hug and kissed her on the cheek. "Oh child, we love you and are so happy you're still alive!" Seeing their grief, Sede began to cry. "Oh, this is so hard to bear. I love Shoda so…"

As Sede tried to compose herself, she remembered Shem's wonderful words of comfort he gave her the night before. "I have something I want to tell you. When Shem told me of the ill news of Shoda, he said such a wonderful thing. Tears were in his eyes when he spoke, and his words were so kind; almost like a prayer. He said, 'Shoda was loved, and may her life be like an arrow that shoots straight to the heart of Yahweh, finding a place of rest in His embrace.'"

A calm settled in their midst, and Mersta softly spoke, "Thank you, Sede, for your words of comfort. Our Shoda is with Yahweh. I have this confidence of heart: We, the Sethites, have a living hope, and I know we will see her again when we are united in paradise." Sede felt Mersta's strength of faith, and it soothed her breaking heart. It had been her desire to give comfort to them, but it was she who had been comforted.

Ne-el drew near. "Dear Sede, I wish to give you something." In her hands was a folded robe. It was very beautiful; embroidered with silver threads and exquisite in craftsmanship. "I made this for Shoda, but now I wish to give it to you. You were like a sister to her. I made this with love and want you to have it."

Sede burst into tears once more, holding the robe to her chest. Trying to find the strength to speak, she choked out her words. "Thank you, Ne-el. I will cherish it always!"

That night Ne-el, Adat, and Sede fell asleep in one another's arms, drawing strength and comfort from the closeness of just being together. When Mersta came to their room, they had already fallen asleep on the furs. Tears filled her eyes when she saw them tangled over one another; their arms and legs bent and folded every which way. Her heart felt a sentimental pang. She remembered when her girls were but babies, sleeping piled together like newborn puppies; head, arms, and legs all jumbled together. She lovingly covered them with bedding furs, kissing each forehead and musing in her heart…that 'children are so very precious.'

Chapter 7

Shoda's Rescue

The village went into a state of mourning. Two of their own were dead. Sede and Shem's wedding would have to wait until Ham and Shoda had been honored. Tolmaka was overjoyed that she had returned and comforted her as she mourned for her dear friends. But none knew that Shoda and Ham still lived.

After the stampede, Shoda lay unconscious from her blow to the head. The ground near her began to shake, not from the pounding of hooves but from footsteps. There, standing over her, was a giant Nephilim. He carried a dead shosposcus across his shoulder, and when he saw Shoda, he flipped her over with his foot. He watched the rise and fall of her chest and dropped the shosposcus. After he bound her hands, he tightened a gag around her mouth and then stuffed her inside a net from his belt. Over one shoulder he hoisted the shosposcus and over the other he slung Shoda, dangling in the net.

When she came to, the first thing she felt was something pressing against her face. The weaving of the net cut into her face as she swung in a back and forth motion. In the confusion of the moment, she tried to scream, but only a muffled noise came from beneath the gag. Struggling to free her hands, she pulled at the ropes only to exhaust herself. What she saw when she looked through the net was the aftermath of the stampede. Dead carcasses lay bloodied where they fell, and a million hoof prints covered the ground. She scanned the open prairie, frantically looking for Ham and the others. Had they been trampled? Were they alive? Would they know to look for her?

She twisted in the net to see who was carrying her. To her horror, she realized it was a Nephilim. He was a brutish giant, similar to the one they had killed in the valley. His smell was horrific to the point of making her gag. It was the stench of sweat and rotten meat. His long hair hung over the net and slapped her with each long stride he took. Where was he taking her? Would he kill and eat her? Fear and dread gripped her heart. In a helpless panic, she prayed within herself, 'Oh Yahweh, help me, for I am lost if you don't!'

The sun had almost set when she heard the faint sounds of wailing, shouting, and the crack of whips. She couldn't see where they were going but only knew it was farther and farther from Ham and the others. The smell of smoke filled the air, and she knew they were close to his campfire. Dread filled her as she realized she had become a captive. Another cry rose up within her. 'Oh Yahweh, I need you….'

Meanwhile, Ham climbed down the tree that had saved his life. He had been dazed by the blow to the head and couldn't remember how long he had been lying over the branch. Dead shosposcus spotted the ground to the horizon. His shout called out to the others—over and over—only to hear the echo of his own voice. Fear filled his heart as he began to look for his pack. Were they still alive? He followed the direction that the herd had run, looking for their tracks. After what seemed like hours, he realized there would be no finding them. He stopped to gain his composure and wiped the tears from his face. His head still hurt, and he felt a sense of helplessness. What had become of them?

With his head bent low in sorrow, he opened his eyes. What was this? He could hardly believe what he saw at his feet. It was Shoda's sling. He dropped to his knees and held it, pressing it to his heart. "Shoda," he whispered, his voice cracking from the pain of loss. Looking through his tears, he saw strange footprints leading away from where he knelt. He recognized them. They were Nephilim. Could this mean she was taken and still alive? Could he dare believe it? A thrill of hope filled him as he held her sling to his chest once more. Rising to his feet, he followed the tracks. The weight of the giant's body had pressed footprints deep into the soft earth, making them easy to follow. He began to run, knowing he had several hours of daylight left. He didn't want the wind to come up and cover the trail. But as the sun began to set, so did his hope. 'I don't see them ahead. How will I track in the dark?' As the sky lost its last light, he brought himself to a stop. "Oh Yahweh, how will I find her in the night?"

Shoda's Rescue

Darkness had now covered the land, and his only resolve was to make camp and begin early in the morning. As he was searching in the dark for something to build a fire, he heard faint sounds in the distance. He tripped and fell on his chest. A small seqwetta bush was snagged in his sandal. Realizing what it was, he pulled it up. Shaking the dirt from its roots and stripping the branches from the stem, he sparked his flints to light the roots, making a flaming torch. 'Now I can see the way!' Holding the torch close to the ground, he continued to track the giant.

The closer he came to the distant sounds, the more recognizable they became. They were the sounds of captivity: cracking whips and wailing. Was Shoda the one who was crying out? Pain pricked his heart. When he saw the light of the camp, he extinguished his torch. Creeping on his belly, he made his way to the edge of the rocks that overlooked the valley. From his vantage point, he had a perfect view of the whole camp. Many small fires burned to light the perimeter, and in the middle were corrals filled with the captured. All of them were bound. He counted three groups: men, women, and children. Patrolling the perimeter were giants, each carrying a torch and spear. Could Shoda be with the women? He had to know.

Slowly he made his way down the face of the rocks to the valley below. Crouching in the cover of the tall grass, he waited for the camp to fall asleep. After the fires burned low, he crept toward the women. Slowly he moved on his belly, but he suddenly stopped. A patrolling guard passed. He was so close he could see the hair on his legs. Inching his way, he tried to spot Shoda. There were probably fifty women huddled together in their corral, slumped over, and trying to sleep. He could tell by the symbol on their clothing that they were all Sethites. Which village had they plundered to capture so many people? Could Taasa-toka have been attacked while they were on their hunt? His thoughts were full of jumbled questions.

As he scanned their sleeping faces, he spotted her. Joy swept through him, and he sighed in relief. She was alive. Slowly he inched his way forward. Waiting for another guard to pass, he slid under the rope barrier. Grabbing Shoda from behind, he covered her mouth with his hand. Waking with a start, she struggled. But panic quickly changed to recognition as she mumbled softly under his hand.

Cutting her ropes, he freed her hands. Tremendous relief overwhelmed her as she hugged him and began to cry.

The woman beside them woke with a start. Just as she began to speak, Ham motioned with his finger to his lips. They looked around to see if any of the other women had seen them. None had. She whispered in a panic, "Take me with you, please!" Ham looked at Shoda, who nodded and rubbed her wrists where the ropes had dug into her skin. Cutting the woman's ropes, he said in a hush, "We must go quickly!" Holding his finger to his mouth, he added, "And quietly!" They edged their way backward until they could no longer see through the grass. Both women began to softly cry. "Oh, I never thought I'd see you again!" sobbed Shoda. The other woman clasped her hands in prayer, crying softly, "Thank you, Yahweh, thank you!" Ham motioned again to keep silent. "We must keep moving. Follow me."

Crawling on their knees, they reached the rock ledge where Ham first saw the camp. Believing they were finally safe, he asked them what had happened. Shoda explained about waking up inside the net and realizing that a Nephilim had captured her. When they reached the camp, she was dropped from the net and thrown in with the other women. Zilla, the other woman, had been captured from the village of Tagma. Nephilim raiders had attacked their village just yesterday. They had been bringing more people all day, adding to those who were already captured from Bethla-seska and Nishka. Pressing them for more information, he asked, "Where were they taking you?"

"I'm not sure," answered Zilla, "but I think I heard them say something about taking us to a ship."

Ham and Shoda looked at each other, perplexed. "Ship? What is a ship?"

"I don't know, but that's what they said," she added.

"We shouldn't linger here," cautioned Ham. "We must put distance between them and us. When I came this way, the land was flat. We'll be able to run in the dark and not fear falling into holes or off a cliff. Let's go!" They rose to their feet and began to run, stopping only to give Zilla a chance to catch her breath. Although Ham and Shoda were seasoned hunters, Zilla was not.

It was early the next morning when the Nephilim discovered two of their captives had escaped. The camp was in confusion as they began yelling and sorting through the corrals. Shouting orders were given, and they counted, looking for the missing. They found the bent grass where they had escaped, and the captain sent two guards to track them. "You'll hunt them down and bring them back. I won't be known as one who let a Sethite escape through my fingers. And remember; I want them back alive!"

They scaled the rocks to the top of the plateau and looked to the horizon in hope of spotting them. Their footprints were the only evidence left behind. One laughed as they ran, "How easy is this? Their footprints will lead us straight to them!" The other grunted in his burly voice, "Stupid humans. They know nothing of covering their tracks. It almost takes the thrill out of the hunt. I wish we didn't have to return them. I'd have great pleasure in skinning them alive."

Ham led the women through the night, past the dead carcasses from the stampede, and into a small valley. He recognized the area and knew which direction led to their village. The sun was rising when they stopped to rest by a small stream. Here they would take shelter in the overhanging trees. Ham knew they must find food and prepared to leave. "You're not going without me, are you?" Shoda said with a smile. Grinning, he handed her the sling. He knew he wouldn't win if he insisted she stay. They looked at Zilla. "Will you be okay if we leave?"

"Yes, I'll be fine. Just don't be gone too long." With a smile, she jested, "I'm looking forward to being a guest in your village tonight!"

"We'll be back soon," Shoda said, reassuring her.

Zilla saw them run side by side and disappear over the hill. Exhausted, she settled under the bushes beneath the trees and closed her eyes. Sleep came soon enough. It was early evening when Ham and Shoda returned to find a nice fire burning. Zilla had used her flints in anticipation of their return. "Sorry we took so long. Game was scarce." A small rabbit hung from Shoda's waist belt, and Ham carried a grouse by its feet.

"I was beginning to worry for you," Zilla said with concern in her voice. As she dressed their kill, she told them about the raid on her village and some of the stories she had heard from the other women. Their villages had been plundered and their families killed. Nothing remained. It was all destroyed by fire.

Everything that they had held to, of family and their way of life, was gone. The world had become a crazy place of raiding, killing, and uncertainty!

The food strengthened and revived them, and when they finished, Ham suggested they leave early the next morning. Zilla protested. "Can't we travel tonight as we did last night, running in the dark?"

"I wish we could," he said, "but the terrain is different from here to the river. It would be unsafe. In the morning, when we pass through the valley, we'll find the river and then follow it upstream to the village."

Shoda took Zilla's hand to reassure her. Patting it, she soothed her, saying, "We'll be okay. We'll leave in the morning. Tonight Ham and I will stand watch so you can sleep. I'll take first watch. Be assured, Zilla, morning will come before you know it, and then we'll be on our way."

As they slept, Zilla and Ham's breathing was slow and steady. Shoda crouched by the fire and watched their sleeping faces. Thanksgiving filled her heart as she thought of Ham. He had come for her, and another Sethite had been saved. As she pondered their escape, she heard a twig snap. Looking into the dark, she scanned for movement. Slowly rising to her feet, she nudged Ham. He woke with a start, and she spoke in a whisper, "Something is out there!"

Ham touched Zilla to wake her. "Wake, Zilla. You must hide while we look around." Startled, Zilla scrambled beneath the thickets and waited. From her hiding place, she could see the surrounding area lit by the glow of their fire.

Shoda and Ham crept, circling the camp. Slowly they made their way through the trees. All of a sudden a great roar exploded as two Nephilim charged. They had been waiting for them. Zilla held her hand over her mouth to keep from screaming. She saw both Shoda and Ham pulled into the open and pushed face down on the ground. One giant had his knee against the back of Shoda's neck, and the other had his foot pushed into Ham's back. They bound their hands and gagged them. Zilla saw them struggling, but they were no match against the giants. While they were knotting their ropes, they laughed and said, "Your campfire led us right to you. It almost takes the sport out of hunting!"

The other chuckled. "Yes, we've got you. They'll be even happier that instead of two women, we bring a man!"

"Shall we look for the other one?"

"No, let's not waste any time searching in the dark. We don't want to miss the ship at Zadanim. I want to be on that ship!"

Shoda and Ham struggled while they were stuffed into nets and slung over their huge shoulders. Zilla cried as she heard their footsteps grow softer and softer. "Oh, Yahweh, they're gone. What should I do? What will become of them?" She bowed her head and sobbed. As the night grew long, she finally fell asleep.

It was the call of a hawk that woke her in the morning. Looking through the thickets, she saw the smoldering campfire. The sun was rising, and she knew she had only one recourse. Slowly she crawled from her hiding place and stood to her feet. Tears filled her eyes as she replayed the memory of Ham and Shoda being carried away. Crying, she turned her face to the morning sky. "I'm alone, Yahweh. Help me find Shoda and Ham's village. They are the only people I have left. Maybe their kin can help them!"

Remembering what Ham had said about following the valley to the river, she would be able to find their village. She took what meat was left at the smoldering fire and wrapped it in her robe. Grabbing Ham's water skins, she started across the valley. It was late in the day when she arrived at the river. She would have to hide until morning for, unlike Shoda and Ham, she was no hunter/warrior. When the sun rose, she followed the river, going upstream as Ham had said. It was late in the afternoon when she saw thin threads of smoke rising in the distance and heard the faint sounds of a village.

She began to run, running faster and faster. The gatekeeper saw her at a distance and ran to meet her. Collapsing at his feet, she breathlessly told him she had been captured by Nephilim and that Ham and Shoda had been taken. Carrying her in his arms, he took her to Noah's hut. Pounding on the door, he called for Noah. Breathlessly, Zilla rehearsed her capture and how Ham had rescued her and Shoda. They had been captured and carried away by Nephilim raiders.

"I must call the elders together. My son still lives! Send word to Gruetat, and call the elders," he charged the gatekeeper.

Noah led Zilla to the council fire, where the elders waited. Again Zilla retold the events of what had happened in Tagma; how their village was burned and the survivors led away captive. Bethla-seska and Nishka had also been raided. She told how Ham had set her and Shoda free and how they were ambushed at their camp by two giants.

Tolmaka addressed the council, "We must send out hunters at once. I know of this place, Zadanim. It's near the Great Sea. If we are to save Ham and Shoda, we must leave immediately!"

All the elders nodded in agreement. Tolmaka's pack would rescue their own. It was the elders' decision not to send Zara. She was too young to risk such peril, and Gruetat wouldn't be going either. He had hurt his ankle just that day and couldn't endure such a journey. Noah sent them on their way with his blessing, "May Yahweh go with you and show you the way. May He bring to me my son, and may Shoda return to her father's embrace!"

Chapter 8

Zadanim

It was late when Tolmaka returned to his hut. Shem and Sede had fallen asleep by Dosta's fire, waiting to know why the council meeting had been called. Tolmaka burst through the door in wild excitement, waking the sleeping with a start. "We must leave immediately!" he blurted, and he frantically began to gather his spear, knife, and leather bags.

Sede and Shem looked at each other, puzzled. As he continued to gather his things, he hurriedly explained what had taken place at the council meeting. Sede's heart leapt, and a burst of adrenaline exploded within her! Grabbing Shem by the forearm, she trembled with excitement. "Shoda and Ham are still alive!"

Dosta quickly prepared food for their journey, mumbling to herself and holding back her tears. Grabbing their water skins, Sede and Shem hurried to the village stream. As they filled their skins, Sede's joy overflowed. "They're alive…. I can hardly believe it. We have to find them!"

"If the wind doesn't cover their tracks, we'll be able to follow their trail. Shem saw his hands shaking with excitement as he secured the lip of the water skin. "We'll find them, Sede. Our pack will bring back their own!"

She sensed his resolve and determination. It made her heart thrill. Leaning forward, she touched her forehead to his, adrenaline still racing through her. "Ha-la-lah, we *will*!"

When they left the village, it was still dark. Even in the light of the moon, Shem knew the way to their last hunt. As the sun began to rise, they quickened their pace, running even faster. They reached Ham's abandoned campsite then found the plain where the stampede had happened just days before. The dead shosposcus were now picked clean by scavengers, and their bones were the only witness that a stampede had taken place. Following the Nephilim tracks, they arrived at the ridge that overlooked the valley below. It was now late in the day, and the sun was beginning to set.

The deserted camp was left in shambles: smoldering campfires, torn up corrals, and dead captives left where they fell. Tolmaka saw the horrified look on Sede's face as she realized these Sethites would be left for scavengers. In compassion, he grasped her shoulder. "We must look to the living, Sede; the dead are with Yahweh." Lifting his eyes to the horizon, he saw a cloud of dust. "They're pressing hard to get to Zadanim," he said. "We must hurry. Their ship must leave in the morning!" Taking a drink from their skins, they continued their run westward.

It was late in the night when they met the people, being herded like cattle. They moved in the shadowy light of torches, making it hard to see their faces. The air was filled with the noise of children wailing and the gruff shouts of the giants yelling at them to keep up. "This is a nightmare, Father!" Sede said in a panic. "How will we ever find them?"

"Yahweh will show us the way, my child," he reassured her. "Let's look for the men. We'll free Ham first, then Shoda. Let's move to the perimeter…go!"

They moved through the tall grass, coming into place alongside the men. Only a curtain of grass now separated them. The helpless walked with their hands bound, stumbling and weeping as they were prodded forward.

Japheth nudged Tolmaka in excitement. "I see him. Over there, in the middle of the men. We need to get his attention, and I know how." Tolmaka knew what he meant and gave a nod of approval. Cupping his hands to his mouth, Japheth sent the bird call their pack used in the hunt. With all the noise, Ham hadn't heard him. He sent the call once more as the men began to pass. This time Ham looked toward the grass, surprised to hear the sound he knew so well. Calling once more, Ham now saw them crouched in the grass.

A giant cut through the crowd of the men, his great feet pounding angrily on the ground. Men flew out of the way, avoiding being stepped on. Someone had tripped and fell, causing those behind them to stumble over his body and pile up. This was the distraction Ham needed to slip away. The commotion was so great that those who were beside him didn't notice when he stepped into the tall grass and simply disappeared. Just a stone's throw away was Japheth. He knelt beside him and held his hands out to cut the rope that bound his wrists. As soon as the rope fell, they threw their arms around each other in relief. Breathlessly he muttered, "We must free Shoda!"

Tolmaka touched his shoulder and nodded. "We will. Let's go!"

They crept through the grass to where the women were passing. They continued following until Sede finally spotted her. "I see her!" she whispered in excitement. "There she is!" Relief filled her to see her friend but pain too. She looked so helpless, bound and hurried along with all the others.

Shoda tripped and regained her balance. The giant guard came up behind her and gave her a push with the handle of his whip. "Hurry along, you!"

She felt herself fly forward from the strength of his nudge. Falling to the ground, the woman behind her started a chain reaction of stumbling and falling on top of one another. A heap of bodies began to pile up. Strangely, the same distraction that had helped Ham's escape would now help her. The guard became angry and raised his whip to strike the woman on top of the pile. Shoda was help-lessly pinned beneath them all. The giant tossed the women from the pile by their arms and legs, throwing them over his shoulders; landing on the ground with a thud. As she struggled under the weight of the women's bodies, she noticed two figures crouched in the tall grass. It was Ham and Japheth. The rest of her pack knelt behind them and motioned to her. Surprise and joy filled her as she realized they had come for her.

As the Nephilim grabbed the woman on top of Shoda, she dangled midair by the leg. Drawing a hidden knife from her belt, the woman slashed his hand. He bellowed with pain and dropped her to the ground. Shoda scrambled through his legs and disappeared in the grass. Through the commotion, none of the other women noticed her slip away; they were too distracted by the roaring giant.

"Lie still," whispered Tolmaka. "We can't be seen!" They froze as huge legs passed where they lay. As Japheth cut Shoda's ropes, she grabbed him around the neck and hugged him. "Thank you, thank you!" she sobbed.

Sede then grabbed her and whispered with tears in her eyes, "I'm so glad you're alive!"

Tolmaka hushed them. "We must be still. If they hear us, we perish. Back away!"

As they inched slowly backward, they saw the last group of children stumbling along to keep up with the hurried pace. "How can we free them?" Sede tearfully asked. Her heart broke to see them herded like animals, terrified and alone.

"I don't know," Tolmaka answered. "But we have to try!"

As they drew near the lights of Zadanin, Sede caught the scent of something strange. "I smell something unfamiliar. What is that?"

"That's the smell of the Great Sea. It's the smell of salt water," Tolmaka whispered. "We've arrived!" The lights from the street torches revealed a city none of them had ever seen before. Their lodges were strange and foreboding. As far as the eye could see, one long hut extended down each side of the street. Hanging from every door was a skull painted with strange markings, with bowls of foul smelling blood at the stoop. Through the open windows, they could see the naked dancing and chanting to the strange drumbeats that filled the air. The people had similar physical characteristics: elongated heads. Sede felt sickened and remembered what her father had told them about Nephilim inner breeding with the Cainites. Was this a city of the offspring of Cainites and Nephilim?

Moans rose in the air when those standing along the streets began cutting themselves with knives and groaning with strange sounds as blood flowed from their open wounds. A darkness that could be felt pressed against the frightened pack. Sede felt a tightness in her chest and the hair on the back of her neck stand up. Blinking in unbelief, Shem turned to Tolmaka and choked out his words… "What is this place?"

"This is the ungodly city of the Cainites, my son. This is the place I saw when I was a young man, lost from a hunt. I was fortunate to escape with my life. None but a few who are taken ever return to their villages. And when they do come back, they come back changed!"

The guards paraded the captives through the street while Cainites came pouring out of their doors. They ran to them, chanting strange words and touching them. It was though they drew some invisible power with just a touch. The children were the ones they most desired to touch. The Sethite women wept as they walked, bowing their heads. Hopelessness filled the men, knowing they were doomed. The exhausted children stumbled forward, dazed by the noise and the strange behavior of the evil that surrounded them. They all knew they were lost to this dark and evil world.

Tolmaka turned to the others and said, "They'll take them to the ship. We must find the pier before they arrive. Our best chance to save them will be there!" They stayed in the outer perimeter of the city and quickly made their way to the beach. There they saw the huge ship tied to a crude pier. As giants stood sentry, Cainites busied themselves on deck with preparations to leave. Tolmaka breathed a prayer. "Yahweh, what should we do?"

Shem turned and smiled. "I think I know. You see that ship? It's made of wood. And wood burns. We should set it on fire. This will give us a distraction to free as many as we can!" Tolmaka smiled and nodded. "Sede, you go with Shem and set the ship on fire. The rest of us will stay here and free the people."

The tumultuous roar of the Cainite's filled the air as they followed the Sethites to the ship. From the shouting Nephilim, cracking whips, crying women and children, and the Cainites' wild leaping and dancing around the Sethites, it was utter mayhem. Shem and Sede crept behind barrels and boxes piled near the pier. Slipping into the water, they made their way to the back side of the ship. The water was cold, unlike the warm river water they were used to. Looking up, they saw the railing of the ship and the attached rope for the anchor. They began climbing the rope, stopping only when they heard a sound. Crawling over the railing, they took a quick look around.

"I'll take that torch, open the hatch, and throw it below. We'll burn this ship from the bottom up!"

Sede nodded with an excited, "Yes!"

"You move to the front and start your fire there," whispered Shem.

As though some unseen hand guided them, they moved without thinking about what to do next. The men on deck seemed to move in such a way as to allow them to pass right by them. With torch in hand, Shem tossed it below.

Unbeknownst to him, it held barrels of lamp oil as cargo. As Shem backed slowly away, a huge explosion blew him off the ship and into the water. Sede, too, was blown over the railing without even using the torch in her hand. The confusion that followed was what they had hoped for.

Tolmaka and his pack crouched behind the cargo that still needed to be loaded. They signaled the men and women huddled from the explosion.

"Follow us," called Tolmaka, pointing to the emblem on his skins. Recognizing the symbol, smiles of relief filled their faces.

With the Nephilim distracted and racing toward the burning ship, the Sethites were able to quickly move to the cover of the barrels and boxes. Ham and Japheth cut the ropes of the men, who in turn, set the women and children free.

"We must move quickly!" Tolmaka whispered. "Follow me!" He led the way as they followed him into the tall grass.

Shem and Sede swam away from the burning ship and followed the shoreline to join the others. While they ran on the beach, she gave him a little nudge with her shoulder. With a smile that communicated admiration she said, "You did great, Shem!" He met her eyes with a warm smile. They stopped when they heard voices and realized it was Tolmaka and the freed Sethites. Stepping into the grass, they joined them and continued to run farther away from the city.

The Nephilim went wild when they discovered their captives were gone. Their roars were deafening. The captain blew his horn, and eight giants rallied to attention. Grunting, he tossed nets at each of them and passed out long hocked poles. "Take these nets and poles. Tonight you hunt." With gritted teeth and clenched fists, he ordered, "You will find them and bring them back! There's another ship coming in the morning. We'll sail with them!"

With torches in hand, the Nephilim grabbed their nets and poles. Sweeping out in different directions, they moved through the rustling grass. One giant grunted excitedly, "I love to hunt Sethites; they're such easy prey!"

The other laughed. "Yes, and I love the helpless look on their faces when I tighten my hold on their throat and their feet dangle in the air!"

They both laughed and swept through the grass. It wasn't long before they found the trailing end of their escaping captives. One threw a net over four men running together, while another found a group of women huddled together and netted them. Families were swept up by more nets. Only the children scurried too fast for the giants to catch, ducking and darting in and around their legs.

"We'll never catch these small ones like this," bellowed the captain. "We'll have to burn them out!" With a smirk on his face and a sinister laugh, he lowered his torch and set fire to the grass. Like a match to kindling, the grass ignited. The breeze spread the fire toward the desperate. Screams rose in the night as children began running in all directions. With their long, hocked poles, they raked the children in by the neck and stuffed them in their nets. It took little time to round them up.

Tolmaka turned to see the fire sweeping toward them. "Hurry, we must escape to the water's edge. There the flames will have no power over us!" Only Tolmaka, Shem, Japheth, and Shoda stepped on the beach as the flames consumed the tall grass behind them. "Oh Shem!" gasped Tolmaka. "Where are Sede and Ham?!"

Shem whirled around in unbelief, and panic gripped his heart. She had been just behind him. "Nooo!" he screamed. "Sede. Sede!" he screamed with even more panic, moving toward the fire. "Where are you…?" He lunged into the fire only to have Tolmaka pull him back as both fell to the ground. Slapping the flames from Shem's burning skins, Tolmaka felt helpless panic. His chest burned as though he'd been stabbed in the heart. His daughter—his beautiful daughter—was gone. He raised both hands in the air, and a cry rose out of his throat that he couldn't control. "Ahee!" It was a cry of pain, love, and loss!

Shem bent his head back and with his whole heart and soul cried, "Sedeeee!" His cry burned hot as any flame that consumed the grass. His Sede was lost to him—gone.

Shoda dropped to her knees and covered her face with her hands, crying. "Ham…Ham. You saved me, but by saving me, you were lost. Oh, my friend; my betrothed. Sede, Sede, my sister, my friend!" She lowered her head to the ground and wept with painful tears.

Japheth knelt beside her and wept his own mournful words. "Dear brother. How can you be gone? Sweet Sede. Oh, beautiful, sweet Sede!"

The four stood for a long time watching the fire burn in the distance. Japheth shouted in anger, "Why did we try to save the Sethites when we could have left and been safe!" A long silence held their hearts.

Shem put his hand on his shoulder. "We would have never been able to live with ourselves if we hadn't tried." Japheth lowered his head and wept, nodding in agreement.

Tolmaka clasped Shem's shoulder and said, "I love you, my son. You have spoken true words. We had to try." Heaviness filled their hearts as they began the journey home. Their lives had been forever changed this night. Each had lost someone: a daughter, a promised husband, a promised wife, a brother, a friend, and a sister. How would they ever live without them? This question fell upon each heart as they turned silently to the east.

They didn't speed their return home, for the news they bore would only bring sorrow. Healing needed to come to them before they could extend it to others. They hunted the second day and made camp that night. It was Tolmaka who knew they must talk and release the pain they carried. "Come, children, and sit with me here at the fire. Let us draw strength from one another."

Shem was thankful that he would counsel them. He couldn't speak for fear of bursting into tears.

As they sat cross legged, Tolmaka looked intently at their sad faces. Tears filled his eyes. Not only was his own grief near, but he sensed theirs too. "Two days ago we each lost a piece of our heart. Never will our lives be the same. The question we must ask ourselves is…how do we step into our future without them?" Their sorrowful faces looked at him, longing for the comfort of his words. Shoda began to cry, and Japheth reassuringly put his arm around her shoulder.

Tolmaka consoled her, "Yes, our tears we give them; for they are worthy of all that is in our hearts. We have been a pack for many years and have learned to depend on each other for our very lives. Let us now depend on each other for comfort and consolation." He stood with his arms extended and beckoned them, "Come children, receive the embrace of a father." They stood, and one by one, he held them as they cried on his chest. It was what they had needed to release their tears and receive the embrace of someone who knew what they felt. When the last had been held, he turned to Shem. "Will you give me your embrace?" Shem began to cry as he held Tolmaka, his strong arms embracing his leader's shoulders. Tolmaka wept bitter tears for he held such love for his daughter. Japheth and Shoda bowed their foreheads on Tolmaka's back as they wept with him. This was not just their loss but his too.

When his tears had been spent, he spoke. "Let us ask Yahweh to help our village in their lament for the dead; for Sede and Ham were dearly loved by our people." With tear-filled eyes, they looked heavenward into the night and, linked arm to shoulder, formed a circle of prayer.

Tolmaka's deep voice rose as he spoke his words: "Yahweh, Father of Adam, we lift our prayer to you. We sorrow here in this wilderness place for our dead, but the village will greatly mourn when they hear that two of their young have died. Help them in their grief. Comfort their hearts and may they draw upon one another in this time of sorrow. Thank you for the lives of Sede and Ham. They came from your heart and have returned to their resting place in you. We offer thanksgiving that we knew them and loved them, and now we release them back to you." Silence enfolded them as they held Tolmaka's words close to their hearts.

When the sun rose, they had but a half day's journey to the village. Though comforted by Tolmaka's embrace and prayer, their loss was still with them. Shem fought back tears for he longed to hold Sede as he had the night the Watcher returned her from the desert. His heart was just beginning to make room for his future with her. His feelings of affection had grown, changing from friendship to love. And now all that had been taken from him. He felt the loss of her but also the life they could have shared together. He knew Yahweh was preparing her too. He could see it in her eyes when she looked at him and in the blushing of her cheeks when he held her hand. But now, he felt frozen.... It was though his heart had turned cold and numb.

When the gatekeeper saw them approach, the tower horn sounded their return. There was much rejoicing as they entered the gate. It was only after they heard of the death of Sede and Ham that the village began to mourn. As was the custom, they would mourn three days; then three days of celebration would follow. Huts displayed the black banners of mourning and hung them from their doors. On the black cloth were painted three white tears; each tear signified the grief of family, the village, and the world. All three had lost the presence of the one who once lived among them. All day long the musicians played the soothing "Love Song for the Dead." They never tired of their playing. They believed it was a gift to the dead; in their loving memory.

One by one, elders visited the huts of Noah and Tolmaka, speaking words of love and comfort to them. Dosta and Ezmere, too, had elder women who consoled them. It was on one of these nights that Dosta visited Shoda. Draped neatly over her arm was the robe Ne-el had given Sede when they had believed Shoda had died. Tears welled in both their eyes as Dosta gently extended the lovely robe. "Thank you, Dosta. When I wear it, my thoughts will be of Sede, my dearest of friends."

Dosta gently wiped the tear that rolled down Shoda's cheek. "My most precious Sede will never marry and wear such a robe. She would want you to have it." They both held each other, unable to speak. The loss was so very deep....

After the three days of mourning ended, Noah spoke to Gruetat. As the leader of his people, he would present the "custom to honor the dead." This Sethite custom was an attempt to continue the "seed" of the dead brother. His betrothed would marry a living brother, and they would dedicate their firstborn as his namesake. Shoda had been pledged to Ham. Ne-el had been pledged to Japheth. Only fifteen, Ne-el was not of the age of maturity according to Sethite tradition. Seeing Ne-el was not old enough to marry, Noah proposed they allow Shoda to marry Shem or Japheth, thus honoring Ham. This would enable one of them to dedicate their firstborn son as his namesake. Noah called his sons to council to discuss who would marry Shoda. Shem still mourned the loss of Sede, and Japheth saw that it would be grievous for a sorrowing groom to comfort a new bride. His heart also ached for Shoda; he knew she had loved Ham. He had not found a love for Ne-el for he knew she was too young to set his affections on. He realized his heart was open to fulfill this honor he could give to his dead brother. In faith, he trusted that Yahweh would give him love for Shoda.

As the elders discussed the custom, Japheth stood and bowed before them. "I wish Shem this time to mourn his loss and consent to Sethite custom. I will honor Ham and name my firstborn son as his own." Shem stood to his feet and faced his brother. With tears in his eyes, he embraced him. "My brother, not only do you honor Ham, you honor me. Thank you for giving me time to find peace with Sede's death. May Yahweh richly bless you." The elders then called Shoda to stand before them. They asked her consent to Sethite custom. Bowing, she said, "May the love I find for Japheth be an honor to Ham. I consent to union with him and pledge my firstborn son be named as Ham's." Noah stood and clapped his hands three times and proclaimed, "As it has been said, so let it be done. The union of Japheth and Shoda will crown the three days of celebrating the death of my son and Tolmaka's daughter."

The village was abuzz as the elder women were called together. They would begin Shoda's preparations. Mersta, Ezmere, and three other elder women gathered at Gruetat's hut. Shoda felt a pang of loss when she hung her skins on the peg in her room. She would be a hunter no more. She, like Sede, had loved the life of the hunt. By the end of the third day of preparations, she had been instructed about the intimacy between a man and a woman and prepared herself for her union with Japheth. Her cheeks blushed from innocence, for she knew intimacy existed but knew nothing of the details. Her innocence, like all Sethite maidens, had been carefully guarded until the set time for her to know. This was now her time. One of the elder women had taught her food preparation; another the "art" of washing clothes—or so she humorously called it. And the third shared the knowledge of childbirth and the wisdom of child rearing. In her heart, Shoda ached for Sede's companionship. She had always been there to share her innermost thoughts with. She missed her friend....

Chapter 9

Voyage to the Unknown

As the village mourned and prepared for Shoda and Japheth's wedding, little did they know that Sede and Ham still lived. Snared by the nets of the Nephilim, they had not perished in the flames but were captured with the other Sethites. Fear gripped Sede's heart as she struggled against the pressing net that dug into her face. The weight of the other women's bodies pressed against her, making her feel as though she were suffocating. She tried breathing through the weaving of the net but couldn't fill her lungs. She tried to relax her body, but fear was greater than what her mind told her to do. Tears ran down her face as she cried within herself, "Oh Yahweh, save me from this horror!" Where were the others? Had they been captured? Were Father and Shem still alive? Were they safe? She closed her eyes with the painful thought of it. What of Shoda, Ham, and Japheth? Her head pounded from the tension of her thoughts.

The giant shifted the weight of the net, and she was now on top of the other bodies. At least now she could breathe. The women beneath her struggled to find a place for arms, legs, and heads. The Nephilim had strung two of the filled nets from the hocked pole, suspending it across his shoulder much like the women of the village carried water skins from the stream. It wasn't long before they arrived back in Zadanim. The giants dropped the nets with a thud and began to pull the women out by their arms and legs. Three groups were formed again of men, women, and children. There were far less Sethites this time; many had been lost in the fire. Sede searched the women's faces, looking for Shoda. Disappointment, then relief, filled her when she didn't see her. Perhaps she was still alive and had escaped.

From where she sat, she could see the huddled men. She searched their faces, darkened with the soot of the fire. Fifteen, sixteen, she counted. Wait. Was that Ham? Yes, it was. Hope was kindled, and she tried to call out to him through the commotion. It was impossible to be heard above the chaos around them. She remembered their pack signal used earlier that night. Cupping her hands to her mouth, she sent the call. He raised his head to see what direction the familiar sound came from. When his eyes met hers, she drew her hand to her heart and moved it slowly out to him. He smiled briefly but was interrupted by the crack of a Nephilim whip. Both settled back, feeling some relief that they weren't alone.

Silence fell over the captives as, one by one, they fell asleep. Some huddled in small groups; others curled up in fetal positions. It surprised her, but her thoughts were of Shem. Her heart ached to have him hold her. Her memory slipped back to the campfire along the river after he told her of Shoda's death in the stampede. His arms had felt so good around her, his heartbeat so reassuring. She had felt so safe and comforted. Oh, how she wished he was with her now....

Suddenly, she woke with a start. It was the sound of yelling and whips. It took her a few seconds to realize where she was. The stark memory of last night flooded over her, filling her with dread. The sun was just beginning to rise as the captives began to stir. The brutish guards shouted their commands and herded them into the water next to the burnt shell of the ship. "Wash yourselves!" they gruffly shouted. The people tried to drink the water but spit it out. They had never tasted salt water before. After washing the best they could, they were forced back to the beach. Baskets of bread and water skins were thrown at each group of captives. The cold, shivering people desperately scrambled over each other for food and water.

As Sede chewed on a hard piece of bread, she looked up to see a ship gliding toward the city from the sea. She was awed by the sight of it. It was beautiful with its white sails full of the wind, extended out like the wings of an eagle. The ship's sides were covered with shining gold paint reflecting the rising sun. 'Oh that this ship could take me home!' she thought. 'This must be the ship the raiders were waiting for.'

There was much shouting and grunting as four giants tugged on long tow lines. Slowly the burnt shell of the ship was pulled out of the way. The new ship inched its way to the pier. As whips cracked, the frightened Sethites were herded aboard the ship. They stumbled and fell down the stairs as the giants pushed and shoved them below deck. No longer separated into groups, all shared the same space. Family's found each other and huddled together as well as people reuniting from their villages. When Sede and Ham found each other, they hugged in relief.

She asked first. "Tell me what you know of last night and if you saw any of the others alive."

Ham rehearsed the events that led to the grass fire. "We were all together, and I was following Japheth through the grass. When the fire swept toward us, confusion and flames separated us. I searched to find a way around the fire but became surrounded by other captives. That is when we were netted!" With questioning eyes, he clasped her hand and said, "Tell me what you know."

"Shem and I made it back from the burning ship and found Father and the others in the grass. The noise and confusion was so great I thought you were with us too. As we looked through the grass, we saw the beach and moved in that direc-tion. It was when I was following Shem that I suddenly felt a quick pull around my neck. A giant had snagged me with his hook. He then stuffed me in a net with other women. Shem continued running, not hearing my scream. I called after him, but he was moving too fast. Within seconds, he was gone. The others must have made it to the beach because they were so close!" She began to cry. "I have to believe they made it to the beach. I don't think I could bear it, knowing they perished." She lowered her head to his shoulder, tears streaming down her face.

Ham put his arms around her in reassurance. "I believe they made it. I'm sure they're all right. We're alive, too, and together."

Footsteps and shouting could be heard overhead as the ship's crew began to ready themselves to sail. Sede lifted her eyes, listening to the noise. "We must think of a way to escape before we get too far from this place. There'll be no familiar landmarks once we're in the middle of the Great Sea." They both looked around to see how they might escape. Ham circled the perimeter of the enclosed cargo hold, looking for more hatch doors. Sede made her way up the stairs, pushing on the overhead hatch. Locked from above, it wouldn't budge. They both checked the port holes that spotted the lower ship's wall only to realize they were too small for a body to squeeze through. As both sat down, they leaned against the wall and sighed; they were trapped, and there was no escaping.

A horn sounded, and as the noise overhead quieted, the ship moved away from land. She rose to look from the port hole. The breeze brought the smell of salt water to her nostrils, and she could see seagulls gliding high in the air, cawing their song to each other. As she closed her eyes, she heard the soft, muffled cries of her fellow Sethites filling the crowded cargo space with their sorrow. A hollow dread settled in her stomach. There was freedom out there beyond the port hole but bondage inside the ship. She grasped her seed pouch around her neck, thinking of home. "I will return home," she whispered to herself. "I am Yahweh's seed, in the lineage of the 'Promised One' to come."

Hours passed as the captives sat in silence, the ship gently rocking them. The cries of the children had been soothed, and a mother gently stroked her daughter's hair as she slept in her lap. A young man held his wife to his chest. The kiss of love touched the top of her head, and a single tear rolled down his cheek. Sede sensed his hopelessness and despair. They were all captives, not knowing where they were going or what lie ahead. She closed her eyes and fell asleep, the ship gently rocking and swaying in the night.

* * *

Confused excitement could be felt in the great hall as the buzz of many voices echoed off the walls. The priest stood on the platform and moved his hands to silence the servants. "The 'Sea Wind' hasn't arrived with the captives. We will prepare for the coming of the 'Golden Bird.' Captains, see to your servants!" The servants scattered as the commands were given. Large, fragrant pools shimmered like glass, while brilliant flowers floated on the surface, waiting for the first toe to enter. Tables of folded robes lined the wall, with a pair of sandals resting atop and two small bowls stacked behind them. They held grooming tools and paint with brush. Preparations were under way for the captured. The priest handed the messengers their scrolls and commanded: "Dispatch these to the great houses of Atlantis. The auction will take place in two days. Fresh Sethites are the prize for those who will pay!"

The sound of a ringing bell echoed off the marble floor, while the messenger waited at the door of Playtheus' mansion. Hurriedly, the servant opened the door. "Yes?"

"There's a message for all the great houses of Atlantis!" boomed the messenger. Extending a scroll he gave the command, "Make sure you give this to your master." Turning, he hurried on his way, grasping his armful of scrolls.

Hearing the bell, Playtheus rose from his resting place on the veranda. The morning sun was beginning to rise, and the city below glowed with light reflecting off the rooftops. A beautiful flute melody rose from somewhere below. The servant entered the room and bowed. "A message sent to all the great houses, my lord." He stepped forward and presented the scroll.

"Umm, what great word do we have here?" his deep voice mumbled as he unrolled the scroll. "Oh, there's to be an auction in two days of fresh Sethites!" With sudden excitement he commanded, "Call Tailius; I want to speak to him!" As the servant quickly left, Playtheus stretched his arms and yawned, his magnificent form silhouetted against the light of the rising sun. At the railing, he viewed the city below. Groaning within himself, he said, "Umm, the hungry yearn to be satisfied!" The tattoos on his arms began to glow intermittently as he groaned once more.

Tailius hurried to his room and bowed. "Yes, my lord?"

"Prepare my chariot. I wish to visit Toleshba." Moving swiftly through the streets, the chariot soon arrived at Toleshba's mansion. Symbols were engraved on the black pillars that lined her mansion, and strange feathers and pouches moved in the breeze, suspended by glistening strings. They swayed and moved as if to beckon him to her entrance. Leaving the servant with the chariot, he stood before her door. A sense of foreboding filled the air as the door slowly opened by itself. A strange breeze pulled on him as if to draw him in.

"Playtheus, I knew it was you. I could feel you coming."

He gasped. Her beauty gripped him, and he couldn't take his eyes off her. It was as if a power had descended on him the moment he saw her. Even though his eyes were fixed on her, he was aware of things happening around him. The "Invisible" began moving and whispering. The room itself seemed to be slowly spinning.

As her beauty transfixed him, she smiled knowingly. Her forehead tattoo glistened a sparkling green. "You've come to ask me something. Say on."

As though waking from a trance, he shook himself and collected his thoughts. "I had another dream of her last night, and today I received word that fresh Sethites will be arriving in two days!"

One side of her mouth lifted with a small smile. "Ah yes, the 'innocent'!" Her many tattoos began to glow, flickering as though they were alive. Her eyes danced with soft flames with just the thought of them. "You want to know if she is among them."

"Yes, I do." His yearning eagerness was evident in the tone of his voice.

"Wait here. I'll be back."

She left through a side door as he stood in the middle of the dimly lit room. The whispering "Invisible" began to move behind him. He wanted to turn and see them but felt frozen in their presence. He could feel their breath on the back of his neck, their invisible hands touching him. Just as he gasped, Toleshba appeared, carrying a small box. Instantly they were gone!

"Come here, and I'll read the signs for you. Are you willing to give me my price?"

"Yes, I am willing," he said, trying to sound certain.

With his arm extended, she touched one of his tattoos with her finger. It disappeared from his arm and appeared on hers. "Ah," she sighed. "This is a nice one: 'Purity of Heart'!" She paused to savor what she had received. Her face glowed with enhanced beauty that stunned him. He felt the draw from his own soul and looked down at his arm. He had lost an "innocent." His face darkened briefly, and he shuddered.

"Why are you surprised, Playtheus? You know that those who acquire the 'innocent' are enhanced, and those who surrender them are diminished. This is the price that any pay for our knowledge."

She was the wife of Masta-lovid, one of the fallen angels. She bore the mark of witch on her forehead and possessed his knowledge, but he possessed her soul. This was the price she paid to be his. This was the price she paid to have his knowledge. She opened the box and withdrew the stones. Each were etched with strange symbols. Rolling them between her hands, she closed her eyes and began to whisper her words of enchantment, words spoken in a language he had never heard before. The stones began to turn hot red. Rolling them until they began to sizzle, she threw them on the table. "Ah, I see her. Yes, it *is* the one who you have been waiting for, the one from your dreams!" Bending closer she looked at the stones as if she saw more. She darted a surprised look at him. "I see why you were willing to wait for her. She is truly an innocent with great powers. I dare say she is marked by…" hesitating to speak the name of God, she reluctantly said, "…the 'Most High.'" She shuddered and trembled as she spoke His name. "She is a 'Tella-la-no-ah.' To possess her will give you great power. She will mark you among the 200 as a 'Mighty One.' They will seek you out because you possess her innocence." As she finished her prophecy, she continued, "Your long wait is over, Playtheus, and well worth the price you paid!"

Having gotten this exciting conformation, he left with adrenalin hotly pumping through his chest as his heart pounded wildly. After all this time he would finally possess the one who had haunted his dreams. He hardly noticed when the chariot arrived at his mansion; his breathing had intensified, and the whole world seemed to scream with the excitement he felt. In but a few days she would be his. As he stood before his mansion, he raised his fists to the sky and roared, "She will be mine. And with her innocence, I will be declared a 'Mighty One' in the earth!"

* * *

The horn blew, and the noise of footsteps and shouting could be heard overhead. Sede woke and peered through the porthole. She motioned for Ham to come and look. They had arrived at a pier. Unlike the crude dock they had left, this one was magnificent. Bordering the water's edge were carved stone arches and lush green gardens with falling water. A magnificent Nephilim sat atop a beautiful creature. Its mane and tail flowed in the breeze as it took flight. The wings on each side of its forelegs gracefully rose and fell as he circled high above. The many Nephilim on the dock were not ugly and grotesque like the ones who had captured them but beautiful and regal with flowing robes and golden bands around their heads. As humans moved among them, they showed no fear but rather respect, bowing as they greeted them. Truly, this was a place like no other. Ham, too, was wide eyed, staring in awe at what he saw.

The ship stopped with a small thud against the pier, and the hatch flew open. With shouting and the snap of whips, the Nephilim drove them to the ramp. At the dock, the priest's captains led them along a narrow street to the Great Hall. It was frightening. The buildings they passed were so tall and strangely shaped. Even the sounds in the air were different. It sounded like the rumbling voices of a marketplace, chattering, with no distinct words. Whimpering cries came from the children as they were pulled from their parents' arms, and Sethites were sorted once more. When Ham was led away, he caught Sede's eye. Tears fell as he motioned with his hand to his heart and slowly out to her. She returned the gesture thinking, 'Will I see you again, Ham?'

Chapter 10

The Market

In the Great Hall, every woman was given a servant that led them to one of the fragrant pools. Gently they began to help them undress and ushered them into the water. Refusing her servant's help, Sede removed her skins. Never before had she been naked before others. It made her feel vulnerable. She covered her breasts with her hands but then stopped herself. 'No. I will not let them shame me!' She removed her seed necklace and rolled it tightly in a ball, hiding it in her hand. As a servant gathered their robes, skins, and sandals, a pang of loss pricked her heart. Hot tears filled her eyes as she clutched her necklace to her chest. 'Of all that I brought with me, though I lose my skins, this one thing I will leave with!' Stepping into the water, she moved toward the other women.

The servants worked gently, sponging and washing the remaining soot from Zadanim's fire. Fragrant oil was poured on their hair, smelling of heavy spices that stirred the soul. As the fragrance filled the air, she felt anger rise within her. 'Are we being prepared as a sweet smelling sacrifice for their gods?' She looked over the other women being groomed. 'Doesn't anyone else see that we are being prepared for something or someone?' She felt the heat of anger in her cheeks. The folded robes and sandals were passed out, and the women were relieved to be covered once more. Looking around, so as not to be seen, she slipped her necklace over her head and under her robe. The women were then seated on low stools, where their servants combed and braided their oiled hair. Ornaments of jewels and carved ivory were woven in and through their braids, creating a unique look for each woman. It felt strangely different from the simple braid she was accustomed to, and the heady smell from the oil sickened her.

Just then a strange man entered the room. He wore an elaborate robe embroidered with symbols and a golden turban that covered his elongated head. She realized he was a Nephilim, for he also had six digits on his hands and feet. Evil emanated from him. Her servant whispered, "The priest has arrived." He gave the command, and the women were lined up. The servants stood ready, holding a brush and bowl of paint. One by one, the Priest stood before the women. Closing his eyes, he chanted strange words and then paused as if waiting to hear something. Turning to the servant, he spoke the symbol that was then painted on their forehead.

Puzzled, Sede asked her servant, "What is he doing?"

She whispered back, "He has the power to discern each woman's virtue. With this mark, the Renown at the market will know what virtue they are buying."

A look of horror swept over her face. "Virtue can be bought? What market? What's a Renown?" she innocently asked, searching the servant's face.

The servant put her finger to her lips to silence her questions. "You're next," she whispered.

The priest stepped in front of Sede, gazing into her eyes. His breathing became marked and his chest rose and fell in sudden excitement. "Tella-la-no-ah!" he gasped, hardly believing what he was discerning.

The servant's eyes widened. She looked at the priest, then at Sede, and back to the Priest. "Tella-la-no-ah!" she whispered in wonder.

Slowly he closed his eyes and began chanting different words from what he had spoken over the others. Sede was confused. Why had he reacted so strangely to her? Why was the servant in awe of her? As he slowly opened his eyes, he looked long into hers. Then again, he whispered "Tella-la-no-ah."

Trembling, the servant made the mark on her forehead.

When he had finished marking the women, they were ushered into a beautiful room set with food on low tables. Deep jewel-toned cushions surrounded the table, and lovely music filled the air. Strange food was set before them she had never seen before. The other Sethites, too, looked at each other with puzzled expressions. Sede chose fruit and what looked like the cakes that Dosta made her. Thinking she was drinking water from her goblet, she swallowed deeply. Spitting, she realized it wasn't water. It had a strange fermented taste. Looking around the room, she tried to understand what was happening to them. Why were they suddenly being treated as guests, washed and fed? What was this "market" that the servant had spoken of and the strange symbols on their foreheads? Her attention turned to eating, and she began listening to the lonely melody filling the room. It pulled at her heart. She felt so alone....

After they had finished eating, the Priest entered the room, raised his hands, and clapped twice. The servants led them to a dimly lit room where fur-covered cots lined the floor. The women gladly lay down, welcoming the comfort of something clean and soft. Guards stood sentry at each door—a message that they wouldn't be leaving. During the dark, lonely night, Sede heard the women whispering and their soft cries. With a longing heart, she whispered her own words into the night, "Yahweh, help me to find a way out of here. This is such a strange place... I long for Father, Shem, and my home." As she looked through the window, her thoughts took her back to her own room where she saw the stars at night. The furs on her cot always made her feel safe. "Tonight, Yahweh, *you* keep me safe." A strange peace swept over her, and she felt her heart strengthened. A gentle breeze brushed her cheek, lightly feathering the fur next to her face.

"I will, Sede...and you *will* find your way back home."

Joy filled her as she brought her hand to lips, tears filling her eyes. For the first time since she was taken, she felt the presence of Yahweh. With a tearful voice she whispered, "Oh thank you, Yahweh, thank you." She pondered how lost she was yet how loved. The God of the universe knew where she was and had spoken to her. She would be safe and return home.

Waking to the sound of footsteps moving past her cot, she realized the servants were rousing the women. As they stood to their feet, the priest stepped to the platform. "Listen to me, women of captivity. As of today, you are no longer Sethites but people of Atlantis. Today you will be dispersed among us." A frightened "NO!" echoed as the women responded in horror. Cries filled the air as they held each other in fear. Sede realized something was about to happen.

Quickly, the women were hurried down a narrow street behind an open arena. When they entered through the archway, cheers erupted. The noise was deafening. Just seeing that many people in one place was a frightening sight. They stood in line and, and one by one, were ushered up the steps to stand alone. Shouts rose and hands waved wildly, motioning to be recognized. A horn blew signaling the purchase. The woman standing in front of her began to cry. Her body was visibly trembling; she knew she was next. Out of compassion, Sede touched her shoulder and leaned forward, whispering in her ear, "You must trust Yahweh. He is our only hope!" Turning to see who had spoken to her, she looked long into Sede's eyes. With remembered knowing, she felt composure replace fear.

"Yes, we the Sethites put our hope in Yahweh!" In gratitude she embraced Sede and wiped the tears from her face. The guard grabbed her arm, ushering her up the steps where she stood alone. The noise of the arena encircled her. Although the cheers and shouts accelerated and hands flew into the air, a still calm enveloped her like an invisible shield. As their eyes met, Sede saw her composure and a dignity that only comes from knowing who you are. When she was led from the platform, she looked back at Sede, peace radiating from her face. It was the kind of peace that only comes from a heart that trusts Yahweh.

Strengthened by what she saw, she remembered the peace she had felt just the night before. A calmness settled over her as she took the last step to the platform. Lifting her face to the crowd, a profound hush fell over the arena. An eternal moment passed as she turned slowly and looked out over the multitude. Unbeknownst to her, a beautiful glow radiated from her whole body. The painted symbol on her forehead glistened white as light streamed from it. Then suddenly the silence turned to a roar; the crowd went wild with the fevered desire to buy her. The Priest finally stepped forward to still the hysteria. Stunned by the crowd's reaction, she wondered why they responded differently to her than the other women. Why was she different? (Part of the power of the innocent is that they don't realize what they possess. She radiated the beauty of innocence but was unaware of it. The pure and humble of heart are mighty!)

The Market

The Priest took her by the hand and began parading her in a circle, smiling as the crowd accelerated their cheers with shouts and waved their hands. The deafening noise continued until the horn blew and Playtheus stepped forward. The moment his foot touched the platform, a hush that could be felt descended on the crowd. All eyes were on him. Sede could hear the pounding of her own heart as he walked toward her and extended his hand. Stunned, she stood there just looking at him. He was a Nephilim, the like she had never seen before. He was beautiful but yet terrible! Seven feet tall, his appearance was strikingly masculine. His dark hair came to the shoulders, and a gold band circled his head. His physique was muscular and bronzed, and the tattoos that covered his arms glistened with amber light. A golden sash was tied at the waist of his white robe that came to the knees. His braided sandals covered his calves and were made of golden, polished leather. But the most alarming were his eyes. They were piercing, crystal blue. When he looked at her, it was though he could see to the depth of her soul. What did he want? Why did he have his hand out to her?

He stepped forward and ushered her down the steps, gently grasping her arm. A thrill rushed through him as he felt her skin for the first time. He led her through the archway of the arena as the crowd erupted once more with roaring cheers. In the chariot, Tailius waited with a Sethite maiden. Sede recognized her from the ship. When the servant saw Sede, his mouth dropped open. "You… you…are beautiful!" He stuttered, not realizing he was speaking out loud.

"Yes!" Playtheus uttered in breathless excitement. "And she's finally mine!" He was heady with the thrill of seeing his dream unfold before his very eyes. As he stepped into the chariot, he put his hand on hers and gently squeezed. She drew her hand away, shocked that a stranger would touch her in such a manner. His touch felt strange and cold, making her tremble. When the chariot pulled away from the arena, she looked back, longing to see Ham. Had he been sold? Was he safe?

As they moved through the streets, she tightened her grip on the side of the chariot. The wheels beneath them loudly clacked over the cobblestones. 'What is this strange thing that carries us? Where is this Nephilim taking me?' Her heart was racing. She could feel his penetrating eyes on her, and she purposely looked away. People shouted greetings to him as they passed in their chariots. Others, walking along the street, stopped and bowed, showing their respect. Everyone she saw bore a strange symbol on their foreheads.

They passed through the market with its busy activity and noise and saw wondrous structures. Huge stone statues lined the front of large marble buildings. Water cascaded from sculpted stone fountains, splashing into beautiful blue pools. They passed a large amphitheater filled with people listening to musicians play their harps and flutes. Sede had never seen such sights. Even though what she saw was beautiful, she felt the coldness of unfamiliarity. What a contrast from the simple huts that lined the streets of her village. What a contrast of sound. There were no familiar sounds of children laughing and playing, and she suddenly realized she hadn't seen any children. She turned to the other Sethite. "I see no children. Where are their children?" The woman blinked in unbelief, looking up and down the streets, searching for the sight of them.

They left the noisy streets and saw beautiful mansions built on the hills and bluffs overlooking the city. They looked like white jewels embedded in the emerald landscape. The chariot slowed and then came to a stop. Playtheus stepped down with a smile and extended his hand. "Step down and see your new home." Lifting her eyes, she beheld what lie before her. His mansion, beautiful and white, shined with a polished glow as if it were made of pearl. Silver filigree bordered the door as well as the top and bottom of the pillars. Statues graced the massive grounds, and the gardens extended to the city below. Servants were busy grooming the hedges and tending the fountains. What she saw was beautiful and grand.

Tailius opened the great front doors and bowed, motioning with his hand to enter. Sede felt the trembling hand of the other Sethite. As they walked hand in hand toward the door, the woman's knees buckled out of fear, and she started to collapse. Sede caught her by the arm. "There, there, we have each other to draw strength from," she whispered. As they drew closer to the open door she asked the woman, "What is your name?"

"My name is Ka-sta."

"I am Sede-quete."

The Market

Two male servants stepped toward Playtheus and bowed. "Take the women to their chambers and prepare them for me," he commanded. Watching Sede walk away, he followed her every move. "She takes my breath away and is everything I knew she would be!" he whispered to himself.

The servants stepped quickly before the women and led them through a beautiful corridor lined with silver torches. On the walls, a painted mural displayed Nephilim in grand poses. At the end of the hall were their rooms.

As the servant ushered them through the tall double doors, Sede saw two rooms that were joined by another door. Strange furniture filled the room. Luxuriously padded cushions were thrown together on a low silver platform with legs. Against one wall was a large bed, covered with satin and furs. Dangling jewels hung from the sheer canopy. Centered on the opposite wall was a massive marble fireplace with a low-burning fire. Silver torches were positioned along the walls, and a large arch opened to a veranda that overlooked the city below. Sheer curtains hung from the top of pillars surrounding a small bathing pool and gently swayed in the breeze. By all appearances, it *was* beautiful.

"We must prepare you for our master," the servants said, eager to begin. They seated the women on a low, padded bench. Taking a bowl of water, they sponged away the markings on their foreheads and loosened their hair from the braids and ornaments. Slowly, the servant combed through Sede's fragrant hair. His hands trembled just being in her presence. Her hair hung long, full, and shining. She thought it odd that a male would be serving her.

He left the room and returned with a garment draped over his extended arms. It shimmered with light, reflecting the golden threads woven through the shiny fabric. Jewels and small bells dangled from the hem's edge. Ka-sta was led by her servant through the adjoining door to her room. As Sede listened to their muffled voices, she felt comforted to have a Sethite near.

The servant motioned for Sede to stand and prepared to help her change. She felt uncomfortable dressing in the presence of a man. She held her robe, refusing his help. "Send for a woman!" she demanded. "I won't let you undress me!" She wadded a handful of robe to her chest, holding it in defiance. He smiled and bowed, leaving the room. After he left, she quickly removed her seed necklace and hid it beneath the bed pillows. Just as she turned, a female servant appeared at the door.

Smiling to know she had refused the other servant, the woman bowed. "I am A-thia. I will help you dress." As the servant began to dress her, she marveled at Sede's presence. "You are an 'innocent,' aren't you?"

"I don't know what you mean," Sede answered.

"This is why you wouldn't let your servant dress you. It is this way with all Sethites who come to my master's house. Your friend requested a female servant as well. Modesty is a precious virtue of the innocent; it is valued by the Renown." Realizing she had said too much, she worked silently, helping Sede slip out of her robe and into the garment the other servant had brought. The fabric hung delicately over her body, accentuating her lovely shape. Being a hunter had made her body well-sculpted and toned yet beautifully feminine. When the servant turned her back, Sede slipped her seed necklace from under the pillow, over her head, and beneath her gown.

The servants then led the women down the long corridor to the banquet room. There, servants hurried about, attending the table and bringing food. Sede and Ka-sta were led to cushions by the low table. "Please stand and wait for Master," the servants instructed.

The women looked at one another in wonder, their eyes going up and down each other's bodies. "This is so unlike my Sethite garb. I miss my skins," Sede said with longing.

"And I, my own handmade robe," chimed Ka-sta. Their conversation was interrupted by Playtheus, who hurriedly entered through the archway.

Smiling, he gestured with his hand for them to sit. His eyes followed Sede's every move, marveling at her beauty. The musicians began a melody on their harps as Playtheus reclined across from them. Leaning on a pillow with one elbow, he smiled and began conversation. "So, tell me of yourselves." He grabbed a cluster of grapes and began to eat, motioning with his hand for Ka-sta to begin. She looked at Sede, wondering what he wanted of her. "Come, my dear. Tell me your name. Where are you from? What did you do in your village?"

Swallowing hard, she timidly answered, "My…my name is Ka-sta, daughter of Falko. I am from the village of Beth-la-hay. My…my…duties were weaving of fabric and making of robes." She began to cry. "I want to go home. Home to my kin!" She lowered her head, weeping with her face in her hands.

"Come, come, my dear. This is your home now, and I have bought you. I am now your kin." She continued to weep as he turned to Sede, who was his real interest.

Setting the grapes aside, he looked intently at her; his eyes filled with softness as he beheld her beauty. There was a glow about her countenance that was so stunning. From where he sat, he could feel her virtues. Briefly the symbol reappeared on her forehead and glistened a sparkling white. A warm, smooth rush ran through him, and he shuddered. "What is your name, my dear?" he asked softly.

Sede felt anger rise within her. Looking at him squarely, she defiantly answered, "My name is not 'my dear'!"

"Well then, tell me what it is!" he said, enjoying her sudden defiance.

"My name is Sede-quete."

Amused no longer, he closed his eyes and whispered to himself, "Sede-quete." 'I have heard her name fall from her own lips.' He had known her only in his dreams, but now, for the first time, he knew her name.

"I am a Sethite from a wilderness village. I am the daughter of a great elder, and I am a hunter among my kin." She looked at him defiantly once more, then reached for an apple.

"Tell me of your people," he asked.

Sede knew that if she revealed the name of her village or her family, they might be at risk. She would tell this Nephilim nothing. She turned to the musicians, chewing as she listened and ignoring his question. Amused by her continued defiance, he smiled.

As if remembering something, he sat up and clapped his hands. Five women entered, stepping delicately. Dressed in beautifully sheer gowns, they moved into position, waiting to begin. The transparency of the fabric revealed what lie beneath. Jewels dangled from the gowns, covering the area of the body that Sethite women save for the eyes of their husbands only. As the musicians began to play, and as if by cue, the women began their dance. The melody was strangely seductive, making Sede's heart pound. As the music continued, the air in the room began to tingle. It was as if the music, the sheerness of the dancer's gowns, and their alluring movement had some kind of hypnotic power over her. She felt her cheeks flush. Ka-sta looked at her wide-eyed. She was feeling vulnerable too. Playtheus watched as Sede's eyes followed the dancers. He drew some strange delight from her shocked reaction and reddened cheeks.

The dancers slowly turned and swayed to the music; their alluring moves showed no modesty. As the music softly intensified and drums began to beat in counter rhythm, Sede felt her heart pound in rhythm with the drums, and her cheeks felt hot. As the dance continued, each dancer began to remove jewels from their gowns, revealing what lie beneath. They dropped each jewel at Playtheus' feet. As they circled him, they stroked his neck with their fingertips, releasing a sigh. When the last jewel had been dropped at his feet, the dancers began to untie their gowns. Sede felt a tingle in the air once more, and a sudden rush of emotion surged through her.

Surprised, she looked at Ka-sta and said, "Did you just feel that!?"

"Yes. What is happening?"

As the gowns fell at their feet, the dancers stepped toward Playtheus, joining their hands. They circled and swayed before him, not ashamed of uncovering themselves but rather finding pleasure in it. A look of astonishment was apparent on Sede's face. The stark lack of modesty was unbelievable to her. She felt confused by what she saw and what she was feeling. She leaned over to Ka-sta and began to whisper. Pleased by her look of astonishment, Playtheus smiled.

Clapping his hands twice, the music stopped, and the dancers stood quietly before him, breathing softly from the energy and excitement they felt. He drew one dancer near. Kissing her palm softly, he smiled then released her to stand with the others. "Sede-quete, you seem shocked with their nudity and lack of modesty." He reached for another grape and began to talk as he chewed. "When they became my 'innocents,' the innocent virtue I took from them was their modesty. It satisfies me greatly. The symbol of 'Modesty' was painted on their foreheads at the market. I bought them for this purpose. When I see their unrestrained modesty, I again taste of its sweetness. When they are immodest, they have pleasure too, as you can see." He motioned his hand toward them, each dancer breathing softly from the pleasure they felt. "You see these tattoos," pointing to his arm. "This represents their modesty I now possess." Five small tattoos circled his arm like a band, pulsating and glistening with an amber glow. Sede and Ka-sta looked at each other in confusion. Playtheus softly laughed, realizing they didn't understand what he had tried to explain.

"Ka-sta, would you like to know what your symbol was on your forehead?" Surprised that he had spoken directly to her, she quickly looked down.

"What?" she timidly asked.

"Your symbol was 'Purity of Heart.'" He hesitated, then a small smile formed across his lips. "I chose you for this very purpose: to experience your purity and savor it. After you have been transformed, like my dancers here, I will savor your purity every time I see you choose to be anything but pure in heart. You will in turn find great pleasure in this!" Ka-sta blinked in unbelief. She looked at Sede with fear in her eyes. He smiled, seeing her reaction.

"Sede-quete, would you like to know what was written on *your* forehead?"

"No, I would not!" she said hotly. She stood to her feet and turned to leave, the bells on her hem tinkling softly.

"Wait, wait," he softly laughed. Clapping his hands, Tailius appeared. "Take Sede-quete and Ka-sta to their chambers." Looking at the dancers, he said, "You may go as well, my dears." The dancers again circled him, and each stroked his cheek as they passed to leave. Their voices could be heard as they giggled and laughed, slipping down the corridor nude, delighted that their immodest behavior had made the women uncomfortable.

Smiling with satisfaction, he leaned back on his cushion and folded his hands behind his neck. As he watched Sede follow Tailius down the hall, he mused, 'She's truly as beautiful and innocent as I dreamed, and I love the fire of her spirit!'

While they walked down the corridor, Ka-sta began to cry. "I'm afraid and want to go home. He is so large, and I feel so small when I'm around him!"

Fighting her own fears, Sede whispered, "Don't be afraid, Ka-sta. We'll find some way to leave this place and return home. As I told someone today, 'Yahweh is our only hope.'" Sede opened the door between their rooms. "If you need me tonight, wake me, okay?"

Exhaling the tension she felt, Ka-sta exclaimed, "Thank you, Sede-quete. I'm relieved I'm not alone."

A night robe had been laid out by her servant, and Sede gladly shed the strange clothes she had worn. She welcomed the quiet and slid under the soft furs. Exhausted from the unbelievably confusing day, she fell asleep.

Chapter 11

Playtheus' World

When she opened her eyes, she could hardly believe she had slept so soundly. Two servants stood at the door, waiting for her to wake. It was the male and female servants from the night before. Recognizing them, she said, "Oh, it's you two!"

Fro-mos smiled at A-thia, remembering her insistence for a female servant to dress her. He bowed and said, "Today you will leave with Master. Ka-sta will stay here." He stepped forward with a tray of fruit and meats.

She chose some meat and chewed it hungrily. With her mouth still full, she asked, "May I have some water? I don't want what you serve to drink. It tastes strange to me." Fro-mos smiled while he poured water into her goblet. He knew she was probably unaccustomed to the taste of wine. She drank deeply. Another servant appeared at the door and announced, "He is calling for her. We must not keep him waiting!"

She hurriedly dressed and followed Fro-mos.

Playtheus stood tall and proud in the chariot waiting her arrival. With piercing blue eyes, he looked intently into hers. "Today I will show you my world and who I am!" The chariot made its way through the city and up a long winding road that gradually ascended the mountain. There, on a protruding cliff, was a majestic building. White as pearl, its tall pillars surrounded a grand veranda that wrapped around its exterior. Cascading from beneath its foundation was a waterfall spilling down the mountainside and coursing its way to the bay. It was amazing to behold—breathless even. When he saw her wonder, he smiled with pleasure. "This is Champion Hall!"

The chariot pulled into the stables beneath the Hall. There, servants stood at attention near their master's chariots as the horses pawed the ground and whinnied with the sound of strength. Tailius bowed and took his place beside his chariot.

With pride, Playtheus took Sede's hand and escorted her to the grand spiral staircase. As they ascended the wide marble steps, their footsteps echoed into the height above. A gigantic mural followed the curve of the wall, portraying the images of Nephilim in striking pose. Golden symbols were inscribed over their heads, and different scenes were depicted behind them. The images of these Nephilim were the likeness of perfection: masculine, virile, and beautiful. At the top of the staircase, two gigantic statues held the supporting archway on their muscular stone shoulders. Their heads were bowed beneath the assumed weight.

The archway opened to a great open room. The light and sounds greeted them as they approached. From the center of the vaulted ceiling hung an elegant chandelier. It was made of crystals that glowed with light that seemed to come from within the stones. Across the room, tall pillars lined the extended veranda that overlooked the city below. On this balcony were fountain statues of sculpted couples. Water fell gracefully from the urns they held and made the peaceful sound of running water. Many doors lined the circular interior walls, each hosting a strange golden symbol. These were the same symbols that were above the heads of the Nephilim on the mural.

This great room looked to be a gathering place for socializing, abuzz with music and servants offering food and drink to those around them. Couples visited and slowly danced to the music that filled the air. Human females hung on the arms of their male companions, captivated by their strong and powerful presence. The Nephilim females in the room were exquisite in beauty: tall and fair, exuding a sense of supremacy. But it was the human females that possessed something that the female Nephilim lacked. This human quality seemed to satisfy the males in a way the others could not. The males glowed with the energy and light they absorbed from their human companions. There was a visible exchange that flowed between them. The women emitted, and the

Nephilim absorbed. These Nephilim were similar to Playtheus: regal, powerful, and perfect in their masculinity. A sense of grandeur and elegance permeated the air.

As they stepped through the archway, all stopped, and every eye fell on Sede. There she stood poised by his side. The breeze gently blew against her gown, revealing her beautiful form, and her hair softly feathered in the breeze, sending its fragrance to Playtheus. Inhaling, he smiled as he looked over his fellow Renown. 'Umm…this is my moment!' He could feel the longing eyes of his fellow Nephilim, captivated by Sede's lovely purity. The tattoos on their strong arms began pulsating and glowing with golden amber light. As if compelled by some mysterious force, they left their companions and began to slowly press toward her. Feeling vulnerable, she stepped behind Playtheus. "Here, here, Sede-quete. They just want to behold your innocence." He clasped her hand and drew her back to his side, proudly smiling down at her.

Puzzled by what he said, she looked up and questioned, "Behold my innocence?" As she stood there, a light began to shine from her forehead. The symbol 'Tella-la-no-ah' appeared, and blazed in brilliant white. A deep hush descended accompanied by a soft "ah" as they gazed on her with wonting eyes.

"This is my innocent," Playtheus proudly announced. "My prophetic dream is unfolding!"

Sede felt them respond. They began touching her arm, her shoulder, her back—sighing with an "umm" at the touch of her. They seemed to find some kind of power and pleasure in just a touch. It reminded her of the Cainites from Zadanim with their desire to touch the Sethites. They slowly began to whisper among themselves. Their hungry desire for her was becoming evident. It could be felt in the room. Sensing their mounting fervor, Playtheus smiled and clasped her hand as he escorted her through their midst. Without saying a word, and as if someone had snapped their finger, the Nephilim regained their composure. Just as suddenly as the symbol appeared on her forehead, it disappeared. Backing away, they returned to their companions but were compelled to look over their shoulder to gaze at her once more. She was relieved by the distance that was now between them. She felt their hunger, and the fear of them made the hair on her neck stand on end. She had felt this same fear when she had been cornered by a pack of hungry tallmars during a hunt.

Playtheus turned his attention to Sede and desired to explain the activity and purpose of Champion Hall. He began, "The elite among us are called the 'Regal Renown.' These are the Nephilim who possess the knowledge of their angelic fathers. The rest of my brother and sister Nephilim are called the 'Renown.' They, too, are majestic Nephilim but do not possess angelic knowledge. Here we gather and socialize. Behind these doors, the Regal Renown use the knowledge their fathers gave them. We each have a special knowledge—a special work. Some of my brothers work with great architecture, breeding, astrology, the seas, and one of my favorites: the manipulation of the soul through music. Last night you felt the hypnotic power of the music, did you not?"

She darted a quick look at him, suddenly realizing that he was the cause of the strange power that had tried to overcome her during the women's dance. Like lying in wait for prey; setting a trap; anticipating the hunted; waiting for the right time to strike; she recognized this strategy from hunting. He was doing the same thing; only she was the hunted. She froze as the reality of his craftiness became evident to her.

"Diatus granted me the power of his knowledge last night. I found great pleasure in what I saw it do to you." She was beginning to see his manipulations and concluded that the whole experience with the dancers was no more than the craftiness of a snake observing its helpless prey.

"Let's begin your tour, Sede-quete," he said as he motioned with his hand. He knew the Regals would be most eager to meet her for they held him in high regard. Briefly, they would explain their specialized knowledge and accomplishments, accomplishments that no mere man could achieve. And there was no denying it. The knowledge to create these wonders was truly not of this world.

He opened the door of Architecture and introduced her to Trihedron. His father and mother were across the room, admiring scale miniatures of their son's architectural wonders: the city of Atlantis, Champion Hall, the Pavilion, and statues that lined a great highway. But his greatest accomplishments were his gigantic sphinx and pyramids. Trihedron led them to his parents to introduce her.

Kalibar-buk glowed with sparkling blue light as his eyes searched within her. He was seeing deep within, and she felt his evil intrusion. She stepped back in fear.

"Here, here, Sede-quete. He is seeing within," Playtheus said smiling. "All is bare and naked before the Mighty 200."

Trihedron's mother, Sahad-oden, smiled, admiring Sede's virtues and innocence. "You are most fortunate, Playtheus. She is rare indeed!" He smiled, knowing her words to be true.

Trihedron then showed Sede his wonders in miniature, explaining the challenges he had faced in creating them but also his father's knowledge that had solved them. He boasted of his privileged and favored position of being chosen by his father to possess his knowledge. She was appalled by his lack of humility and sensed his shallow heart. She could see his standard of greatness was based on the knowledge he possessed and not integrity of heart. Playtheus sensed her boredom and bowed in respect to Trihedron and his parents, desiring to continue her tour.

When they entered Diatus' room, she immediately felt something unseen surround her. A tingling, compelling sensation enveloped her as the mystical melody filled the air. Sheer fabric draped from the vaulted ceiling above and was drawn back to cascade down the wall. The breeze blew from the open veranda, waving the fabric in motion with the music. The lighting was by candlelight, and the deep scent of musk and spices filled the air. She felt the same hypnotic sensation she had felt when she watched the dancers. In the center of the room was a beautiful sculpted fountain. Diatus was depicted in stone, playing a flute over embracing couples at his feet. Water gracefully cascaded from his flute, gently falling on the stone couples below. Around the base of the fountain was a low bed following the curve of its circumference. It was luxurious—six feet wide—and made of rich, sericeous blue fabric. Several couples reclined on the pillows, embracing as they responded to the music.

Musicians stood nearby playing a romantic melody. As the music accelerated in warmth of mood, so did the intensity of the couples' embrace, revealing the music's power. Sede blushed for she had never seen the intimacy of caressing and kissing so openly displayed. Playtheus and Diatus looked at each other with coy smiles. They both felt the attack on her innocence and found delight in seeing it assaulted.

Playtheus looked intently in her eyes. "Can you not feel the music draw from the very depths of your soul?" She blinked, wide-eyed, not wanting to admit that what she was feeling was exactly what he said. As they readied to leave, Playtheus smiled and bowed to Diatus. "Most gracious brother, your work is my delight. I honor you."

"And I you, my brother. For you alone, Playtheus, have the knowledge of the innocent that feeds us all."

She was relieved to feel a release from the music's influence as they entered the next door. They stepped into the dimly lit room of Apogee. Playtheus whispered to her, "It was Apogee's findings that confirmed my dreams of you. He has the knowledge of the stars and can read the future."

His room was grand in size. In the shadows, Sede could see scrolls neatly stored on shelves that lined a whole wall, which he later boasted contained the names of stars, their power, and the rotation of the constellations through the universe. Twelve tables made of black marble lined the perimeter of the room; the sign of the Zodiac was embedded in gold on the tops. The dome ceiling was a deep bluish black with stars replicating the universe. The dome slowly revolved, revealing the rotation of the stars and the solar system in different seasons. It was from the sparkling stars that the room had its light. Sede felt suffocated by the air in the room. It seemed to press in on her with a dark, ominous feeling. She noticed goblets of blood on his table. Just the sight of it made her shudder. She could only imagine why blood would be in a goblet. (Sethites have an abhorrence to drinking blood. They were taught that "life" was in the blood.)

Apogee was pleased to see Playtheus and greeted him with enthusiasm. "Come, Playtheus. I have determined your 'innocent's' future as you requested!"

He led them to a large parchment spread over a table. On it were strange dots, having lines drawn from one point to another and crisscrossing in different directions. Apogee looked at Sede with excitement. "Never have I read such a future! You live for a very long time and in great happiness and prosperity. Your children rule and reign—filling the earth!" Playtheus beamed, thinking this to be true of their future. She blinked in unbelief. How could anyone know the future but Yahweh? This had to be the sorcery of fallen angels.

While Apogee was talking, Satsum-kedesh and Felmeth stepped out of the shadows. "Ah, Father and Mother. Come meet Playtheus' new 'innocent.'"

Sede looked at him, troubled that he referred to her as Playtheus' 'innocent.' As they approached, she again felt evil encroaching upon her. It made her skin crawl. Satsum-kedesh began to glow brighter as he approached her, filling the room with blue light. Apogee's mother was radiant in beauty; her eyes were powerful in their searching gaze. They both circled her while Playtheus proudly watched. It was as if they were beholding all she was. She felt so very vulnerable.

With great reverence, Playtheus bowed at the waist. "Great One, she is my prophetic dream fulfilled. Her name is Sede-quete." He took her hand and kissed her palm. Sede was appalled.

"The fates have smiled upon you, Playtheus, to have such a one. May my son be so fortunate!"

Playtheus was pleased to have such recognition from one of the Mighty 200. He bowed and then said, "Thank you, Great One. May it come to pass as you have said." Wishing to show her more rooms, he bowed and left Apogee and his parents.

Sede was beginning to feel drained by all the evil that she had felt. Not only was it suffocating and intrusive but she felt weakened by it. She wondered how much more she could endure meeting these evil beings. Playtheus opened the door of Fathom and Shoal. They were the twin sons of Masta-lovid and great navigators of the seas. Their father had given them his dark knowledge of the seas. They knew the tides, the currents, and the mysterious "paths" of the oceans. They had the knowledge of navigating by the stars when nothing but water surrounded them. The room was filled with the things of the sea: great shells, nets, and good-sized replicas of their great ships. Sede recognized the "Golden Bird" and the "Sea Wind" she and Shem had burned. There were other ships too of different hull designs and masts. Great maps were painted on the walls as well as a double life-size mural of Masta-lovid and his sons. It was a depiction of them standing at the bow of a ship as it sailed through stormy seas. Wind was blowing their hair, and the look of power was on their faces. She felt so very small in the midst of such greatness.

Fathom greeted them, for Shoal and Masta-lovid were out to sea. His eyes widened when he saw Sede. He inhaled deeply and then uttered, "More fair than a westerly wind."

Playtheus smiled in delight. Oh, how he gloried, knowing his "innocent" was the desire of them all. Fathom boasted of his knowledge and his own greatness, but she cared little for what he had to say. The only things of interest were the maps of the sea that had been painted on the wall. He boasted that Atlantis was the center of the world and how all the sea ports catered to him, his father, and his brother. She saw the port city of Zadanim. Oh how she longed to return home. When they left, she breathed a sigh of relief.

As they stood before the next door, somehow she knew it was his. "This is my door," he said with pride, gesturing with his hand at the glistening symbol. "It reads: 'The Innocent.' All Nephilim seek me out. They desire and need the virtuous innocence of mankind. All the glowing tattoos you see on their arms—I made that possible for them. They value me greatly because only I have the knowledge to give them innocence. All these beautiful human companions here today I provided them with. I gave each Renown a companion of their choosing. I have found that my brothers prefer human companions over our sister Nephilim. Humans possess a secret quality that our female Nephilim lack; that secret something is 'innocent virtues.' My brothers drink from their innocence and are satisfied, making them glow. Their arms bear their tattoo symbol. The female Nephilim benefit from my services because I provide them with an inborn need for innocence. Yes, my work is with the souls of mankind, to take and possess their innocence."

As he opened the door, he said, "Come, I will show you my work." Her head reeled at what he was saying. It was all so strange, all so unbelievable. For the first time since she was taken, she felt truly afraid. He and the fallen angels had called her his "innocent," and now he had just said that his work was taking the innocence from the soul of man. She suddenly realized what he was planning. He wanted to take her innocence. Her face grew pale, and she felt the room starting to spin. The whirling increased until everything went black. When she opened her eyes, she was on the floor, and Playtheus was leaning over her. "Sede-quete, Sede-quete, you've fainted. I'm afraid this has all been too much excitement."

"Come, we'll walk in the gardens." Leaving the Hall, he led her to the gardens. She felt great relief to be in the open air and away from the distress she felt inside. As she looked over the gardens, she thought that perhaps she'd never seen anything so beautiful. She had seen the natural beauty of the mountains that surrounded her village, but this beauty had been planned. The trees and bushes had purposely been planted to create designs and patterns on the rolling hills. The colors, too, were spectacular. The shades of green and yellows in the trees and shrubbery contrasted so beautifully with the crystal blue of the fountains and pools. Oranges and reds from exotic flowers were brilliant, bordering the white, pillared gazebos. It was there she saw couples sitting in seclusion, casually talking with each other. It seemed so tranquil. Even the large birds that gracefully moved over the open green lawns seemed to be part of the plan of this place. Their tails were opalescent purple and blue and fluttered in the breeze, and their song called out as if to welcome those who chose to walk among them. Amidst all this beauty, her thoughts fell back to what she had just witnessed inside. 'What a perplexing contrast. How can such beauty be in the same place with such wickedness? This is so confusing.'

As he talked, she walked silently beside him, thinking but not listening. Her thoughts drew her back to what he'd said inside. His work was to take the innocence of man, and he had called her his "innocent."

"Sede-quete, are you listening?"

"What?" she said.

"Are you feeling better? Come and sit with me, and I'll tell you of my dream."

He led her to a peaceful gazebo. The sound of a nearby fountain could be heard, and a light mist from its spray moved in the breeze. Everything around them spoke of peace, but while they seated themselves, she felt a creeping dread rise from within. He remained silent for a while and then spoke. "I want you to look at me, Sede-quete."

Hesitantly, she raised her eyes to his. "I'm going to tell you about us. For many years I've had a dream—the same dream—over and over again. In this dream, you came to me. You gave me something I was missing in my life. You possessed the power that I needed, and this power gave me the ability to be transformed. You resisted my yearnings for surrender at first, but finally you gave yourself to me by the act of your own free will. In giving me your innocence freely, the power of that innocence was magnified 100 times above the innocence that can be taken unwillingly. When we united, a great burst of power was manifested, and all who beheld it stood in awe as I became a 'Mighty One.' I saw your mark in my dream, the mark of 'Tella-la-no-ah.' That marks you as one of the most powerful of humans. If a 'Marked One' will freely surrender their innocence to a Renown, there is no end to what I can do or what I can have. The value of your innocence is worth more than 100,000 children bred for their innocence!"

She listened, puzzled and confused. All his words were spinning in her head. They made no sense to her. Suddenly she felt her necklace resting against her chest. Looking down at her robe, she remembered. Memories flooded back of the Watcher who told her it was a gift and Yahweh's own words about the "Promised One" to come. Playtheus had just told her about his dream, but she had her own dream—and he had no part in it!

Slowly, she began to regain her composure and then turned to him. Looking him squarely in the eyes, she challenged him. "So all I hold dear and all that makes me, me—all I hold to of dignity and strength—will be reduced to a tattoo on your arm?" He blinked, realizing what she said was the truth. For an instant, he saw his own selfish depravity. He saw his blind lust for power. He knew that what he wanted would cost her everything and him nothing. His thoughts annoyed him, and he dismissed them.

"Oh Sede-quete, not only a tattoo but THE tattoo. This great tattoo will rest on my forehead; they are so rare that only the 'Mighty Ones' have them. You will share in my power and glory. We will be stronger together than I could ever be alone!"

His words were hollow as he spoke them, evil dripping from every word. A cold chill went through her as she looked at him. The beauty she had seen in his face was darkened. For the first time, she saw the evil he was. He was totally corrupted. There was nothing human about him: no compassion; no mercy; no selfless love. 'I will fight this Nephilim with my last breath!' she thought. 'I will never give any of myself to him. His dream will be to his own ruin. *My* dream will come to pass. I will *never* surrender to him!'

Playtheus looked at her with longing eyes; something deep within him yearned for her. His breathing softly deepened as he searched her face. Leaning forward, as if to kiss her, he slowly closed his eyes. His tattoos began radiating a warm glow. Startled, she slid away. Opening his eyes, he realized she was frightened. Slowly, he withdrew. Looking at her with continued longing, he composed himself and said, "It's getting late, and we should go." He caressed her cheek with his finger. "Let's go back to our home."

As they stepped into the chariot, Playtheus felt his pent up emotions explode! He felt a void inside that was screaming to be satisfied. Unprepared for what he suddenly felt, he knew what he needed was at his mansion. With urgency, he commanded Tailius, "Make haste, Tailius; make haste!" He drove the horses hard in their return, speeding through the streets. Playtheus clenched the sides of the chariot, feeling a growing fervor. His passion had been aroused by his desire for her. Turning, he gazed upon her in all her loveliness. He was so hungry for her. Looking down at his arm, he saw where the tattoo had been that he had surrendered to the witch. The absence of that "innocence" gnawed at him. He needed to be satisfied. He had to fill the void of what he'd lost. His plans would be ruined if he forced Sede-quete. He knew he needed her willing surrender for the full power it would give him.

Pulling back on the reins, Tailius brought the chariot to a halt, the horses gasping for breath. Playtheus bolted from the chariot and ran to the entrance of the mansion, yelling for his servants. Sede stood in the chariot, dazed by the shaking speed she had just experienced. Tailius took her by the hand to help her down. "Come, I will help you get settled." Opening the door for her, he motioned, "This way to your room."

After they entered her chamber, he bowed to leave. "Wait," she said hesitantly. "How long have you been here—here in Atlantis?"

Stunned that she had spoken to him, he answered, "I was taken five years ago."

"From what people did you come?"

"I was of the Sethites, as you."

"Tell me, of what tribe?"

"Of Tagma. I and my betrothed were to be married, but all that came to an end when I was taken."

She suddenly remembered the name. "We saved a young woman who was from Tagma. She had been captured in a raid but was freed by my kin. It was before I was taken. Perhaps you knew her? Her name is Zilla."

Tailius' face blanched. "She…she was my betrothed!"

Sede gasped. What a wonder this was. She could see how visibly shaken he was and the pain he still carried from his loss. He grabbed the pillar to steady himself. Compassion overwhelmed her, and she rested her hand on his shoulder. "Brother Sethite, I sorrow for you."

With longing in his eyes he asked, "Is Zilla well? Did she marry another?"

"Your village was attacked but a week ago and burned by Nephilim raiders. My kin rescued her, and she now lives among my people. She is a maiden still."

Joy was obvious on his face. "Oh, to know she is well and still lives as a Sethite. It brings me great joy!" He paused. "You know, my name is not really Tailius. All slaves are renamed when their innocent virtue is taken from them. My Sethite name is Dollo-maah." A tear rolled down his cheek, and he struggled to regain his composure.

"How was your innocence stolen?" she asked. His eyes looked down. "It all happened in Playtheus' room at Champion Hall. He withdrew my innocence by his sorcery and against my will."

"What has it done to you?"

"I have lost a piece of my soul. My innocent virtue was 'Loyalty.' Master desired this virtue for the service it would bring to him. I would be his loyal servant. In stealing my innocent virtue, I have become harnessed and controlled, much like the horses used to pull the chariot. Once they were wild, free, and strong. I have lost my strength and freedom as they have. I am bound to be his servant until such a time as he releases me. I don't see that ever happening."

"Brother, I am so sorry for this evil that has come against you." With Sethite love and compassion, she tightened her grip on his shoulder. As he looked into her eyes, her countenance began to glow. He stood in awe of what he saw. He had seen many "innocents" come and go from the mansion, but never had he seen one like her.

She began to speak from the depth of her heart. "Hear my prayer, Yahweh. You know the evil done to my brother, Dollo-maah. You are the 'Most High'; the One and only True God. Restore to him what was stolen. You are our only hope!"

As Sede continued to look in his eyes, his face began to shine. A peace settled over him, and he felt healing enter his soul. He had been made whole by the power of Yahweh. "My innocence and virtue—they've been restored!" he whispered in holy wonder. He closed his eyes and silently moved his lips, "Oh Yahweh, you are most wonderful. Thank you." The presence of the Lord filled the room, and they stood in awe of the miracle that had just happened.

When the moment seemed right, Sede spoke, "I plan to leave this place. I want you to come with me. I want to help Ka-sta too."

"With all my heart, I want to go with you, but how would we ever find our way home? Atlantis is an island; our home is in the wilderness mainland."

With confidence, she answered, "Yahweh told me the night I was being prepared for market that I would return home. I believe Him. He will show us the way, but there is one thing that you must do before we plan our escape. I came with another Sethite, who was sold the same day I was. His name is Ham. Do you think you can find out where he is?"

"I will try," he said. A bell rang, and he knew he had to leave.

"I must go, but we will speak again. How can I ever thank you, Sede-quete?"

"Your thanks be to God who delivered you, and please call me Sede, for that is my name among my pack."

With a broad smile, he responded, "Call me Dollo, for I, too, was a hunter among my kin!" They looked at each other in amazement that they had this common bond. Still smiling, he bowed and backed toward the door, leaving the room.

Playtheus was in a frenzy as he raced into the mansion. "Call for Ka-sta," he shouted to his servant, throwing his cape aside. Racing to the gardens, the servant quickly brought her and bowed as he closed the door. Ka-sta stood sweetly before him while he lay before her on his cushions. Her face shone with purity of innocence. "Come, sit here, my dear, by me." He patted the cushion beside him. Hesitantly, she moved toward him but then stopped. "Come, come, sit here," he insisted, patting the cushion once more.

As she listened to the music, a strange feeling began to move through her: a weakening. The music in the air embraced her with a soft, hypnotic melody. A flutter began to stir within her, moving mysteriously through her body. Her cheeks flushed a lovely pink, and she slowly knelt beside him on the cushion. The purity of innocence was shining from her face. She shuddered as he looked deep into her eyes.

Softly, he began to speak in a language that she had never heard before. He spoke his words to her shoulder, her neck, and her mouth. His eyes followed his words. He took her hand and raised her palm to his lips, kissing it gently. Chanting his words again, she *felt* them. They felt warm and smooth as oil. He leaned to her ear; his warm breath made her shiver. His spoken words penetrated her being, stirring her, wooing her. She felt light headed as her body began to sway ever so gently. Something was happening to her…she was beginning to surrender. His eyes widened in delight. 'Yes, she's responding!'

She felt his warm breath as he whispered his words in her ear once more. Then he called to her, wowing her inmost being. "Come to me…come to me, Ka-sta." She closed her eyes as her heart pounded. He spoke again, whispering his strange words and breathing them in her ear. She shuddered. A yearning to surrender rose within her. She had never known such feelings—these yearnings from this unknown place within her. It was strangely hot and fierce, yet smooth as silk.

Slowly, ever so slowly, she leaned toward him. He felt the warmth of her spoken words. "Yes, I give myself to you. I am yours. Come, take and drink deeply of my 'Purity of Heart'!" A coolness swept through her as she felt him draw from her soul. Barely touching his lips to hers, he inhaled deeply. A mist left her mouth as he drew her innocence and virtue from the depth of her being. A tattoo began to materialize on his arm, glittering the golden symbol of 'Purity of Heart.'

"Ah," he sighed as his body shivered. The rest of his tattoos glistened lightly as he continued to savor his new "innocent." He whispered softly, "Umm…no longer hungry…no longer longing. The 'innocent' have satisfied!"

Leaning back on the cushions, he exhaled deeply and closed his eyes. Ka-sta, too, leaned back, feeling the full impact of what had happened on the inside of her. Both lay quiet and still. After but a few moments, he faced her and softly spoke. "You have freely given your innocence to me. You are mine for as long as I choose. You will serve me in selfless abandonment."

"Yes, my lord, with selfless abandonment." She gently touched his cheek with her small hand. "I live to do your every bidding, Playtheus. All of who I am is now yours."

He threw his head back and roared in delight. "You I will call my 'trophy' innocent." A strange smile crossed his lips as he thought of what he had just taken from her. 'How easy a prey are these Sethites. They're helpless against my power and knowledge. They possess such greatness and are totally unaware of it. This, too, is a virtue of their innocence.' His thoughts began to turn toward Sede-quete. 'She will give herself to me in the same way. I know she possesses far more power than this one. When I possess her power, I will rise to be named a 'Mighty One' in the earth. She will ravish my passion more than this one or any other ever could.' He felt a fevered rush and closed his eyes to savor the thought. He became aware of the music filling the room around them and the fire slowly burning in the marble fireplace. He listened to the slow and steady breathing of the new "innocent" laying at his side.

'Umm…my power is great, and Sede-quete shall make it greater still!'

Chapter 12

Champion Hall

As Sede stood in the doorway between the bedrooms, she looked at Ka-sta's bed. She wasn't there yet? Feeling fatigue from the strange day, she slipped between her bedding furs. 'My hope has been stirred,' she thought. 'When Dollo finds Ham, we'll plan our escape.' She fell into a deep sleep. When she stirred, the lovely sound of distant music seemed to greet her. A lovely fragrance of trellis flowers blooming on the veranda filled the air. For just a moment she thought she was in a dream. When she opened her eyes, she saw Fro-mos and A-thia. Tears filled her eyes. She was not in a dream but still a captive. They stood waiting for her to wake. They held clothes and a tray of food.

Stepping forward, Fro-mos spoke, "Master desires your presence this morning."

Rising, she chose an apple from his tray and asked, "Where is Ka-sta? She didn't sleep in her bed last night."

Bowing, Fro-mos replied, "Last night Ka-sta surrendered her innocence to Master. She will now sleep with him. She has become his companion."

Sede froze in her steps and whirled around. "What!?" She looked at his face and could see he had no surprise in what he'd spoken. To him it was a matter of fact. Her thoughts were spinning. 'How could this be? When did this happen? Ka-sta and Playtheus!'

Fro-mos led Sede to Playtheus' chamber and opened the tall doors. She felt bewildered, wondering what she was about to see. "Come in, come in, Sede-quete. I want you to meet Polisha!" he announced with enthusiasm. Ka-sta stepped from behind the veranda's pillar. Sede gasped at the sight of her. Her first thought was: 'Changed in every way.' Surely this was not the same Sethite she knew?

"Hello, my dear," said Polisha as she confidently walked toward her. Grabbing her around the waist, she sashayed her in a circle. Her touch felt strange and awkward. Sede cringed. Searching Ka-sta's face, she sensed the absence of innocence. She looked strangely alluring. Taking Sede's hand, she brushed it against her own cheek. "You, too, will know the pleasure of being his. We will share him in every way!"

Sede couldn't believe what she was saying. Ka-sta was so different. So changed. Playtheus watched a single tear roll down Sede's cheek. 'Oh, the depths of this woman. To freely give her emotions to someone she hardly knows. I can only imagine what she will feel when she surrenders to me.'

Playtheus broke her shock. "Today you will accompany us to Champion Hall. I wish to show my brother Nephilim my new 'trophy'!" Smiling, he stroked Polisha's cheek while her eyes danced at the touch of his hand.

When a different servant brought the chariot before the mansion, Playtheus seemed puzzled and asked, "Where is Tailius?"

"He is not feeling well. I am here to serve you, my lord."

"Very well; let's be on our way." While they passed the market and began the ascent to Champion Hall, Sede was appalled by Ka-sta's behavior. She caressed Playtheus in such a seductive manner. It made her blush just being in their presence. What had happened to this innocent Sethite?

The three arrived at Champion Hall and stood in the archway of the great room. All eyes fell on Polisha. The look of awe was evident; her presence was commanding, confident. Playtheus stepped forward, parading her, her hand held high in his. He circled the crowded room as Nephilim began touching her as she passed, their tattoos glowing brilliant amber. A warm flame burned in Playtheus' eyes as his new tattoo glistened on his muscular arm. It made Sede sick to her stomach. She turned her head in disgust. He had changed her to sport. All a human holds to of dignity, strength, and honor had been ravished from her. Thankful their probing eyes were not on her, she backed against the wall, seemingly forgotten for the moment. Bowing her head, she whispered her prayer: "Cover me from their evil eyes, Yahweh. Make me invisible to their every gaze."

Looking again at Polisha, she felt such sorrow in what she saw. She began to think of Tailius. 'I didn't see this corruption in him. He said his innocence was stolen. She gave hers freely. Perhaps there is a difference in what happens within the soul. I wonder if Polisha could be restored to Ka-sta as Tailius was to Dollo.'

Playtheus stood in the middle of the Nephilim who had encircled them. Waving his hand in the air, a transparent image appeared above them. The image was Ka-sta as she stood before Playtheus after the servant brought her from the garden to his chamber. She stood small and still—so pure, so innocent. All Nephilim were awed by her gentle beauty. The symbol from the market briefly appeared on her forehead, which they recognized as "Purity of Heart." Waving his hand once more, the image disappeared. He raised her hand in his, proudly saying, "This is some of my work, brothers and sisters. With my father's knowledge, I have the power to transform the most innocent, just like the one you saw, into what you now see before you."

All eyes followed Polisha as Playtheus continued to parade her. A soft "umm" filled the air as they admired the transformation.

He then nodded to Diatus, who in turn, nodded to the musicians. The soft music changed into a mysterious, drummed rhythm. The eyes of the Nephilim widened as they listened. Their souls pulsated with the beat of the drums. Ever so slowly, a hot fierceness began to settle within their chests, and beads of sweat moistened their brow. They looked with longing eyes on this captivating human. Playtheus released Polisha's hand to stand solitary before them. At that moment, every Renown had one single thought…they wanted her. Playtheus stepped back to watch his "trophy." He had revealed a secret to her, a secret that none knew but those who possess the dark knowledge of the innocent. And now he would see how she would use it.

With eyes ablaze, she whispered strange words and leaned slightly forward, inhaling deeply. Supernaturally, she drew in their fevered desire for her. Silver strings of "desire's light" were drawn from each Nephilim chest. From all over the room, the strings of light lifted and joined into one single strand. She inhaled deeply the single strand of light, filling her lungs. Her eyes flickered with power. Capturing her breath, she slowly tilted her head back and lifted her arms, gently arching her back. With her beautiful hair swaying behind her, she slowly began to turn in a circle. She looked magnificent as she turned. Every eye was upon her and held spellbound. As the drums continued their fervent beats, she then, with an explosive burst of power, exhaled the captured desire she held within her. The ignited specks of light shot into the air from her exhaled breath, falling in small jolts on each Nephilim's chest. As if stuck by lightening, they lifted their heads and roared with power! The sound was deafening as it echoed off the walls, ceiling, and floor. Sede held her hands to her ears. The vibration from their roars sent waves through her body, filling her with terror.

The drums deepened their pounding, louder and louder. Nephilim began leaving their companions and moving in unison toward Polisha. Circling her, they pressed forward, every hand reaching to touch her. At that very moment, Playtheus stepped through them, taking her by the hand once more. "Isn't she ravishing?" he taunted.

Hearts pounded as they watched him move her through their midst. Their fevered desire followed her every move. Playtheus looked at Diatus with a smirk and slowly nodded. For their own amusement, they had manipulated and played the whole room. Sede trembled as she beheld this strange magic. She felt her own heart pound with the drums. Their hunger for Polisha was frightening to her, like wolves circling their prey. The saddest of all was Polisha, who encouraged and relished their hunger. 'This is no more than divination,' she thought. 'Will he stop at nothing in perverting her?'

Playtheus raised his voice to be heard. "You have sought me to help you possess the 'innocent' for yourselves. I was given this knowledge to satisfy *you*, my brother and sister Nephilim." Their tattoos began to glow as they roared in response to him. Raising his voice, he began to shout, "Great is my father. And great the 200. Great is their knowledge and power. Great is my father and great the 200. Great is my father and great the 200!" Cheers and roars erupted as they all began to join in praise and worship. Their voices were so deafening that Sede held her hands to her ears.

Suddenly Talimus-qua-tam materialized before them. "Father!" uttered Playtheus, bowing reverently. Two other Nephilim bowed in respect and responded with "Father." He glowed from the inside out, glistening with bursts of blue light. Sede remembered the Watcher who had given her the seed of Eden; he had glowed in the same manner. This angel was fiercely beautiful, and all the female companions shrilled in spontaneous excitement. The look of desire was evident on their faces. He stood tall and proud, his dark hair flowing about his shoulders. A magnificent symbol glowed red on his forehead. His piercing blue eyes reflected the power that strove to escape from his being. As he began to speak, Sede's ears burned. She felt an evil unlike no other! It pressed in on her, and she felt as though she would suffocate. Though he was cloaked in light, his beauty was a deception. His very presence made the hair on her neck stand on end. Trembling in fear, she pressed harder against the wall, wishing she could pass through it to escape.

"Today my son has honored me, showing this great praise of me and the Mighty 200." They hung on his every word, awed by his power. "I am pleased to see the knowledge I gave my son created this wonder before you!" He waved his hand toward Polisha. She quaked with delight that he acknowledged her. "This power to transform first came from our great leader. He used this knowledge to transform Adam and Eve, who willingly gave their innocence to him. He granted me this knowledge, and I, in turn, granted it to my son." Looking proudly at Playtheus, he smiled and grabbed his shoulder in affection. "Only those who possess this secret knowledge know its great power!" The tattoo on Talimus-qua-tam's forehead began to glow even brighter as his eyes pierced Playtheus'. "You are well on your way to becoming a 'Mighty One' my son. As it made our leader and myself great, so it will make you great!" With awe, all Nephilim bowed at the waist to Playtheus.

Talimus-qua-tam then turned to Polisha. "You have drank the desire of the Nephilim, but I will drink of your essence!" His piercing blue eyes flashed with power as he focused his attention on her. A hush fell in the room, and not a breath was heard. As if pulled by a great unseen power, she moved forward, gliding but an inch off the floor. Stopping in front of him, her eyes widened as she looked at his mouth. An anticipating moment gripped the room. She began to breathe shallow and fast, her chest rising and falling with each breath. She was now in full surrender to what was about to happen. Her breathing accelerated into gasping breaths. Clasping her face with his hands, he drew her face closer still. Inhaling deeply, he drew from her trembling, parted lips. Supernatural light from her arms and legs rose and gathered to her chest and through her throat, bursting forth from her mouth into his. After he inhaled, a powerful luminescent light exploded from his body, blowing those around him backward with a blast. In that instant, he was gone, disappearing as quickly as he had appeared.

Bodies of dazed Nephilim lay on the floor, stunned by his mighty display of power. Shaking themselves, they stood to their feet. As they collected their thoughts, they looked at each other and erupted once more in unison: "Great is Talimus-qua-tam and great the 200. Great it Talimus-qua-tam and great the 200!"

Playtheus took the shaken Polisha by the hand and walked toward Sede. He had an amazed look on his face. "My father's power is great. As his son, I will possess the power we just saw when I become a 'Mighty One'!" He smiled at Sede with sinister confidence, his eyes piercing hers. She instantly knew that *she* was the key to him becoming a 'Mighty One' and remembered what he had said the day before in the garden: 'With your innocence, Sede-quete, I will be a 'Mighty One'!'

While Playtheus was escorting Polisha and Sede from the room, he briefly bowed to Diatus. "Your work was most effective, brother. The knowledge and power your father has given you is evident to all!"

With a smirk, Diatus returned a bow. "And you, my brother, have shown us a spectacular display of the knowledge your father has given you!"

When they arrived at the mansion, Tailius greeted Playtheus as he stepped from the chariot. "How is it you are well so soon, Tailius?"

Bowing, he answered, making up the first thing he could think of, "The gods must have blessed me, Master."

Playtheus suddenly stopped and turned to look at him again. "You look strangely different. What is it?" Playtheus looked at the tattoo on his arm. The symbol was still there, but there was no amber glow.

Tailius quickly looked at Sede and then down. "It must be the blessing of the gods, Master," he said as he bowed once more.

Still heady from the display of his transformed "innocent" and his father's praise, he dismissed the tattoo. "Show Sede-quete to her chamber. She will dine with me and my ravishing 'trophy.'" He took Polisha's hand and kissed her palm. "You did well with the knowledge I gave you, Polisha." She shuddered to know she had pleased him.

As Sede walked with Dollo, her head was spinning from all she had witnessed at Champion Hall. She had seen the supernatural power of Yahweh come down and consume their sacrifice and the glory cloud of His presence. She had trembled at the presence of His Watcher and felt His loving power when He spoke to her on the night breeze. Never were His power or acts evil as she had seen and felt today. 'What a contrast of powers,' she thought. 'Yahweh's power brings peace and a sense of wellbeing. His power *gives* life. This dark power brings fear and only *takes* from others to exalt itself. This Atlantis world is empty, corrupt, and evil.' She pondered still… 'Those who rule live only for sensual pleasure and satisfying their endless thirst for power. My people are scorned and are merely something to be transformed to please them, like Polisha. Using their dark knowledge, they twist and pervert Yahweh's creation. They have no power to create anything. They use something that has already been created, twisting and perverting it. Surely you will judge them, Yahweh, and bring this evil world to an end.'

Dollo saw her distress. "Take heart, Sede. We will leave this evil place and be with our kin once more. We *will* go home!"

As they continued down the corridor, she felt strengthened by his words. Thinking about home, she asked, "Have you found Ham?"

"Yes, Sede, I learned he was sold to a Regal Renown."

She stopped. Grabbing his arm, she nearly yelled, "Tell me more!"

"The Priest at the arena told me he was sold to Castius. I've been to his mansion when Master did business with him. This Regal specializes in species breeding. He not only crossbreeds animals but also animals to humans. He alters the seed of life within them."

"How is this possible?" she asked.

"I don't know, but just like everything else in this place, it happens."

"I long for the pure and simple," she groaned. "This corruption is suffocating!"

"It's been so long since I've seen or felt anything pure or simple," reflected Dollo. "I have hope once more to experience them, thanks to you, Sede." He looked at her gratefully. A bell rang, and he turned to leave. "We'll talk soon," he said and closed the door behind him.

When she had finished eating, Fro-mos led her from the banquet room and asked, "Did you enjoy Master's presence this evening?"

She couldn't bring herself to answer. Her throat was tight with distress. If she talked, she knew she would burst into tears. When he closed her door, she ran to her bed, burying her head in the furs. "Oh Ka-sta, Ka-sta!" she cried. During their meal Sede had seen more of the corruption that had settled in Polisha's soul. Her behavior was anything but pure. Sede had kept her eyes lowered, ashamed to see what she was doing and saying.

Playtheus knowingly smiled, seeing how uncomfortable Sede was in her presence. "Come, come, Sede-quete. She is spreading her wings. She is discovering her newfound freedom. I delight to see her transformation. When you see her shameful behavior, I am savoring her lost 'Purity of Heart.' This is part of the power I possess—to continue to savor what humans have freely and willingly given me. She, too, finds pleasure in what she is doing."

Sede felt his evil. It was suffocating. "Stop!" she shouted, covering her ears.

Polisha came behind her and pulled her hands away from her ears. She warmly whispered, "Don't be afraid to surrender yourself to him. He is wonderful beyond belief!" Her eyes danced as she spoke.

Sede grabbed her arm. "Ka-sta, you can change. Yahweh can heal you!"

Polisha looked at her in amazement. "Why?! Why would I want to be healed from this?" She slowly waved her hand toward Playtheus. He smiled as his eyes met Sede's.

"You see, Sede-quete, an 'innocent' freely given to me is mine forever. Her 'free will' gave her the power to choose. Those who unwillingly surrender are different. There still remains a free will within them even though I possess the virtue of their innocence." Sede began to see why praying for Ka-sta would do no good.

Sede continued to cry with her head buried in the furs. She would be leaving but not with Ka-sta. Ka-sta no longer existed. She had become someone else. It would be Ham, Dollo, and herself who would find freedom.

"Wake, wake," said A-thia, as she lightly touched her shoulder. Opening her eyes, she saw her servant leaning over her. "I'm sorry to wake you, but Master has given orders to leave soon. We must hurry to prepare you." A-thia quickly helped her dress, and she ate walking down the corridor.

'What could be so urgent?' she thought.

As she stepped into the chariot, Dollo nodded to her in recognition. Sede smiled in return. Playtheus and Polisha came hand in hand, hurrying down the mansion steps. "I have an appointment with Castius. We must hurry. Drive on, Tailius!" Dollo flicked the reins, and they hurried on their way.

They arrived and hurried up the grand staircase. Passing through the crowded room, all Nephilim eyes followed Sede. She felt as though they were wolves sniffing the wind for prey. She walked even closer behind Playtheus, who led them to Castius' door. This was one door at Champion Hall she hadn't seen. When they entered, Castius and Playtheus greeted each other with a powerful clasp of arm to forearm handshake. "Ah brother, you want me to make this happen for you?"

"Yes," Playtheus said. "I long to have this!"

Castius smiled and said, "And you shall, brother; you shall!"

They were led farther back into his massive room, passing beautiful, ornate cages that housed strange and exotic animals. A large, deep pool graced the middle of the room. Pillars surrounded the edges, and flowering vines hung from the circular supports. The light from above made the water sparkle a crystal blue. Peering in, Sede and Polisha saw strange creatures swimming deep below. They had the bodies of women to the waist but, instead of legs, a very large fish tail. As they darted and swirled under the water, Polisha dropped to her knees for a closer look. Bending over the water, she followed their swift movements with an "ooh" and an "ahh." One of the strange creatures came to the surface and spit a stream of water in Polisha's face. Shocked and angry, she stood and wiped her face. "Annoying little creatures, aren't they?" she said, obviously humiliated. Castius knowingly smirked to see their antics.

As Sede looked around the room, she was filled with awe and wonder. Everything was so grand in size and beautiful. Castius saw her reaction and proudly said, "These are my creations. My father has shared his knowledge with me. I know how to blend the seeds of creation. When I have successfully united their seed, I name my creations just as Adam named…" He hesitated but then reluctantly said, "Just as Adam named the 'Most High's' animals. What you see in my pool is the breeding of fish to woman. I have named them 'Mermaids'!" Waving his hand, he motioned them to step forward. Leading them to a large, exquisite cage he said, "These two I call 'Centaurs.' They were bred horse to woman."

The male and female Centaurs trotted toward Castius with smiles on their faces. The female spoke first. "May I breed with that male there?" She pointed to Tailius. "Yes, I would like that!"

The male Centaur reached through the bars and gently clasped Polisha's hand, kissing it softly. "Please may I breed with her? She is so fair."

Castius laughed and said, "Now, now, you two. So eager to breed. This female I have other plans for." He gave Playtheus a wink. "And as for the male, he is Playtheus' servant. He would have to give his consent." Tailius was aghast by the mere suggestion that he could be forced to breed with this creature.

Moving to the next cage, he said, "Ah yes. Let me show you my praise!" Stepping in front of the massive cage, a beautiful, black-winged horse trotted to his extended hand. Reaching through the bars, he stroked the stallion's forehead. "He is bred bird to horse. I have named him Pegasus. Isn't he magnificent?!"

The winged horse lifted his head and whinnied, rearing on his hind legs and pawing the air with his hooves. His wings went full spread. Sede could feel the power within its neigh. He was strange and fierce. This was the very horse she had seen through the porthole of the ship the day they had arrived in Atlantis.

As if remembering why Playtheus had come, he turned and said, "Come Playtheus. Bring her!"

Smiling at Polisha, Playtheus squeezed her hand. "Yes, let's go!" he said. He then turned to Sede and brushed her hair gently from her forehead. "Wait here with Tailius. I'll return soon." He pulled her to himself with his fingers beneath her chin and spontaneously kissed her on the lips. Sede was horrified. It happened so fast she didn't have time to resist. She stepped back with a start. He smiled, knowing he had caught her off guard. He followed the others and closed the door.

Sede looked at Dollo in unbelief. Shaking his head, he said, "It will be a good thing when we leave this place. I don't want any part of some strange breeding experiment with a Centaur. I'm glad they've left so we have a moment to talk. This is the Regal Renown that bought your kin, Ham. We should see him somewhere around here. He works for Castius."

Her eyes lit with surprise. "What? He's here?!" she blurted.

"Shush!" said Dollo. "Let's keep our eyes open for him."

While they waited, they began to make plans for their escape. They would have to find their way to the dock and a ship that sailed to Zadanim. She reasoned, "Surely the ship that brought us sails to the same place it came from. The two days we sailed, we moved in the direction of the setting sun. Surely the way home would be to sail east. It should bring us to Zadanim. We must find the ship with the white sails and golden sides!"

"I know that ship you speak of. It sails every seventh night!" They looked at each other, realizing their time had come. Both grabbed the other's forearms, and without thinking, they both said at the same time, "Ha-la-lah!" and touched foreheads, being the hunters they were.

A door opened to the side of where they were standing, and a man approached carrying a small lion cub with wings. Gently, he put the cub into the cage and turned to leave. As he looked up, he nearly shouted, "Sede!"

"Shush!" they both said as Dollo put his hand over Ham's mouth.

"I can't believe it's you!" he said, visibly shaken by the surprise.

Quickly, Sede filled Ham in on the plan of escape. "You must find out how to get to the pier. In two nights we'll be waiting at the great arch."

Relief filled him as he hugged her. "Oh, to be home again!" he said tearfully.

Looking around, she asked, "What do you do here, Ham?"

He answered hesitantly, "I assist Castius with his breeding." Tears came to his eyes, and she could see he was troubled.

Putting her hand on his shoulder, she said with compassion, "I'm sorry for what you've been through, Ham."

He looked at her and said, "This all looks amazing and even wonderful with these beautiful cages and exotic animals. But I've seen the failed breeding and the suffering that our people have endured because of his experiments. There are caverns full of our dead." He continued with tears in his eyes, "This place is beautiful on the outside but underneath everything you see is a dark and brewing evil!" Sede could discern that Ham, too, had come to the same conclusion she had. Just then a servant yelled at Ham, calling him Bromos. "I've got to go, but I'll be there," he said as he wiped the tears from his face. He left through a side door with the other servant.

Just as soon as he had left, Playtheus stepped through the door with Polisha beaming at his side. "I'm pleased," he said. "Let us be on our way." As they stepped into the chariot, he commanded, "Sede-quete will stand with me." He rested his hand on hers and said, "Today, I do this for us."

"What?" she said as she pulled her hand away.

He smiled and continued, "I've put in motion my plan to have a child with you. In the past, the females I've impregnated have died during pregnancy. Castius has found the problem. He will experiment one more time with Polisha. I won't risk your life. Polisha now lives to serve me, and I wish this to happen. It will be as Apogee has seen in the stars. Our children will rule and reign in the earth. I will become a 'Mighty One,' and you are a 'Tella-la-no-ah.' With that combination, our children will be supreme in every way. They will truly be 'Titans,' so unique that they will be worshiped as gods!"

She felt the heat of anger rise within her. To think that she would ever agree to have children with him was unbelievable. This was confusion and madness. In her hot anger, she prayed within herself, 'Yahweh, destroy this wickedness with its wicked.'

She stepped down from the chariot in silence. Playtheus eagerly searched her face for a happy response to his words. "I am exhausted," she said flatly, not wanting him to know what she was feeling.

"Yes, yes of course," he said. "Tailius will show you to your chamber." She looked at Dollo, not believing what Playtheus had just told her for he had heard it too.

As he walked her to her room, he sensed her anger and anxiety. "We'll leave this place in two days, Sede. All the distress you now feel will be but a memory to forget. We must plan this just right so we don't miss the ship's departure." As she focused on what he was saying, her thoughts began to clear. They *would* leave this dreadful place. Hope had been stirred within her once more, and she bid him goodnight.

Chapter 13

Exploited Children

It was a beautiful morning as the chariot moved slowly out of the city. It was good to hear only the wind in the trees and an occasional bird. The sun was warm and comforting, relieving the tension in her body. 'Oh, to be in open spaces once more!' she thought.

Playtheus looked at her as she stood beside him. She was so beautiful with the breeze blowing against her, making the sunlight dance off her long, flowing hair. He sensed her pleasure and smiled. This was the day he wished to show her his work in the country. He had been planning each day with the intention of preparing her. He wanted her free surrender and companionship. In his dream, he knew she would rule with him. Today would help prepare her for that purpose.

The chariot pulled in front of a country mansion. Similar to those in the city, it stood grand, polished white, and perfectly manicured. The warm sun, the light breeze, and the smell of fresh cut grass filled her senses and brought a smile to her face. As they walked through the mansion, their footsteps echoed in the grand foyer. It felt cold and hollow compared to the open outdoors. Passing through, they stood at the railing of the veranda, overlooking the gardens below. What she saw brought delight to her soul—children everywhere!

A broad smile lit up her face, and he felt great happiness. She looked over the open, lush green gardens and saw children playing in the sun: laughing, skipping, and dancing. Playtheus saw the happiness that exuded from her. "For the first time, Sede-quete, I see your happiness!"

She briefly looked at him but returned her attention to the children. "I had wondered where the children were. I thought it strange there were none playing and running in the streets as they do in my village."

"I brought you here today, Sede-quete, hoping to give you an understanding of my work. All the children that are bought or born in Atlantis are brought here. This mansion is but one of many I own. Here in the country, they are nurtured and prepared. I have purchased many Sethite women to breed for me, giving me children." She turned to him in shock. He continued as if there was nothing wrong with what he had said. "I have found that there is a vast difference between the two people groups on the earth. The Cainites are a vile people and possess corrupted virtues, if you can call any virtue that. Their virtues are not innocent. I prefer Sethites. It is they who possess true innocent virtues. Occasionally I purchase Cainite children under the age of 4. Any older than that I cannot use. Their innocence after that age is corrupted. All the children here receive a tattoo upon the forehead, as you can see. They are asked to choose one of the Mighty 200 to favor and worship. The symbol on their forehead is the mark of the god they have chosen. After I've withdrawn their innocence from them, they leave this place and join Atlantis society, honoring the Renown son of the god they have chosen."

Sede realized yet again that the beauty of what she saw only masked the evil beneath it. The beautiful mansion and its grounds, the playful laughter of the children, and the peaceful order all masked the evil festering underneath. Her face flushed white, and she looked at him with an unbelievable look of horror.

"What do you do with the children?" she said, almost afraid to ask.

Looking down into her troubled eyes, he flatly said, "I withdraw their innocence, and it becomes mine."

She searched his face, trying to understand what that meant.

"Because we are angelic *and* human, Nephilim have a bred in thirst for innocence, for we have none of our own. To not have innocence would be a torment to us. Always there would be this ravenous need in our soul. It is what empowers us; it satisfies the human part of us. The innocence of the children is then transformed within us, giving us our virility, our voracious appetite for pleasure, our strength, and our glory!" His voice crescendoed with each word he spoke. She looked down at his arms. His tattoos glistened as if ignited by what he had spoken. She felt the heat of them just standing near him. With widened eyes, she trembled. "This is how we differ from the Nephilim 'low ones,'" he continued. "They have no access to innocence for themselves. They sense it in humans but have no knowledge of how to withdraw it for themselves. That is why they are so barbaric and wild in cruelty and violence."

He continued, absorbed in what he was telling her. "Children's innocence within a Nephilim is brief, lasting only one cycle of the Zodiac. Once gone, the desire burns hot within us to have the power of the 'innocent' renewed. These children are a continual source of replenished power for us. Once their innocence has been withdrawn, they become servants for the 'Renown': working in their fields and in their mansions, doing commerce, and some, at adulthood, becoming breeders for me. Fro-mos and A-thia came from one of my country breeding mansions. They know no other life but to serve me and are happy to do so. Castius also desires my children when they have grown, wanting them for his breeding. The Renown honor me and highly praise me because only I can satisfy them with this continual source of power. I am the one and only Renown who has the knowledge to withdraw the innocence from mankind. This makes me great among my brothers. This ability I possess has set my destiny in place. One day soon, I will be declared a 'Mighty One,' a title all Renown desire but very few attain."

It was as if she could hear no more. She looked out over the children, her heart overwhelmed within her. She saw pregnant women, bellies large with child. They moved among the children, bending down and kissing their heads. The children happily returned them an offering of a flower. Sede's eyes filled with tears. Her kin, the Sethites, bred for the pleasure of these abominations. She began to cry.

"Oh come, Sede-quete, you will see this differently in time. You will come to see the great potential for power in using them. I am showing you this to help you see how I value you." She looked at him with questioning eyes, half afraid to ask what he meant. "I once told you that you were worth more than 100,000 children bred for their innocence…remember?" Shocked, she suddenly remembered. "Come, let's go down and greet them."

As she continued to cry, she shook her head. "No, I cannot."

"Very well," he nodded and turned to leave. "I won't be long."

As she stood on the balcony overlooking the children beneath, she saw them happily run to him. As he walked toward them, they hugged his large legs and offered him flowers and smiles. Patting the large belly of a woman near him, she returned a smile as they conversed. All seemed to enjoy his presence. 'How could these women be so deceived?' she thought. 'Where was their desire to return home and honor Yahweh with their lives? How had they come to be so blinded?' As she stood there, she felt so lost, so alone…

"Sede." She heard her name softly spoken.

"What?"

As she turned, she felt his presence. There before her stood the radiant Watcher she had seen at Eden's wall! Love and peace flooded her soul, and she began to weep. All the sorrow and sadness she had felt instantly melted away. Within a moment of time, the atmosphere of sorrow had shifted to peace and love. The fragrance of his being filled her lungs with holy pleasure, for he carried the aroma of heaven. She couldn't speak, and her knees started to buckle, weakened by the power emitting from his being. He stepped forward and touched her shoulder. Immediately strength exploded within her.

"Oh," she shuddered, as she looked at him in amazement.

"Sede, I have come to encourage you. Yahweh has sent me. 'Let not your heart be troubled and don't be afraid.' You have seen a great evil today. Yahweh, too, is grieved, grieved to the point He regrets that He made man. He *will* judge this place and all who willingly worship and serve the 'fallen ones.' They have done a great evil taking to themselves human wives that bore them Nephilim. Their quest for power will exceed what you are now coming to understand. They will utterly destroy all that is good and holy in the world. You will leave this place in two days. I have been sent to make a way for you. Ham and Dollo will be saved as well. Here, child, receive the gift of 'grace' Yahweh has sent for you." Touching her shoulder, a powerful light flowed from his hand, sending its warmth and strength through her. She instantly stood tall. Strong. Renewed. Slowly, he vanished in a mist before her.

Instead of the Watcher, she now saw Playtheus walking toward her. What he saw made him stop! A brilliant white light glowed all around her body. Awed by her presence, he exhaled. Unable to help himself, he said, "You never cease to amaze me Sede-quete. Your power is great!" Smiling, he took her by the hand and led her through the mansion to the waiting chariot. She was silent as they returned, filled with wonder in all the Watcher had said. She felt the warm comfort that remained from his presence and the strength from the grace she had received. She would be going home, far from this dreadful place. The Watcher would make a way.

Chapter 14

Seduction of the Innocent

The day had come to an end. A lovely melody filled the air as the servants attended their food. Sede still carried the glow from the grace the Watcher had brought her at the country mansion, and a comforting calm had settled within her. She busied herself with eating. Playtheus could say nothing but watch her as she ate. He saw a difference in her but couldn't decide what it was. Polisha, on the other hand, trembled in Sede's presence. She felt a strange remembering—a nagging regret. Something about her glow reminded her of something, but she couldn't quite find its definition within herself. Unwilling to look Sede in the eyes, she could tolerate her discomfort no longer. Excusing herself, she retired to Playtheus' chambers.

"I'm pleased we can recline together," he said. "Tell me your thoughts. You saw many wondrous things today." Grabbing a small pear from the table, he paused, waiting for her response.

Sede looked at him in wonder. He acted as though she had pleasure in what she had seen that day. He had no idea how grieved she was over the children. She hesitated but then said, "I would rather hear your thoughts," hoping to divert his attention from her.

This pleased him greatly, thinking she was truly interested in what he had to say. "What would you like to know?"

"I was wondering of this place, this Atlantis. How did it come to be? How does it maintain such wealth?"

Smiling, he leaned back with hands behind his neck and sighed, "Ah, Atlantis!" With dreaming recollection, he began, "It all began when our mighty fathers chose to live upon the earth. They desired a dwelling place of their own making, seeing that…" he hesitated to say the name of God but continued, "Seeing that the 'Most High' had pleasure in creating a world and filling it with *His* children, they, too, desired to create a dwelling place and fill it with *their* children. They looked upon the daughters of men and saw that they were lovely, just as I look upon you now." He paused to let his eyes slowly move up and down her body. His face softly expressed what his words were saying. "These lovely women they took for wives, and bore them children, the Nephilim. The women paid a price for their surrender to our fathers. Some wives bore them 'The Beautiful.' They are the Renown among us. The price they paid was their souls. They surrendered them. Some became witches, using the knowledge given them by their husbands, the angels. Some of the wives bore the 'low ones.' We Renown call such creatures 'Hagonoths' and lay no claim of them being our brothers. They are the unintelligent, beastly giants. In their aggressive and fervent anger within the womb, their mothers died in childbirth. This is the price these wives paid. These simpleminded creatures have no greater use than hunting, warfare, and raiding. They have no place in Atlantis. I have no use for them. To me, they are a disgust. They take, raping and pillaging, consuming vast amounts of resources. They defile the Sethite women that could have been useful to Atlantis. Our culture is one of willing surrender. We savor the act. I still savor Ka-sta's surrender. The sweetness of her innocence is still with me." Closing his eyes, he groaned deeply, "umm!" Sede looked at him wide-eyed, sensing his evil pleasure. He continued, "Our great fathers wanted us to have our own city. Trihedron built it for them with the knowledge his father gave him. It was first called, 'The City of Sons' but was later renamed Atlantis. Our fathers have their own city called the 'City of Lights.'"

She continued her diversion with another question. "Tell me of Atlantis' wealth. How does the city maintain such grandeur?"

"Yes, our wealth. The Hagonoths serve the purpose of raiding the villages of both Cainites and Sethites. They bring us the captured, selling us the ones that were not spoiled by their defilement. The greatest wealth from these villages are the people themselves, used, as I said, for service, breeding, and possessing their innocence. But the village grains, animals, gold, spices, and ointments are of value too. Those that are captured and pose a problem to us work as slaves in the mines, maintaining a steady flow of gold to our wondrous city. In gratitude and love for our great fathers, once a year we Renown offer an 'innocent' as a burnt sacrifice." Sede was horrified and held her breath. Was there no end to the evil that lay beneath the surface of this place? He continued as if what he had said was natural and matter of fact. "We worship our fathers for giving us life, this city, and our great wealth. They have established Atlantis for us, their children, and there is no end to the wealth they lavish upon us!"

He stopped and smiled. "I see what you're doing, Sede-quete."

Trying to appear composed, she answered him, "What do you mean?" but realizing her diversion had been detected.

"I see you would have me talk so *my* questions will be diverted." Her face blushed red at being exposed. "I love your virtues. They have no end in surprising me. Like your innocent blushing just now. They are like the many facets of a diamond, each so surprisingly beautiful!" He took her small hand in his, and looking down at it said, "And you are as valuable as a diamond to me. Because of you, I will shine as a 'Mighty One'!" She marveled at his ability to think only of himself and how she would be used for his glory.

"Come, Sede-quete, walk with me." He stood and helped her to her feet. Nodding to the musicians, they began to play a strange and lonely song. Its haunting melody followed them as they entered the corridor. The light flickered from the silver torches, making the figures of the Renown seem to move on the mural. She recognized the first Renown. It was Castius. He stood tall and bold beside his beautiful, black-winged horse, one hand resting on its back. His strange symbol for breeding was above his head. "Ah, Castius. Isn't he beautiful in power?"

Sede didn't answer but looked at the next. It was Diatus. His symbol glistened above his head, and a flute was held to his pursed lips. Strange symbols floated in the air from the flute, falling on the couple embracing at his feet. It reminded her of the fountain in his room at Champion Hall. "Umm, I use his power often. Can you feel it now? It follows us as we walk."

She shuddered as she felt the music surrounding her, embracing her. As they walked farther, she saw the next Renown. Her mouth dropped open, and she gasped.

It was Playtheus. His symbol for "the innocent" was above his head. In his proud pose, he stood with legs apart and arms crossed at his chest. At his feet, a maiden extended her outstretched arms on his muscular leg. Her uplifted face shone with adoration. She blinked, not believing what she saw. The maiden was *her*! It was her exact likeness! The same symbol from the market was painted on her forehead! She had walked past this mural every day and had never seen this. She froze in shock.

"You seem surprised, Sede-quete. I had this painted after my first dream of you many, many years ago." Smiling, he crossed his arms at his chest and looked proudly at the painting, admiring his greatness. "Yes, this is who I am." Then his mood changed, and he began to dreamingly gaze at the painting. "Each day for these many long years, I passed this painting and thought of you...waiting for you."

She felt lightheaded as though she would faint. The painting—it looked exactly like her! It was the same symbol on her forehead that had been painted from the market. She exhaled, collapsing at his feet. Her hands clutched at his leg to stop her fall. Still smiling, he looked down at her. "See, just like the painting!" She turned to look, realizing they were now in the same pose as the mural. She was horrified. Quickly, she brought her hands to her lap and looked down.

He bent down and scooped her up in her strong arms, carrying her down the corridor to her room. Her mind was whirling in unbelief. And now he was carrying her. She heard the music surrounding her once more. The lovely, haunting melody seemed to be stroking her with invisible hands. "Sede-quete, I still wait for you. I wait for you to come to me. Come to me," he whispered. He started breathing strange words that floated down and settled on her body. She felt her soul weakening as his words penetrated her. She could hear his heart pounding through his robe. His seductive powers were wooing her, and she knew it. He lowered her on the furs, resting her gently on her bed. The room seemed to be spinning. She felt his breath as he drew to her face. Dazed and confused, she wanted to shake herself from the power he was using. Her heart was racing. 'I must get free of him. I am *not* his. My heart, my life, my love—they belong to Shem!'

She drew the strength to cry out within herself. 'Yahweh, may the grace you gave me today strengthen me. I resist this evil. Break this power over me. You are my only hope.' A loud "*No. I cannot!*" erupted from her throat.

Startled by her sudden ability to break his power, he stood to his feet. Then settling himself, he took her hand and said, "Why do you resist me so? You know my dream is true. You saw the painting. You *are* mine."

"No! I'm not yours!" she shouted, pulling her hand out of his.

Seeing that his sorcery had been broken and his moment lost, he smiled down at her. "You *will* come to me. And when you do, it will take your breath away. I have waited these many years…I will wait but a little longer. You are glorious, Sede-quete, and you *are* mine!" Pausing at the door, he looked at her with a deep knowing. He must wait for *her* free surrender. As he gently closed the door, she heard his footsteps grow softer and softer.

She spoke into the darkness of her room. "Oh Shem. Shem. I am yours and yours alone. You have the true power of love over me, not sorcery or divination. I long for your words of love…for the wooing of *your* heartbeat. I will rest in *your* arms. The seed of my womb will be yours, not his. Our child will pass on the seed of promise for the 'Promised One'!" She felt a great power settle within her chest as she breathed deeply. Her gift of grace had delivered her and had now filled her with power as she spoke her prophetic words.

She rose from her bed, walking in the shadowy darkness to the veranda. The stillness of night surrounded her. There was no sound from the city below, only the quiet night. Lifting her gaze, she marveled at the vastness of the stars of heaven. She began to feel so free…so very free and powerful. She spoke her words into the night: "Though I be held a captive, I am free in you, Yahweh. Free in a way this world beneath me could never know!" As her eyes fell on the twinkling lights below, she felt pity rise within her. "They know only pleasure and power. Every day *it* is their master—driving them—never enough!" With joy, she clasped her hands to her chest, holding her seed necklace. "How grateful I am to know you and your ways, Yahweh. Instead of empty pleasure and power, you give lasting love, comfort, and purpose. Oh, my heart is full of love for you!" She lifted her head and hands to the sky and began to whirl, spinning and spinning with joy bursting from her thankful heart. Her laughter echoed into the great sky above, echoing to the very throne of God.

Chapter 15

High Companion

Today was the day. Her day! This day she would leave Atlantis and see it no more. Joy filled her heart as she woke, remembering the Watcher's words, 'I have been sent to make a way for you.' Yahweh had proved Himself strong rescuing her from Playtheus' plan. His attempted seduction last night would become a memory to forget, as Dollo had said.

Fro-mos and A-thia stood at her door, greeting her with a tray of food once more. They had come to enjoy her quiet ways and looked forward to their conversations. As they served her day after day, she told them of her life as a Sethite and what her people believed. They showed great interest that the Sethites worshiped only one god. When she spoke of Yahweh, they felt their hearts yearn to know what she knew. They could see in her a faith that was alive and not mere ritual or ceremonial observance. She was different from those who had lived in the mansion before. They marveled at her free spirit and the kindness and compassion she showed. Today they would take great pleasure in preparing her for Playtheus. He had given command that she was to be declared his "high companion."

The preparations would take all day. At the Pavilion tonight, he would present her as his "high companion" and manipulate her to freely surrender to him. This honor of "high companion" was only bestowed on the Renown's favorite and most precious companion. Sede was a "Tella-la-no-ah," and by possessing her, he would elevate his status. Once more she was being used. This was but another piece of his plan—his plan to glory and greatness as a "Mighty One."

Fro-mos dismissed himself as A-thia led Sede to a room she had never seen before that overlooked the city below. In the center of the grand room was a special pool surrounded by pillars and open to the sky. A light, warm mist rose from the water's surface, and sheer curtains gracefully moved in the warm morning breeze. Sede smiled at the loveliness that greeted her.

Bowing, A-thia motioned her hand to the pool. "Fro-mos and I have prepared your heated pool with rare spices and oils. Come, I will help you down." Sede untied her robe, letting it fall around her feet. The sun streamed through the open pillars, warming her body. She paused and closed her eyes. Lifting her face and palms to the sun, the warm light seemed to embrace her, feeling so very good. As the calming rays settled upon her, she exhaled and smiled in pleasure. A-thia rolled her robe to the waist and held Sede's hand, helping her step into the pool. Submerging her body, she greeted the water with a soft "ah!" Warm, smooth oil floated on the surface, feeling so good, and the fragrance had an intoxicating effect. Taking a deep breath, she felt soothed and calmed.

As she relaxed in the water, she began to slowly glide, enjoying the water's warmth. "Ah, this is wonderful," she exhaled, as A-thia smiled and beheld her sweet innocence. Of Sede's days in Atlantis, this was the first time she'd been alone to just relax. It *was* wonderful to feel the simple pleasure of bathing and to be away from the demands of Playtheus.

As she peaceably enjoyed her quiet time in the water, she was unaware that Playtheus stood nearby. In the shadows of the pillars, he watched. His attempts to seduce her had failed. He knew that tonight he must seal his union with her in order to gain his title as "Mighty One." As he watched, his heart burned for her. She was so lovely. Perfect in every way. Her silhouetted body was breathtaking against the light of the sun as she stood with her hands and face lifted to heaven. She *did* take his breath away.

The water moved so gracefully over her skin as she glided beneath its warm misty surface; touching her; caressing her; as he wished he could. He had been with many beautiful women, but she…she captivated him like no other. She was his match in every way. Seeing her in all her loveliness made him want her all the more. He shuddered at the thought. He felt a yearning growing within, compelling him to step down into the water and pull her to himself. 'I must leave,' he thought, 'or I'll join her in the pool. I can't take her. She must surrender willingly to me. Only by the act of her own "free will" can I gain the full power of her innocence.' He had never denied himself anything, but more than this instant gratification he wanted to be named a "Mighty One." He knew he would have to wait. Turning to look once more, he saw her step from the pool. Releasing his desire, he exhaled and quietly slipped from the room.

Sede stepped from the water, and A-thia patted her skin, leaving a moist sheen from the oil. Unfolding her garment, she proudly extended her hands to reveal its beauty. "See what Master has given you to wear?" The morning light reflected the golden threads that were intricately woven through the deep purple satin. The gold glistened as the fabric moved in A-thia's hands. Resting nearby was a filigree band of gold. This would crown her head. A delicate bracelet and sparkling sandals seemed to be waiting her touch.

As A-thia began, her patient hands worked slowly and gently. She fashioned Sede's hair in a relaxed style, allowing most of her long hair to cascade down her back with just a touch of gentle curl. The filigree band fit perfectly around her forehead. She slid into her gown, and when A-thia had finished securing the back, she slid the bracelet up her arm, resting it near her shoulder. From the band hung a single diamond that glistened as Sede moved. The very tip of her jeweled slippers sparkled beneath the hem of her gown and reflected the light as she took each step. Standing back, A-thia admired the work she had done in preparing her. "You look lovely, mistress!"

Smiling sweetly, Sede looked down to see the beautiful gown she now wore. "Thank you, A-thia; I feel lovely!"

Fro-mos had entered and left the room many times throughout the day, bringing food and drink for Sede and A-thia. When he entered to remove the last tray, he beheld A-thia's finished work. He was taken aback by Sede's transformation. He remembered the modest girl that had clutched her robe that first night she arrived. But now this lovely woman stood before him—so gracious, so poised, so beautiful. She sweetly smiled, knowing he was admiring her.

"Master will be pleased," he said, smiling at A-thia.

"Yes, I believe he will," she responded with pride.

Sede pondered as she looked at Fro-mos and A-thia. They stood there so humble and eager to please her. "I want to thank you for serving me and being so kind. I'm truly grateful." She knew she might not see them again before she left. Their quiet care had brought her a small measure of comfort in all the craziness she had experienced. She felt sorrow for them. They would probably never leave this place.

Fro-mos opened her doors, and as they led her down the corridor she stopped, remembering. "Oh, I've forgotten something!"

Quickly, she left them and slipped back into her room. Sliding her hand beneath her pillow, she withdrew her seed necklace and hid it within her gown. She returned, and with a breath of excitement, said, "*Now* I'm ready!"

Playtheus himself had been preparing for the occasion. He spent a good part of the day giving orders for the Pavilion preparations. A special visit was made to see Diatus. He would be requiring his "work" for this special occasion. In his own grooming, Playtheus, too, prepared. He soaked in his own scented pool, the oils leaving him smooth and fragrant. Upon his wishes, he chose a garment that would complement Sede's gown. His was made of a glistening gold fabric with a deep purple sash that crested his chest; tying at the side. His robe came to the knees, where his golden sandals tied. His hair hung loosely at his shoulders, accented by a single gold band that circled his forehead. His light blue eyes were stunning in contrast, with his dark hair and bronzed, oiled skin. He stood tall and dignified— beautiful even—as he waited for his servant to present her.

And now the moment had come. Playtheus heard Fro-mos turn the latch of the door. As the tall doors slowly opened…there she stood! In silence, they beheld each another. Sede couldn't help herself. Of all the evil she knew existed in him, what she saw was beautiful. He *was* breathtaking! She caught herself, realizing she was allowing him to see her pleasure. She quickly looked down.

Smiling, he knew. He stepped toward her and led her into the room. As she stood before him, he slowly circled her. He saw what Fro-mos had seen: a total transformation. He was looking upon his queen. He circled her once more, his eyes taking in her every delicate detail. Drawing near her neck, he inhaled. The fragrance of her body made him tremble, and he remembered her beauty while she bathed. His eyes followed the curve of her neck to her soft shoulder and then the glistening sheen of her sculpted arm. The diamond on the arm band sparkled as he touched it softly, sending forth a faint tinkle.

As he came from behind her, he bent down and suddenly clasped her face with his hands and kissed her. In his kiss, she felt his desire for her. It happened so fast she didn't have time to protest. Shocked, she pulled away.

"I've been wanting to do that since the first day I set eyes on you. You are mine, Sede-quete, and I will now present you to *my* world!" The momentary pleasure she had seen in him totally evaporated. The stark reality of who he was hit her once more. "Here, I wish to show you something."

Reaching for a small, jeweled chest, he lowered it from the mantel. Pausing, he stroked it softly.

"What is it?" she asked.

He stroked it once more. "This is your past."

Her brow wrinkled with question. "What do you mean, my past?" As he slowly opened the chest, her heart leapt. Folded neatly within were her hunting skins. "How? How did you get them?" Her surprise was evident in her voice.

"I paid handsomely for them from the priest at the market."

She paused, wondering why he would refer to them as her past. "What do you mean…this is my past?"

Looking at her intently he said, "This is what you used to be. But tonight I'm going to show you who you *are*. I am presenting you as my 'high companion.' You are my queen!" He returned the chest to the mantel and with commanding authority said, "I show you your past and your future, and I hold them both in my hands." He extended his hand and said, "Let us be going!"

They entered the chariot, and Tailius slapped the reins against the horse's backs. As they glided over the streets, Sede's feelings were screaming at her. She felt deeply hurt seeing her skins used to manipulate and control her. Those skins represented the life she loved and the people she held dear. He could keep them in a chest, but she would never forget. They represented who she still was: a Sethite; the daughter of Tolmaka; a hunter among her kin; and promised wife of

Shem! As they moved along the street, she was sullen in mood. She dreaded what she would be put through only to boost his pride.

The chariot slowly came to a stop in front of the Pavilion. Beautifully dressed servants rushed to attend them, helping them both from the chariot. As they stepped forward, they began to climb the massive marble steps toward the entrance. Each step was six feet deep and hosted a grand marble statue of a Renown, one on each side of the step. Sede recognized the likeness of some of them. It was an extreme display of their own self-importance, and it disgusted her. As they took the last step to the entrance, it was though her breath was sucked from her lungs. She gasped!

Before her was something she could have only seen in a dream. The sight and sound of it were almost too much to take in. A magnificent, spacious room filled with sparkling colored lights, music, and beautiful dancing couples opened before them. Caught in the wonder of the moment, she watched the dancers as they moved to the music in such a wondrous way. The only dancing she had known was the "Dance of the Maidens" from her village. These dancers were not dancing individually but together, facing each other with hands at the shoulder and waist. She could hardly believe what she was seeing! Their graceful movements were a thing of beauty.

The Renown and their companions were breathtaking, and the companions' gowns could only be described as a mystery. Although each gown was made of white, shining fabric, a different light radiated from them—a light that came from within the woman's soul. These brilliant lights were in shades of lavender, pale green, pink, blue, and amber. There were a multitude of different shades.

As the flecks of colored light radiated from them, they seemed to be absorbed by their Nephilim escorts. Not only were these Nephilim immaculately groomed, but they exuded a manliness that took her breath away. She felt the pull of their masculinity on her, just as she had felt when she saw Playtheus in his chamber. Was it sorcery that made them so virile? She then remembered what Playtheus had said: 'It is the children's innocence that gives us our great virility.' She sensed that innocence did hold a mysterious power. As she continued to watch, the air itself seemed charged with energy coming from the exchange of these couples; the women emitting light, and the Nephilim absorbing it. She felt its hypnotic effect. As the music played, it filled the air above them with a sense of grandeur and opulence. Oh, such beauty and elegance. She didn't want to admit it, but she liked what she saw.

As they stepped through the entrance, the music abruptly stopped. A hush fell, and companions began to whisper in their partner's ear while every eye fastened on the "Prince" and his new "queen." They looked stunning as a couple; Playtheus: tall, handsome, and proud; Sede: beautiful in purity and innocence. She was unaware of it, but sparkling flecks of light radiated from her. Just as the companions had emitted colorful lights from within their souls, she, too, radiated light. Her gown emitted not just one color but the colors of the rainbow. The bursts of colored light far surpassed the lights of the companions. Everyone stood silent and amazed. What they were seeing was the manifestation of a righteous soul! Playtheus smiled, looking down on her loveliness. He groaned softly as he absorbed her light, closing his eyes to savor what he felt. There was no equal to her in the room. She alone was exceptional and rare. As he looked over the crowd, it was to his great delight that he alone possessed such a one. The music began to play once more, and all returned to their dance and conversation.

Talimus-qua-tam approached them, with Ba-nea at his arm. She was Playtheus' mother and "high companion" of Talimus-qua-tam. Sede felt his dark presence. It made her want to crawl some place inside herself and hide. Although she felt his evil, the light that streamed from her intensified, growing more brilliant as he approached. (For darkness does not overcome the light, but the light dispels darkness!)

"Ah, my son. This is your queen." As he circled her slowly, she felt his intrusive eyes penetrating her, searching the very depth of her being. "I'm pleased," he said.

Sede felt as though he wanted to plunder her soul. She shuddered, feeling totally exposed to his searching eyes.

Looking at Playtheus with great approval, he said, "My son, she is truly 'Tella-la-no-ah.' She will make you great. When you unite with her, you *will* be a "Mighty One," and we will plan your ceremony. At the set time, I will make the arrangements at Horizons Gate. I see the innocent, pure delight within her, and you'll do well to drink of her fully!" Sede quaked at his words. He bent near her neck and closed his eyes, deeply inhaling. As he inhaled, she felt him pull at some deep, hidden place within her. But in that same place, she felt her anger rise. And though she didn't speak the words out loud, an unspoken "No!" rose up within her.

He opened his eyes with a start! With a smirking smile, he said, "She actually resisted me, Playtheus!" Smiling once more, he continued, "You'll savor this one greatly!" He looked at Sede once more, knowing she was no match for him. He cared little to possess her for himself. He wanted his son exalted as a "Mighty One," and she was the key to make that happen. Of all his many sons, Playtheus was his praise among the 200.

As Talimus-qua-tam continued to talk with Playtheus, Ba-nea faced Sede, sliding her hands into hers. She looked intently into her eyes, and the tattoo on her forehead blazed a brilliant crystal blue. She, too, saw deep within her. Sede felt Ba-nea's eyes searching the recesses of her soul. They didn't plunder as Talimus-qua-tam's had. Smiling sweetly, Ba-nea whispered, "You are fair, my dear. Your innocence sends forth a most fragrant aroma!" As she continued to look into Sede's eyes, she gasped. "I know who you are!"

Sede searched her face, not understanding what was happening. But just as suddenly as she had seen Ba-nea's reaction, she now saw calm composure. A veil of secrecy now covered what she knew. Sede sensed her power and was in awe of her ability to control her emotions and knowledge. Smiling again, Ba-nea said, "I am happy for my son. You will give him what his heart yearns for: a love he does not yet understand." Sede was puzzled by what she meant. She spoke with such certainty, and her words seemed to be a mystery; a mystery that could be understood only by the wise. There was something about Ba-nea that made her suddenly feel safe, but still she knew she was part of this world—this strange and evil world of Atlantis.

Playtheus took Sede by the hand and led her about the room, stopping to converse with different Renown and their companions. He gloated with delight in the reactions of Apogee and Trihedron. Their response to Sede's beauty and presence was like one who saw the most desirable thing in the world but knew they could never have it. He could visibly see the same longing in Fathom and Castius. He knew they secretly wanted her and envied, too, that she was his. Playtheus scanned the room. Seeing Diatus, he nodded. The couples moved back, and the room cleared.

Taking Sede's hand, he led her to the middle of the floor. Nodding once more to Diatus, the music began. Sede felt a strange, yet wonderful thing as the melody permeated the air. The music seemed to embrace her, sending a tingling sensation through her. Wave after wave after wave of warm, soothing, invisible hands stroked her. What felt like smooth oil slowly flowed within her being. It was rapturous. Her whole body responded. She could feel herself weakening to its power. She wanted to resist but couldn't. The hypnotic music was holding her captive.

She felt a panic. How could she possible resist such power? It gripped her, leaving her vulnerable and emotionally bare. She then had a sudden thought. 'If I surrender to this power, I'll be lost!' In that very second, she made a decision. 'I'll embrace this power and use it against him. I feel myself weakening to it, but if I possess this power before it possesses me, perhaps I will endure.' Wave after wave of pleasure continued to sweep over her as the music embraced her. Closing her eyes, she felt the power that was pressing in on her, and she intentionally pulled it to herself, taking **it** captive! A low rumble of power exuded from her being. In that moment, *she* now possessed the power that had come against her.

Closing her eyes, she inhaled deeply, then released her breath in a smooth, controlled sigh. As Playtheus took his next breath, the sweet, strange fragrance that had come from her was inhaled by him. He staggered. Something had happened. He felt it instantly. As she slowly opened her eyes, she raised them to meet his. Her piercing look searched deep within his soul. She could see as Talimusqua-tam and Ba-nea had seen within her. She saw his greed for power and lust for pleasure, but she saw other things as well. He had places of vulnerability. She felt power rising in her, mounting in strength. She realized, '*I* have power over *him*!' Something inside her knew she could get whatever she wanted from him. This invisible, warm oil that had flowed through her had ignited something: a strength, a power, a fire! She knew she could have Playtheus at her bidding.

As Diatus' music had wooed Ka-sta's will, it had wooed hers. But instead of his music wooing Sede to surrender, she exalted her "will," and now this power had surrendered to her. She felt the strongest urge to consume Playtheus' being. 'What is this sudden, strange strength within me and this hungry desire to consume his essence? Something has happened to me. I've been changed!' Playtheus sensed something was happening in her too, for he felt himself weakening to her power. Surprised, but warmly eager, he responded, "Umm, my queen!"

As the music still surrounded them, embracing them with its beautiful, haunting melody, they stopped dancing and stood facing each other. She slowly, with commanding confidence, raised her hands to his face and drew him to herself as if to kiss him. Her eyes were focused on his lips. The music swirled around them, enveloping them, Diatus' sorcery permeating their very souls. Playtheus' moment for Sede's surrender had come. He held his breath, waiting. In the silence of the moment, he strained to hear her say, "I am yours." She drew him ever closer, as if to touch her lips to his. Whispering with her beautiful breath, she softly commanded, "Be *mine*." It was she who would possess him!

Like an unpredicted volcanic eruption, Playtheus exploded with ecstasy! Throwing his head back, he laughed with thrilling rapture. Every emotion in him was alive and sizzled. *She* had control over him. *She* was pursuing him, circling him as prey, lying in wait for *her* moment to strike. The room seemed to spin around him in indescribable wonder. For the first time in his life, he was being hunted as he had hunted his "innocents." How was it possible that any woman could possess such power, such control, especially over a Regal Renown? Within himself he knew, 'She is truly my equal…in every way.' She drew him close, pulling him to herself. He felt her heart pounding against his chest and her hands on the small of his back, pulling him tightly to herself. His body responded to hers, witnessing within himself that she had the power to excite him. His eyes widened, for it was he who was now vulnerable.

Mesmerized, he stepped out, leading them in dance. Moving in perfect harmony, they floated over the huge floor, her eyes piercing his and his heart pounding. He had been hunted. He had been captured. She wanted to consume him as he had wanted to consume her. Everything he had dreamed was coming true!

As they danced, the music continued to embrace them. They were both lost in a world of their own. One was no greater than the other, but both were equal in beauty, power, and strength. But then, ever so slightly, she felt a strange knowing beginning to come to her. It began at first as a slight impression and then a strong awareness. Something was breaking through the power of Diatus' sorcery. All the power she had over Playtheus was beginning to melt away. She was being released. She began to feel a great relief sweep through her. For though she had captured this power in a desperate attempt to survive, it had no true place within her heart. It was not part of the world she knew. This power was of the Nephilim world.

She looked about the room, wondering what or who was releasing her. There against a pillar she saw him. It was the Watcher from the Garden of Eden and the veranda at the country mansion. He stood there radiant, light streaming from his inmost being. It was only Ba-nea who saw him and bowed reverently at his feet. Those around him seemed unaware of his presence, their eyes cloaked by his command. As Playtheus turned her with the music, her eyes returned to the Watcher again and again. Her soul began to fill with the presence she knew so well. It was Yahweh. As if an explosion went off within her, Diatus' sorcery was blown away by Yahweh's presence! His presence was a million times greater in wonder and pleasure than Diatus' sorcery could ever be. At that moment, she felt like the most powerful person in the world. In His great love for her, Yahweh had watched over her and saved her when she was too weak to save herself.

As Playtheus continued to whirl her, Sede lost sight of the Watcher. He had disappeared, and Ba-nea now stood alone and still, her hands clasped to her heart. But even though he had disappeared, he had left Sede with a restored mind and soul. This whole place, with its beauty and splendor, was nothing more than a deception, beautiful on the outside but evil within. This was just as her father had told her about the "Evil One" himself; he comes as an angel of light, disguised in beauty but corrupting evil within.

They continued to dance as her composure calmed her. She began to think of her escape. She knew Playtheus was convinced she wanted him. He would be easy to convince that she was ready to surrender. When she returned to his mansion, she and Dollo would find their moment and flee. It was just a matter of waiting for the Watcher to make a way for their escape.

When the dance ended, Playtheus led Sede to the golden platform, his eyes filled with wonder at the power she had over him. Raising his voice, he began his declaration: "Tonight I present to my honored father and mother and all of you, my fellow Nephilim, my choice for 'high companion.' From this day on, I declare Sede-quete as my Queen!" He felt chills run through him as he spoke her name. Applause exploded throughout the room, and the air was electrified with shouts of praise. Raising her hand high in his, he began to escort her in a grand circle. As they circled the room, he looked upon her—so lovely, so beautiful. He continued to absorb her radiating light, making him pulsate with pleasure. Bending down, he whispered, "This night you shall be mine in every way. Tonight I become a 'Mighty One' through our union. I will drink of your innocence, and you in return, will be transformed before my very eyes. I will savor your lost innocence, and we will consume each other in endless pleasure!" He closed his eyes and groaned deeply.

She trembled at the evil within his groan. She realized how close she had come to being trapped by Diatus' power.

"You are trembling, my queen. Here, let me hold you!" He scooped her small body up in his powerful arms. The crowd went wild, cheering once more as he began to whirl her in delight. Bending his head back, he roared in victory, "Sede-quete. You are mine forever!"

Chapter 16

Escape from Atlantis

It was well into the night when the chariot pulled in front of Playtheus' mansion with the night beautiful with stars. Fifty servants lined the path to the entrance, holding high their silver torches and creating a flaming runway for the couple. Music lilted in the air from somewhere inside. Sede looked in wonder at the grandeur that awaited their arrival. He had anticipated his night, and he would have extravagance. "Here, let me help you down!" he said with excitement in his voice. Playtheus circled the chariot. What was this? He noticed Tailius bent forward, whispering to Sede. A frown pressed his eyebrows. With displeasure and insult, he rumbled, "Why are you speaking to my queen?"

Tailius trembled at his angry tone. "It was nothing, Master," he nervously muttered.

Playtheus' anger escalated, and he felt his neck get hot. "Well, it must have been something for you to be whispering!" He looked down on his arm where Tailius' tattoo still remained. The symbol of loyalty was visible but no amber glow. Confused by this change in his tattoo but too angry to reason, he turned to one of the servants holding a torch. "Take him to the wine cellar and lock him in. I'll deal with him in the morning!"

The servant stepped forward and grabbed his arm, leading him away. Sede realized his suspicions were aroused. "Now, Playtheus, he was just complimenting me on the beautiful gown you chose for me, that's all. Let's not ruin our night of magic and wonder."

His eyes widened as her power continued to sway him to her will. Smiling, he dismissed his anger and focused on her.

Sede, Seed of Eden

Stepping forward, he took her hand and, with a broad smile, ushered her down. "Come, my queen. See what I've prepared for us!" When the servant opened the great doors, Sede's eyes beheld the unexpected. Along the circular wall of the foyer were musicians. Their wondrous music was amplified by the vast height of the ceiling and the marble floor and walls. The music seemed to press into them from all sides; it was glorious. Servants stood intermittently between them. Slowly, they fanned silken sashes that reflected the warm glow from the chandelier light. The slow, rhythmic motion of the silken scarves and the warm romantic melody was most hypnotic.

Playtheus took her at the waist and drew her to himself. "Umm, Sede-quete. This is our night!" He drew her around the room, flowing to the music that pressed into them. When the music slowed to a stop, he beckoned her servants to come forward. "I've prepared a special gown for you, Sede-quete. Your servants will help you change and then bring you to our bridal chamber." A-thia and Fro-mos stepped forward and led her to her room.

On the bed lie a beautiful gown, much like the one she had seen on his dancers. It was transparent in sheerness, with diamonds dangling to cover the most private areas of the body. As A-thia lifted it, the light from the burning fireplace reflected off the diamonds. Looking up, Sede gasped, "Oh it's beautiful!" Slowly turning, she watched the flickering lights dance off the ceiling and walls, reflecting the brilliance of the diamonds. As she absorbed what she was seeing, it again occurred to her that what was beautiful on the outside only masked the evil that lie beneath. This beauty only masked Playtheus' intentions of seducing her heart. The torched runway to the mansion, the romantic environment in the foyer, and now this wondrous gown were all part of his subtle plan. Had it been with the right man, her heart would have been won.

A-thia nodded to Fro-mos to leave so she could begin her service to Sede. He bowed and backed away from the room. "Wait, Fro-mos. I want you to do something for me before I enter Master's presence."

Pleased that she would ask him for anything, he bowed and said, "How may I serve you?"

"Go to Playtheus' chamber and bring me the jeweled chest on his mantel. I will also need a quill and parchment. Don't let him know you've taken the chest…I wish to surprise him!" Happy to serve her, he bowed and left the room.

Turning to A-thia she said, "Come, help me find my way to the wine cellar. I wish to choose a special wine to serve Playtheus when we recline in our chamber." A-thia led her down the dimly lit corridor beneath the mansion. As they approached the door, she turned to A-thia. "I would like to choose the wine myself. Please wait at the entrance."

As A-thia walked back to the entrance, Sede removed the wooden plank that secured the door. A surprised Dollo greeted her. "How did you get here without being seen?"

"Fro-mos and A-thia know nothing about Playtheus' orders concerning you," she answered with confidence. "Stay here until I leave, and then wait for me by the fountain at the front entrance." Almost forgetting, Sede grabbed a bottle of wine and hurried down the corridor to meet A-thia.

By the time she and A-thia had returned to her room, Fro-mos had brought the jeweled chest and writing materials. Playtheus knew nothing of him entering his room for he was eagerly waiting for her in the bridal chamber. When Fro-mos closed the door, A-thia reached for her gown to dress her. "Not just yet, A-thia. I wish to write a love letter to Playtheus. You may dress me soon. Please wait outside my door. I wish to have privacy while I write."

When A-thia left, Sede quickly changed into her skins. A wonderful feeling swept over her as she felt them next to her skin once more. She ran her fingers over the Sethite symbol on her chest. "Yes…this is who I am," she whispered to herself. She slipped her seed necklace over her head, resting it once more next to her heart. Quickly, she wrote on the parchment and placed the scroll in the jeweled chest next to the gown. Slipping from the veranda, she climbed down the trellis and made her way to the mansion entrance.

There, Dollo crouched by the fountain, awaiting her arrival. A look of surprise swept over his face. No longer did he see a queen but a Sethite hunter. "Sede, you *are* a hunter!"

"Yes, brother, and both of us will have to use all our hunting skills to avoid being caught this night!" They quickly left, making their way through the dimly lit streets to the dock.

Meanwhile, Playtheus waited in the bridal chamber. Everything was to his approval. The musicians played softly in the darkened corner, and his dancers stood ready to be summoned. The room had a warm, yellow glow from the torches, which were positioned to allow the mood. He leaned back with his hands behind his neck, anticipating her arrival. "Umm," he sighed. Everything had come to its zenith: all the many years of dreaming of her; his patient wooing; her surprising transformation at the Pavilion; and the romantic reception at his mansion…all had brought him to this moment. Leaning forward, he chose a cluster of grapes from the tray. He thought of her as he ate them one at a time. 'Each of her innocent virtues are as these grapes, and I will savor the smoothness of every one!' Up until now, he had only sensed her virtues, but in a few moments, he would *know* them all.

As he finished his fruit, he looked about the room and wondered at her delay. Summoning Fro-mos, he sent him to see why she tarried. A-thia still stood outside Sede's door, waiting for her mistress to finish the letter. After their exchange at the door, Fro-mos returned and relayed A-thia's words. "Ah, she's putting her heart to pen. This pleases me!" Waiting no longer, he rose and eagerly walked the corridor to her door. He would delight in ushering her to their chamber himself.

A-thia bowed as he approached. "Master."

"I wish to see my queen," he said, looking at the closed door.

"Yes, Master, she's almost ready for you." Waiting no longer, he turned the handle. Confusion struck him when he entered the empty room. On the bed was her lovely gown and the chest from his mantel. What did this mean? Where was she? He looked quickly around the room; then, in a panic, he rushed to the veranda. Turning, he glared at A-thia. "Where is she?" he demanded.

A look of horror flashed from her face. "I don't know, Master. She asked me to wait outside her door as she wrote her letter."

His eyes swept the room once more and fell on the small chest resting next to her gown. In confusion of why it would be here instead of his mantel, he felt compelled to open it. With trembling hands, he slowly lifted the lid. Instead of her skins, he saw a scroll. He somehow knew it held a message for him. Walking to the fireplace for better light, he unrolled the parchment.

> To Playtheus,
>> The one whose dream has brought him to his own ruin. I, Sede-quete, take back my past and willfully possess my future. I belong to another. He is the great Shem, a Sethite and hunter among his kin. *He* will drink deeply of my innocence, and every last breath of who I am…I will freely give to *him*.
>
>> Sede,
>> Sethite hunter among her kin.
>> Child of the "Most High" God!

He heard the air exhale from his lungs. A feeling of ruin flooded over him, and he staggered on his feet. He couldn't believe this was happening. In horror, he looked at the letter and began to shake with anger. His rage rose and exploded. A great and mighty "NO!" erupted from his throat as he crumbled the letter in his fist, bringing it to his lips. He felt such pain. Hot tears filled his eyes. No one had ever done this to him before. No one had denied him anything. No one had ever had this kind of power over him—to trap him and to betray him. His mind was spinning. She was gone… Gone! All his plans for becoming a "Mighty One" were now dashed. His anger boiled once more. He both hated her and loved her. She had set her trap and waited for the right moment. He had been hunted and played. She had turned his world upside down. Yelling in confused rage he roared in anger once more, "NO!" The sound echoed through the empty rooms of his mansion, only echoing the great hollowness he felt. He left her room, tromping down the corridor and shouting for his servants.

* * *

Ham paced in his small room. This was the night of their escape, and still he hadn't discovered the way to the docks. He had carefully questioned two other servants about directions but neither knew the way. He was unable to search the city for himself for he was not allowed to leave Champion Hall. It would have to be Yahweh who made the way for him.

And that "way" was about to come. A messenger pounded on Castius' door. A search was under way. Playtheus' queen was missing, and a search party was being organized. Ham smiled. His escape was already in motion. Instead of finding the docks himself, he would be escorted there.

Relief filled his heart as he moved through the streets with the others. The days since his capture had been a nightmare. As they moved through the streets, his mind raced back to the day he was bought at the market. After leaving the arena with Castius, he and Jokta, another Sethite, sped toward Champion Hall. There they waited for Playtheus' arrival. Playtheus would have just enough time to service Castius before he reclined with his own newly purchased "innocents": Sede and Ka-sta. When he arrived, Castius and his Sethites were waiting. With a broad smile, he slapped Castius on the back and spouted, "Come, my brother, and the 'innocent' will satisfy!"

Inside, an opulent room surrounded them. Everything was made of purple, gold, and white marble. Lovely couches and chairs were arranged throughout the room, and from the dome ceiling, hung an elaborate gold chandelier casting beautiful light from the delicate stones that hung and swayed in the breeze. Recessed archways formed the perimeter of the room, where magnificent mural paintings depicted the most regal of the Renown. At their arms were their breathtaking companions. The artist had captured their essence, for greatness exuded from their image. A haunting melody filled the air as flutes and harps released their mystical notes. The silhouette of the musicians could be seen through the sheer curtains that hung from one of the recessed archways.

Playtheus ushered the Sethites to recline on gold velvet chairs. He asked each of them if they would surrender their innocent virtue, explaining the benefits to willing surrender. They would be the highest of servants and given honor within Castius' mansion. Through their service to him, they would remain under his care and protection for life. With willing surrender, they would have access to the city of Atlantis and all it had to offer.

If they unwillingly surrendered, their plight would be confinement to Champion Hall, serving him there. Here they would assist with breeding and giving care to his creations. Ham knew his own heart. He could never willingly give any part of himself to anyone but Yahweh. He may be a captive, but he still could choose refusal. He set his will against surrendering and hoped against hope that somehow he would find a way to escape this place and return to his family and kin.

With tears in his eyes, he responded to Playtheus, "I will not surrender what you're asking of me. You are going to take something from me I don't understand. But know this: You will never take what belongs to Yahweh!"

Castius and Playtheus blinked in surprise. Rarely did they hear such strength from a Sethite. A small smirk rose on Playtheus' face. "Fight me all you will; I still have the power to take your innocent virtue, and I will, even if you don't willingly surrender."

He looked at Jokta and mocked, "Any speeches from you?"

The trembling Sethite knew who was in control. He wanted nothing to do with breeding and working with strange creatures. In his village, he worked with parchments, teaching children the art of reading and writing. He saw no way he would ever return to his home. He had no home. It had been burned to the ground by Nephilim raiders. "I choose to freely give what you are asking of me. I surrender my virtue to serve you."

Playtheus smiled. He saw this over and over again with these Sethites. Some resisted; some didn't. In the end, their innocent virtues became his to give to whomsoever he chose. And so it was that day.

Before he began, he motioned for Castius to recline on a large couch. It looked as if it were made for royalty. Rich purple tapestry covered the well-padded surface, and elaborate carvings in gold crested the back of the couch as well as the legs. While the music moved and swirled around them, Playtheus spoke his words of divination. The words blended with the music and fell on them, penetrating their souls. He then leaned forward and inhaled deeply, drawing the misty, swirling light from Jokta and then Ham. He paused for a few seconds, savoring the sweetness of their virtues. He felt his own soul tremble with the purity and beauty that was now in him.

Standing over Castius, he then released their misty virtues as Castius deeply inhaled. He trembled with pleasure as he savored what he had now received from his new "innocents." Two bright amber tattoos materialized on his arm. One symbol read "Loyalty" and the other "Faithfulness." The effect was immediate. Playtheus smiled at the obvious. Castius was instantly enhanced, his masculinity pronounced with strength and compelling virility. The breeding tattoo of Castius appeared on both of his servants' foreheads. Ham felt the heat of it as it formed.

During the exchange, Playtheus saw within both Castius and his "innocents." With the power and knowledge his father had given him, he had the ability to see within the soul. It played out like a scene. He saw the reenactment of the secrets of their hearts—secrets that they themselves had hid from everyone. He saw Castius secretly meet with Diatus' companion, luring her to his embrace. He also saw his plans to seduce Apogee's companion. All Castius' secrets were laid bare before his knowing eyes.

For the mighty beings these Renowns were, this was the most vulnerable moment they had no control over. Playtheus had learned to respect this vulnerability for it was the one thing he could do to honor his fellow brothers. He knew that when he came to them for their services, they, too, would show him honor and respect. This was probably the greatest reason he was so highly regarded among them. They were aware he knew their most secret of secrets. The 200 knew too; that he alone was the catalyst that held the world of Atlantis together. Without his service, their beloved sons would not have the virtues and glory to be truly mighty in the earth. His service brought regal beauty, strength, and majesty. He was a "Prince" in the eyes of the 200, and for this reason, they welcomed his coming appointment as "Mighty One" in the earth.

Jokta's secrets, too, were laid bare. Playtheus saw him secretly take gold that wasn't his, hiding it in the ground within his hut. When the village sought to find the gold, he denied knowing anything about it. He had wrestled with the guilt of what he'd done, having deep remorse. He had failed to confess his wrong while his kin still lived, and now that they were gone, he had no way to make things right.

He saw Ham's jealousy of his older brother. This brother sat in the seat of honor beside his father at council meetings. The elders sought his opinion, while

Ham was not acknowledged. He envied that his brother would be the future "father of their people," whereas he would be but an elder. Playtheus watched another scene play out, when his brother was honored by visiting elders at their festival. Ham had stood at a distance and watched, feeling envy over the honor given to his brother and not him. But he saw too that he loved his brother. As the next scene appeared, he saw the reenactment of Ham's brother selflessly saving his life on a hunt, even in great peril to his own. 'Always these Sethites struggle with their conscience,' he thought. 'This is an aspect that refines their innocence. Once they resolve their guilt, their virtues are purified. Oh, how I love to see this played out within them.'

When Castius had recovered from his transfer of innocence, he stood to address his new servants and give them their new names. Ham he called Bromos, and Jokta he named Landros. Ham struggled to hold back his tears. Not only was he a captive and his virtue and innocence stolen, but he no longer owned his own name. He had instantly felt the change that had taken place within him. Something in him had been harnessed and his inner freedom stolen. And he was right, for it had.

In the days that followed, Ham saw the work of Castius. He *did* breed animals to humans and one species of animal to another. What was showcased at Champion Hall were his successes, but Ham saw his failures: distorted humans with strange animal parts left to suffer cruelly from the torment of knowing they had been altered. They had both the soul of a man and the nature of an animal residing within them. They cried out with moaning and groans, the inner turmoil of two opposing natures battling within. They knew no peace, day or night. Some never drew a breath of life, for they were stillborn. Some Sethite women had their wombs ripped open by ravenous creatures within them. All the dead were piled as trash in the caverns deep in the mountain. Their bodies were fed to savage beasts that were bred to sport for their arena games. Seeing all this and being forced to participate in it was like a nightmare—one he wished he could wake from.

He did have access to Castius' private room where he kept his parchments and maps. From journeys on his flying horse, Castius had developed detailed maps of the known world. He used these maps to aid traveling merchants and sailors, which he was pleased to do. This gave him recognition and acclaim with the 200 as well as his fellow Renown. On the maps, the port cities were marked with golden stars. He read the name of the largest star, located to the south on the mainland. It read Wadi-al-Jarf. It was in a region marked Aegyptus. Near the star were three curious triangles and several small figures. One of the figures was a crouched lion. It had the head of a man. Another figure had arms folded across the chest of a man but the head of a hawk. More breeding experiments he presumed. Both of these small figures faced the direction of the isle of Atlantis. As he studied the map he recognized the port city of Zadanim. He saw the distance between the island of Atlantis and Zadanim. It stretched far across the Great Sea.

He also saw the major inland caravan trails, connecting the known world. All the trails led to what looked like a great city. Its name was circled in red. It read: "City of Lights." Along this trail were small figures of statues too numerous to count. Studying the map closer, he calculated the Sethite regions of Estoploph, Agkib, and Makedaz. From their location, he saw the river that ran past his village. With longing, he ran his finger along the line that marked the river, estimating the location of Taasa-toka. It was the day he saw Sede and Dollo that hope was stirred within him of returning home. Since that day, it was all he thought about. He would see his father and mother again. He would be with his kin once more. These thoughts filled his mind while he followed the other servants to the dock. With anticipation, he watched for their signal.

Chapter 17

The Journey Home

Dollo knew his way to the docks. He had gone there many times to pick up goods for Playtheus. They crept through small back streets, crouching and hiding at any sound. The city was asleep, and very few moved about. They saw the occasional drunken Cainite sailor and a few patrolling Nephilim guards. Within an hour they arrived at the great arch where they would meet Ham. The "Golden Bird" was tied to the pier, waiting for dawn. It thrilled Sede to see the great ship. She knew it was her way back to Shem; back to her father; and back to the people she loved. "Look at it!" she whispered. "That's our way home!" Dollo smiled, feeling the same excitement.

Two huge giants slowly paced the wharf that led to the quiet ship. It seemed the crew had left to spend the night in the city. It was them they had seen, drunken and lying in the streets. While they crouched and waited, they debated how they would climb aboard the ship and where they might hide. They continued to wait another hour but saw no sign of Ham.

Finally, Dollo said, "Maybe something has happened, and he won't be coming."

"That's not possible. I *know* he'll come. The Watcher told me all three of us would escape this place and return home."

Dollo's eyes widened when she mentioned the Watcher. "You've seen a Watcher?!"

"Yes, Dollo. He comforted me when I was in distress and told me he'd make a way for us."

"I've never seen a Watcher, but a few of my village elders have. Yahweh had sent one to give us the word of the Lord and comfort us when we had to rebuild after a Cainite raid."

"Yes, that's what he did for me," she whispered. "His comfort and guidance is why we're here tonight."

They were suddenly interrupted by a mounting noise. It was growing louder and louder. Shouts echoed, and the light of torches lit the night sky with the flaming light. The guards left their post by the ramp and approached the crowd. They were looking for someone. Dollo looked at Sede in a fear. "I know it's Playtheus. He's looking for you and probably me too. Who else would have the influence to mount such a search?"

As the crowd seemed to multiply, they knew they had to find a better hiding place. From where they hid, they would be easily spotted. "Follow me, Sede; I know a secret chamber in the arch. We can hide there." Waiting for the right moment to run, he led her to the door and pulled the hidden latch. The stone door slowly opened and then closed behind them. A slit in the stone made it possible to see out but hard to see in. "This is a good place," he whispered. "We can see everything from here."

By now a crowd had assembled at the wharf and began searching the area. The order was given for servants to board the ship and turn it inside out. As torch lights moved past the stone door, Sede saw him. It was Playtheus. He looked anxious and angry. The sight of him made her tremble. "He looks out of control!" she said trembling.

"It'll be all right, Sede. We'll be safe here. Very few know of this secret place."

"How did you discover it?" she whispered, trying to calm herself.

"An old servant of Master showed me one day. He was my one and only friend in this place. As a boy, he played on this wharf when the arch was built. He died two years ago."

Sede sensed the sadness in his voice. Her compassion was stirred.... How dreadful would it be, being here as long as he had, and having only one friend? And then, to have him die? "I'm so thankful you'll see Zilla again," she said, trying to offer comfort.

He smiled as though reflecting on a memory. "Yes, my betrothed. She's the joy I live for."

Smiling at his comment, she peered through the slit once more. Hardly able to speak, she blurted, "I see him. It's Ham. He's with Castius' servants. They must have been called to help with the search."

"How can we let him know we're here?" he whispered. "I don't know, but we need to think of something."

The search continued for a half an hour, leaving nothing unturned. When Playtheus realized everything had been searched, he proclaimed with a loud voice, "We'll continue the search to the north part of the city. Follow me!" The noisy crowd turned and followed; his angry steps pounded the ground as he walked.

Sede suddenly remembered how they alerted Ham once before, when they hid in the tall grass near Zadanim. "I know how to get his attention." Putting her hands to her mouth, she gave their pack's signal call.

Ham froze in his tracks. He knew that sound. As the other servants continued to follow Playtheus, he crept to the side, hiding behind a statue. He waited until they were out of sight and then made his way to the stone arch. The only thing he knew was the familiar sound had come from this direction. He crept close to the wall, fearing the watchful eyes of the patrolling giants.

"Ham. Ham!" whispered Sede. "We're in here!" Ham followed the sound of her voice and then saw a stone door slowly open. Sede ran to him and grabbed his forearm, breathing in relief, "Ha-la-lah!" Broad smiles broke out on all their faces.

Dollo whispered, "We must find a way to board the ship and then find a good hiding place before the crew returns."

Sede had an idea. "Let's climb the anchor rope. That's how Shem and I boarded the ship we set on fire in Zadanim. The anchor will be on the backside of the ship. Let's go!"

All three crept to the water's edge and quietly swam to the rope, avoiding the guards. Climbing over the railing, they hid behind stacked barrels.

"We must go below," Dollo whispered. "We'll find a hiding place there." Waiting for the guards to turn, they opened the hatch and quickly made their way down. Barrels and boxes filled the space; small kegs of wine lined the wall, and large pieces of dried shosposcus meat hung from rows and rows of hocks. "This is great!" Dollo whispered with excitement. "We'll have food and drink for our voyage home."

Ham saw the large barrels and had an idea. "I think we should empty three barrels to hide in, just in case they search the ship once more. We'll have time to empty them before dawn." They found large pieces of leather shosposcus skins and began filling the center with grain from the barrels. Gathering the edges together, it made a crude bag to haul the grain up the steps and then poured over the railing. When they made their last trip up the stairs, the first light of dawn was beginning to glow from the east. Slowly, they closed the wooden lids that covered the barrels, concealing themselves inside. They had found their hiding place for the next two days.

Much commotion was heard overhead as the crew arrived and readied themselves to sail. Shouts and banging could be heard as more supplies were brought below. Soon the belly of the ship was packed. A loud horn blew, and the sound of footsteps softened as those above set sail. They were on their way at last. As morning turned to night, the stowaways remained hidden. In the dark womb of the barrels, each had time to think: about what they had experienced in the awful world of Atlantis, how it had touched them, and how it had changed them.

Dollo had been there five years. He had seen all kinds of Sethites come and go through Playtheus' mansion. He saw the terrible way Playtheus' power was used to change his people to profit the Renown. His old friend La-pheth, who had shown him the stone door in the arch, had died in his arms. His last words were of his childhood tribe and kin, and he still missed them in death. He had dreaded the thought that he would have the same fate: to die in a strange land, away from the ones he loved. But every day he had thought of Zilla. Thoughts of her were the only thing that kept his sanity. It was she who now gave him hope for a life after Atlantis. As each hour passed, it was an hour closer to seeing her. Yahweh had not forgotten him. Meeting Sede was proof of that. He had known deliverance from Playtheus' hold over his virtue, and now he was going to be a true Sethite once more. Oh, the freedom to be who he was created to be: a Sethite, an elder, a hunter among his kin, and husband to his beloved!

The Journey Home

Ham's thoughts brought him back to the market where he was bought by Castius. He had possessed his virtue and even robbed him of his name. He shuddered as he remembered all the bodies of the failed experiments. It was a horror to think of it once more. He could still remember the despair he felt thinking he would never see Shoda and his family again. When he saw Sede's face that day at Champion Hall, he knew they would somehow find a way home. Now it was happening. He was leaving—leaving all the confusion of Atlantis. Even his old torments of not being honored because of birth order were no longer paramount in his mind. For it would be better living unnoticed in his village than living a life in Atlantis. Oh, the joy of being with his family once more. The first thing he planned to do was ask permission to marry Shoda. Then he could have a fresh beginning and a new life with her.

And there was Sede, full of the memories: the fire in the tall grass of Zadanim, sailing to Atlantis, and the strange market where she was sold to Playtheus. Ka-sta, poor Ka-sta—forever changed. All those visits to Champion Hall, with the Renown's evil hunger for her—she shuddered recalling it. The children—oh, the children; her heart broke with just the memory. And then her close call with Playtheus' seduction and how Yahweh had given her the grace to resist him. She now understood the Watcher had been watching over her all the time: when Diatus' power had gripped her in the Pavilion, showing her how to flee the mansion last night, and finding a place to hide while Playtheus searched for them. Even now she saw his hand at work, providing them a hiding place and provisions for their journey home. She had been changed. She knew it. Even though Playtheus had not stolen her innocence, her innocence had been affected. She was no longer the sweet, innocent hunter whose only world was her father, Shem, and the village. Now she had the knowledge of a bigger world—a world that was utterly corrupt. She held to Dollo's words: 'These would be memories to forget.' It was her prayer, there in the darkness of the barrel, that somehow, with Yahweh's healing help, her simple life and heart would be restored.

By morning the three decided they no longer had to hide. No one had entered the lower deck, perhaps because it was too full. They would spend the last day of their voyage free to climb over the cargo and stretch their legs. As they shared their experiences with each other, they realized how they had been saved from danger, and even death, by the mysterious hand of the Watcher that now guided them home.

* * *

Playtheus had been up all night with the search party, trying to find her. When dawn broke over the city, he realized his searching was in vain. It was as if she had disappeared. He hadn't slept, and his emotions had been ripped to shreds. Exhausted, he collapsed on her bed. It was the one place that made him feel close to her. She had slept there for nearly a week—a brief time but, for him, an eternity of being alive. Looking around the room, he remembered the night he carried her here, the night he thought she would surrender. Pulling the furs to his face, he inhaled. The smell of her fragrance was still there. He could still remember the thrill he felt presenting her at the Pavilion and then the feeling of satisfaction in the bridal chamber knowing she would be his in minutes. But then, to find she was gone, reading that her love and life she would give to another…this was not his dream fulfilled. This was not his destiny's desire. She was to surrender her innocence to him. She was to give him the power to be a "Mighty One." He had wanted her for the power she would give him, but for the first time, he realized he loved her. She was his equal in every way. Her fire, her spirit were as fierce as his. Moaning, he sighed, "Oh Sede-quete, Sede-quete, I have to get you back!"

As the day wore on, his mood was flat. It was as if someone had sucked the life out of him. He didn't feel like eating but rather called for Polisha. Perhaps her "Purity of Heart" innocence would sooth him. She brought him temporary relief. The sweetness of her lost innocence calmed him, and her caress soothed him briefly. But deep down, he knew…no other woman could ever satisfy or be his Sede-quete. He had the thought to visit Toleshba once more. Perhaps she could help him find her.

He called for Tailius only to learn he had escaped as well. Summoning his chariot, Fro-mos took him to Toleshba. Again the door opened by itself, and he saw her compelling beauty. With knowing eyes, she waited for him to speak. "I need your help, Toleshba."

"Yes, I know. She's gone. And you…you want her back."

He was surprised she knew, but being so needy, he confessed, "Yes, I want her back!"

"The price you will pay…umm…it will be great. I require of you your new innocent. The 'Purity of Heart' there on your arm."

Playtheus looked down at the tattoo. It glowed as he thought of her. He remembered how he felt when his first 'Purity of Heart' was surrendered. He suffered, craving her loss. The void in him gnawed to be fulfilled. He knew he would feel Polisha's absence and again feel ravening hunger once more. She had been his "trophy," his praise among his brother Nephilim. But for Sede-quete, he would have surrendered them all, every last tattoo, if she had demanded them.

"I continue to enjoy the last 'Purity of Heart' you surrendered," she continued. "I find her most empowering. I wish this one to be my companion. This 'Purity of Heart' will be a delight to defile!"

He looked at her in all her coldness, realizing the depth of evil that existed in her heart. "She will give me great power with her innocence!" Her voice trailed off, leaving the impression that she knew more than what she had said.

Slowly lifting his arm, he surrendered Polisha. As Toleshba touched the tattoo, the absence of Polisha's innocence was felt immediately. Toleshba's face glowed with enhanced beauty, and a strengthening within her was immediately evident. His face darkened briefly, and he felt the void.

"Later I will send for my new trophy. Have her ready."

He felt the pang of hearing her refer to Polisha as her new "trophy," knowing *he* had given her that name. But she was no longer his.

"Now, your missing love!" she said with a snicker. She knew she had gotten the better deal from the bargain. He would get information, but she had gotten a soul. "Yes, your missing love; let's find her." Regaining composure from his surrender, he waited for her to reveal his queen.

"Come here to the fire," she motioned. He moved with her to a fire burning in the center of the room. It was contained in a large brass bowl. The flames were smooth as they rose in the air and crackled with a spark as they descended once more. "We'll see her in the flames," she said confidently. Holding her arms over the fire, she moved them in a slow, waving motion. The flames seared her skin, but no burns appeared. She felt no pain from the heat but rather smiled with satisfaction. She began singing a beautiful melody.

It was hauntingly compelling and stirred his soul. The words in the song were strange and unfamiliar to him. He knew that they each had their own language for working their spells. He had used his words on Ka-sta and Sede-quete. He knew the power they possessed. Watching her, he marveled at her abilities. She commanded such power, such control.

As she continued to sing, Playtheus began to see Sede-quete in the flames. She was with Tailius and Bromos. He remembered him from the transfer of his virtue to Castius. This was the Sethite that had shown a strong spirit of defiance. They were in an enclosed space: among barrels, wooden boxes, and other cargo. She looked so lovely and happy sitting there while they talked and laughed. He saw her in the skins she had taken from his jeweled chest. It changed his whole impression of her. He saw her for the hunter she was and sensed she had this whole different life he knew nothing about. It made him long to be a part of it. As he watched, the flames rose and fell, and the image changed to one above a ship looking down. It was the "Golden Bird" moving on the Great Sea. Its full white sails reflected off the deep blue of the sea, while seagulls called as they soared high above the mask. It looked so beautiful. A smile rose on his face as he looked at Toleshba. "I see her and know where this ship will sail. Toleshba, you've done well!"

"Yes, Playtheus, I know. I always do."

As he was leaving, she caught him by the shoulder. Her touch sent a cold and icy chill through him. When he faced her, she taunted him, "You know, Playtheus, we have something in common."

"Oh? What's that?" he questioned.

"We share the intimacy of knowing our 'Purity of Hearts'!"

He shuddered at her hungry coldness for the innocent. He saw her for the devouring she-wolf she was.

"Umm, the pleasure of having them is great, is it not?" she softly groaned. As he walked to his chariot, he shook her influence from him. He felt as though he might be devoured himself. Commanding Fro-mos, they made their way to Champion Hall. He wished to see Castius.

Champion Hall was again full of conversation with the pleasure seeking Renown enjoying the companionship of their lovely humans. When Playtheus entered, eager eyes met him, thinking he had brought them some new "delight" for their entertainment. Walking past them, he opened Castius' door. He found him helping a young man with wings, obviously one of his creations. Castius watched as he gently extended his wings and then waved and flapped them, rising from the floor and hovering midair.

Seeing Playtheus, he left him. "My brother, what can I do for you today?" He saw the urgency in his face.

"I continue the search for my queen and must borrow Pegasus."

"Oh brother, I share Pegasus with no one. But I do have Pergisus. You may use her. She is Pegasus' mare and will serve you well. Like Pegasus, she has the ability to perceive your thoughts, knowing your every wish." He led him to her beautiful cage. She was a magnificent chestnut mare, with wings matching the color of her coat. She whinnied as they approached. "See. She knows your thoughts already. She's eager to fly!"

Playtheus paused, remembering. "I have just come from Toleshba's and discovered your servant Bromos is with my queen. When I find her, I'll return him to you."

"I wondered where he was. His virtue has left me. I feel the grievous, gnawing absence."

"If I don't return with him, I'll help you replace him with another. Just bring one from the market, and the 'innocent' will again satisfy, my brother."

Standing on the large, extended balcony outside her cage, Playtheus swung his body and mounted Pergisus. She flexed her wings and raised her head, whinnying in the wind and rearing on her hind legs. She gently swooped over the city, while Playtheus felt the surge of freedom from the speed and the height at which she could fly. As they circled Champion Hall once more, far below Castius waved and became but a speck on the balcony as they flew away. She circled the canyon walls, flying over his mansion, then out to sea.

They flew over miles and miles of open water. To break the monotony, Pergisus occasionally swooped near the surface, skimming her hooves and sending small sprays of water shooting into the air. She whinnied softly, enjoying the freedom. Playtheus, too, felt great freedom in the open sky, with the wind blowing in his face. They flew for a long time, seeing only an occasional whale, their great backs rising and falling below the surface. But then he saw it! There it was, in the far distance, so beautiful with its white sails against the blue of the sea. Diving from the great height, they descended.

As they neared the ship, the stowaways heard sudden shouting and commotion overhead. "I wonder what's happening? We won't be landing until the morning!" Dollo said in a panic.

Excitedly, they stumbled over the barrels to peer through the portholes to see what those above had seen. High in the sky was a large flying horse with a Nephilim on its back. It was an amazing sight to see. Sede had seen Pegasus and knew it must be one of Castius' creatures. But why would someone be flying this far out to sea? Horror and dread struck her like lightening. She knew. Although she couldn't see his face, she knew who was riding on its back. It was Playtheus. Somehow he had found out where she was. Looking at the others with a white face, she spoke her fear. "He's found us!"

They reflected the same look of horror. "What are we going to do?" Her voice quivered, panic evident in her tone. "There's too much cargo on deck for him to land on the ship," assured Dollo. "He'll try to capture us at Zadanim." Through the portholes, they saw him fly east. "Yes, there. That's where he's going…Zadanim. He'll be waiting for us there."

They sat in silence, thinking of what they could possibly do. Water surrounded them everywhere, and Playtheus would be ready when they tried their escape at the dock. With the feeling of helplessness looming over them, the ship continued east, a fair wind blowing them ever closer to Zadanim.

The sun had set, and the sky had turned a restful dark. Only speckled stars and a crescent moon gave light. The ship cut through the silvery shine of the calm, smooth sea. Far, far into the distance, they saw the glow of Zadanim's lights. Sede felt a mounting panic rise within her and started to tremble.

"Sede, Sede, we'll think of something," Dollo said, seeing her distress. Ham grabbed her reassuringly around her shoulder and gave a comforting squeeze. "Yes, Sede, we haven't come all this way to be captured again."

Looking through the porthole, she watched as their ship cut through the water. It looked so peaceful in the reflected moonlight. As she thought of the water, she had a sudden thought. "I think we should swim to shore." Both men looked at her, knowing it was impossible.

"It's too far!" "We'd be too exhausted to reach the shore," they chimed, one right after the other.

"Not if we took those small wine barrels to float beside." She pointed to the small wine barrels stacked against the ship wall.

A broad grin broke out on Dollo's face, "You're right. That might work!"

Ham nodded in agreement.

"The crew is surely asleep. We could sneak on deck and over the ship's side!" she added. Smiling, they locked arms and spontaneously whispered with excitement, "Ha-la-lah!"

With adrenaline pumping through them, they grabbed a small wine barrel and moved slowly up the stairs as the boards beneath their feet creaked with each step. Dollo cracked the hatch door. The sleeping crew were sprawled over the deck. Motioning with his finger over his lips, he nodded for them to start. Each carried their barrel under their arm and tiptoed over the sweaty bodies. The only sound was their snoring interrupted by an occasional snort. When they reached the railing, they took a deep breath and dove into the water, releasing the barrels to float on the surface.

The noise startled the sleeping crew, who jumped to their feet and ran to the railing. Floating on the surface were three barrels. The captain woke with a start and yelled at those standing nearest the railing. "Why didn't you secure that cargo? We can't drop the sails for just a few barrels!" He cracked his whip, lashing at the startled crewmen. They scrambled and tripped over each other, scattering in every direction.

As the ship continued in the breeze, it moved farther away from the floating barrels. As they slowly brought their heads to the surface, it could no longer be seen in the moonlight. With excited but hushed voices, they sputtered, "Yes, it worked!" Laughing and holding onto each other's shoulders, they bobbed in the water. Sede playfully splashed them as she swam to grab her barrel. With the stars above them to guide them, they happily began the long swim to shore, stopping only to rest on the floating barrels. They would probably have to swim all night, but they were free and on their way home.

As the sun began to rise, they felt the current pulling them to shore. In the rolling, crashing waves, they were washed to shore. Struggling to stand, Sede shouted above the roar of the surf, "Oh, to have solid ground beneath me once more!"

The other two laughed while their bodies were tossed and rolled onto the beach. "Let's hide the barrels in case someone looks for us," Ham shouted above the surf. Quickly, they hid the barrels in the tall reeds that grew along the beach. "Let's find fresh water. The wine we've drank these last two days is disgusting!"

Sede and Dollo chuckled, "Yes, let's!"

Not far away they saw a rocky plateau and climbed to the top. From the ridge, they could see in every direction. To the east, they saw smoke rising from the city of Zadanim; the forest was to the west, and to the north was the Great Sea. To the south was the river. Ham smiled, remembering Castius' maps. "Let's follow the river. It will lead us home."

They looked at each other. "Home!" Yes, they *would* find it. They *would* be with their kin once more and see the faces of the ones they loved.

* * *

The sun was setting when Playtheus landed on the beach of Zadanim. Pergisus snorted in relief at the chance to rest, her shiny coat glistening wet with sweat. Patting her neck, he gave her words of praise. It had been a great ride for both of them. He had heard of Zadanim and knew it attracted the lowest of the low, being the farthest port of sea in the known world. From here, the great wilderness stretched inland. It was from this wilderness that the Nephilim raided, finding helpless villages to plunder.

Zadanim was known to be the capital city of the Cainite people and a major outpost for the Nephilim Hagonoths. Atlantis' influence was not evident, for it was primitive in architecture and customs. It had a temple, market, council hall, and sprawling suburbs for both Cainites and Hagonoths. All of the one story buildings were of plaster and painted red, signifying their great love for blood. It was a culture rooted in sacrifice, blood-letting, and unrestrained eroticism. Only the temple rose high above the rest of the city and showed artistry and reflected the semblance of some kind of culture. It wouldn't be a city he would have chosen to enter, but this is where he would find his queen. He would tolerate their hospitality until the ship arrived in a few hours and then leave with her.

The people of the city ran to see this wondrous sight: a flying horse and a Regal Renown. They were accustomed to the Nephilim Hagonoths, rarely seeing a Renown. The leading elder, Daagus, greeted Playtheus, thinking him to be a god flying from the famed "City of Lights," the city of their gods. With great pomp, they welcomed him. Strange music filled the air as the crowd threw flowers and bowed before him in the streets. Their wild behavior at just the sight of him was alarming. On several occasions, Daagus used his scepter to beat back Cainites crawling to kiss Playtheus' feet. With pride, Daagus gave him a tour of the city. He was shown the port, the marketplace, and the great temple. It was in the temple that Playtheus discerned what the Cainites most valued.

The temple interior was surprisingly magnificent in architecture, unlike its outer appearance. The altar was inlaid with gold and jewels, with thirteen steps leading to the sacrifice platform. Symbols of the gods were engraved on the pillars that surrounded the room. It was here they offered their sacrifices to the gods. "It is my pleasure to show you our most sacred place!" Daagus spouted. With much pride, he waved his hand outward. "Here we honor your father and the other mighty angels. Our culture is a culture of pleasure, pain, blood, and fertility. All our maidens must prove their fertility before they are given in marriage. Our priests impregnate them, and after they have proven their fertility by giving birth, they are then allowed to marry their hopeful husbands. Their newborns are offered upon this magnificent altar to the gods, with the hope that they will bless them with many children and long life. We Cainites offer all our firstborn to the gods!"

As Playtheus listened, a priest brought a baby forward to be offered. "Would you like to witness one of our sacrifices?" he asked, hoping to please Playtheus. Looking at the baby, Playtheus was appalled at such a waste. This child could have been used for its innocence instead of wastefully offered by these barbaric people. "I believe I would much rather feast with you," he said, hoping to rest and eat rather than watching them spill blood.

Daagus waved his hand forward to usher him through the streets to the council hall. By now all the elders had gathered, along with the most influential and elite among them. They sat at long feasting tables, awaiting his arrival. They wore their finest furs, jewels, and feathers. On their foreheads were tattooed the symbol of the god of their choice. When he entered the room, they all reverently stood and bowed. An exquisite gold crown was handed to Daagus, who bowed and did obeisance, placing it on Playtheus' head.

As they ate, Daagus called for the maidens to dance. From their elevated position, Playtheus and the feasting elite could see the dancers enter the great floor beneath them. Fifty maidens excitedly took their pose, waiting for the drums to begin. The only clothing they wore was a skirt of bones dangling from a leather belt around the waist. Their bodies were completely covered with paint in shades of yellow, red, orange, and blue. Some wore head dresses of feathers and others the horns of beasts. The light from the torches made their shiny bodies glisten in the light.

As the drums began, the dancers moved in perfect unison. Their every raising of the hand, bending of the knee, and turning of the head was masterfully executed. It surprised Playtheus. He watched, intrigued by their abilities. They formed different designs, clustering in groups that moved as if the designs were alive. With the magic that surrounded them and the combination of colored paint, their movements looked as though they were rising and falling flames responding to the wind. Deep-sounding drums now joined with the softer drums. The depth of sound carried a magic Playtheus could feel. He thought of Diatus, knowing that certain sounds have a power of their own.

The Journey Home

The dancers continued in precise unity of movement. They were amazing in their ability to express not only with their bodies, but with their sounds as well. They released groans and sighs at just the right time. Playtheus felt himself respond, making him shudder with desire. Deeper and deeper the drums beat as their movement kept step with the quickening beat. Their groans grew louder and louder. Drawing small daggers from their skirt of bones they slashed their forearm and the blood flowed. They exhaled with trembling sighs. It made Playtheus' heart pound with desire. He was being drawn into their magic. Fully aware of what was happening, he knew the words that broke a spell and spoke them. Immediately he felt the magic break from him. He was not here for pleasure, but to retrieve his queen.

With his mind now clear, he saw the purpose of their blood-letting. As if it sounded like one voice, the dancers spoke enchanted words in perfect union and enunciation. Demons began to rise from the earth, hovering around them, caressing them, and savoring their blood. The feasting Cainites responded in wild frenzy, charging the air with thrilling expectation. They began ripping their robes and furs off themselves, joining the maidens on the floor below. They cut their flesh and entreated the pleasure of the demons. It was a mayhem of noise and confusion; Playtheus was sickened by what he saw. This was the reason he wanted nothing to do with the Cainites. They were all like this, defiled and utterly disgusting. They had no place in his city, in his culture, or in his world. He could stand no more. He pulled Daagus aside and demanded they go to the dock.

When they arrived at the beach, he saw the "Golden Bird" gliding toward the dock. Playtheus gave the order that when the ship docked it was not to be unloaded until everything was searched top to bottom. He would oversee the details. The ship was tied off, and Daagus' servants ran aboard searching every inch of the ship. As Playtheus stood on deck, word came from below: Three large barrels had been found empty of grain but no stowaways. After questioning the captain, he was told the only strange thing that happened during their voyage was three barrels that had fallen overboard. He hadn't seen any stowaways.

Playtheus was furious. How could this be? He had seen Sede-quete in the flames at Toleshba's. He had seen the "Golden Bird." He ached to look upon her face once more, to see the softness in her eyes, and to smell the fragrance of her skin. The absence of Polisha's innocence was gnawing at him too. Had he given her up for nothing? Had Toleshba played some wicked trick on him? He had been there since nightfall, and now the sun was beginning to rise. He could hear the city in the distance, still wild with their pleasure and pain. He walked along the beach and looked to the horizon, trying to clear his head. Taking the gold crown from his head, he tossed it in the sea. She had escaped again. He considered what the captain had said about the three barrels that had fallen overboard. Did they escape with the barrels? Did they swim to shore?

Mounting Pergisus, they took flight. He would follow the shoreline, flying high. Surely he would see them from above. He searched all that morning, flying over the beach and grassy marshes. As he continued to fly, he saw something far below. Dismounting, he discovered the small barrels and wondered if they could be theirs. He searched for footprints and found them. There they were. He bent down to see three sets of prints. When he saw Sede-quete's small footprints, tears filled his eyes. He saw where she had pushed herself from the ground to stand. He bent and lovingly touched it with his fingers. He ached to hold her in his arms once more, and hope filled his heart of finding her. He followed their tracks to the rocky ridge but lost their trail on the stony surface. Flying inland, he hoped to see them from his high vantage point. But as the day drew to an end, he realized he wasn't going to find them. He knew he had to return to Atlantis. Searching from the air would not be the way he would find her. He had been awake for three days, and his body could hardly stand the need to be satisfied by an "innocent."

Polisha was gone when he returned to his mansion. Toleshba had summoned her, and she was now hers. He called for his dancers, and their beauty and lack of modesty momentarily refreshed him. He savored them far above what he had seen and felt from the Cainite dancers. He would surround himself with the beauty and pleasures of his world and forget for a brief moment his pain for Sede-quete. Tomorrow he would go to the market and buy another "Purity of Heart" Sethite. He would not go another day without one. By the end of the evening, he would woo her and find the satisfaction his Nephilim cravings were screaming for. Finding his queen would have to come another way, without Toleshba's help. She had proven a grave mistake. Although she helped him see Sede-quete in the flames, what he had gotten was not worth the price he had paid.

Chapter 18

A Pledge Is Made

A sense of excitement filled the village. The day of the wedding had come. Although Shoda and Japheth had agreed to marry, they had not yet spoken to each other. That time had now come. Noah and Gruetat made arrangements for Japheth and Shoda to meet before the wedding, where they would exchange their intimate pledge before sharing it with family and kin. Under the great oak outside the village, in quiet and solitude, Japheth approached Shoda. Extending his hands to hers, she willingly took them and said, "Brother and friend." She looked intently into his eyes and continued, "I had resolved to see you as my dear Sethite brother and friend, but now I ask my heart, 'Can you be more to me? Can I find a place in my heart to call you husband?' In my grief for Ham and the love I felt for him, I search for a place for you. Help me find a place for you in my heart."

Japheth drew her close and said, "My sister, my friend. I, too, saw you as family and have not yet considered the feelings of love for a wife, knowing Ne-el was not of age for love. I don't have the conflict you now feel, for I know you were prepared to love my brother with your whole heart. With all that is in me, I pledge myself to you, Shoda—to learn to love you and cherish you always. I give you the hope and promise of love. Will you accept this pledge and believe that I can and will love you?"

With tears in her eyes, she responded, "Yes, Japheth, I receive your pledge and believe you will love me. I embrace you, brother and friend, as my husband. And I give my pledge to you to learn to love and respect you. I believe I will see my love grow for you, and we will have a blessed life together. Will you accept my pledge?"

"Yes, Shoda. I accept your pledge." As they stood looking into each other's eyes, a special bond settled within them. They promised their love to one another with the belief that it would grow and be blessed of Yahweh. They would honor their dead but would live for each other, believing love would grow between them.

Shoda was radiant as her father led her toward Japheth. He stood waiting by his father. Lovingly, Gruetat placed her hand into Japheth's. A peaceful, gentle presence surrounded them. Yahweh was near.... Mersta was misty eyed as she beheld the beautiful woman her daughter had become and reviewed her young life in memory. She was such a tender child, sensitive yet having a strength Mersta marveled at. Through her young years, she saw evidence of the strong leader she would someday become and consented when she desired to be a hunter/warrior. Even among her sisters she took the role of leadership, mentoring them with all she had learned from Tolmaka's counsel and the life lessons she had learned working with her pack. And now here she was, exchanging vows with a wonderful young man she would share life's journey with. When they finished their vows, Noah pronounced his blessing over them. To his utter amazement, the glory cloud descended. He gasped, for never in all his years had he witnessed Yahweh's glory on a union. Truly this marriage was being marked as unique.

That evening as the feasting came to an end, Gruetat led the way to the wedding tent he had prepared for them outside the village wall. They would spend their time alone, secluded from others. The Sethites honored the new-lywed with days of seclusion, giving them this special time apart. Singing as he went, Gruetat sang "The Father's Love Song," the song all Sethite fathers sang to their daughters on their wedding night. He honored her not only as his beloved daughter but now as a godly Sethite woman and wife. She would carry on the love he had invested in her, passing it to the next generation that would come from their blessed union.

When they arrived at the door of the tent, Gruetat kissed her sweetly on the cheek and bid her goodnight. Placing his hand on Japheth's shoulder, he said, "Be blessed, my son, for a bright and glorious life awaits you as Yahweh unfolds what He has ordained."

A Pledge Is Made

When the light of his lamp grew dim and his song could no longer be heard, Japheth turned to Shoda. "Come and rest in my arms. Let us find a quiet moment for our hearts to embrace this new beginning."

They settled on the pillows and furs as the quiet night surrounded them. He then gave her the words of his innocent heart: "Although we have the right to unite this night as man and wife, I want to wait until we both desire each other. For I discern that Yahweh has a great blessing in store for us. Not just because we consented to marry for Ham's sake but because our hearts desire to love one another in purity and truth." With tears in her eyes, she saw the strong and honorable man Japheth really was and sensed a depth she had never seen before. She was prepared to share herself with him, in honor of her vows, but now she saw that what they would share would come from the love they would find together. "Thank you, Japheth that you care about our hearts being ready for love and not just the act of honoring the dead. This is the first step of love between us. Tonight I begin my love for you."

As they lay in each other's arms, they fell asleep, overwhelmed by the change in both their lives. Love was born in them that night, and where it began was in Japheth's honor and respect for her.

* * *

Tolmaka had mourned and celebrated with the village honoring the life of his daughter and Ham. But even though he celebrated Sede's life, he longed to hear her voice and once more hear her call him "Abba." He had seen Shoda and Japheth marry that day and knew his beloved daughter would never know the joy of marriage. Hot tears of pain for her loss filled his eyes as he grieved once more. As he pondered her precious life, he began to remember what Yahweh had told her. She would bear the seed that would be in the lineage of the "Promised One." The Watcher in the Cave of Treasures had told him that she should be joined with Shem in marriage. He suddenly stood to his feet. He heard his own mouth say, "No! She cannot be dead. Yahweh has given His word and promise to her!" Hope rose within him, and a great peace flooded his soul.

Making his way through the dark village, he knocked on Noah's door. Shem's footsteps could be heard as he sleepily greeted him. "Come, Shem, we must talk!"

Shaking sleep from himself, he walked with Tolmaka. As Shem listened to Tolmaka's reasoning, his spirit leapt within. He, too, now believed that Sede still lived. "Yes, Tolmaka, I believe Yahweh's words will be fulfilled. Wherever she is, I believe she will return to us. As Shoda and Japheth married today, I, too, will marry your daughter and call you my father."

Tolmaka grabbed his shoulder. "Yes, you are my son. We'll leave in the morning and begin our search at the burnt shoreline of Zadanim. I know when we find Sede, we'll find Ham as well!"

Early in the morning, Shem and Tolmaka left for Zadanim, not knowing what they would find but believing Yahweh would lead them. They passed the bones of what remained from the stampede and the abandoned camp of the Sethite captives. As the day turned to night, they knew they would have to make camp. "We must find water for our skins are nearly empty. The river isn't far from here. It's there we'll make camp." They found a site nestled deep within the trees and speared a dworta drinking at the riverbank. Reclining near the fire, Tolmaka and Shem encouraged each other while their game slowly roasted on the crude spit.

Suddenly, they heard a twig snap. Tolmaka darted a cautious look at Shem and whispered, "Take cover and keep low." Backing into the surrounding bush, they hid from the approaching danger.

With stealth, two dark figures approached the perimeter of the camp and crouched by a tree. "Circle left," one whispered, "I'll go right." Each moved quietly as they circled the camp. When they met each other by the same tree, they agreed it was safe and stepped forward. Tolmaka and Shem lunged forward with spears in hand, pressing the tips against the intruders' backs. They could feel the sharp points piercing through their robes. Just then, they heard someone else say, "Drop it. Both of you!"

Tolmaka and Shem dropped their spears and turned, recognizing the voice. It was Sede! "Sede…it's you!" Everyone was in a state of shock, each not believing what they saw. Tolmaka and Shem reached forward, pulling her to themselves, hugging her, and crying like young boys. "Oh, Sede, Sede. You're alive. You're alive!"

Ham and Dollo were speechless as they turned around to see what was happening. Dollo looked at Ham in confusion. He didn't know who these two men were that held Sede.

She spoke first. "Dollo, I would like you to meet my father and Shem, my betrothed." With broad smiles, they clasped each other's forearms in greeting: "Ha-la-lah."

Shem then grabbed his brother and embraced him in his strong arms. "Oh Ham, this is nothing more than the hand of Yahweh. You're both alive!"

Far into the night they told of their experiences as captives, stopping only to eat more dworta and throw more wood on the fire. Sede shared about the Renown Nephilim that had bought her and the great evil she had seen in Atlantis. She told how their people were used for their innocence and turned into servants and slaves. "All of Enoch's writings are true," she said. "The evil 200 live, and we've seen their sons, both brutish giants and refined Renown." Tolmaka and Shem listened in wonder. She held Shem's hand as she told him about how she thought of him during her captivity and longed to return. With her other hand, she held her father's and told him how she longed to hear his voice once more and feel his loving arms around her. Tolmaka began to softly cry, realizing Yahweh had kept her safe against all that had risen against her. He had found a way to bring her back to them.

Ham told of his experiences as a servant and how Castius defied Yahweh by corrupting the seed of creation. And Dollo shared his five years of captivity, telling stories even Sede and Ham marveled at. Above all that he shared, he was most grateful that Yahweh had brought Sede into his life, for now he would be with Zilla, his beloved.

As they began to settle next to the fire, Tolmaka called Sede to his side. "We must talk, my daughter."

As she sat next to him, he shared with her his experience in the Cave of Treasures and what the Watcher had spoken. It was the Watcher who had instructed him concerning her marriage to Shem, and it was now time to see it come to pass.

"Yes, father, I'm ready to marry. While I was held captive, I realized that I am ready to start a life with Shem. I look forward to seeing Yahweh's word fulfilled in our lives. I want to be a wife and mother."

Tolmaka opened his arms for her, and she slid close, next to his heart. "Oh daughter, I love you so…."

She felt his love as he wrapped his arms around her. How glad she was for this time with him. She sensed that after this night, her life would begin with Shem.

They both settled down near the others, Sede lying between her father and Shem. For the first time since her capture, she felt safe. Putting her hand on her father's back, she whispered, "Goodnight, Abba."

Tears filled his eyes hearing her call him Abba once more. It had been the longing of his heart to hear those words.

Turning to Shem, her eyes searched his face. Ever so tenderly, he brushed her hair from her forehead. With a soft and loving tone, he whispered, "Goodnight, my fair one; you are mine once more."

She moved into his open arms, resting her head on his chest. His heartbeat was so comforting, his strong arms so safe. 'This is the heartbeat I've longed to hear,' she thought. 'These are the arms I've longed to hold me. I'm home at last.'

As morning broke, Shem suddenly remembered that Shoda and Japheth had married believing Ham had died. "I must tell him, Tolmaka, to give him time to prepare his heart before we return to the village. We'll follow a short distance from you."

Sede turned to see Ham crying while Shem held his shoulder. "What's happening, Father?"

"We thought you had both perished in the fire of Zadanim. Our village mourned for three days and then celebrated your lives. According to Sethite custom, Ham was to be honored in death, so Shoda and Japheth agreed to marry and bear seed in his name. Shoda and Japheth now celebrate their union in the wedding tent. They are man and wife."

"Oh Father. Shoda and Japheth are married?! My friend is a bride?!" Her mind was awhirl, "Oh Ham… his heart must be broken," and she looked behind her once more at Ham. Tolmaka listened as she tried to make sense of what he had just told her.

"Well, Daughter, they married to honor him. I'm sure he doesn't see that right now, but that was their desire…to honor him. Noah discussed the 'custom of honoring the dead' with the council. Shem and Japheth had the choice to marry Shoda. Shem's grief was too great for you. He couldn't."

She looked back at Shem, wondering about what he had suffered thinking she was dead. She remembered how she had felt when she hung in the Nephilim net, thinking he might have died in the fire.

"He loves you dearly, you know." Searching his face, she sensed he knew more than what he was saying. "He was willing to live life without a wife if he couldn't have you, Sede." He smiled lovingly as he watched her reaction. "I'm glad he's to be my son. I know of no other man I would trust to love and care for you. I thank Yahweh for him." She squeezed his hand and sighed in relief. With all he had said, and amidst all these changes, it was so very good to be home again.

* * *

Japheth and Shoda woke early that morning. "I have an idea, Shoda. Let's pack our things and journey into the mountains. There we can spend time in the forest we love."

She smiled. "Yes, I would like that!"

They packed their things and followed the deer trail to the plateau. From there, they began their ascent up the mountain. It was a joy to hunt as one, finding food for the evening, making camp together, and getting to know each other in a new and wonderful way. That evening as they sat around the fire, they both sensed a presence. It was wonderfully familiar. They had felt this presence when the glory cloud descended at their wedding. It was the loving presence of Yahweh. "Oh Japheth, I feel His wonderful presence, don't you?"

"Yes, I do. Come, my wife. Let's kneel and give thanks for the gift of His presence and our new lives together." As they knelt in their innocence, they spoke their thanksgiving out loud. As they continued to speak, something truly wonderful began to happen. They began to sing their words instead of speaking them. They seemed to know the melody and simply surrendered as the words flowed from their hearts. "Yahweh, what a wonder you are to surround us with your presence. I sense the future you have planned for us and that it is just now beginning. We offer ourselves to you. Use our lives to bring you glory. We worship you in the midst of your holy presence!" After they had sung their words of love to Yahweh, they held each other, knowing their worship had become a song of praise.

While they closed their eyes and were lost in the moment, a Watcher materialized before them. When they looked up, they saw him! Startled, they held each other. They had never seen an angel before. "Don't be afraid, children. Yahweh has sent me."

As he spoke, they felt love and comfort enfold them. With wonder and awe, they watched as the Watcher raised his palms, bidding them to rise and stand before him. "Yahweh has seen the gift of surrender you have given and your heart of worship. He has sent me to bless you." He stepped toward them; they felt weakened and began to collapse in his mighty presence. He touched their shoulders, and they were instantly strengthened. Placing his hands on each of their heads, he said, "May Yahweh bless you and keep you. May His countenance rise upon you and give you peace."

They felt warm, liquid love flow from his hands through their bodies. Tears rolled down their checks, for never had they felt what they were now feeling. Heaven and earth had touched. The Watcher lifted his hands and took a step back. He continued his message: "Yahweh not only wanted to bless you, children, but He also wants to give you this warning. The time is coming when the whole earth will be filled with violence, and all will corrupt themselves. He has told you so that you will be strong in the face of it. Obey your father in all he says to do. Yahweh has given him His word for the future. Peace be to you now. Grow in love for each other!" He gently blew the breath of heaven upon them, and they felt the beauty of holiness. He paused and smiled, radiating a pure, soft light. Like a mist, he then disappeared, evaporating into thin air.

Japheth and Shoda were shocked and looked at each other in wonder. They staggered to sit down as they held each other from falling. They sat in silence for a long time, trying to take in what had happened. Finally, Japheth leaned his forehead to touch hers. "My wife, love for you will grow as he has said. This night I set my heart to love you. You are *my* blessing!"

"And I set my love upon you, my husband. You are *my* blessing." They slowly kissed a sweet and loving kiss…their first kiss.

Chapter 19

Nersha

Playtheus had found temporary satisfaction with another "Purity of Heart." Her innocence had been smoothly inhaled, and he thought perhaps her comfort was what he needed. Similar to Polisha, she had been pure in heart but transformed, a totally changed woman. He tried filling the emptiness with many new "innocents" only to find they lacked "Tella-la-no-ah." He stopped going to Champion Hall because he was shamed by the Renowns' questions about his high companion. All that made him a proud Renown had been brought low. For the first time in his life, he had been humbled. It had been a week, and still he remained in his mansion, sulking and depressed. "I must find her," he groaned. "I'll seek Father for help." Summoning his chariot, he prepared for the long journey to "Horizon's Gate": the mountain retreat of the Mighty 200. There his father lived with his mother and his many concubines in their mansions surrounding his kingdom. Surely his father would assist him for his passion was to see his son named a "Mighty One" among the 200, and Sede-quete was the key.

He journeyed three days with his servants and arrived at the portal, guarded by the beasts of Arnon. Grotesque, they were fierce in appearance, having two heads and razor spikes protruding from their hides. They were greenish red, and fire blazed from their nostrils. As he approached, he cried out the commandment: "To-zistro-zolis!" Bowing their heads in submission, the beasts backed away, their ancient chains rattling as they moved. It had been a long time since he had visited his childhood home. It would be a comfort to be there once more.

Ba-nea welcomed him with open arms and a beautiful smile. "My son, how good to see you!"

"Mother, it is good to see you as well."

Ba-nea was fair beyond words. Her beauty was even more remarkable than Toleshba's. It held those who saw her spellbound for all the wives of the 200 drank the draught of "Estan-knoh." It enhanced their beauty and prowess, giving them a mysterious air. He had recognized her powerful influence over his father even as a child. "What brings you, my son?" She already knew but wanted him to reveal his heart to her.

"My 'Tella-la-no-ah' has fled, and I need Father's help to find her. Is he here?"

"Yes dear. I will call for him." Closing her eyes, she sent her request. She could communicate with thoughts, sending them to whom she pleased. "He will be here soon," she said with a loving smile. She raised her hand to his face and gently stroked his cheek. "Not to worry, your father will help you. He has high ambitions for you, you know." She smiled once more, indicating she knew more than what she was revealing. "Ah, here he comes now!"

Within just a few seconds, Talimus-qua-tam appeared in the doorway. Playtheus looked in wonder at his mother. Her power was magnificent.

"Ba-nea, you have welcomed our son…good!" Stepping forward, he gripped his son's shoulder in welcome. "Son, I sense your burdened heart. Come. We will walk." Before he left, he paused before Ba-nea. As if drinking in some unseen pleasure, he drew on the light she was emitting. A low rumble resounded, and he softly groaned. Raising her hand to his lips, he kissed her palm while the tattoo on his forehead burned red hot. "My wife, you are most fair!"

"Yes, I know," she responded with a knowing smile. Her eyes flashed with power, and the tattoo on her forehead glistened a brilliant crystal blue. Playtheus sensed this was some game they played between themselves. He had learned many things observing their ways. He perceived their mysterious intimacy, and it made him desirous to pursue his own.

He beckoned his son, "Come, let us walk."

Playtheus followed his father to the mansion gardens. Music filled the air, and beauty surrounded them. The grounds were vast. The surrounding hills were spotted with the beautiful mansions of his concubines, and below them lay the sculpted garden grounds. Trees that the earth has never seen lined the perimeter. The tall crystal trees moved in the breeze, their delicate leaves brushing against each other and vibrating their own distinct sound. A beautiful harmony filled the air as they swayed in the warm breeze. Their colors were of amber, emerald, sapphire, and crystal clear diamond, each glowing with colored light from within. One particular tree was made of black onyx and vibrated only when Talimus-qua-tam spoke. Its melody sent forth a deep and powerful sound. There were animals that graciously strolled the grounds, never seen by humans. Fanning their wings, these majestic and graceful creatures sent forth an aroma that filled the air with a scent that stimulated every cell of the body. Playtheus felt better just being in this familiar place. As they walked together, Talimus-qua-tam exuded great power that Playtheus eagerly absorbed, comforting his troubled heart.

"Father, my high companion has fled, returning to her village. I tried to find her through Toleshba and even surrendered one of my innocents as payment, but it was all for nothing. She tricked me."

"I'm not surprised, my son, for such is the way of witches. I'm pleased your mother never fell to the temptation of becoming one. She is rare among our wives, a 'Tella-la-no-ah' herself. She has kept many of her virtues hidden, even from me. Her powers are an envy among the wives and the admiration of my fellow 200. I chose her well."

Playtheus discerned the power she had over his father. He had seen this same quality in Sede-quete: a reserve; a strength; a part of herself she kept hidden within. He had always been curious why his mother was the only wife of the 200 that glowed crystal blue from her forehead tattoo and not green as the others. It was because she alone had unwillingly surrendered to a fallen angel, and her "Tella-la-no-ah" had given her the power to conceal her virtues.

Bringing his thoughts back to his own needs he searched his father's face.

"You will still become a 'Mighty One' my son. I have a plan."

"Tell me of this plan, Father."

"This plan is a female."

Playtheus' curiosity was aroused. "Tell me of this female. Is it Sede-quete?"

"No, but you will use this female to find her."

"Who is she?"

"I will show you. She's here now."

He clapped his hands, and several servants ushered a stunning female to stand solitary before them. He was in awe of what he saw. She was beautiful beyond description, and…she was a Nephilim. She stood as tall as he, and her proportions were perfection. Her gown accentuated the curvature of her tiny waist and gracefully draped from her shoulders, revealing her beautiful skin. Her light golden hair cascaded to her waist, and her eyes sparkled a sea green. They held him captive as he looked deep within. Her lips were inviting, a most beautiful pink. Playtheus looked at his father. "She is truly breathtaking. But why a Nephilim Renown? Why not another human female?"

Talimus-qua-tam smiled. "There is a reason, Son. She is the fairest of Nephilim females. Castius has groomed her since her birth. She is the epitome of his breeding. Surely he will be declared a 'Mighty One' himself for this great achievement. Apogee told him she would fulfill a special purpose. He read it in the stars. That purpose is you, my son. She possesses a rarity that no other female Nephilim has. Do you not sense this special quality about her?"

Playtheus closed his eyes as if delving into his senses. He searched deep within to see. "Yes, I see it!"

His father smiled. "She possesses virtues from her human mother. No other female Nephilim ever had this gifting. These virtues will satisfy you, for they are mixed with the angelic!"

Playtheus drew near and circled her, his father watching with pleasure. He leaned in, close to her neck, and inhaled. "Ah, you are fair. I smell the aroma of your essence." he sighed with unexpected pleasure.

She smiled with confidence. "Yes, I know." He gently ran his fingertips down her arm feeling her soft skin and shuddered with excitement.

"It's now time, my son, for you to learn to partake of the essence of the soul. As I learned, I will now teach you."

He had seen his father partake from Polisha at Champion Hall, and it thrilled him that the time had come for him to be given this knowledge. He felt every fiber of his being rise, straining to be satisfied.

"Repeat these words: 'Zahlo-yobo-yah-qwest-ah!'" The words were hidden from the ears of those who stood nearby who saw only his lips moving. But Playtheus heard and then repeated them. He sensed the power that now surrounded him and leaned close to her lips. Inhaling deeply, he drew from her soul. A mist of light rose from her legs and arms, swirling within her chest. In excited anticipation, he inhaled through her parted lips.

"Satisfy yourself deeply, my son!"

Playtheus continued to draw, deeper and deeper, until she began to shudder and sigh. "Yes, my lord, drink deeply. I, too, am receiving great pleasure from what you are drawing from me. I desire to satisfy you." She moaned, sending a surge of heightened excitement through him.

Talimus-qua-tam smiled, knowing that his son was now entering a new phase of his knowledge. He had now passed into the realm of the "Mighty Ones" and the pleasures they experience.

Playtheus staggered on his feet from the power and satisfaction he now possessed from this Nephilim. "Father, this is a wonder!"

"Yes, my son. I have longed for you to grow to this level of understanding and am pleased you have arrived. This 'partaking' is far beyond the inhaling of the 'innocence.' You will find it to be more satisfying." He proudly watched as his son continued to savor what he had withdrawn from her.

"Drink again, my son!"

Playtheus leaned forward, repeated the dark words, and drew heavily from her once more. She shuddered with great quaking and then collapsed in the arms of the servants.

"Yes, Playtheus; when you draw, draw until there is none left to draw!"

Playtheus trembled with ecstasy and power and staggered on his feet. His father proudly steadied him by his arm. "Yes, that was good. Come. She will recover, and you may drink once more if you like. There is an endless supply in the soul." Playtheus staggered while his father held his arm and they continued their walk in the gardens.

"This female was chosen especially for you. You were given permission to have her *before* being declared a 'Mighty One.' This is a rare privilege and was only allowed by the agreement of all the 200. It makes me very proud. Through her, you will satisfy your heart's desire!"

He stepped near his father and with whispered breath said, "But Father, my dream revealed Sede-quete would make me a 'Mighty One.' She is my heart's desire."

"Yes, I know, my son. This female is the instrument you will use to find her. Apogee has seen it in the stars. This female is a direct link with you reuniting with your queen. When you find Sede-quete, bring her here, and I'll perform your ceremony declaring you, my son, a 'Mighty One' in the earth!"

Playtheus raised his head and roared, "I *will* be a 'Mighty One.' I *will*!" He glowed in power, and flicks of light burst into the air, releasing the angelic power from within his being.

Smiling in pride, Talimus-qua-tam's body responded with brilliant blue light. His son was truly a "Prince" among the angels' sons. How few of them could boast of such beauty and majesty in their sons? There would be no great sons if not for the work Playtheus did for them: giving them innocence to possess from the children and virtues from the captives. Playtheus had not yet perceived how important he really was to the plans the 200 had for their children's greatness. It was their plan and strategy to see their progenies replace the meager human race that the "Most High" had created. The angels themselves would be fruitful and multiply, filling the earth with *their* seed. They would eventually replace the seed of man so that the "Promised One" would not be able to come from a pure human lineage. It was their plan to eliminate the threat Yahweh had made concerning their leader when he gave Eve the promise that "her seed would crush his head." This is why they were willing to show Playtheus this great favor before he was officially named a "Mighty One" in the earth. He was the key to their whole world.

As they entered the mansion, the female Renown stood poised and waiting for them.

"Father, I don't believe we've been properly introduced. What is her name?"

"Playtheus, I would like to introduce you to Nersha."

Nersha stepped forward and gently caressed his neck and came but an inch from his lips. Whispering, she breathed, "*I am your perfect match in every way.*" Her words stabbed his heart like a knife! Unknowingly, she had said exactly what he had said of Sede-quete when he opened his heart to her. It tore him to his very core. Sensing the shift in his mood she asked, "What is wrong, my lord?"

"Nothing, my dear" he said, veiling his heart from her. "Yes, Father, she will do nicely." Playtheus was determined to do whatever it took; he would use anything, or anyone, to get his Sede-quete back, even this beautiful Nephilim with her rare virtues.

"Take her home to Atlantis and become better acquainted. She has been given to you for your pleasure and the fulfillment of your future."

Playtheus bowed before his father. "When I come again, Father, I will bring my queen, Sede-quete, and be declared a 'Mighty One'!"

Turning to leave, Playtheus paused before his mother. "Here, Mother, I give you this for safekeeping. It is my most treasured possession. Someday I will return for it." He extended a wrapped box, which she lovingly received. She returned a kiss to his cheek. Clasping Nersha's hand, he quietly left, returning to Atlantis.

Playtheus soon learned this new knowledge was far superior to the simple knowledge of withdrawing the innocence from humans. It brought greater pleasure and satisfied his needs in a deeper way. He found that he preferred the essence over the innocence of the soul, just as his father had said. He was proud that he was learning the ways of the "Mighty Ones" even before he was declared to be one. He perceived he had the favor of the 200.

When he became accustomed to Nersha's essence, he began to experiment with humans in the same way. They didn't have the stamina that Nersha had, but he was delighted that they recovered quickly. It was true…they had an endless supply. He shuddered to think how Sede-quete would give him endless pleasure with her precious "Tella-la-no-ah" essence!

But as time went by, Playtheus saw Nersha as a double edged sword. Her essence was sublime, but her jealousy was aflame over his interest in other females. Even though she knew Nephilim had an incessant appetite for women, she became enraged if he showed interest in spending more than one night with them. She used the knowledge she had overheard at Horizon's Gate to manipulate him. She constantly reminded him that she alone was the key to his future and only her angelic essence would satisfy him like no other.

Her most grievous jealousy was when she learned a secret from their intimate talks. He had unwittingly confessed that his heart belonged to another, a human named Sede-quete. He even showed her the mural in the corridor, reflecting the dream he had of her years before. This was the same woman she overheard him mention to his father at Horizon's Gate. She sensed his deep love for her and desired to have the place in his heart that this mere woman had. The fire of jealousy burned and became fierce, even after he announced her as his high companion at the Pavilion. Though he went through the motions of presenting her as his queen and gave her the title, Sede-quete still had his heart. Her pride was assaulted, and she knew she would always be second to her. She knew it was for appearance sake that she had been appointed as his "high companion." Playtheus needed to regain his influence among the Renown once more, and she was the new novelty. They all sensed her virtuous qualities and were deeply envious. She was the first female Nephilim to possess her own virtues. This had reestablished his prominence before them. Not only was she jealous of his love, but she was angry that she was being used to promote his greatness. She loved him, and yet, through her anger, she hated him. She was to herself, also, a double edged sword.

Gradually, Nersha began to devise a plan—a plan to capture Sede-quete and destroy her forever. With her gone, she would then possess Playtheus' heart and be cherished by him as he had cherished Sede-quete. Only then would they rule united, with nothing between them. This plan would take time and preparation. While he was busy performing his duties to the Renown, supplying them with innocence and virtues, she began to spend her days training as a warrior. She excelled and quickly proved to be mighty in skill and spirit, for she was part angelic in her being. She soon had the admiration of the famous Renown Warriors and went to battle with them, destroying a rebellious uprising by warring Cainites. They returned to Atlantis with great pomp and acclaim. She gloried in the recognition it brought her and used it to further manipulate Playtheus.

Nersha

She approached him one evening when he was walking in his garden. He often spent quiet time walking alone and thinking about Sede-quete, reliving their memories over and over in his mind. The sun was setting over the mountains, and the evening breeze blew the sweet fragrance of the flowers in the air. The sound of soft music rose from the city below, setting the mood for peace and calm. She came alongside him and slid her hand into his. He turned to give her a smile. They continued to walk, and she began to softly speak. "I wish to talk with you, my lord."

"Say on, my fair one," he responded.

"I have learned the skills of a warrior and wish to lead an army. With this army I could raid the frontier wilderness. It is my desire to gain greater wealth and recognition for you among the Renown. Together we will establish our glory among them. You here in Atlantis and me in the frontier."

Playtheus smiled. He sensed there was more to her plan than what she was divulging. He had come to recognize her subtle skill of manipulating him and knew her motivation was not really about pleasing him but satisfying some secret desire she had. As she continued to talk, he welcomed the idea of having peace from her constant jealousy over other women and agreed to her wishes. Although he would miss the satisfaction from her essence while she was gone, he knew he would be satisfied by the multitude of human female companions within his harem. He also realized that he would gain greater acclaim among his brother Nephilim by this plan. So he consented and bid her farewell. He often thought of what his father meant when he said she would help him find Sede-quete. Perhaps in Nersha's conquests of Sethite villages, she would be discovered. Little did he realize how deep her jealousy was. She would never allow them to be reunited.

She traveled to Zadanim where she employed an army of brutish Hagonoths. These giants were most eager to please her, for they sensed her virtues, and it excited them. Nersha had a dominating personality and was clever in manipulation. It wasn't difficult to gather a following, and she appointed a particular giant as their captain. His name was Grog. He was ruthless and knew how to motivate his soldiers. Though mighty among his peers, he was like putty in her hands. His delight was to hear the words that fell from her lips. They revered her, bowing down and worshipping her as a god. With this willing army, she would raid Sethite villages until Sede-quete was found and then destroy her.

They began the systematic raiding of all known regions, pushing deeper and deeper into the wilderness. Many, many Sethites perished in these raids, and multitudes were enslaved and sold in Atlantis. As "The City of the Sons" became saturated with an abundance of Sethites, it was her decision to allow the Sethites to remain in their villages, and she imposed Nephilim rule over them. (The Watcher had told Japheth and Shoda and Tolmaka, while he was in the Cave of Treasures, that a great evil was coming to their villages. *This* was the evil that was spreading through every village.)

She allowed her ruthless army to take liberties, exercising any desire they had. These barbaric soldiers knew nothing more than to rape and pillage, making Sethites live in great fear and dread. Their crops and livestock were routinely stolen, and they barely survived on what remained. Before Nersha left any village, she always lined up the females and searched for Sede-quete; she knew her likeness from the mural in Playtheus' mansion. She never tired of the thrill of capturing another Sethite village, and her jealously and hatred for Sede-quete drove her with relentless zeal.

Chapter 20

Sede's Day

Sede opened her eyes as the light filtered into her room from the open window. 'This is the dawn of a day like no other,' she thought, 'the dawn of my new life with Shem.' She felt a fluttering within her chest and a wave of excitement. She had been in seclusion for three days while going through her "days of preparation." Ezmere, Dosta, and Adah, along with the other chosen elder women, came to instruct her. They gave her the knowledge of the "way of a man with a woman." She blushed a great deal during this time for she hadn't considered such things or had an interest in them. But now the time had come for her to know.

Each day she soaked in special baths, prepared with spices and oils. Dosta was more than pleased to show her the secrets of cooking and the spices she used to bring out the wonderful flavors Sede had enjoyed all her life. Adah showed her the "art of washing clothes," or so she humorously called it. But robes did need to be washed a certain way or they become needlessly worn. Other elder women spoke of pregnancy, giving birth, and child rearing. By the end of three days, she felt as though her mind was full, and there wasn't room for any more. She was thankful, though, for someday she, too, would instruct her daughters as she had been instructed.

She thought about her last day of preparations when she was soaking in her bath. She had requested to speak to Dosta privately. The other women smiled and nodded in respect, leaving quietly, and Dosta stood with folded hands in front of her, waiting for her to speak. "Dosta, you have given me such wonderful love since I first knew to call you aunt. Thank you for all you've done for me and Father. I love you dearly."

A single tear rolled down her cheek as she listened. Sede could see the rise and fall of her chest and knew she was having a hard time holding back her emotions. After a long silence, Dosta replied, "Oh my precious child, I love you too. It has been my joy to care for you and see you become the woman before me. Your mother would have been so very proud of you."

Sede was silent for a few moments, moving the spices that floated on the surface of the water back and forth with her hand. "Tell me of my mother, Dosta. I so wish I had known her…Father doesn't speak of her. I sense her loss is still with him, and I don't wish to grieve him with my questions."

"Yes, he does still carry grief for her. She was everything to him. They hunted together, you know?" She giggled a little giggle, remembering a pleasant thought, and then continued, "She and your father had many wonderful years together, and their happiest days were when she was pregnant with you. Both of them were giddy with joy. They had hoped for a girl for she never got over the loss of her sister Marah. Somehow, she thought that through you, she would have her again. It seems kind of strange to think that way, but I understood. Your father could have never survived the loss of her had it not been the great joy of seeing you for the first time and holding you in his arms. He sees her in you, Sede; he has told me this himself." Sede smiled, for he had told her the same thing.

"Do you know how Marah was taken?" she hesitantly asked.

Dosta looked out the window as if recalling the memory. "Your mother told me the story…. She was a young hunter at that time, and Marah, a mature maiden. Your mother loved to spend the day with her sister when she had a respite from hunting. And it was on one of those days that they decided to spend it in their favorite place in the forest. They knew of a place along the river where wild berries grew and wanted a day of fun and play as they gathered berries and swam. It was on the forest path that they encountered a Watcher. Lettah said he was magnificent in beauty and radiated a brilliant light. Perhaps because Lettah was younger than Marah, the angel showed no interest in her. But he did in Marah. There was magic shrouded over their conversation. Lettah heard none of their words, only the moving of their lips. Something in the air then lulled her to sleep. When she woke, the Watcher was gone, along with her sister. Lettah was hysterical and could hardly speak when she got back to the village. She was depressed for months after that and really never got over the loss. Her last words before she died were words of love for her lost sister."

Sede began to weep for she felt the sadness in what had happened to her mother and aunt. Her mother could never have fought the power of the angel; Sede knew that firsthand. And because she was a young hunter/warrior, she probably felt she should have tried to defend her sister. And her aunt—she probably still lived, snared in the power and control of some dark angel and corrupted like Ka-sta. "Oh Dosta, that is so sad."

"Yes dear, but we should think of happiness today. Let's put these words aside and think about that handsome, strong man waiting to lift your veil and look into the eyes of perfect beauty." She giggled, making Sede giggle too. It was a welcome thought for her heart was now prepared to be his wife. She wondered if he, too, was considering such things. He was being prepared by his father's council as well as the elders. She knew what she had learned in the past three days and wondered what he had learned about being a husband and, someday, a father.

And now, here it was, the morning of her wedding. Looking around her room, she saw her hunting skins hanging on a peg near her curtain door. Her bow was propped against the corner of the wall. A pang of loss pricked her heart. No more hunting. No more following the tracks of prey or catching their scent in the wind. No more "going out and coming in."

She saw her wedding gown and veil draped over the wooden trunk. She rose from her cot and admired the beauty of the fabric. She stroked the folded veil. It was shiny, sheer, and so very soft to the touch. Jewels dangled from the edges, reflecting the light that was now streaming into her room. The colored lights danced on the wall as her fingers moved the jewels. She stopped to ponder the magic of the moment and watch the lights as they danced about her room. 'This veil will cover my innocence until we enter our bedchamber,' she thought. She felt a flush in her cheeks. The scent of her body rose, and she inhaled. The fragrance was heady, exciting something in the depth of her being. The elder women said this delicate aroma would be Shem's delight and that his desire would rapture her. She felt a flush in her cheeks once more and a fluttering within her chest. Soon Dosta, Ezmere, and Adah would come to her room and dress her. As she stood by her veil and pondered, she looked out of the window to the sky. She wished she could send a message to Shem and say, "Today we start our lives together. Do you hear my heart? I love you."

Within a few moments she heard voices behind the curtain. Ezmere and Adah had arrived. As she stood and grasped the curtain, she paused…'Yahweh, bless us this day.' The women were busy discussing the feast and all the food the village women had prepared. Tolmaka had spared no expense and employed many of his kinsmen to help with all the festivity.

When the women saw her, they paused and smiled. "Good morning, young bride," Dosta said, bubbling with joy. "Good morning, my daughter," Ezmere happily chimed in. "Good morning, young beauty," Adah echoed.

Sede smiled sweetly. "Good morning, mothers of my heart." All three women giggled and opened their arms to her, their hug forming a loving circle around her.

"There is much to do," said Dosta, "so let's begin!"

The ceremonial drums began to beat in unison, and the crowd of kinsmen settled on their mats for it showed great honor to be seated while the bride and groom stood. All eyes fell on Sede and Tolmaka. Holding her by the hand, they walked forward. The tiny bells on her hem tinkled as she took each step. His heart filled with pride as he looked through her sheer veil and saw her sparkling eyes, alive and filled with wonder. He hadn't seen anything so beautiful since the day he married Lettah. She smiled sweetly and squeezed his hand. A tear rolled down his cheek, and he cleared his throat. He whispered softly, "I love you, Sede. Your mother would be so proud of you."

"I love you too, Father," she said as she returned a smile.

As they stood before Noah, Tolmaka brought Sede and Shem's hands together. She remembered what the Watcher had told her when they had talked at Eden's wall. This very thing is what Yahweh had done when He had brought Eve to Adam. He had brought their hands together and blessed them. Tolmaka's loving, deep voice whispered to them, "I speak my blessing, children, as you come together as man and wife. May your lives together know great happiness."

A soft, warm breeze fluttered her veil, pressing against the curve of her nose. She sensed Yahweh in the breeze. A hush—and then she heard His still, small voice speak: "As your father has blessed you, I, too, bless you this day, my child." She closed her eyes to capture His words.

Stepping back, Tolmaka stood beside Ezmere. Placing his hands on Shem and Sede's shoulders, Noah spoke with a great voice. "As Yahweh told our father Adam: 'A man shall leave his father and mother and cleave to his wife. The two shall be one flesh.' May the joining of these lives be the fulfillment of Yahweh's words."

Tolmaka handed long, narrow strips of leather to Noah, Shem, and Sede. With the leather strip in hand, Noah held it high, moving it to the right and the left so all could see. "This one strand of leather represents the life of Yahweh. Shem brings his life and Sede hers." They lifted their strands in unison. "As these three strands are braided together to make one cord, the life of Yahweh is woven within them. 'Two are better than one, and a threefold cord is not easily broken'!"

As Noah, Sede, and Shem began to braid the cord, Noah proclaimed, "This is a covenant between you and Yahweh. It shall not be broken!" When they had braided to the end, Noah tied them, forming a circled cord. "What God has joined together, let no man unbraid!" Turning, Sede and Shem faced each other as Noah placed the tied, three-stranded cord over their heads, resting it upon their shoulders. Placing his hands on their heads, he whispered for only them to hear, "Be blessed, my children, and live to see the glory of the Lord your God!"

Shem lifted the jeweled edge of Sede's veil, letting it fall around her shoulders. In her eyes, he saw the softness of her love and the beauty of her innocence. He couldn't help it but softly gasped. His response to her stirred something deep within her soul as when "deep calls unto deep." 'He sees who I truly am,' she thought.

He softly spoke, "You are my future, Sede." Without thinking, they both closed their eyes and gently touched foreheads. At the same time, they both breathed, "Ha-la-lah."

With a broad smile, Noah raised his hands over his head and clapped twice. "Let the celebration begin!"

The crowd gave a shout, and the musicians began to play in joyful song. Like the flow of water down a stream, their kinsmen moved toward the council fire, where the feasting began. Shem and Sede stood silent, still caught in the moment that belonged to them. Tolmaka touched their shoulders and whispered, "I love you, my children."

Shem squeezed Sede's hand and said, "Our love is with you, Father." That was the first time she heard their love spoken as *our* love. What a wonderful feeling, knowing that she and Shem were now one. Noah and Ezmere hugged them and whispered their love in their ears, joy filling their hearts for them. They had seen their joy fulfilled. (For every Sethite parent had this one heart's desire: to see their children reach this milestone—stepping into marriage and perpetuating another generation.)

Throughout the rest of the evening, kinsmen showed them honor. Tokens and gifts were brought and laid at their feet. Sede felt admiration at Shem's graciousness. From this moment on, the village would recognize him as her husband and an elder that would lead their family. As was the custom, Shem and Sede rose to dance "the dance of husband and wife." Standing side by side, with hand to forearm, they moved in unison as they stepped and turned to the lively music. All who watched clapped in rhythm to the beat, rejoicing with them. But it was Tolmaka and Noah who reveled in greater joy. From where they stood, they began to turn and whirl in dance, lifting their heads and hands. Their laughter and joy rose in the night to heaven itself. It was this joy that reflected every Sethite father's heart. Their beloved children had come full bloom: beautiful in purity, strength, and glory.

After Tolmaka had bid the last kinsmen goodnight, he stood before them. "Rise children. It is time for you to enter your bedchamber." Clasping each of their hands, he helped them rise from where they sat. Shem and Sede held hands and followed him as his torch lit the way. As a gift of love, Tolmaka had prepared a large tent near a grove of trees overlooking the village. As they walked, he sang "The Father's Love Song." Gruetat had just sung it for his sweet daughter, and now it would be Tolmaka singing for his. Sweet memories came back to him of Lettah's father singing for her and the special night that had been theirs. And now he was singing for his beloved Sede. His deep bass voice softly echoed in the quiet, moonlit night, its sweet melody embracing their hearts…

I lead you to the sacred tent
You, my daughter, the bride
Innocence has bloomed, and now full grown,
Sweet intimacy awaits inside

Come bride and groom, bring your hearts
And tremble the path unknown
There is no other night like this one
For it was made for you alone

'This is sung for me,' she thought, 'that I may enter this new life with my father's blessing.' She felt bonded to the moment. "I will remember this always!" She squeezed Shem's hand, and the soft moonlight reflected the sweetness of her smile. He, too, held this moment dear. This was a time like no other. His innocence, too, had come full bloom, and together they would discover what Yahweh meant when He said, "The two shall become one flesh."

Tolmaka raised the tent curtain, exposing the softly lit interior. A small lamp burned at the far end of the tent, and furs covered the floor, along with a multitude of pillows arranged for a bed. A low table was set with fruit and meats to eat at their leisure. The sweet aroma of beloma filled the air. Their two weeks of provisions were bundled neatly in the corner. Tolmaka smiled sweetly as he turned to leave. "Cherish this night" he said, resting his hand on Shem's shoulder. Kissing Sede's cheek, he tearfully whispered, "I bid you goodnight, my beautiful daughter." He began to sing again as he left and his song softened until she could hear it no more.

They took each other's hand and stood in silence, looking into each other's eyes. Shem spoke first. "I haven't had a moment to tell you how beautiful you looked today, Sede. When I lifted your veil, I saw the softness of our love and the beauty of purity. It made my heart leap!"

She felt her face flush, and that same flutter of emotion welled up within her that she had felt earlier that morning. He bent down and kissed her softly. The warmth of his lips sent a sensation through her she had never known. Then she realized...this was their first kiss. It was a kiss of a man for a woman—a kiss that communicated desire. She was experiencing feelings she had never known possible. This was love as it was intended to be, not like the sorcery used by Playtheus to pull it out of her. This is what Yahweh intended when a man and a woman came together with bonded hearts. The elder women had done their best to prepare her for this night, but she was surprised that desire and been in her all along. It had been in her...sleeping. Now it was awakened, and everything in her wanted to respond to him.

She felt a surrendering weakness come over her as he led her by the hand to the bed of pillows. "Come, Sede, tell me your heart."

As they reclined, he drew her to his chest and held her in his arms. She felt the warmth of his body and the beating of his heart, and she smelled the fragrance of his body. It was of fragrant oils and spices. He, too, had prepared for her. As she gathered her thoughts, she spoke, "I feel a surrendering within me that is new to me. I've never felt this way before. I feel as though I could give myself completely to you. There is a yearning within me to be one with you."

"I, too, have felt the power of desire to be one with you, Sede. This desire has also awakened in me. How wonderful that we can experience this together, each of us pure to one another. I am pleased to give myself to you, my bride." He lifted her hand to his lips and gently kissed her folded fingers.

"And I am pleased to give myself to you, my husband." Touching her forehead to his, she closed her eyes and softly exhaled, savoring the moment. She tenderly thought, 'This is the love my father told me of: a love that a woman can give a man to make him complete. When he told me about such love, I could only imagine what it would be like. But now I know. I am able to love and be loved in return. How wonderful that Yahweh would make it so.'

And so it was that night, in their softly lit tent, Sede and Shem experienced love and unity as it was meant to be: in purity, innocence, and beauty.

Chapter 21

Set Apart

Sede woke to the sound of a bird's lovely song. From a tree overhanging their wedding tent, the song bird sang its morning praise. The first thing she saw when she opened her eyes was Shem's peaceful face. His eyes were closed and his breathing slow and steady. She lay there just looking at him—so handsome, so strong. A sudden rush went through her as she remembered last night. Her cheeks blushed, and her body reminded her she had given herself to him. The elder women had told her of the pain she would feel from the intimacy with a man. They said it was but the first pain of love; childbirth would be love's pain as well. He had been so gentle with her, his touch so wonderful. She blushed once more just thinking of it.

Shem stirred. As he opened his eyes, he knew she had been watching him sleep. "Good morning, my fair one, my bride." He smiled and gently leaned forward, giving her a warm kiss. A sudden rush went through her as she waited for his words, wanting to hear more. "Last night was wonderful…was it not?"

She smiled and, just as he had done, leaned forward and kissed him softly. "Yes, my husband. Last night *was* wonderful!"

Opening his arms, he beckoned, "Come, let me hold you." She moved into his warm arms, delighting in the unity she felt with him. Lovingly, he kissed her on the side of her cheek. "Sede, you were so wonderful last night. Your innocence rose to embrace me. Oh, it was ecstasy to me!" She felt him shudder. "I'm amazed that we'll have a lifetime of pleasure in our times of oneness."

She felt great comfort that he had shared his heart and revealed his most intimate thoughts. He had felt no embarrassment in what he had said, which gave her confidence to speak her own heart. "Shem, your words are love to me, making you great in my eyes. I, too, look forward to a lifetime of enjoying this amazing unity of love. Our love cannot help but grow like the seed your father spoke of—the seed that will grow into a great tree bearing much fruit." He smiled and gave her a gentle hug.

She pulled her seed necklace out from under the pillow. "Here, I want to share with you. It's my most precious secret!" Opening her hand, she revealed the seed that Yahweh had given her. She rehearsed her encounter at the wall and drawing the seed from Eden's pool. "The Watcher told me this seed was a gift and I would come to understand its meaning in time. He called it 'seeds within a seed.' Here, listen to the sound of heaven."

She held the seed to his ear, and he heard for the first time, the music of heaven. Pleasure was in his expression, and she knew he was being blessed. "Oh, this is amazing, Sede!"

"Yes, and it holds deep meaning for me. Yahweh told me that I am the one, in this generation, to continue the lineage for the 'Promised One.' Through my seed, the lineage will continue until Eve's prophetic promise is fulfilled."

He looked in wonder at her. Here was a young woman who had been told the greatest of secrets and had kept it secret. He realized in that moment that she was his treasure indeed; to have a woman that would hold Yahweh's confidence over any others. "Thank you, Sede, for sharing this precious secret with me. I am so honored that Yahweh would choose you, and in a way…me; for it will be our union that will create this seed!" His feelings gripped him and turned into an emotional release.

He began to weep. The presence of Yahweh surrounded them, and the atmosphere shifted, coming alive with a love they could feel. It was a holy moment…a moment realizing the precious privilege that had been given to them. She held him close, and she, too, began to weep.

As they held each other, someone spoke to them from outside the tent. "Come forth, children of the 'Most High'!" Lifting the tent curtain, they saw an angel. He was the same Watcher who had appeared to her and returned her to Shem in the forest. Trembling, they beheld him as he glowed with a light that radiated from within. They felt themselves absorb the light, filling them with strength and a tangible love that soothed them. "Yahweh has sent me to lead you to a cave and instruct you. This is a special cave, known only to a few selected elders among the Sethites. Your father, Sede, was there but a short time ago."

They quickly gathered their things and followed him through the forest. Excitement filled them, knowing they were going to be shown this sacred place. All Sethites knew about this cave, but few knew where to find it. When they reached the mountain, they began their ascent.

Halfway up, they saw the entrance. A flat ridge spread from the opening, almost like a platform, and from there they could see to the horizon. The panoramic view was spectacular in beauty and wonder. It was as if they could see the whole world. The angel announced, "This is the Cave of Treasures. Here is where Yahweh led Adam and Eve when they left the Garden of Eden. This is where they lived their lives." Pausing, he looked to the distance. They sensed he was contemplating a memory. He then continued, "This place knew the birth of their children and the beginning of humanity. Their sons and daughters played within these walls, calling it home. This cave knew great joy but also sorrow. This is where they mourned for Abel. They lost both their sons that day. After Yahweh confronted Cain for murdering his brother, he left for the land of Nod. He took his sister, the one promised to Abel, and there he began the people known as the Cainites. This cave has known the beginning of all things. Here, secrets are hidden that Yahweh wishes to reveal to you."

Pausing at the entrance, the Watcher spoke the words of heaven and waved his hand before him. They were amazed as the dark cave became illuminated with light. Behind the stone walls, ceiling, and floor was a brilliant white glow. The stone surface seemed to dance with light, and Yahweh's presence permeated the air. Sede remembered her father telling her of his experience and the great wonder he felt as he discovered the secrets within. "Come, the eyes of your flesh have been unveiled, and you now see with the eyes of the spirit. You see the cave as it truly is, the way Adam and his family saw it."

Holding hands, they stepped forward in awe as the Watcher led them to a golden table at the far end of the cave. There, a body lay wrapped in white linen cloth. They didn't have to ask; they both knew who it was. It was Adam. Their spiritual discernment had been heightened by just being in the cave. "Yahweh wishes to show you his body. A time is coming when you will be asked to return and take him with you."

Shem had a puzzled look.

"You want to know what I mean, don't you?"

Shem was surprised he'd perceived his thoughts. "Yes, I do."

"I have visited your father, Noah, and have instructed him concerning the future of this world and the judgment that is coming to the unrighteous. When the time is right, you will be asked to return and save Yahweh's treasures. Adam's body is one of those treasures."

Sede and Shem's hearts burned with deep yearning. Asking at the same time, they said, "May we touch our father, Adam?"

"Yes," nodded the Watcher, "you may touch him."

The moment their fingers touched the linen cloth, heavenly music filled the cave. It was harmony upon harmony of resounding love echoed from heaven itself. A burst of frankincense filled the air, causing them to stagger on their feet. It was rapturous. Oh, never had they experienced such glory. They looked at each other, hardly believing what was happening. Tears ran down their cheeks as they felt the deep emotion of being in Adam's presence. They had touched the father of mankind.

"Oh Shem," Sede whispered in tearful emotion, "I stand in awe that Yahweh would show us such things!"

Shem couldn't speak. He had no words to express what he felt. They inhaled once more the heavenly frankincense, and their thoughts stirred within them. Oh, that they could stay here forever in this place of glory!

The Watcher continued to instruct them. "There is a great evil coming to your villages. I tell you this now so you will be able to endure it when it comes. Help your father in any way he wishes, for he will need your support and strength in the days that lie ahead. Yahweh is about to send His judgment upon the earth, just as Enoch wrote. Now, children, I give you Yahweh's blessing." As he towered over them, suddenly they saw his wings appear. He extended them out and around them as if to embrace them. "May Yahweh bless you and keep you. May his countenance rise upon you and give you peace. Be blessed, children; grow in love for each other!" The Watcher suddenly evaporated, and the cave was instantly changed. The light that illuminated through the stone surface was now gone. The table with Adam's body could no longer be seen, only the dark damp of an empty cave. Sede and Shem looked at each other in surprise. It had happened so fast. He was there, and then he was gone! The cave that had been filled with light was now dark!

"Come Sede, we must return and tell the others of all we have seen. They need to be warned of the evil that is to coming to our village."

Shem was alert to the trail. He knew the time would come when he would be asked to return.

They made camp as night began to fall. Sede started the fire as Shem built a shelter from fallen branches. "Come into our wedding tent, my bride," he said with a joking smile. She returned a playful laugh, allowing him to usher her by the hand. As they sat beneath their shelter and gazed into the fire, they shared their thoughts of what the Watcher had shown them. He savored the presence of the Lord he had felt and still had a warm glow of love about him. She, too, felt a wonderful peace settle within. Oh the music, the fragrance, the presence…their experience had been both wonderful yet terrible. What was this evil that would come against their village and the great judgment on the earth? Sede had seen firsthand the evil that abounded in Atlantis. She remembered asking Yahweh to judge them. Would this be an answer to her prayer?

Suddenly, they heard a twig snap. Something, or someone, was approaching. They looked at each other and, without a word, slowly backed into the bushes beneath the trees. The call of the conoka bird broke the silence. Just then, Japheth appeared with Shoda by his side. "Hail, Shem!" he said jokingly.

Shem sighed in relief and shook his head as he stepped forward. "Hail, little brother." He grabbed him by the back of his neck, giving his head a playful shake.

Sede squealed in delight. "Shoda, Shoda!" It was the first they had seen each other since Zadanim's fire.

Hugging her and whirling around, Shoda shouted, "You're alive. You're alive!" Tears rolled down their cheeks as they held each other. After their excitement had settled, they gathered around the fire and shared what they had both experienced with the Watcher. "It looks as though Yahweh is preparing us for what lies ahead," reasoned Shem. "It must be both great and terrible!" They considered his words that echoed their own sentiments.

As their mood settled, each brother held their wife and faced the fire's light. Japheth began to ever so gently rock Shoda in his arms, humming a haunting melody. Shoda began to hum along and then began to sing. Her voice lifted, gently rising above the trees into the starry night…

> *The "night" is calling…*
> *Our hearts hear your song:*
> *Come young lovers*
> *To each other you belong.*
>
> *Draw your lips near young love*
> *And breathe your words so fair,*
> *With warm embrace caress*
> *Two wooing hearts that care.*
>
> *As most intimate love is shared*
> *And your bond made stronger,*
> *Love grows in splendor*
> *And two hearts grow fonder.*
>
> *Recline all night in sweet repose*
> *Your head upon the chest will lie*
> *Till morning sings its song*
> *And your love released with a sigh.*

Sede watched them, sensing that something very special had happened between her friend and Japheth. She was happy that Shoda, too, had found love in the arms of the man who would be her husband in life's journey. Her heart was moved as she continued to listen to her friends sing the haunting love song.

She looked into Shem's eyes and saw again his tender love for her. Resting against his chest, she listened to his heartbeat. 'Yes, this is the sound of comfort to my soul.' She remembered the night in Playtheus' mansion, speaking her words into the night...'It is Shem's arms that I long for. It is Shem's heartbeat that I want to hear. It is his love that will embrace me.' She took his hand and drew it to her heart, whispering beneath her breath, "I love you, Shem. It is you I live for. Every last breath of who I am...I give to you."

She didn't know it, but he had heard her whispered words. He felt her love enter his heart and sooth him in a way nothing else could. She had a depth of love for him that echoed his own love for her. He could hardly believe that this was happening to him. He had found love. And the strangest of all...it had been with him every day in a young woman that had been his hunting companion and friend. All this wonderful love had been sleeping within both of them, waiting to rise and meet each other. He could hardly contain himself knowing they would have this love...forever.

In the morning, they decided that Shem would return to the village and tell their father the message from the Watcher. He would then return and fulfill his sacred time with Sede as would Japheth concerning Shoda. He left and met with Noah and Tolmaka. After he had given them the Watcher's warning, he returned. He was at peace knowing his father and the elders would make the right decisions. There was no knowing when this impending danger was to happen, and if they returned to wait with the others, they would forever lose this "set apart" time between them.

* * *

Noah sent word throughout the village, calling the men to the council fire. The village stirred with excitement as the men left their huts and began to gather. Noah stood, and a quiet settled over the men. "Tonight I have called you, my brothers, to give you the word of the Lord. Yahweh has given a warning for our villages. His messenger, a Watcher, has appeared to Tolmaka and also my sons, Shem and Japheth. The message to each of them is the same: 'There is a great evil coming to our Sethite villages.' I need to warn each one of you to be alert and protect your families. The gatekeeper will not allow travelers to enter until we have heard more from Yahweh. I am going to leave in the morning for Taasa-matak and warn them. I will be taking my family. Shem and Japheth are still in their sacred time of seclusion. Their presence here would not change what we must decide. Tolmaka will take his sister as well as Dollo and his wife to Bal-enah. Gruetat and his family will go to Fel-peth. Erud will remain here as head elder. In five days we'll return. These village elders will seek Yahweh, and when they hear anything, they will send word to us. Now comfort one another that Yahweh has warned us. Go to your huts. Pray this night for each other and Sethite villages everywhere!" In anxious, soft whispers, the men returned to their families.

Early the next morning the elders gathered; voices were hushed as they helped the three caravans load their camels. When all was ready, Noah raised his voice to bid them farewell. "Pray for our journey as we will pray for you…'Took-la-say, a-la-nay!"

The elders echoed in unison, "Took-la-say, a-la-nay!" Noah, Tolmaka, and Gruetat began their two-day journey, each parting in different directions. The elders watched until they were out of sight and then barred the gate until their return.

After two days of traveling, Tolmaka and his company were greeted at Bal-enah by the gatekeeper. "Please take me to Sed-osah for I've journeyed to speak to him."

"Follow me; I'll show you the way." The excited guard quickly led them through the busy streets. Standing at the door, he knocked. Recognizing him, Sed-osah's wife bid them to enter.

They joined his family for their evening meal, and after their children retired, Tolmaka spoke his message. "I must share with you a warning sent by Yahweh to Noah, his sons, and myself. We have been warned that a great evil is coming to our Sethite villages. We need to alert the other villages and pray for each other. Have your hunter/warriors prepare for the unexpected. Noah has requested that each leading elder seek Yahweh. When you receive His words, send the message to the other villages. Tomorrow you must call your elders together and give them this warning."

Exhausted from their long journey, they settled on their furs around his hearth. Sleep came quickly, but dawn as well.

In the morning, Sed-osah called a council meeting with his elders; there Tolmaka repeated Noah's words, calling them to prayer for each other and their kin in other villages. Sed-osah offered a sacrifice to Yahweh, and they joined hands around the altar and sang. Joy burst forth when fire fell from heaven to consume what had been offered.

Tolmaka and his company left the next morning, pleased that his message had been received. Bal-enah would prepare themselves and seek Yahweh for Sethites everywhere.

Chapter 22

The Unexpected

Shem returned to the campsite where the others waited in expectation. He told them of Noah, Tolmaka, and Gruetat visiting the three surrounding villages and warning them. They in turn would warn other villages. Gradually, word would spread to every Sethite region.

"We could go back," said Japheth, feeling that maybe there was something they could do to help.

"I know what you're feeling, brother, for I, too, feel I should do something about what we've been told. But what difference would two more young elders make when the true responsibility lies on Father and our wisest elders? They want us to honor our wives, and I am pleased to do so." He grabbed Sede around the waist and drew her to his side, kissing her sweetly on the lips. Shoda and Japheth smiled, recognizing the gesture of new love.

Japheth and Shoda had found their moment of unity the night the Watcher had appeared to them. Desire had risen within their hearts, and when they united, it was though they were bathed in the presence of the Lord. Their spiritual ears were opened, and they heard the song of heaven. It seemed they were transported to heaven itself. From that moment on, each had the ability to sing the song of the Lord, a song that spontaneously rose within their hearts. They could sing the melody and knew the words even though they had never learned them. It was Yahweh's gift to them for honoring each other until love had found its place within their hearts.

As the brothers looked at each other, they seemed to realize this special time could never be replaced; it would be something they would only experience once.

Each couple bid the other farewell as they returned to the forest to experience their time "set apart."

As the day blended into the next, Sede was lost in the wonder of how she felt being with Shem. At times she felt a rush of passion welling up within her. It was so wonderful but also a little confusing. She wasn't sure what to do about it. Should she approach him or wait for him to approach her? It was all so new to her. She felt herself blushing often and yet delighting that she could satisfy her husband and find the same satisfaction herself. She came to the conclusion that love was a mystery that would take a lifetime to discover. She had only just begun. She would have to be patient with herself and let love unfold its mystery as *it* pleased.

One night they found a river; it was so beautiful in the moonlight. "Let's swim!" she said in sudden impulse. She had her clothes off and was in the water before Shem could respond. Laughing, he threw his clothes off, joining her with a splash. The water felt so good moving around them; it was though it was caressing them. While he held her in his arms and the water swirled about them, they kissed the kiss of love. They each felt the thrill of passion rise within and looked at each other in surprise!

"Sede, isn't this wonderful? I can hardly believe I feel these things and that you are experiencing them too!"

She smiled, remembering her father's words. 'She could give him something that nothing else in life could. She was able to make him complete as a man.' And oh, how he made her complete as a woman. She never dreamed that in that hidden place within her, she would find a full satisfaction that only he could give her.

As they continued to talk, they heard voices farther down the river. Shem gave the conoka call, and Japheth answered with the same. Sede and Shem laughed as they made their way to the riverbank and dressed. Meeting Japheth and Shoda, he jokingly spouted, "It seems we were meant to meet. Who could guess that throughout this great wilderness, we would be at this very place at this very time?"

They looked at each other with a knowing and said at the same time, "I think we should return to the village." Both women giggled for they knew too. It was time to return.

The Unexpected

As they followed their own tracks back to the village, they sensed their lives would never be the same. This would probably be the last time they would be together in the wilderness. Shoda turned to Sede. "I will always remember you this day, Sede—you in your hunting skins. I've loved our adventures together."

"Aye," Sede said with a smile. "I also treasure the memories of the hunt." A tear rolled down her cheek as she fought back her emotions, for though she wanted to be married, she would always be a hunter/warrior at heart. "Perhaps through our children, we will see our lives renewed. It will be them who will rise in our village to hunt for us."

Shoda gave a playful laugh as she bumped her shoulder to Sede's. "Yes, and you'll probably be their teacher!" Their bond was clear; they knew each other's hearts.

As they descended from the forest plateau, they saw smoke rising in the distance in the direction of their village. "Hurry!" Shem said in a panic. "I fear trouble for our people!" All four ran as they descended from the hills, stopping at Shem and Sede's wedding tent. They dropped to the ground, realizing the village was under siege. Their hunting skills were instantly engaged as they scanned the valley below, assessing what they saw.

And what they saw struck horror to their hearts. It was the chaos of a raid. Nephilim giants had their people crowded in pens as others herded their cattle, sheep, and camels. The pens held young women and children. A large troop of giants swept through the streets torching the huts, and soon the whole village was ablaze. Sede's first thought was for her family. Where were her father and Dosta, Noah and Ezmere?

Through the confusion of what they were watching, a Nephilim galloped through the charred archway on a large horse and dismounted. It was a female Nephilim, the likes of which they had never seen before. She was majestic in beauty and carried an air of power. The sun reflected off her polished breastplate and her golden helmet.

"Un…believ….able," said Shem, almost unable to spit the words out. She shouted orders and waved her spear for the women to line up. Slowly, she passed in front of each one, lifting their chin with her finger and looking intently into each face.

"She must be looking for someone," Shoda whispered.

"Yes, but who?" said Japheth.

Sede felt sickened in the pit of her stomach. "I think she's looking for me!"

They turned and looked at her in surprise.

"You?" questioned Shem.

"Yes. Playtheus is relentless. It wouldn't surprise me if he's behind all this!"

"This must be what the Watcher meant when he warned us that an evil was coming to our village," Shem whispered.

"Oh Yahweh, what is to become of our people?" she moaned, trying to hold back her tears.

The four kept hidden for over an hour as they watched the abuse of their kin and were helpless to stop it. It was then that the female leader gathered the village elders. Their hands were bound to a pole, and one after another, a brutal giant began whipping them until their robes turned red.

"I can't stand this," Sede cried. "I know they want me. I need to go down there and stop this. If they have me, they'll let our people live."

"No!" Shem said sternly. "I can't let you do that." He grabbed her arm as she struggled to stand to her feet. Just then, the elder who was being beaten was cut free from the post and pointed toward the wedding tent. She blew her horn and shouted a command, pointing in their direction.

"Time to go!" whispered Shem. Each of them crept backwards, trying to conceal their presence.

They ran up the trail they had descended, building up speed as they went. The sound of the horn grew louder as the Nephilim began to close the gap. Shem called out as they ran, "If we get separated, we'll meet at the village gate after they're gone."

"Aye," yelled Sede.

"Aye," shouted Shoda and Japheth.

It was now getting dark, and they could see the torch lights of those who pursued them. Breathlessly, Shem yelled, "They're relentless!"

"Yes," shouted Sede. "They want me for a prize!"

He looked back at her and yelled, "Never! Never will I lose you again!"

Sede began to cry as the burden of what was happening began to weigh on her. This was all because of her. All because some lust-hungry Nephilim wanted her. She felt both guilt and anger.

Japheth finally said, "I think we should split up. They'll be confused by four different tracks."

Shem didn't want to let Sede out of his sight; he feared for her safety. He knew, though, that Japheth was right. It was probably their only chance to survive capture. "Sede, promise me that you won't give yourself up to save us. Promise me?" Tears ran down his cheek as he choked out his words.

She saw his love for her and the fear he felt for her safety. "Yes, Shem; I promise."

"Let's do it then!" he shouted. "We'll meet at the village gate."

"Aye," they yelled in unison, each splitting in different directions.

It was as if the hand of Yahweh guided them. They ran through the forest in the pitch black of night and didn't fall or hit tree or branch. When the Nephilim found the place where their tracks split, Grog let out a great roar that they the pursued could feel. It sent a hair-raising chill through their bodies.

Shem prayed as he ran, "Oh Yahweh, keep Sede safe. Bring us all together at the village gate." He felt tears well up in his eyes as he choked back his desire to cry. They ran late through the night, and had they not been hunters, they would never have had the stamina to endure the driving pace. Finally, the light of the torches dimmed and could no longer be seen. Had they given up? Or worse yet, had they found one of them? Shem begun his trek back to the village.

Dawn was cresting over the hills as he stopped at the wedding tent. Looking down at the village, he searched for the other three. All the village people were gone, and only a frightened dog nervously roamed around the smoldering huts. It was a ravished sight. All he had known of Taasa-toka was gone. Cautiously, he made his way down the path. As he climbed over the crumbled wall, he saw some of his kin lying dead at the door of their charred huts. Others lay in the streets, spears still in their bodies. These were fellow hunter/warriors who had tried to defend their people. It grieved him beyond words. Hot tears filled his eyes while he continued down the street to the village gate. The great gate hang sideways on one hinge, still smoldering from the fire. There, sitting against the broken down wall, were Shoda and Japheth. "Where's Sede?" he asked.

"She isn't here yet. Come, sit with us. We'll wait for her together," Shoda said as she motioned for him to sit next to her, wiping the tears from her eyes. They sat in silence, not able to speak. The horror of what surrounded them was too devastating.

While they waited, they saw something in the distance. It was a caravan. As they drew closer, they recognized them. It was Noah, Tolmaka, Dollo, and Gruetat along with their families. Running to meet them, they told them about watching the raid and being helpless to stop it.

"My son, where is Sede?!" Tolmaka asked in a panic.

"She hasn't arrived yet, father Tolmaka. We split up in the forest when we were pursued and agreed to meet here. We've been waiting for her return. Follow us," urged Shem. "We'll take the caravan to the wedding tent. We have provision there, and we'll watch for Sede from the forest trail."

All that day, the men buried the dead. It bore heavy on their hearts to see the devastation all around them and to recognize those who had died. As the hours wore on, Shem kept looking to the hills. When would she come? His heart ached to have her in his arms once more and know she was safe.

Japheth saw his distress and touched his shoulder in reassurance. "She'll come, Brother, she'll come."

But as night began to fall, Shem couldn't hold back; he collapsed at Tolmaka's feet and began to weep. "I fear she's been captured!" he cried. "She's been gone too long. She's a hunter/warrior and would have been back by now."

Tolmaka bent to his knees, holding him in his arms. "Shem, Shem, my son; she'll be all right…and I say this because I believe Yahweh's promises. Yahweh will not fail to perform His word. Tomorrow we'll search for her, and then we'll know for sure. Come, my son, comfort yourself with our fellowship and love."

Shem relaxed in his arms, knowing his words were true. They would wait till morning light and then begin their search.

Tolmaka went with them as they retraced the spot where the four had split up. They followed Sede's tracks to a place where the ground was disturbed with broken limbs, bearing the signs of a skirmish. Looking through the matted grass, Shem bent to pick up something he recognized. It was Sede's seed necklace.

"Ah!" he cried. "They've taken her!" He held the necklace to his chest. He knew she had left it for him to find. It was her sign that she had been there. He took the necklace to Tolmaka, thinking he knew it was hers.

"No, my son. I've never seen this before. It must be something she kept as a memory."

Shem knew then that he had been given something she hadn't even shared with her father. Sede and he were the only ones who knew of the seed of Eden. Hot tears fell from his eyes. His wife, his beautiful wife, was gone…gone. Tolmaka held him as he buried his head in his chest. "My wife, my wife!"

Tolmaka, too, began to cry. "Yes, my son, your wife and my precious daughter…"

With a reassuring voice, Tolmaka declared, "Let us offer a sacrifice on the altar to Yahweh. We will honor Him for saving our lives and acknowledge that His promises are sure. I believe that Sede lives. 'Yahweh is not a man that He should lie or a man that He should repent.' We will see her again!"

Shem felt his faith and conviction, and it brought strength and comfort to his troubled heart. Noah embraced him and nodded. They laid the lamb that they had brought on their caravan on the altar.

As they stood with uplifted hands and faces, fire came down from heaven, and the peaceful presence of Yahweh filled them. Embracing one another, Noah said, "Today we begin anew. We must leave this place and press high into the mountains. It is there we must go!"

"Come, Shem," said Tolmaka. "Sede is in Yahweh's hands. We don't have the power to save her; only He can. We will not go to her, but she will come to us."

Shem knew that not only were his words true but they were prophetic. Only Yahweh could save Sede now. Only Yahweh could bring his beloved back to him. It would be she who would come to him.

Chapter 23

Playtheus' Rescue

Playtheus became restless with his days. He tired of empty pleasure and longed for something lasting. He realized that he was changing and wanted more from life than what could be bought at a market. He cared little that Nersha was gone and kept wondering what his father meant 'that she would find Sede-quete.'

That night as he slept, he dreamed. A mist surrounded him as he stood beneath a great oak tree. As he looked intently through the mist, he saw someone walking toward him. As the form took shape, he recognized who it was. His heart leapt. It was Sede-quete! She walked slowly toward him and clasped his hands. Looking into his eyes, she tenderly began to speak…"Playtheus, you know your own heart and the emptiness that lives within you. You've seen the life of Yahweh in me, and your heart yearns to know this life too. Turn, Playtheus; turn from your wickedness. Embrace the life that awaits you. You can have what you've seen in me. It waits only for you to ask."

When she finished speaking, she released his hands and slowly backed into the cloudy mist. He looked in wonder as she disappeared. As he stood there, a great peace filled him, and he lifted his hands to heaven. He spoke the words of his heart as tears rolled down his cheek, and he felt a "love" he had never known before fill him.

Then the dream changed. He saw Nersha and Sede-quete together in one place. Sede-quete's hands were bound, and Nersha was parading her in the camp of her riotous army. She was boasting of her triumph to her captain and his troops. He felt Nersha's hatred for Sede-quete and knew her life balanced on the edge of a blade. It was only a matter of time before she would know its piercing thrust.

When he woke, he remembered his father's words: 'Nersha will find her.' Calling for his chariot, he soon arrived at Toleshba's. The door opened as before, and he entered as he was ushered into the room by the "Invisible."

"Ah, Playtheus. I'm pleased to see you. I sense your power has grown and that you have a plan. I can see it. It's a powerful plan!"

"Yes, Toleshba, and if you help me, you'll profit much!"

"Say on, Playtheus."

He drew close to her, knowing he had the power to draw on her essence. She felt strangely weakened with his approach.

"What has happened, Playtheus? You're different!"

"Yes, Toleshba, I *am* different, and I won't be tricked by you again. Today we work together. I will get what I want, and you'll get what you want."

Her eyes widened as she sensed she was about to experience a new thing, and it thrilled her. "Tell me of this plan."

He began with a question. "Can you transport us to a certain place and then bring us back?"

"Yes, I can do that."

"Good," he said, "for my plan requires it. Find Nersha in the flames and take us to her. I believe she's found the one from my dreams, **and I want her back!**" His words thundered with power as he spoke them. Toleshba trembled as the power penetrated her. She realized he was not going to play games, and she would have to follow through with what she agreed. Playtheus continued, "In return for finding and transporting Sede-quete back with me, I will give you Nersha for a companion."

The atmosphere shifted after he spoke his words. Joy burst from Toleshba, and bursts of green light radiated from her tattoo. She threw her head back and roared, "Yes!" She trembled thinking that she could have Nersha for her very own. She had heard of her beauty, power, and unique virtues. At that moment, every fiber of her being longed to have her. "Oh Playtheus, my heart's desire would be fulfilled to own such a one!"

"Good," he said. "I desire to give her to you in exchange for the service you give me. Do you vow your pledge to give me what I want?"

Her eyes narrowed when she realized that by making such a vow, she would not be able to manipulate him and get more from their bargain than what was agreed. She looked at him squarely, her eyes set to his, and pledged, "I vow to find Sede-quete. I will transport us to her and then bring you back. For this service, you will give me the female Nephilim."

"Agreed!" he nodded, and their arrangement was sealed.

Toleshba marveled at his strength for she had never seen this in him before. "You have been ushered to the very threshold of becoming a 'Mighty One.' I sense your great power, and I submit to you, Playtheus!"

He raised and set his jaw, knowing that what she said was true. She was no match for him for he had become greater than she would ever be. Leading him to the brass bowl of flames, she sang her haunting song once more, slowly waving her arms over the fire. She could hardly contain herself knowing what she would have once she had rendered her service. "There…there she is!" she muttered in excitement.

Nersha had Sede-quete chained by the neck to her horse. She rode as Sede-quete followed on foot. Nersha wickedly laughed as she pulled on the chain, making Sede stumble and fall. Rage rumbled within Playtheus as he saw how she was being treated. Even though she had left him, he had recovered from the rejection he had felt. All he wanted now was to be in her presence once more, to hear her voice, and to look into her eyes and see the beauty of who she was.

"Now I must say my incantation," Toleshba mumbled to herself. Using strange words that he knew were her words of enchantment, she began. Over and over she said them until they began to feel a tingle. Slowly, their form became a mist, lifting into the air. They floated through the window and into the open sky. As she held his hand, her misty smile reassured him. The feeling was exhilarating for both of them as they flew high above the earth. They flew a great distance and then, far below, he could see the long trail of captives with Hagonoths leading the way. Nersha was on her horse, dragging Sede-quete behind her.

Descending, Toleshba and Playtheus touched the ground right in front of Nersha. The startled horse sensed them before they were seen and reared, coming to the ground with a great stomp. Nervously, he backed up and whinnied as they slowly materialized. The soldiers froze in fear at this powerful display of sorcery, and Nersha was beside herself when she saw them. She knew he had seen her brutal behavior toward Sede-quete. His hot displeasure was evident.

"Greetings, my lord," she said, fumbling over her words.

Playtheus pointed his finger at her as he circled the horse to rescue Sede. "Down...now!" he commanded. She dismounted, trembling in fear. Again pointing at her, he commanded, "You...be still!" She froze in obedience. He rushed to Sede's collapsed body, and with great strength, broke her chains with his hands. Tears fell from his eyes to see his queen beaten and treated with such humiliation. Scooping her up in his arms, he whispered in her pale face, "No more will you suffer by her hand...no more."

Fear gripped Nersha, knowing that she had no place of repentance with him. She dropped to her knees, reaching her hands out to him. Pleadingly she cried, "Please, my lord, I did this for us!"

Pointing his finger at her, he thundered, "No more, Nersha, no more!" He held Sede to his chest and embraced her gently, looking down on her frail body. "Oh Sede-quete, Sede-quete!" he whispered in unbelief at what he saw.

Turning to Grog, he gave his command. "Your reign of terror is over. Return these Sethites to their villages along with all their belongings. **I forbid you to harm them again!**" His voice thundered like the voice of a god and echoed to the far distant hills.

Grog fell to his knees and lowered his face to the ground, groveling before him. "Yes, my prince, as you have commanded!" Weakened by Playtheus' thundering words, Grog struggled to stand to his feet. He turned to his troops and shouted his command. His soldiers gathered the captives for their return.

Sede began to cry, realizing her kinsmen would be saved. "Thank you, Playtheus, for this mercy you have shown them."

"Yes, Sede-quete. I do this for you. I know your heart, even if you think I don't."

She could hardly believe what she was hearing. He sounded different. There was softness and compassion in his voice. Was this the same arrogant Nephilim she knew?

Turning to Toleshba, he said, "It is time." Again Toleshba chanted her incantation over and over again. The four of them turned into mist and sailed through the air. Far below, they saw the captives and giants gazing at them as they flew through the sky. Toleshba smiled as she took Nersha's trembling hand while Playtheus held Sede in his arms, close to his heart. Tenderly, he looked down on her bloodied body lying helplessly in his arms. She looked so weak. Would she live?

Sede's head was awhirl. She had lost a great deal of blood and felt light-headed. She had the sensation of flying but didn't really understand that she was. She looked into Playtheus' face, and it seemed...but a mist. Their flight ended at Toleshba's, where they materialized.

Playtheus released Sede to weakly stand at his side. Nersha saw the love he had for her, and it enraged her. She had wanted that love and now realized she would never have it. He stepped toward her, and she trembled from the power exuding from his presence.

"There is one last thing I will be taking before I leave you with your new master." Nersha's eyes flashed from him to Toleshba and back to him as she tried to understand what he meant. He smiled at Toleshba and said, "Behold, Toleshba, the power of a 'Mighty One'!"

Taking Nersha's face in his hands, Playtheus began to draw on her essence. He did not draw slowly as she was accustomed to but angrily. She trembled, frozen by his power over her. He drew, and drew, and drew even more as she began to stagger on her feet. "Take her arm," he ordered Toleshba. "I'm not done!"

Toleshba's eyes widened, realizing he had power over Nersha *and* her. Deeper and deeper he drew. She began to collapse. "No!" he commanded. "You will stand before me and allow this!" He focused his eyes on hers, and she straightened her stance. Humbling her further, he drew one last powerful time. With an explosion of light, they were all blown backward except for Playtheus. The three looked up from the floor to see Playtheus standing tall, strong, and erect, power radiating from his body. Reaching down, he carefully helped Sede to her feet.

As Nersha stood before Playtheus, she knew she was doomed. "Here, Toleshba; I give her to you." Playtheus took Nersha by the hand and put it in Toleshba's.

A look of horror came over Nersha's face as she realized Playtheus had given her to a witch. "You can't do this to me. I'm a Regal Renown!" she shouted.

"Yes, Nersha, I can. You are within my power to do with as I wish, and I wish to give you to Toleshba." He began to speak words of enchantment over Nersha, binding her to Toleshba. When he finished, he then sealed his words by clapping his hands three times over her. "You will now live to please Toleshba. No longer are you mine but hers alone. You are now within *her* power to do with as she wishes. And I am certain she will take great delight in defiling you. This is your just reward for thinking you could destroy my queen." Looking over his shoulder, he saw Sede struggling to stand, weakened to the point of collapse.

Toleshba lifted Nersha's palms to her lips, kissing them lustfully. She then, like a she wolf, slowly circled her prey. She hungrily gazed upon her beauty, virtues, and depth of angelic potential. They were now all hers. Leaning into her neck, she inhaled, shuddering with the excitement she felt. Nersha felt her warm breath as she whispered in her ear, "Playtheus' words have bound you to me. Your very purpose is now to please me. And oh, you shall!"

Her words sent a cold chill through Nersha, and she shuddered. A dark dread settled within her knowing that she was now forever bound to this horrible witch and all she had planned. Never had a human owned a Renown. This was unthinkable! If ever she had the chance, she would get her revenge. She would make him pay.

"Come, my dear. With my knowing eyes, I wish to search the recesses of your soul and discover your most intimate secrets. They will be open and bare to my eager and hungry gaze."

Oh, the horror of this woman! Nersha's cries echoed down the dark corridor as she was led away only to hear Toleshba's sinister laugh answer back. There would be no release from this hell. She was forever bound to this fate.

Playtheus felt his anger released. He exhaled, knowing he had handled her the way she deserved. His father was right; he had used her to get what he wanted, and what he wanted stood before him. He caught Sede just as she began to collapse. Lifting her in his arms once more, he held her gently to his chest. She actually felt him communicate love through his tender embrace. She was relieved to be out of Nersha's presence. She knew death was near and that Nersha's intent was to kill her.

The horror of what she endured replayed in her memory. Nersha had captured her in the forest and gloated, boasting to Grog and his soldiers of her supremacy. She was a god among them, and who was this frail human she had captured? Nothing. When she brought Sede to the camp where her kinsmen were being held, she stripped her naked, parading her in their midst. Her kinsmen covered their eyes, mourning for her shame. Erud had cried with a loud voice, "May Yahweh cover you with the robe of righteousness, my child!" At that moment, she felt the power of Yahweh come upon her, and she no longer felt the humiliation of shame. She held her head high, and Nersha perceived the strength she possessed. It enraged her. Her attempt to humiliate her had failed. In the heat of anger, she ran a sword through Erud and threw her skins back at her, shouting for her to put them back on. Sede stood tall and strong, making Nersha tremble in a way she didn't understand. 'How can humility of spirit give such strength?' she thought. 'I hate her!'

In the days that followed, she tried every way she knew to break Sede's spirit. Finally, she tied her to a post and beat her with a whip. Sede endured, finding strength through Yahweh. This enraged Nersha more. She chained her by the neck and made her walk behind her horse. "I'm the victor, and you, the weakling conquered!" Nersha savored sweet revenge for the love Playtheus had set on this mere human instead of her, a majestic Regal Renown. She spit on Sede from atop her horse, kicking her to the ground with her foot. Sede knew that when she tired of humiliating her, she would surely run her through with a sword. It was only a matter of time.

Playtheus held Sede all the way back to his mansion, the chariot speeding its way through the streets. His tears fell on her for the joy and pain he felt—joy to see her but pain that she had been beaten and humiliated by Nersha. His arms were red and slick from the blood that ran from her back. Carrying her into the mansion, he called for A-thia and Fro-mos. Happy to see her once more, they were eager to serve her.

"Bring me water, and healing herbs, and linens!" he commanded. As she weakly stood before him, he slowly removed her bloody skins. Her eyes fell to the floor as she knew he now saw her at her most vulnerable. He began to weep, knowing she felt this humiliation.

"I am so sorry you feel this shame before me, Sede-quete, but I want to be the one to clean your wounds." He carried her to his bed, rolling her on her stomach. Slowly and gently, he began to clean the blood from her back, which looked like a mass of bloody flesh. It was a wonder she still lived. In the open gashes, dirt and grass were embedded from where she fell when Nersha kicked her to the ground. She writhed with pain as he carefully washed the dirt and grass away. The blood seeped into the white linen under her and soon turned red. He bent down and kissed her back, and she felt his tears fall upon her. Although he didn't speak, she could hear him softly sob. Gently, he dabbed her back with his cloth. Then, ever so carefully, he began to place the healing herbs over the raw wounds. Slowly, he wrapped clean linen around her chest, holding the herbs in place. Helping her to her feet, he covered her with a robe, his face filled with loving tenderness.

Looking into his eyes, she saw a difference in him—something she had never seen before. There was a brokenness and a humbleness about him. "You're different, Playtheus. What has happened to you?"

He paused, just savoring the sound of her voice. He had longed to hear her call him by his name. "I'm glad that you see this change, Sede-quete, for I have changed. It is because of you that this has happened. I was broken when you left. At first, I was angry because I felt betrayed, but then I began to see how very selfish I had been. I had wanted only power from you and what you could give me. I believe I've learned something that only the human part of me could ever know…I have learned selfless love."

She looked wide eyed at him, realizing what he said was truth. "I'm happy for you, Playtheus, that you have found this truth for only in selfless love can one find love in return." He marveled as she spoke, for he heard the wisdom in what she said.

"Tell me of this man you love…this Shem."

She felt uncomfortable that he would ask her of her husband. She was silent, not wanting to answer him.

"I sense your innocent virtues have changed. Have you married?"

She looked at him in surprise. How could he know such things? Still silent, she searched his face. What was he doing?

"Sede-quete, I sense your suspicion and understand why you think this way. But in truth, I only want your companionship. I am so pleased to be in your presence once more." Bending forward, he kissed her on her cheek. Her face flushed red, and he smiled. "Yes, your innocence is still my admiration. Come, lie down, and be at rest."

She lay on her stomach so her back would not begin to bleed once more. He rested beside her and laid his head on the pillow. Slowly, he closed his eyes and fell asleep. As she watched him, she marveled at his transformation. What had happened to make him so human? She still felt suspicion because she knew that he *was* a Nephilim.

As she rested, she, too, fell asleep. It had been a horrible experience being captured and enduring days of cruelty and torture. At least she could rest and be free from the threat of death. She had no idea how she would ever get back to Shem. Her heart ached to see him, and she worried that he was feeling the pain of loss because she was missing. She knew that had Playtheus not showed up when he did, she would have surely died from her weakened state. She had no strength left in her body to fight anything or anyone.

When Playtheus woke, he felt great joy. She was the first thing he saw when he opened his eyes. She was back, and he felt wonderful pleasure just looking upon her as she lay there so beautiful, so still. He took in her every detail: her eyelashes, the arch of her brow, her beautifully shaped lips, the way her hair fell at her neck, and the warm breath she exhaled. Oh, how he longed to inhale her essence. He closed his eyes, restraining himself. Through the days that had passed, he had learned a self-control that he had never known before. He actually found a strange dignity that came from denying himself immediate satisfaction. He realized that quantity was not as satisfying as the one, precious single experience. This was the desire he had—to have one precious experience with her.

She opened her eyes and realized that he had been watching her sleep. Tears glistened in her eyes as she remembered watching Shem the morning she woke in their wedding tent.

"Oh, Sede-quete, I see your sadness. Have I grieved you?"

Again, she was surprised that he would show her such selfless regard. "No, I'm not grieved, Playtheus."

His soul felt pleasure hearing his name fall from her lips. Smiling, he touched his forehead with hers. Again she felt herself well up with tears, for such was the gesture of her people to show a moment of endearment. She missed her husband and her people. Would she ever see them again?

Playtheus helped her to her old room, where she rested. As the day drew to an end, before she welcomed sleep, she strained to stand and walked to the veranda. Standing still and quiet, she lifted her gaze to the starry night sky. Somehow, being beneath the night sky made her feel close to Shem. She knew that wherever he was, he, too, was looking at the same stars and thinking of her. She whispered her love to him, hoping he would receive what she desired to give. And from that night on, before she slept, she stood at the balcony and whispered her love to him, speaking to him in the quiet of the night.

She spent the next months recovering from the beating that had nearly taken her life. A-thia took her daily to the same warm pool she had used the day she had been prepared for high companion. Each day as she went, Playtheus came and stood in the shadow of the pillars. Resting his head against the cool marble, he watched her as she gracefully swam and relaxed in the misty water. She was so lovely to behold. She *did* take his breath away. No longer did he look upon her with lust in his heart but with awe, seeing the beauty of who she really was: the woman he loved.

A tear rolled down his cheek as he realized he had been given another chance to be with her. He felt such gratitude, a feeling that was new to him. He had never explored the human side of who he was, for the fallen angelic within him was so aggressive. Always *it* demanded satisfaction and more of everything. Only through his contact with Sede-quete had he discovered this beauty that belonged to humans only. Deep in his heart, he wished he were only human. Only then would he have had a chance of winning her for himself. Another hot tear rolled down his cheek as he realized that even his tears were from his human heart. Sede-quete had made this revelation possible. He would be forever grateful to her.

Chapter 24

Memories Made

Their days were comfortable as they spent quiet time with each other. Playtheus had not humiliated her with dancing girls and experiences that shocked her but was gracious and caring. He knew he had been given a special gift: time with her. He also knew there would come a day when she would have to go. In selfless abandonment, he desired to give her memories—memories that would enable her to take a part of him with her for the rest of her life. In this way, they would always be with each other through memories. Most of their days were spent at his mansion, strolling the garden grounds and enjoying simple conversation surrounded by the beauty and quiet of the day. But he wanted to show her things that held real meaning to him—things that spoke to his heart.

One day they rode his magnificent horses on the white beaches of Atlantis. She had never ridden a horse before, but being the hunter she was, she soon learned the skill and could keep up with him. They raced side by side, enjoying the speed and strength of the great creatures beneath them. From the water's edge, speeding hooves sent sprays of water flying in the air. Joy filled their hearts as the wind blew in their faces and the salt air filled their lungs. He turned to see her hair flying and the look of pleasure on her face. 'Oh, to share this moment in her life.' As they slowed, he dismounted, and she followed. Slowly, they began to walk side by side as they led their horses. The tide brought the lapping water to their feet, and the sound of seagulls called from high above. The surroundings were so peaceful and calm.

Playtheus stopped and began to stroke his horse's neck. She could tell he was pondering his thoughts. "Sede-quete, I show you Fallon and Mora. Of all my possessions, they give me something that nothing else can. When I ride, I feel freedom—freedom from all that presses on me from this life I live here in Atlantis. I tried to find freedom through sensual pleasure, but only when I'm on Fallon's back, feeling his strength beneath me and riding with the wind in my face, do I know the great pleasure of freedom!"

Stroking Mora's neck, she listened to his words. She was sensing his heart, and it pulled at hers. He was sharing something he had told no one else. She sensed the beauty of what he had just given her: an intimate look into his heart.

Her thoughts shifted to what he'd said about his horse, and she remembered something the elders had taught about the animals that Yahweh brought to Adam. "Our elders have taught us about a great wonder—a wonder concerning the animals Yahweh brought to Adam. They teach us that at one time, they could speak to Adam with their voices. It was a time when Adam had the eyes of the spirit and not the veil of the flesh."

He looked at her curiously, not understanding what she was talking about. She laughed softly, realizing he didn't have the benefit of knowing their history or the spiritual ways of their people. She spoke again, as if trying to sooth him. "We, the Sethites, have the knowledge of the truth. The rest of the world lies in dark ignorance. There was a time when animals could talk and commune with mankind. Only after Adam's rebellion was that ability lost. He had lost his perfect spiritual perception." She looked sadly at Mora while she continued to stroke her neck. "Wouldn't it be wonderful if she could tell us what she feels when she carries us and feels the wind in *her* face?"

He marveled at the mystery she knew. She came from such a different world than his. His cared only for dark knowledge and the power it could give. Hers was a world of simplicity and innocent truth. There was something compelling about what she was saying. When she spoke about the spiritual perception Adam had lost, his heart burned within him, realizing he longed for such truth and understanding.

He leaned forward, touching his forehead to hers. "I want to know what you know. I sense the love you have for Yahweh. I wish to know Him as you do and have this same love I see in you."

She looked at him with compassion. "I don't know if this is possible for a Nephilim, but you could ask Him. There's one thing I do know about Yahweh… He is a God of great love and compassion, and His ear is open to the penitent and humble of heart."

"How do I ask?" he innocently questioned, searching her face.

"Just open your heart, Playtheus. Speak the words that your heart tells you. Faith is that simple."

He looked into her eyes and saw the purity of her soul and the compassion she was pouring upon him. His heart yearned to know the love she knew. "My heart would say…'I was born of corruption. I am the product of something I had no power over. But this does not excuse me. My whole life has been in pursuit of pleasure and power. With all my heart, I wish to turn my back on all the evil I know and embrace you, Yahweh, the only true God. I humble myself and ask that you would accept my prayer." A single tear rolled down his cheek. He said no more but let his prayer linger close to his heart. Ever so slowly, he felt a calm, warm love settle within him and a clean, pure spirit rise within. He looked at her in amazement. "Something wonderful has just happened within me, Sede-quete."

His countenance changed before her, and great peace emitted from his being that she, herself, could feel. His hands tingled as she felt them cover hers. In his eyes, she saw what had transpired in his soul. It was the love of Yahweh in him. He had a softened look, a resting strength. Could it be possible that Yahweh had shown him loving kindness and tender mercy? Could saving mercy come to the lowest of sinners? Could it be that those who humble themselves are lifted up? Her whole paradigm shifted. Yahweh was more wondrous than she knew.

It had been Playtheus' desire to give her a gift of memories this day, but he realized as the love of Yahweh continued to fill his soul, that she had been a part of a memory given to him. Yahweh had changed his life there on the beautiful white beach of the Great Sea. *This* memory they would both carry for the rest of their lives.

As they slowly made their way back to his mansion, she realized that riding Mora had opened her wounds. Her back was bleeding again. She would have to limit her activity in order for them to totally heal. She was reminded again how close she had come to death from Nersha's beating. As each day blended into the next, her wounds began to seal, no longer bleeding when she turned or twisted. When he felt the time was right and she was well enough to travel, he wanted to show her a truly special place.

They began the journey to a distant mountain in the middle of the island of Atlantis. Their camels traveled many days, stopping only at night to camp. When they reached the mountain, they left their servants behind and began to climb. Sede loved being in the wilderness once more. Every cell in her body seemed to respond to the ground, the trees, the sky, the forest. She was still a hunter.

When they arrived at the mouth of a cave, he excitedly announced, "This is it!" Making their way along the rocky walls, they began their descent through the wide tunnel. The path was as steps leading deeper and deeper into the earth. He held high his torch, leading the way, descending deeper and deeper. Finally, they could see a faint light reflecting from the rock wall far ahead. Turning at the wall, she saw it, a wonder of wonders! How could anyone describe what her eyes now saw?!

Before her was a vast, underground world. In unbelief, she asked, "What is this place?!"

Smiling, he waved his hand before him and majestically announced, "This… is the heart of the world!"

She moved from his side, wanting to see more. Stepping out, she thrillingly lifted her hands and whirled in a circle, laughing for the joy that filled her. "This is amazing beyond belief," she shouted. Her voice echoed through the open valley beyond them. She looked up to see a brilliant, mysterious light. From an opening far above, the light fell on the surrounding valley walls that were covered with gold, silver, and what looked like veins of jewels. They were like a mirror that reflected and intensified the light. The air was filled with the faint mist of a waterfall that fell from a rocky ledge. Lush trees and plants grew that she didn't recognize; their strange and exotic blooms released a fragrance like no other. Suddenly, a flock of birds swooped before them, trilling their song as if rejoicing with her. She watched as they soared high into the air and then fell in unison, gliding over the crystal blue lake.

She paused to let the light fall on her face. Lifting her hands palms up, she felt praise fill her heart. Sensing a breeze, she deeply inhaled the fragrant aroma. Returning to him, she grabbed his forearms and, with excitement in her voice, asked, "How do you know of this place? Tell me!"

Smiling, he brushed her cheek with his finger and said, "This place was shown to me in a dream." He marveled at her wonderful innocence of discovery. There she stood before him…so full of life. Even the air around her seemed charged with an energy he could feel.

"Oh, what a wonderful dream you've had, Playtheus. And that it came true!"

A tear misted his eye as he continued. "Yes, all this was in my dream, and here we are.…"

Excitedly, she stepped forward, wanting to see more. "Come, Playtheus, help me discover your dream!" She grabbed his hand and pulled him. Knowing how his dream was to unfold, he clasped her small hand and led her forward.

They walked the waterline of the lake, beholding the open expanse before them. The air was so fresh…the colors so vivid. It was though they had been transported to another world. And in a way, they had. When they reached the waterfall, she had a sudden thought. "Oh, let's swim!"

Before he could respond, she shed her robe and dove into the water, laughing in delight. Giving in to her spontaneity, he dropped his robe and joined her. Their undergarments clung to their wet skin as they both swam to the waterfall that cascaded from the overhanging rocks. Standing beneath the spray, she laughed, moving her hands and face through the watery curtain. Giving him a grateful hug, she said, "Oh, thank you, Playtheus, for sharing this 'wonder of wonders' with me!"

He closed his eyes to keep back his tears for he *had* dreamt of this place, but what he hadn't told her was that she was in his dream and had just now said what she had told him in the dream. He cleared his throat, not wanting her to see his tears. They continued to swim, letting the cool water sooth and refresh them. As she gracefully glided, he saw the beauty of the woman he loved. She was so lovely.… He felt himself caught up in the wonder of seeing his dream unfold. He was living his dream! Everything they said and did was as "déjà vu." But it was when they dressed that he saw the scars on her back, and pain pricked his heart. It was because of him this had happened to her. He gently touched them and then, not wanting to draw attention to himself, helped her with her robe.

"Let's find something to eat and a place to rest," he said as he tied his sash. Leading her to a tree, they hungrily ate the hanging fruit, laughing as the juice dripped down their chins. He knew a place to rest and led her to a grassy ridge overlooking the whole land below them. It would be there they would recline. She carefully leaned against the mossy rock wall, not wanting to open the scars on her back. From where she sat, the whole panoramic view opened before them. With wonder in her voice, she asked, "Who would have thought that such a place existed? Are you the only one who knows of it?"

"I believe so, Sede-quete. The few times I've been here, my footprints were the only ones I've seen." She paused, marveling that she and he were the only two people in the world that knew.

When he knelt to sit beside her, she rested her head on his shoulder. "Thank you, Playtheus, for sharing such a wonderful secret with me; I will remember it always!"

He felt as though he would burst for the emotions he suddenly felt. This new awakening of his human side was overwhelming. He found it difficult to handle the tears that wanted to flow and the tenderness he felt. With his arm around her shoulder, he drew her close as they sat in silence, watching the flock of birds slowly soar and dive over the water far below. As they sat together, a loving but sad smile crossed his lips. His desire to give her memories had taken root. This place she would treasure and remember for the rest of her life.

As they journeyed back to Atlantis, Sede began to feel an uneasiness within her heart. Playtheus had shared his most intimate secrets with her, and she was beginning to feel the bond it was creating within her. If their time together were to continue, her love for Shem would be compromised. She could never let that happen. She felt no guilt for being Playtheus' friend; for in her innocence, that is how she saw him. But she knew he felt much differently about her. She knew he loved her. She couldn't be a part of wounding him. This intimacy could not continue. Somehow, she would have to find the courage to tell him. It was time for her to return home. Her life was there, not here. She had healed well enough. This last trip had shown her that she could now travel. When they returned to his mansion, she would find the right moment and tell him.

Several days later, as they reclined before their meal, she looked at him intently. "Playtheus, would you tell me something?"

"Yes, anything, Sede-quete. What do you desire to know?"

She hesitantly asked, "Where is this all leading to? What do you expect of me?"

He looked at her with tenderness. "Oh Sede-quete, you are so very wonderful!"

She marveled at the emotion she heard in the tone of his voice. It was his heart she heard. He was silent for a long time, looking down at his hands, not sure if he could speak. After he had gained composure, he cleared his throat and softly said, "What do I expect from you? I expect nothing…I've enjoyed your companionship these many months, making them the happiest I've ever known. I realize that you…" His voice began to crack, but he continued. "I realize you are the love of my life. You're the one I dreamed of those many years ago. I thought my dream was to gain me position and power. Little did I know my dream would reveal my heart's deepest need. You would be the one to show me what real love was."

She trembled. He was sharing his soul. His words were so very vulnerable. She knew there was no way she could return his love. Her heart was, and would forever be, sealed to Shem's. It was him she had thought of every night when she stood on the balcony beneath the stars, remembering their bond the night of their wedding. "Oh, Playtheus, I am so sorry for you. I know I can't return your love. It grieves me to tell you this, but I can't deceive you and tell you what you want to hear." She began to cry, knowing she was dealing with his tender heart.

He rose and sat beside her, putting his arms around her shoulder and gently rocking her as he pressed his cheek against her head. "It's all right, Sede-quete. Love now fills me, and I am able to accept what you're saying. I lived to be named a 'Mighty One,' but now I live only to love you."

Pulling strength from deep inside herself, she found the courage to ask, "Do you love me enough to let me go?"

As they faced each other, he looked long into her eyes, knowing that this day would come. A single tear slowly rolled down his cheek. "Yes, my love. I will see that you're returned. Never would I have thought this possible to give you up, but I now know that if I return you, that alone would be the greatest evidence of what I have told you…that I love you with a selfless love."

She began to cry as she understood he would never know the joy of having his love returned. "Oh, Playtheus, my heart is filled with sorrow for you. You are worthy to be loved!" She fell forward, weeping with her face buried in his chest. As he held her, his voice cracked with emotion. "Tomorrow I will take you to your Shem, and we will see each other no more." She wept with even deeper sorrow, knowing he truly did love her. He loved her enough to let her go.

"I have this one request, Sede-quete, before you go. Would you sleep in my arms this night? Will you give me this one last memory of you?" She pulled herself from his chest and searched his face. She saw his surrender to what he must do and the broken heart it caused. What he asked was not of passion but a deep longing for comfort. She knew that this would be the one thing she could give him instead of her love and felt no betrayal to Shem to do so. This would be from the heart of compassion.

He led her to his bed, where he held her in silence next to him. He pressed his cheek against her head, and although he said nothing, she felt her hair moisten from his tears. Her own tears silently fell, grieving for the sadness of his plight.

Just before he felt the shadow of sleep rest upon him, he whispered, "Thank you, Sede-quete, for making my dream come true. It was you, and you alone, who taught me to truly love." He softly kissed her head and gently hugged her. Drifting into his dreams, he realized that *this* was the "one precious experience" he had desired to have with her: to sleep with her in his arms.

Chapter 25

Ceremony of the "Mighty One"

In the morning, Playtheus took Sede to Champion Hall. He would use Pergisus to return her to her people. As they entered Castius' door, Talimus-qua-tam appeared in a flash of light, startling even Playtheus. "Hail, Father," he said bowing.

"What are you doing?" Talimus-qua-tam thundered, searching his son's face. It was obvious he knew his son's intentions.

Playtheus stepped forward, grasping his father's shoulder with an affectionate hand. "I'm letting her go," he answered tenderly.

"Are you mad, son? You can't do that!"

Sede felt quivering fear as Talimus-qua-tam's anger escalated.

"I must, Father. I can't use her to satisfy my own thirst for glory."

His father's eyes flared flames. "We're leaving!" he roared. Taking his cloak, he threw it around the three of them, and they disappeared.

When he unwrapped his cape, Sede realized he had transported them. They now stood in a large pavilion with a multitude of fallen angels circling the perimeter of the walls. Brilliant blue light radiated from each of them, and their beautiful wives stood at their sides. Just then, a glorious platform began to rise in the center of the room, coming from the floor beneath. Dramatic music filled the air in thrilling anticipation, and Sede quaked at the evil that surrounded her. It pressed on her from every side. Playtheus, sensing her fear, clasped her small hand and squeezed it softly. He whispered down to her, "It will be okay, Sede."

She heard the sound of affection in his tone and marveled that he used her hunting name. Never before had he called her by her people's name. He could have only known her hunting name from the note she had left him the night she fled his mansion. She trembled at his ability to make her feel so very special. She looked trustingly at him and squeezed his hand.

Playtheus was taken aback at the large crowd that had gathered and asked, "What is happening, Father?"

"This is your day, Son. This day you become a 'Mighty One'!"

Playtheus looked around and realized the pavilion had been prepared for a ceremony—his ceremony. Nersha stood by Toleshba with a smirk on her face. She had used her influence to contact Talimus-qua-tam. She had found out through manipulating Toleshba that he was planning to return Sede to her people; she had seen it in the flames. How dare he give her to a witch of all people! Toleshba was in her glory, beaming as she stood between Masta-lovid and Nersha. She slipped her hand into Nersha's and brought it to her lips. Kissing her fingers, Nersha met her eyes with a cold, sinister smile. Toleshba may own her, but Nersha still had the power to manipulate and get what she wanted, and what she wanted was revenge.

Talimus-qua-tam stepped to the platform as cheers exploded in the room. They echoed off the huge ceiling above, making the diamond chandeliers vibrate from the thundering sound. With a grand gesture of hand, he waved outward to the huge crowd before him, beaming that *his* son would be exalted among them.

"Come, my son, it is time!" At his father's command, he stepped forward and stood beside him. As the cheering turned to a hush and a hush to silence, all eyes fell on Playtheus.

"You all know my son Playtheus. Today we declare him to be a 'Mighty One' in the earth. All of you, the Mighty 200, have agreed that he be given this honor!" Again, mighty cheers erupted, roaring throughout the great room. Talimus-qua-tam waited for all to be silent once more. Continuing, he commanded, "Let us begin!"

Ba-nea stepped forward and clasped Sede's trembling hand, ushering her to the platform that brought her eye to eye with Playtheus. Her heart pounded, and it was though she felt every beat. She looked down to her chest to see if her robe was moving. Playtheus reached for her hands and held them tenderly. His look was so loving and reassuring.

As they stood facing each other, Talimus-qua-tam began to speak in a dark language. She felt herself cringe. What was he doing? His words descended inside her, gripping her and holding her captive. Each word felt like strong chains that bound her arms, her shoulders, and her heart. She felt herself resisting and struggling against his words, but all her efforts to resist were futile; she felt an overwhelming helplessness. She knew she had no power to say no to what was about to happen. How would she ever escape this time? What was about to happen would not be with her consent but against her will. As he continued, his chant intensified. Talimus-qua-tam's words broke the restraint she had put on her heart toward Playtheus. She had guarded her heart all this time, keeping her heart for Shem only. Through the power of his dark knowledge, her restraint and guardedness were now gone. She now felt herself yielding to his words.

All watched as a mist rose from both Sede and Playtheus. Sede's mist glistened pure white; Playtheus', a sparking light blue. Their mists swirled above them, dancing with sparkling flecks of light, and they raised their heads to see the two mists blend together. Turning and spinning, their lights intertwined, forming a pulsating, brilliant orb. As the sphere pulsated, it sent forth vibrating waves of love that fell and settled on their chests, making their bodies tremble. Each felt the overwhelming love that had come from the other's heart. Sede felt Playtheus' love, and Playtheus felt hers. Even though she hadn't given her love freely, love still sprang forth. It was Talimus-qua-tam's words that had commanded her heart to do so.

Their eyes sparkled with the deep emotion they were both feeling, and a single tear rolled down Playtheus' cheek. Sede raised her hand to touch it. The moment her finger touched the moisture of his tear, an explosion of feelings went off within her. It was as though it were the catalyst to something hidden deep within her. Her breathing deepened, and her eyes softened.

He could not help but touch her cheek. "Even though, Sede, you have not freely given your love to me, I still feel what the words have commanded your heart to do. The love from your heart is beautiful beyond description. My whole being embraces your love. The love of your heart is as I thought it would be…like no other. I resolved that I would never know your love, but here it is. My heart is now complete and my dream fulfilled." With loving tenderness, they leaned forward to kiss, the dark words commanding her to respond to him. By this kiss, they would forever seal their union.

But suddenly, and with no warning, Nersha stepped forward. Her eyes flashed with the fire and anger of revenge. She was not going to allow this union to happen. This was to have been her moment. *She* was to have been at Playtheus' side. *Her* light was to have mingled with his. *She* was to feel the love of his heart. Jerking a javelin from the hand of a standing sentry, she set her face in fierce determination. With all her strength, she drew back and threw. Those standing near gasped; her movements were so fast they didn't have time to react.

As if in slow motion, Playtheus saw the spear spinning through the air. It was aimed straight at Sede's back. He whirled her around just as the powerful javelin entered his back. Gasps of horror reverberated throughout the room as Playtheus fell to the floor in a heap. Those standing next to Nersha grabbed her, holding her struggling arms. Sede stood dazed. What had just happened? She looked down and saw Playtheus on the floor. He was bleeding from his back. "Oh, Playtheus, what have you done? What have you done?!" Her eyes filled with hot tears of both horror and grief. She slumped to the floor and lifted his head to rest in her lap. Her words burst from her panicking heart. "No…no!" Looking up at Talimus-qua-tam, she screamed, "Help him! Help him!"

He buckled at the knees and crumpled to the floor. "Oh what have you done, my son, my great son?"

Playtheus strained to speak. Grabbing his father's robe at the chest, he pulled him down to his face. "Promise me you will return her to her people. Promise me!" he gasped.

Talimus-qua-tam rested his hand on his son's chest, realizing he was dying. "I promise, my son…I promise."

Looking into Sede's eyes, Playtheus lifted his hand to her face. Gently, he stroked her cheek; the look of tender love was in his eyes. Struggling to speak, he whispered, "Sede, my love, you have made me this day a 'Mighty One.' Not a 'Mighty One' among the 200 but a 'Mighty One' in your eyes. This is my last gift to you…I give my life for yours." Grasping her small hand, he brought it to his lips, softly kissing her fingers. "I love you, Sede."

Closing his eyes, he softly exhaled, and his hand collapsed still holding hers. She drew his head to her chest, pain filling her soul. He was gone…. The grief in her heart was unbearable. She felt such pain! Rocking him, she threw her head back and shouted, "Aeh! Aeh!"

She looked down again, hot tears blurring her vision. She blinked and released the tears only to have them fill her eyes once more. Wiping them away, she looked at his face. Beautiful Playtheus was at rest. Gently, she bent down and kissed each eyelid, the softness of her lips touching his skin. "Playtheus, Playtheus," she whispered. Again she began to cry with deep sorrow, gently rocking him.

Talimus-qua-tam watched as she held him to herself, his grief mingling with hers. He felt the depth of her sorrow and began to cry the tears of an angel. "My son, my great son!" he sobbed. Ba-nea slumped to her knees in unbelief, and he drew her hand to his chest, weeping.

Within seconds, his face changed from the face of sorrow to the face of anger, and he stood to his feet. Turning to Nersha, who still struggled in the grip of those who held her, he roared his command: "Come!" She moved forward in his power, gliding just above the floor. Her body trembled as she hovered before him. With the fierceness of rage, he grabbed her by the throat and began to squeeze and lift her, bringing her to eye level. Her feet dangled in the air, kicking wildly. She struggled, gasping for breath while she pulled at his hands around her throat.

"Stop, stop!" sobbed Ba-nea. She gently put her hand on Talimus-qua-tam's arm. Lowering Nersha to the floor, he released his grip. Turning to his wife, he exhaled deeply and looked at her trembling, his unresolved anger still burning hot within him.

She gently moved him to the side and stood before Nersha. Suddenly, a low rumble was heard as power exuded from Ba-nea's being. It reverberated throughout the room, vibrating the chandelier and crystal goblets and shaking the very foundation of the building. She began to grow in size, bringing her eye to eye with

Nersha. Ba-nea fixed her eyes to Nersha's, staring with penetrating power—a power that dove deep into her quaking Nephilim soul. Nersha was now filled with terror and trembled before her presence.

As Ba-nea drove her piercing look even deeper, Nersha felt the heat of fire. Not fire on the outside but fire within. A flame began in ignite within Nersha's chest and grow. The fire moved through her arms and legs, and her whole body began to violently shake from the power of the heat. Ba-nea's stare intensified. Screams rose from Nersha's throat as her body exploded in a flash of flames! Ba-nea, Talimus-qua-tam, and all who were standing near were blown back from the blasting light and heat. Sede held her arm up to shield her face. All that remained of Nersha was a small pile of smoldering ash at their feet.

Helping Ba-nea stand, Talimus-qua-tam responded, "Well done, my wife. A fitting end for the one who has slain our son!" Turning his attention to Sede, he helped her to her feet. "Come, I will honor you for the sake of my beloved son."

Four sentries stepped forward and carried Playtheus' from the room. As the pavilion cleared of the 200 and their wives, Ba-nea spoke softly, "You will come with us until we have honored our dead." Taking Sede's hand, she led her to their chariot and returned to "Horizon's Gate."

She was given a beautiful room. All the furnishings were made of silver and crystal, and only her bed had color, a deep purple. She had never felt fabric like the covering of the bed. It was velvety soft and seemed to whisper a melody when she touched it. She felt the magic in the room, but somehow it didn't frighten her. Everything that surrounded her spoke of Playtheus. Her heart still felt the pain of seeing him die in her arms. She lay on the bed, listening to the lonely melody of the velvety covering.

A knock at the door brought a servant. Bowing, he announced, "Her Highness!"

Ba-nea appeared in a sad and quiet mood. "May I come in, my dear?"

"Yes, please come in." Sede was so brokenhearted. She longed for someone to speak words of comfort. Ba-nea drew near and sat delicately at her side. The velvety covering changed its melody, and Sede heard a haunting harmony that brought tears to her eyes.

Ceremony of the 'Mighty One'

"Yes, this covering reflects the emotions of those who lie upon it," Ba-nea said sadly. "Your sorrow and my sorrow have mingled and is now what we hear." Sede listened, letting the music minister to her soul. A tear rolled down her cheek as she thought of Playtheus once more. "Oh child, I see why my son loved you. Your 'Tella-la-no-ah' is rare, and you really do love him."

Sede was surprised that she was so discerning. She didn't want to admit it to herself, but her heart was now laid bare, and she saw what was really there. It was true; she did love Playtheus. She had convinced herself that she was only his friend, but she could no longer deny it. This tragedy had caused the truth to surface. Now she saw what had been in her heart. Love had been born in her that first day he dressed her wounds; kissing her back and feeling his tears fall on her; seeing him weep at her embarrassment as she stood before him; all those many months of quiet walks with him; his nurturing her to health; the special memories that were theirs alone. How could she ever admit to herself that she loved two men? She knew that someday she would have to find a place for all of this in her heart. But not now; the grief for him was too strong.

Ba-nea spoke again. "I have something I need to tell you and give you. First, I will tell you. Never have I seen a ceremony for a 'Mighty One' like I have this night. After I became Talimus-qua-tam's high companion, I witnessed the ceremonies for the 'Mighty Ones.' In tonight's ceremony, I saw the innocence of two people who truly loved each other. My son was far from innocent, but his love for you *was*. No orb has ever emitted love before. Yours and Playtheus' was the first. I knew Talimus-qua-tam's words were forcing your heart to open to my son, but your love for him was already there, held back by your integrity for your husband."

Sede was amazed that she had such knowledge about her heart. "Yes, Sede, I know all about you. Perhaps it was your restraint that gave such power to the love we saw tonight. I remember a time when I was as you." Sede was puzzled by what she was saying. "There was a time when I was an innocent Sethite." Sede blinked in amazement.

"Yes, Sede. I was taken and overpowered by the dark words of Talimus-qua-tam. He saw my innocence and beauty, taking them for his own. I had no power to resist, just as you had no power when he spoke his words over you. Tonight, I see in you the young woman I once was. If I could have chosen anyone for my son's love, I would have chosen you. I see that Yahweh's love is set upon you. Thank you, for the change I saw in my son. He said it was because of you. He told me that it was you who taught him how to love."

Sede began to cry…she felt Playtheus so close at that moment. Everything in her wished he was there.

"I have something to give you, child. It was one of Playtheus' most precious possessions." Ba-nea withdrew a small, flat box made of pearl with silver filigree edges and a clasp of two round pearls. It was sealed with Playtheus' signet seal. "He brought this here after you had disappeared, wanting me to keep it for him. The only thing he said was 'It is my most precious possession.'"

Ba-nea extended the lovely box, resting it in Sede's hands. Holding it, she realized he had touched it and purposely placed its treasure inside. He had valued it so much that he had given it to his mother for safekeeping. She could hardly see for the tears that filled her eyes. Wiping them away, she looked once more at the box and brought it to her chest. "Thank you, Ba-nea. It means so very much to me!"

Again she cried as Ba-nea wrapped her arms around her. "Yes, child, wash your grief with tears. You will find their healing soon." She felt the love in Ba-nea's embrace, and it brought her a calming peace.

When her embrace had soothed her, Ba-nea looked at her intently. "Tell me of your life, Sede, of your village and family. Who is the leader in your village? Are your parents well? It has been many years since I have thought of my own Sethite village and my dear family that was lost to me."

Sede welcomed her questions for she longed for her family and home. "I come from the village of Taasa-toka. It's an ancient village, deep in the wilderness. Maybe you visited it long ago for yearly sacrifices? Our leader is Noah, my mother's brother. My father's name is Tolmaka; he is also my pack leader. I am a hunter among my kin. My mother no longer lives. She died giving me life. I never knew her…."

Tears came to Ba-nea's eyes as Sede spoke of her family and life as a Sethite. It stirred her own memories of a life she once had that now seemed but a dream.

Ceremony of the 'Mighty One'

It had been so very long since she had been with someone she could freely speak to about the life she once knew and loved. It was though her memories belonged to another person and not to her anymore. As Sede continued to share, Ba-nea watched her countenance. She radiated such purity and innocence. She had once been like her.

When Sede had finished speaking, Ba-nea gently moved her hair back from the side of her face and kissed her cheek. "Thank you for sharing your life with me, Sede. You are very dear, my child. I'm thankful for these moments with you. I grieve the loss of my beloved son, but I sorrow for you as well. I see within your soul a broken heart. I will leave you to rest and will later send my servants when it's time for you to prepare for the ceremony." Quietly, she left the room, closing the door behind her.

Sede lay down once more. The melody from the covering changed and now reflected only her sorrow. She held Playtheus' box to her chest and closed her eyes. "Oh Playtheus, Playtheus," she sighed. Somehow she knew her heart would break in a thousand pieces if she opened the box at that moment. She would wait until she had the strength to see what he had held so dear. With tears for him still in her eyes, she fell asleep, the music from the covering gently soothing her. Several hours later a soft knock was heard on the door, and servants slowly entered. They had both food and a change of garments. Sede tried to eat but couldn't. They led her to a scented pool to bathe and then dressed her for Playtheus' ceremony.

Pressing the pearl box against her chest, she followed Ba-nea as they made their way outside to the mansion's garden. Before them stood a great altar where Playtheus lay on a royal tapestry with the wood for fire beneath him. He looked like a king in his embroidered robe with a golden crown resting on his forehead. He lay there so still; it gripped her heart. She wondered if she would endure what was about to happen….

Talimus-qua-tam stepped forward and honored his son in death with wonderful words of praise. Ba-nea, too, stood and spoke the words only a mother's heart could say. When it was her turn, she approached the altar, holding the pearl box. Breaking the seal, she opened the box to see what he had treasured. To her amazement it was the golden arm bracelet with the one dangling diamond. It was what she had worn the night he presented her as his queen. She burst into tears, clutching the bracelet to her heart. Her voice broke with emotion as she cried, "Playtheus, Playtheus!" She remembered his words: 'you are like a diamond to me, Sede-quete, your many facets each so beautiful.' She could almost hear the tinkling sound of the diamond when he touched it that night on her arm. Taking the golden bracelet, she placed it in his hand. "I could not tell you in life, but I will tell you in death…I love you, Playtheus…I love you." She leaned forward and kissed his hand. Whispering, she breathed, "Yes, Playtheus, this day you have become a 'Mighty One' in my eyes."

She forced the tightness from her throat and began the haunting melody of her people, "The Love Song for the Dead." It wouldn't be words she spoke as Talimus-qua-tam and Ba-nea had done but a song of love instead. She saw Ba-nea, too, sing the song, only with whispered breath. Her lips moved with each word that was sung. Sede sang in a minor key, the beauty of the melody rising to the heavens like sweet incense for the one she had loved. The power of its beauty stirred the hearts of those who heard it.

Cruel death has challenged love
Your arrows pierce my heart
Where once was life and light
Now only hollow dark

Bitter grief, with burning tears
Fall hot upon my face
All is still within me
Of breath, there is no trace

Time stands still, as if it waited
For my days to know their end
When then your face I see
Our love will triumph then

Ceremony of the 'Mighty One'

This sacrifice I offer you
My heart within my hand
With open palms I lift it up
Sent to you in heaven's distant land

Sede bowed her head and cupped her hands before her. Releasing the love from her heart, a brilliant white orb, glistening with flecks of light, rose from her heart and rested in her hands. As she swiftly lifted her hands upward, the light ascended into the heavens with bursting speed. All who stood near gasped at the beauty and wonder of what she had done. She backed away from the altar as Talimus-qua-tam and Ba-nea extended torches that ignited the wood. A huge blast of flame consumed both wood and body. After the blast, Sede looked to see. Only ash remained. The fire had consumed everything, and now he was truly gone. She stood there stunned, not knowing what to do. Playtheus was gone....

Ba-nea stepped forward and wrapped her own cloak around her. Holding Sede's face in her hands, Ba-nea searched deep into her eyes then kissed her sweetly on the cheek. "Farewell, beloved of my son." Then leaning close to her ear for none to hear but her, she whispered, "May Yahweh richly bless you all the days of your life. May He hold you in the palm of His hand."

As Ba-nea stepped back, Talimus-qua-tam said, "It is time!" Wrapping his cloak around the two of them, they disappeared. When the cloak opened, they were standing on the hill overlooking her village. "As I promised my son, I have returned you to your people. You may go." Wrapping the cloak around himself, he disappeared.

She stood there bewildered, still, and alone. "How am I to find a place for all of this in my heart? So much has happened." Her eyes filled with tears as she looked at the village below. "How can I ever return to my old life? How can I?" Wrapping Ba-nea's cloak around her shoulders, she turned and began walking the path to the forest. She must spend time alone—alone to find her heart once more.

www.ingramcontent.com/pod-product-compliance
Lightning Source LLC
Chambersburg PA
CBHW070327260626
47160CB00003B/971